Mr. PANtS

TRICK OR FEET!

WORDS BY
SCOTT MCCORMICK

PICTURES BY
R. H. LAZZELL

Dial Books for Young Readers
an imprint of Penguin Group (USA) LLC

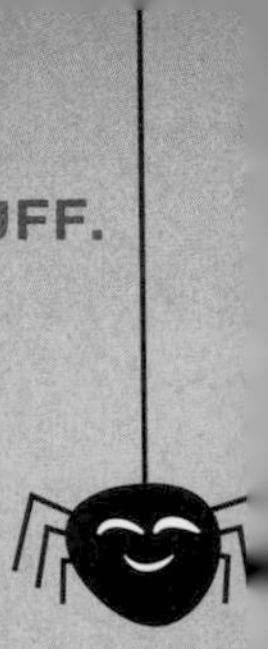

FOR MY WIFE, WITH, YOU KNOW, LOVE AND STUFF.
". . . CLOUDS . . ."   —S.M.

FOR DENNIS AND MEL, WHO WERE ALWAYS AN
INSPIRATION TO ME.   —R.H.L.

Dial Books for Young Readers
Published by the Penguin Group | Penguin Group (USA) LLC
375 Hudson Street | New York, New York 10014

USA / Canada / UK / Ireland / Australia / New Zealand / India / South Africa / China
PENGUIN.COM
A Penguin Random House Company

Text copyright © 2015 by Scott McCormick | Pictures copyright © 2015 by R. H. Lazzell

Library of Congress Cataloging-in-Publication Data   McCormick, Scott, date.
Mr. Pants : trick or feet / words by Scott McCormick ; pictures by R. H. Lazzell.   pages cm.
Summary: As Halloween approaches, Mr. Pants, his mom, and his sisters, share a series of adventures as they choose costumes and get stuck at the airport when they miss their flight.   ISBN 978-0-525-42811-4 (hardcover)
1. Cats—Juvenile fiction. 2. Brothers and sisters—Juvenile fiction. 3. Halloween—Juvenile fiction. 4. Airports—Juvenile fiction. [1. Cats—Fiction. 2. Brothers and sisters—Fiction. 3. Halloween—Fiction. 4. Airports—Fiction.]
I. Lazzell, R. H., illustrator. II. Title. III. Title: Mister Pants, trick or feet. IV. Title: Trick or feet.
PZ7.M47841437Ms 2015   [E]—dc23   2014043737

Manufactured in China on acid-free paper
1   3   5   7   9   10   8   6   4   2

Designed by Jennifer Kelly | Text set in Archer

CONTENTS

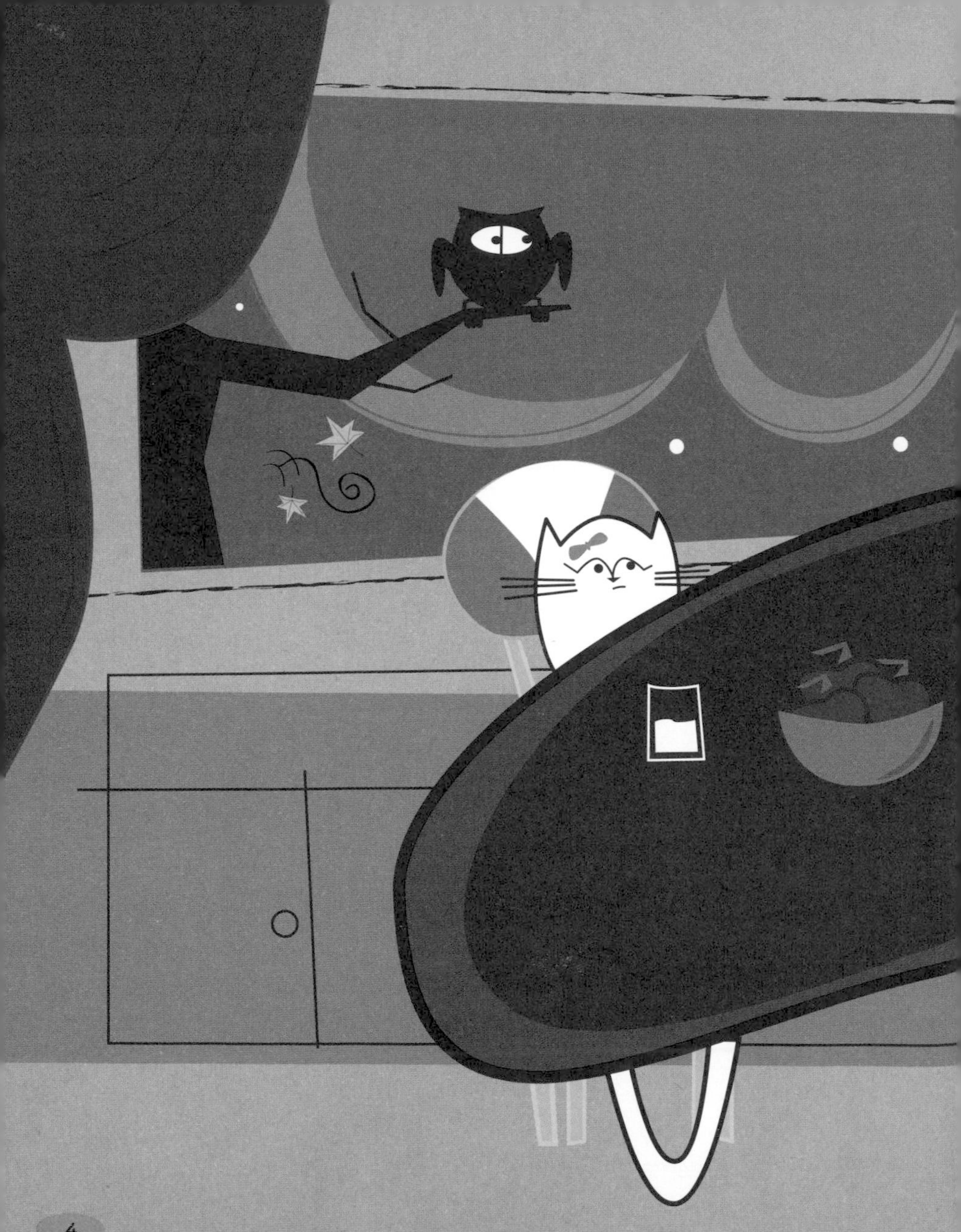

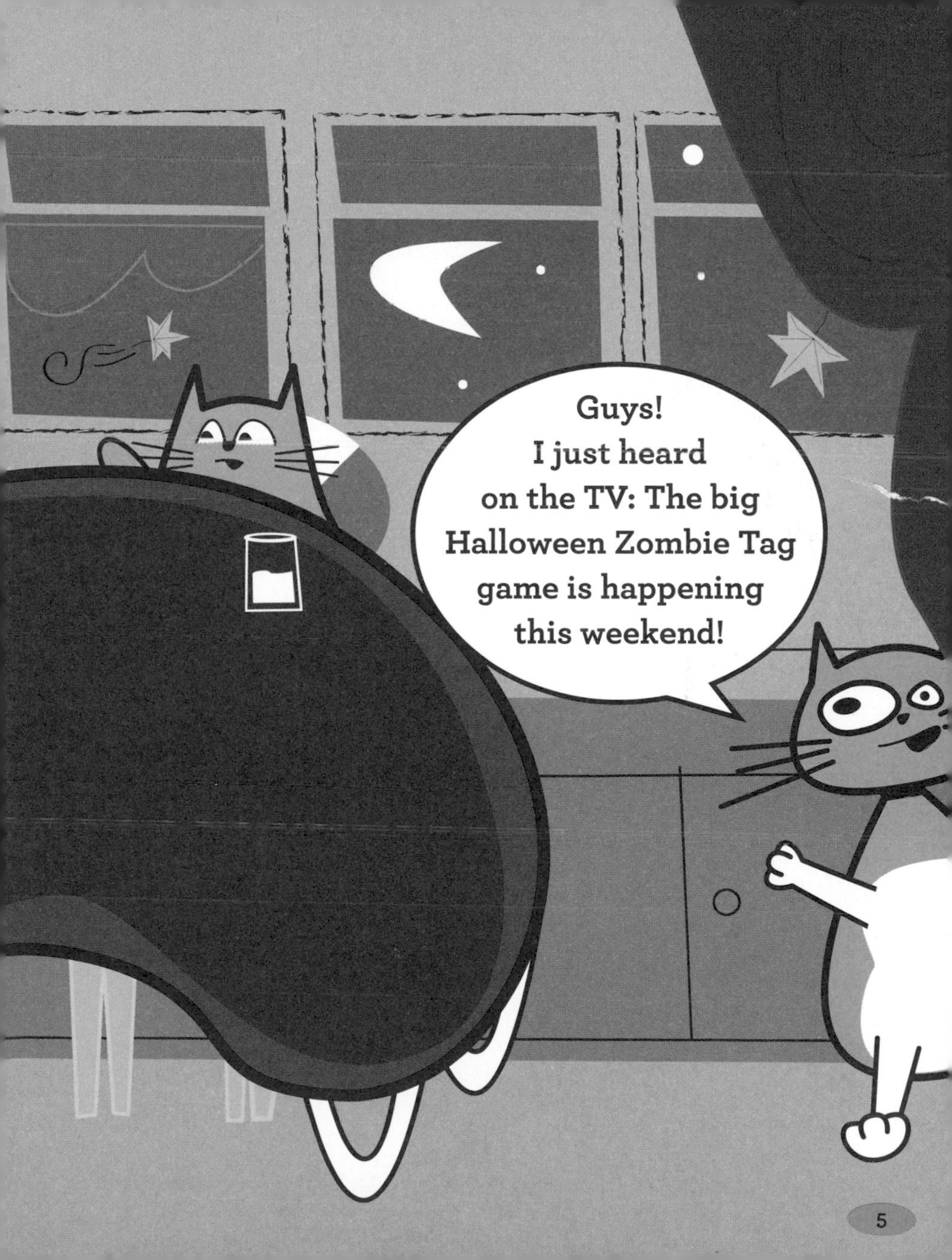
Guys! I just heard on the TV: The big Halloween Zombie Tag game is happening this weekend!

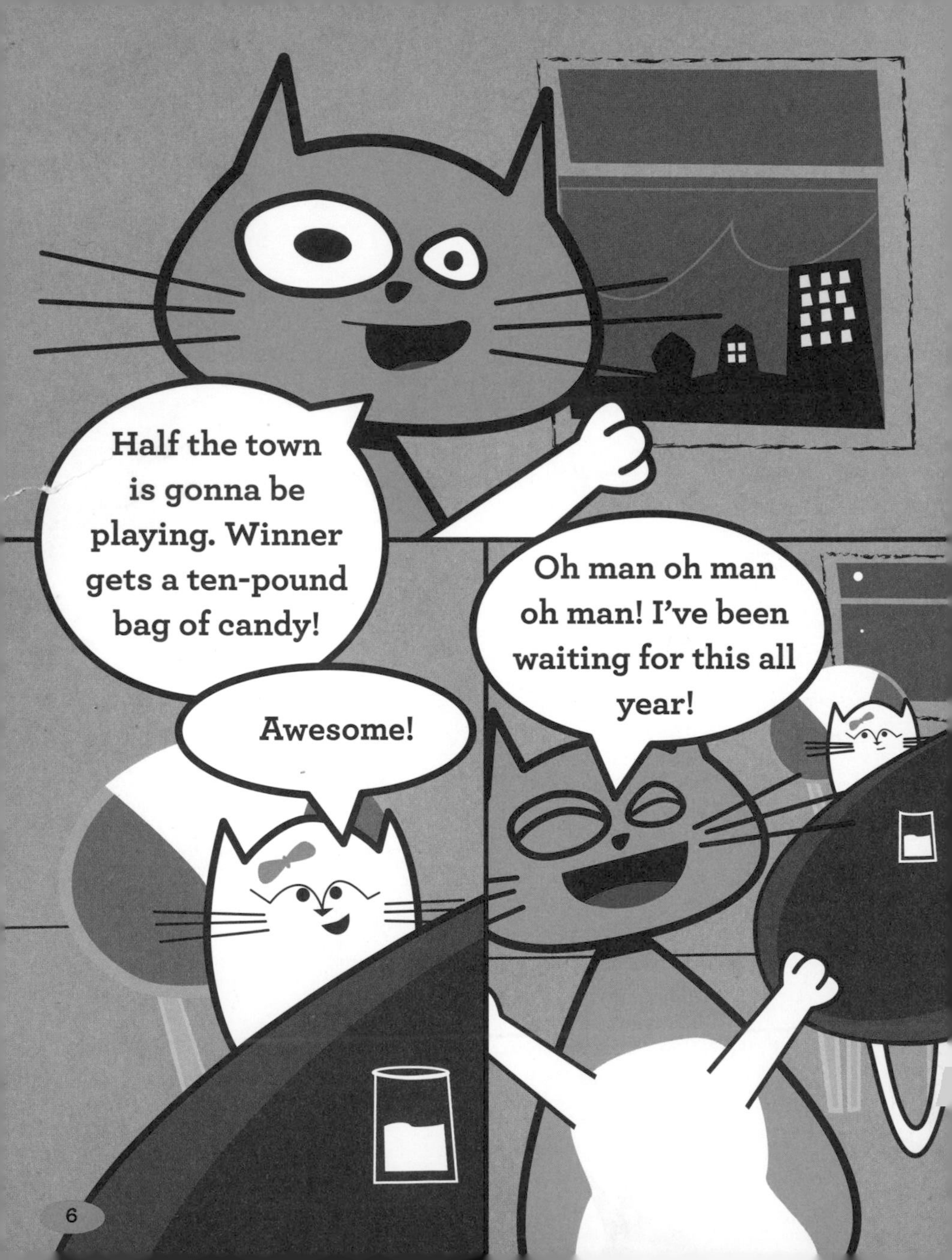
Half the town is gonna be playing. Winner gets a ten-pound bag of candy!
Awesome!
Oh man oh man oh man! I've been waiting for this all year!

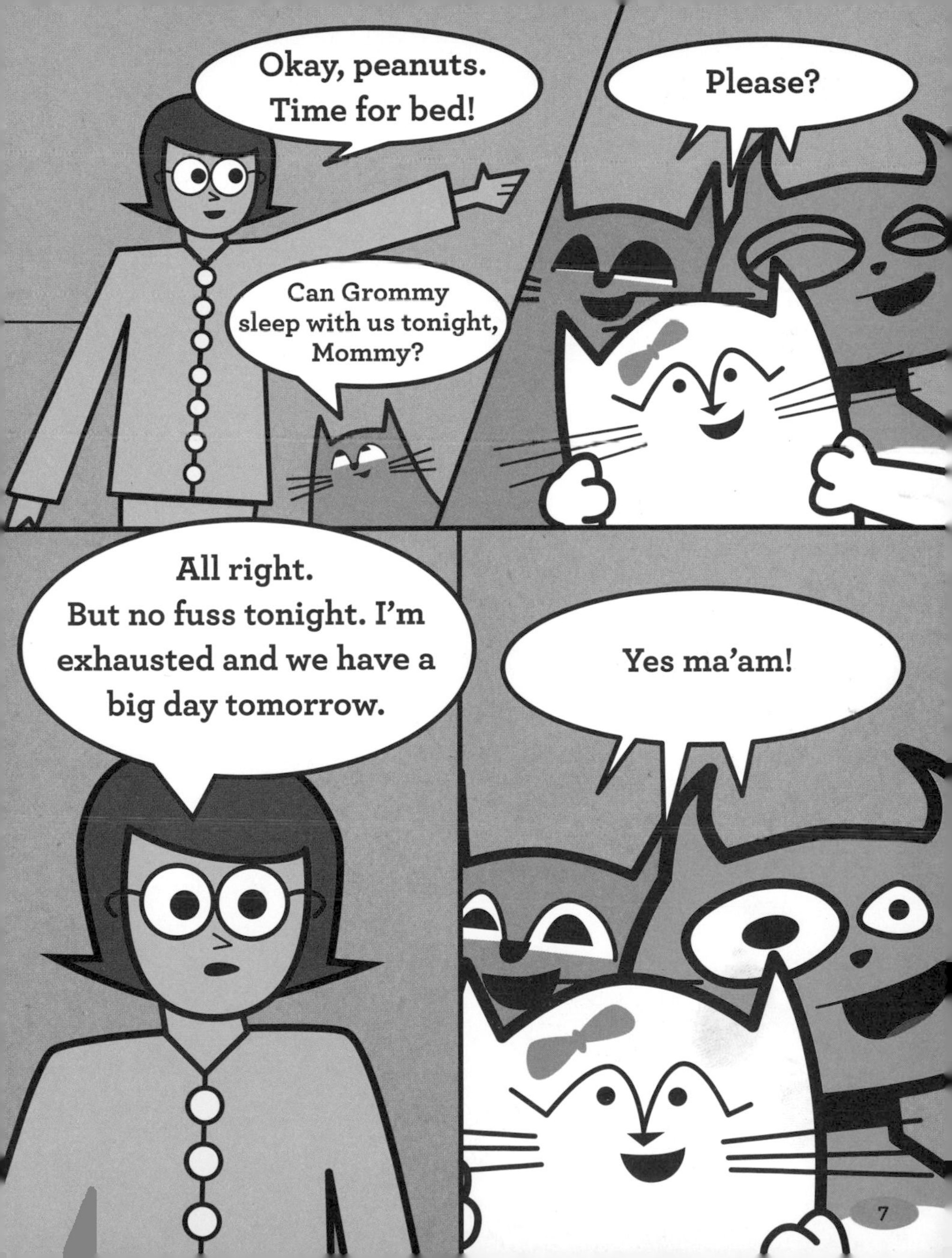
Okay, peanuts. Time for bed!
Can Grommy sleep with us tonight, Mommy?
Please?
All right. But no fuss tonight. I'm exhausted and we have a big day tomorrow.
Yes ma'am!

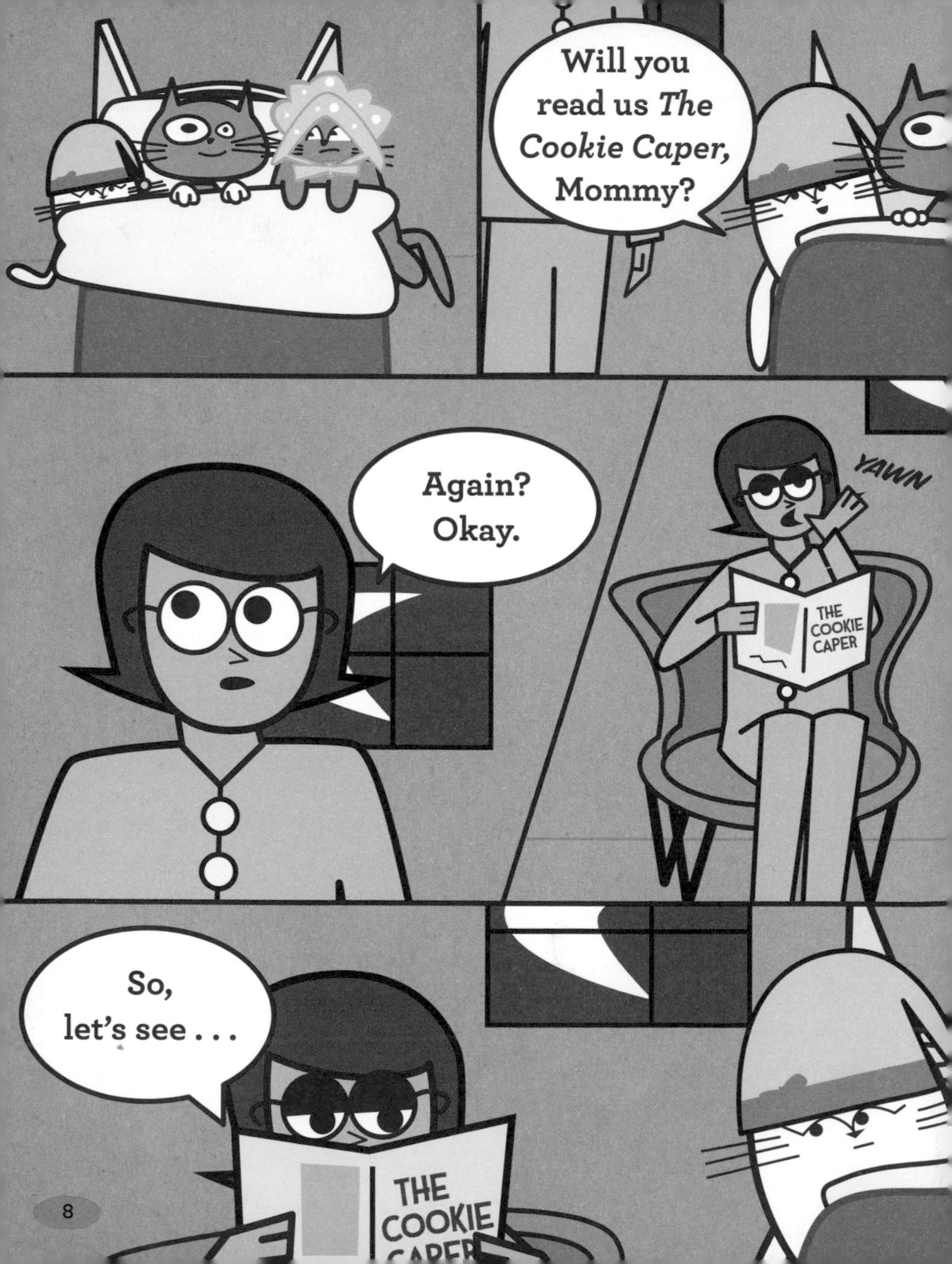
Will you read us *The Cookie Caper*, Mommy?
Again? Okay.
YAWN
THE COOKIE CAPER
So, let's see . . .
THE COOKIE

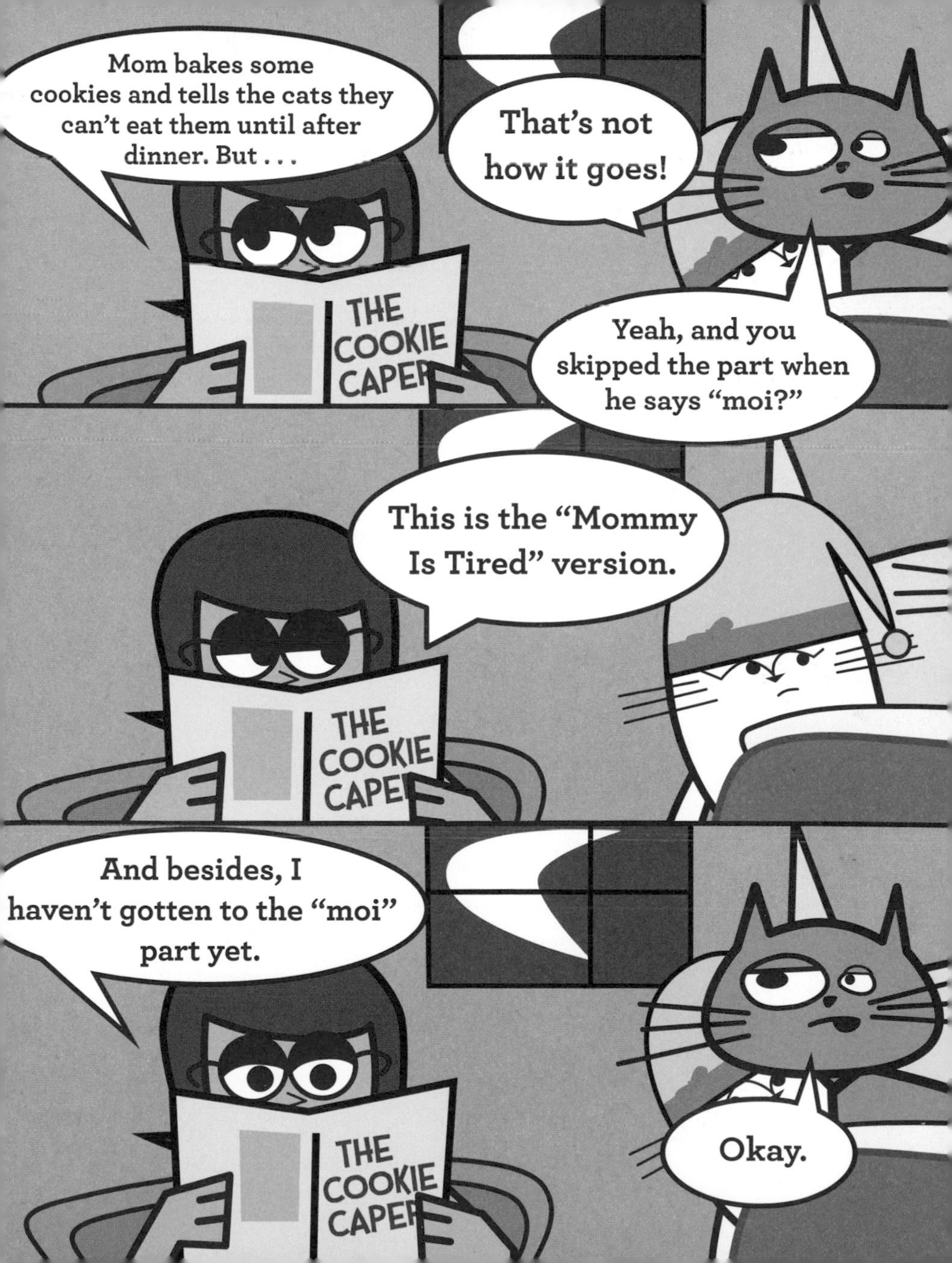
Mom bakes some cookies and tells the cats they can't eat them until after dinner. But . . .
That's not how it goes!
THE COOKIE CAPER
Yeah, and you skipped the part when he says "moi?"
This is the "Mommy Is Tired" version.
THE COOKIE CAPER
And besides, I haven't gotten to the "moi" part yet.
Okay.
THE COOKIE CAPER

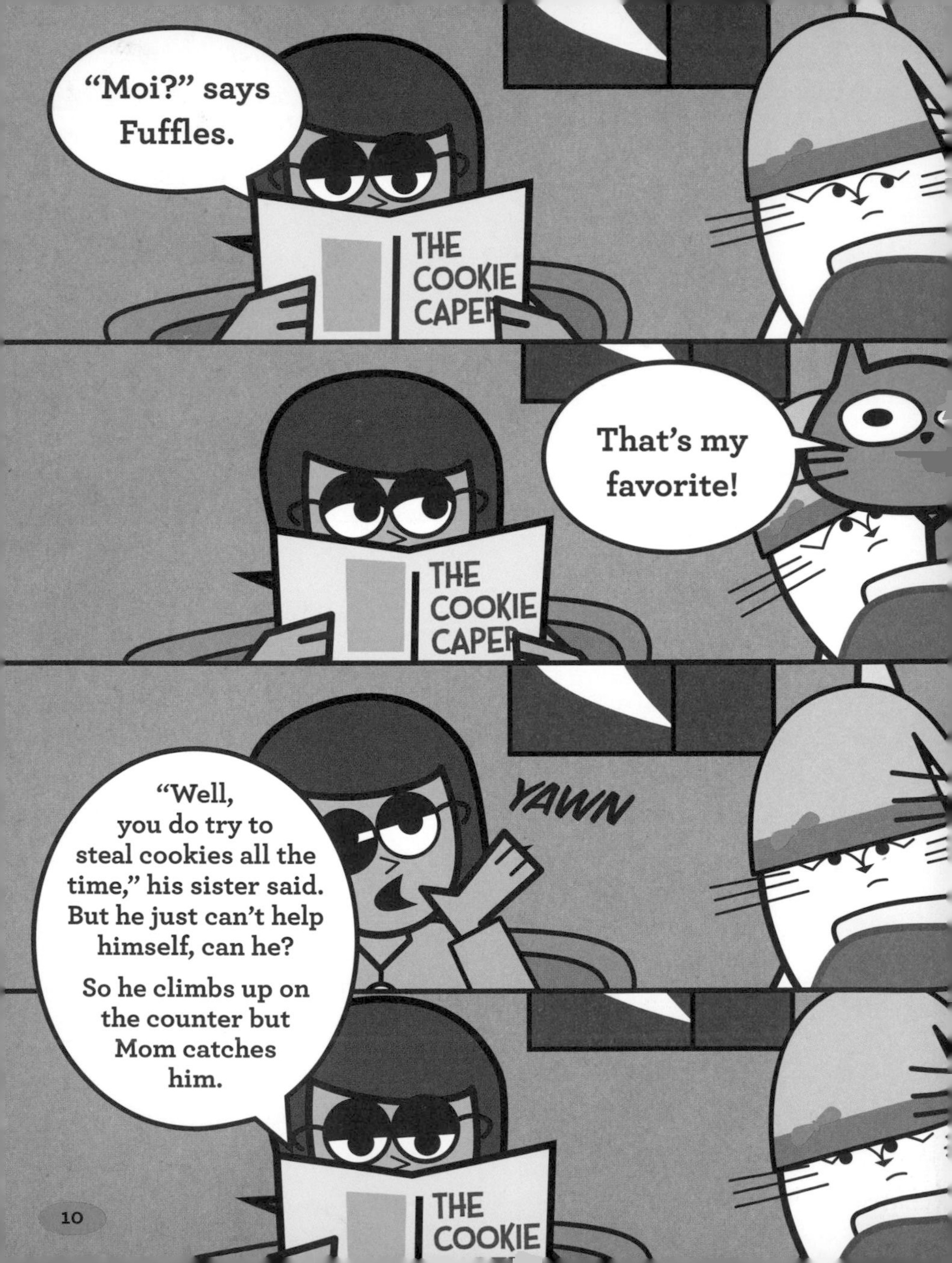
"Moi?" says Fuffles.
THE COOKIE CAPER
THE COOKIE CAPER
That's my favorite!
"Well, you do try to steal cookies all the time," his sister said. But he just can't help himself, can he?
YAWN
So he climbs up on the counter but Mom catches him.
THE COOKIE

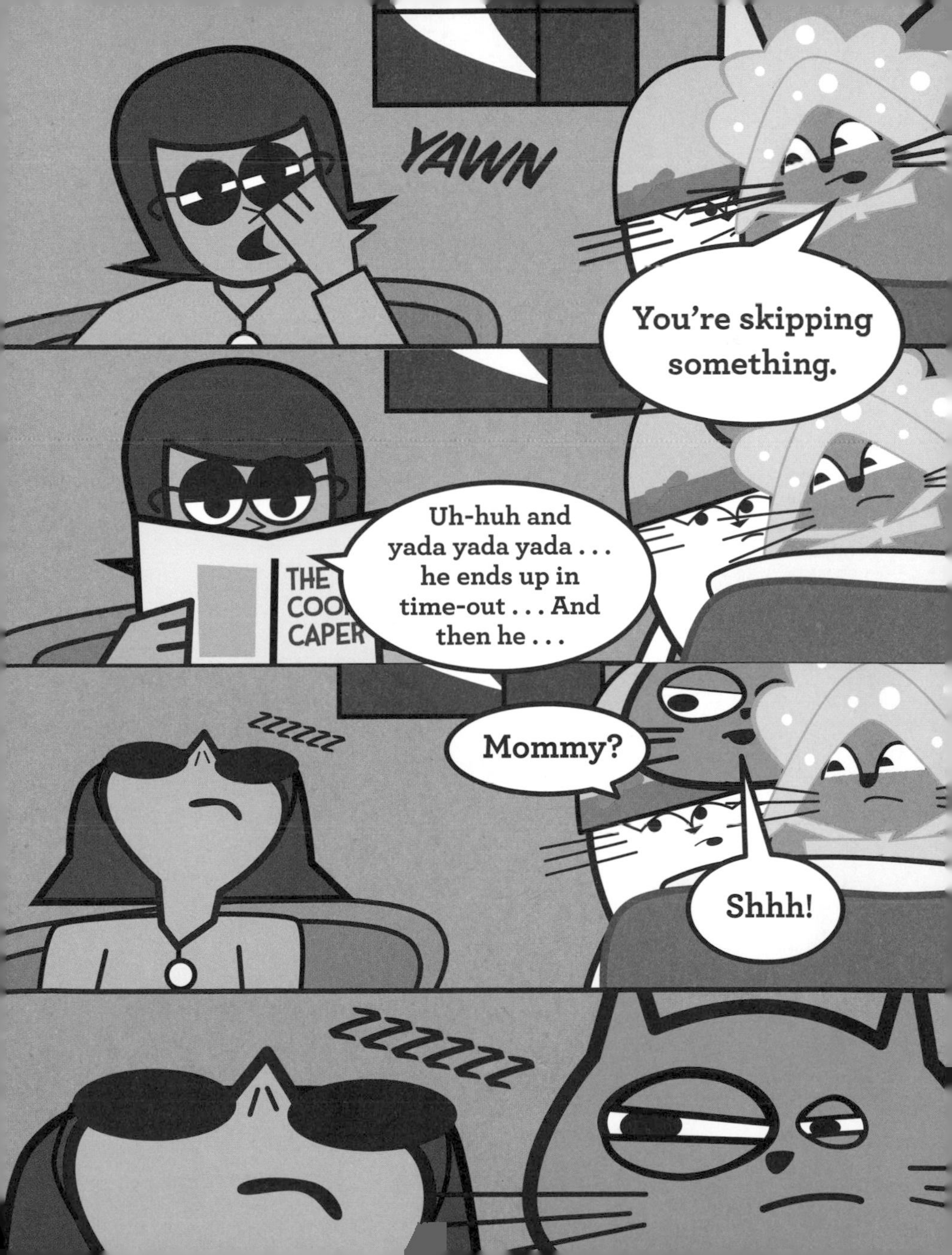
YAWN
You're skipping something.
THE COO CAPER
Uh-huh and yada yada yada . . . he ends up in time-out . . . And then he . . .
ZZZZZZ
Mommy?
Shhh!
ZZZZZZZ

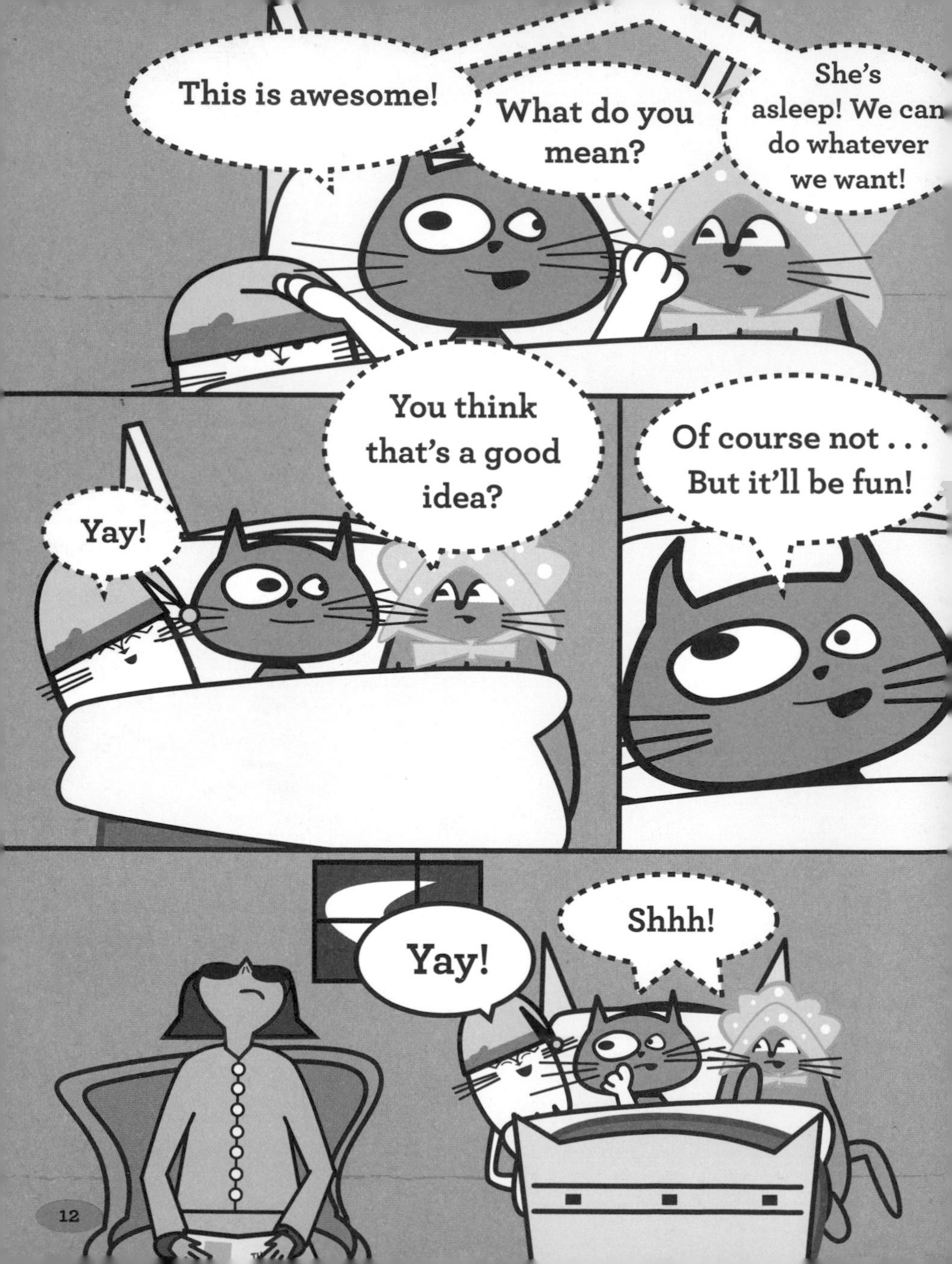
This is awesome!
What do you mean?
She's asleep! We can do whatever we want!
Yay!
You think that's a good idea?
Of course not . . . But it'll be fun!
Yay!
Shhh!

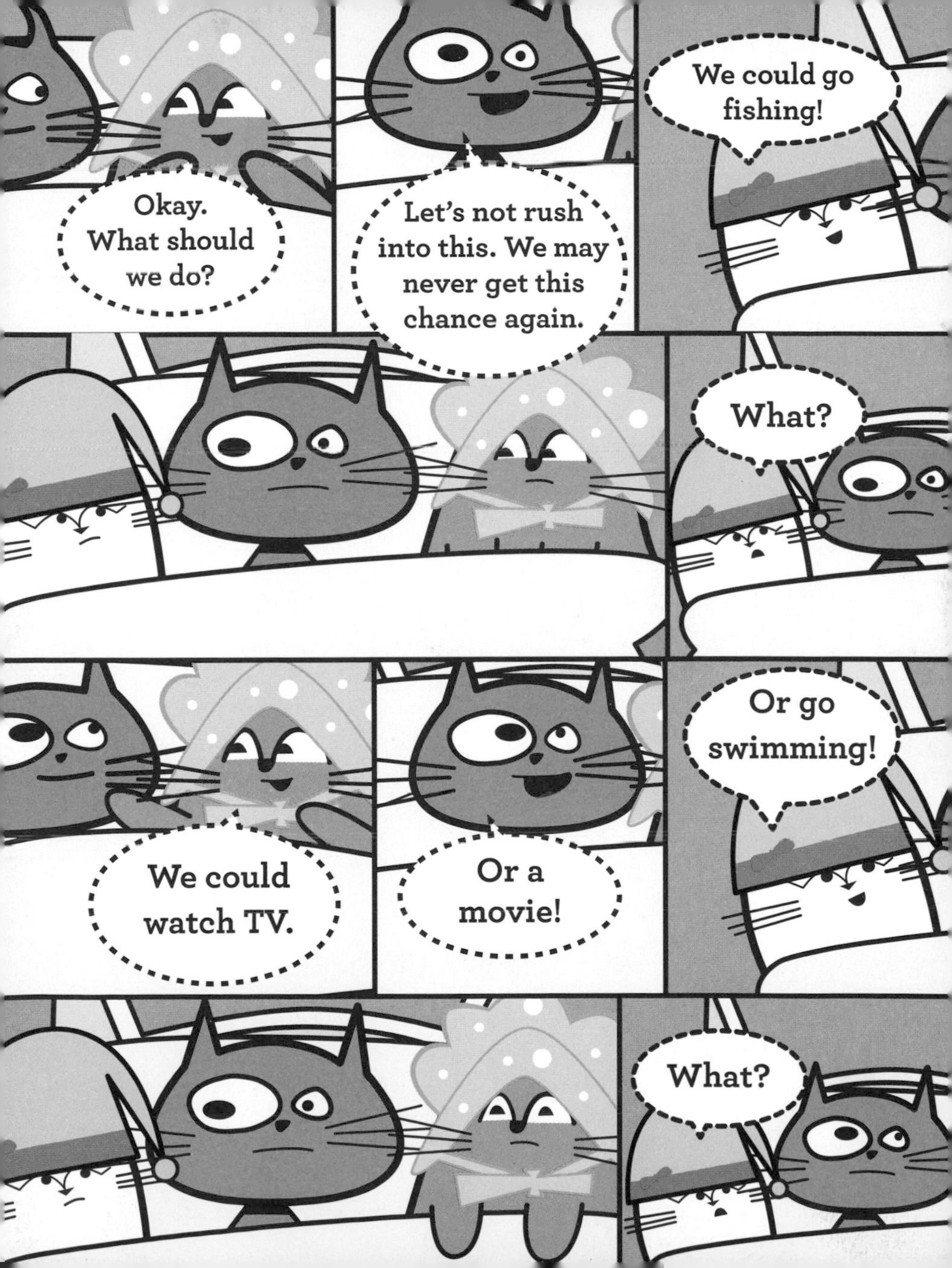
Okay. What should we do?
Let's not rush into this. We may never get this chance again.
We could go fishing!
What?
We could watch TV.
Or a movie!
Or go swimming!
What?

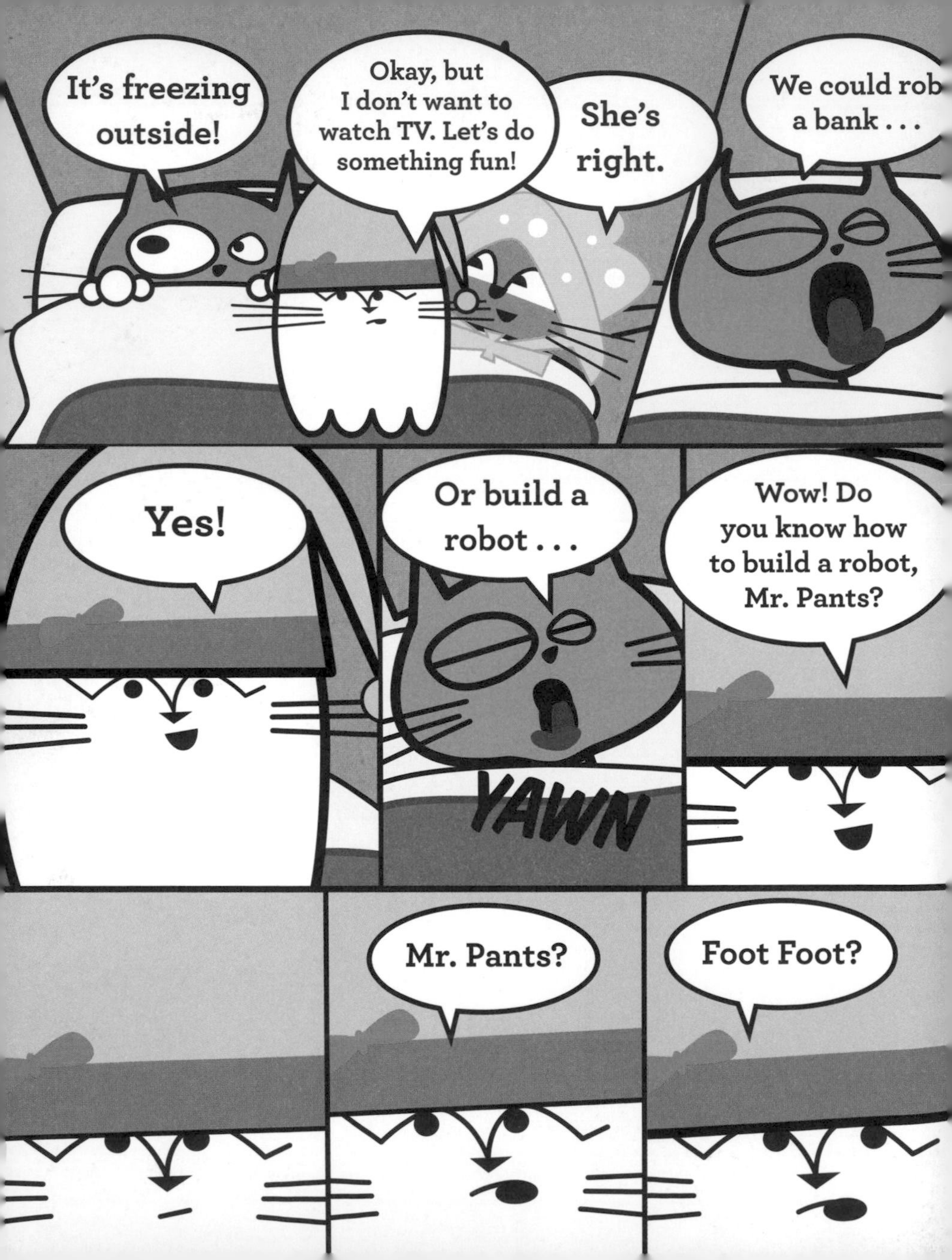
It's freezing outside!
Okay, but I don't want to watch TV. Let's do something fun!
She's right.
We could rob a bank . . .
Yes!
Or build a robot . . .
YAWN
Wow! Do you know how to build a robot, Mr. Pants?
Mr. Pants?
Foot Foot?

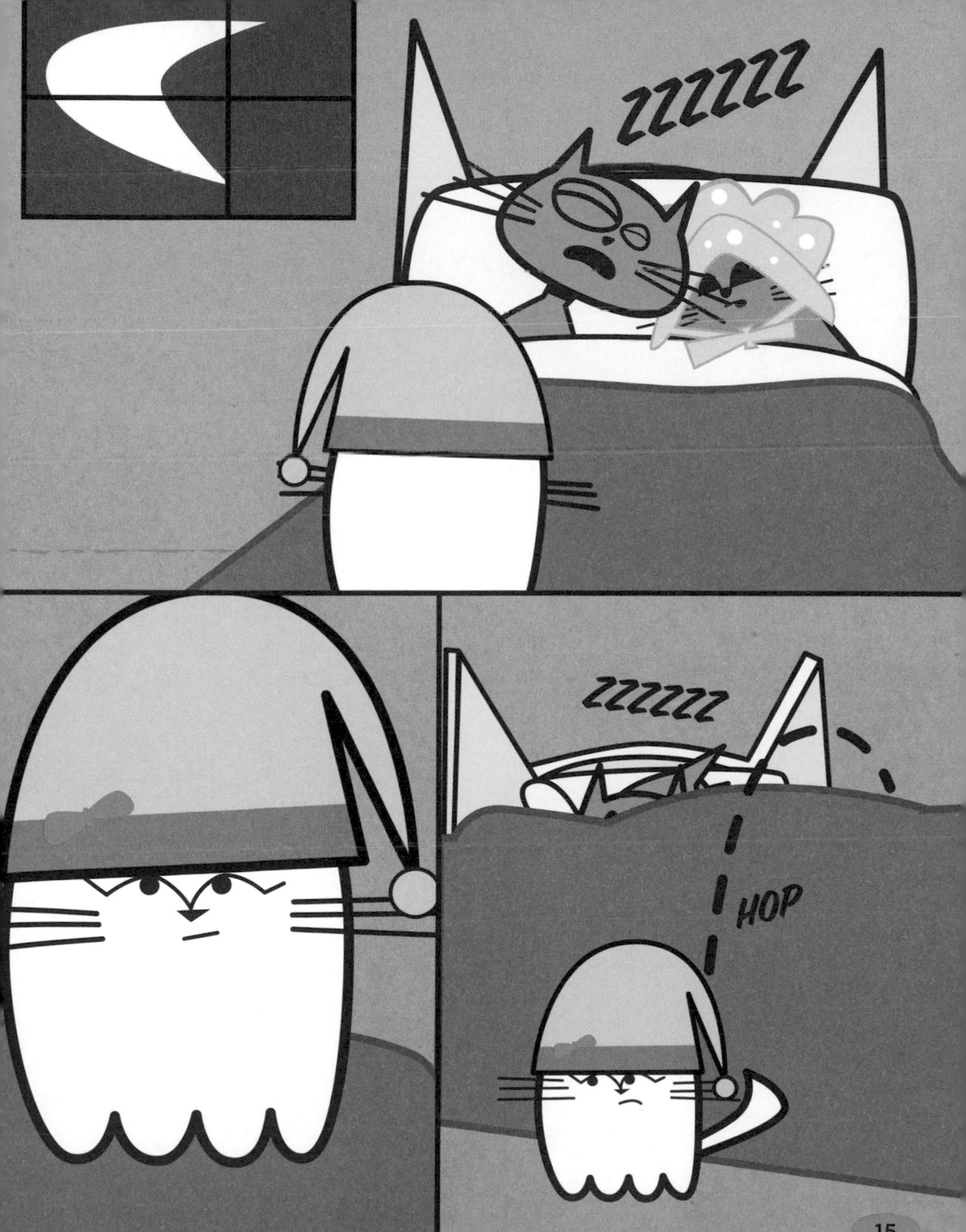
ZZZZZZZ
ZZZZZZ
HOP

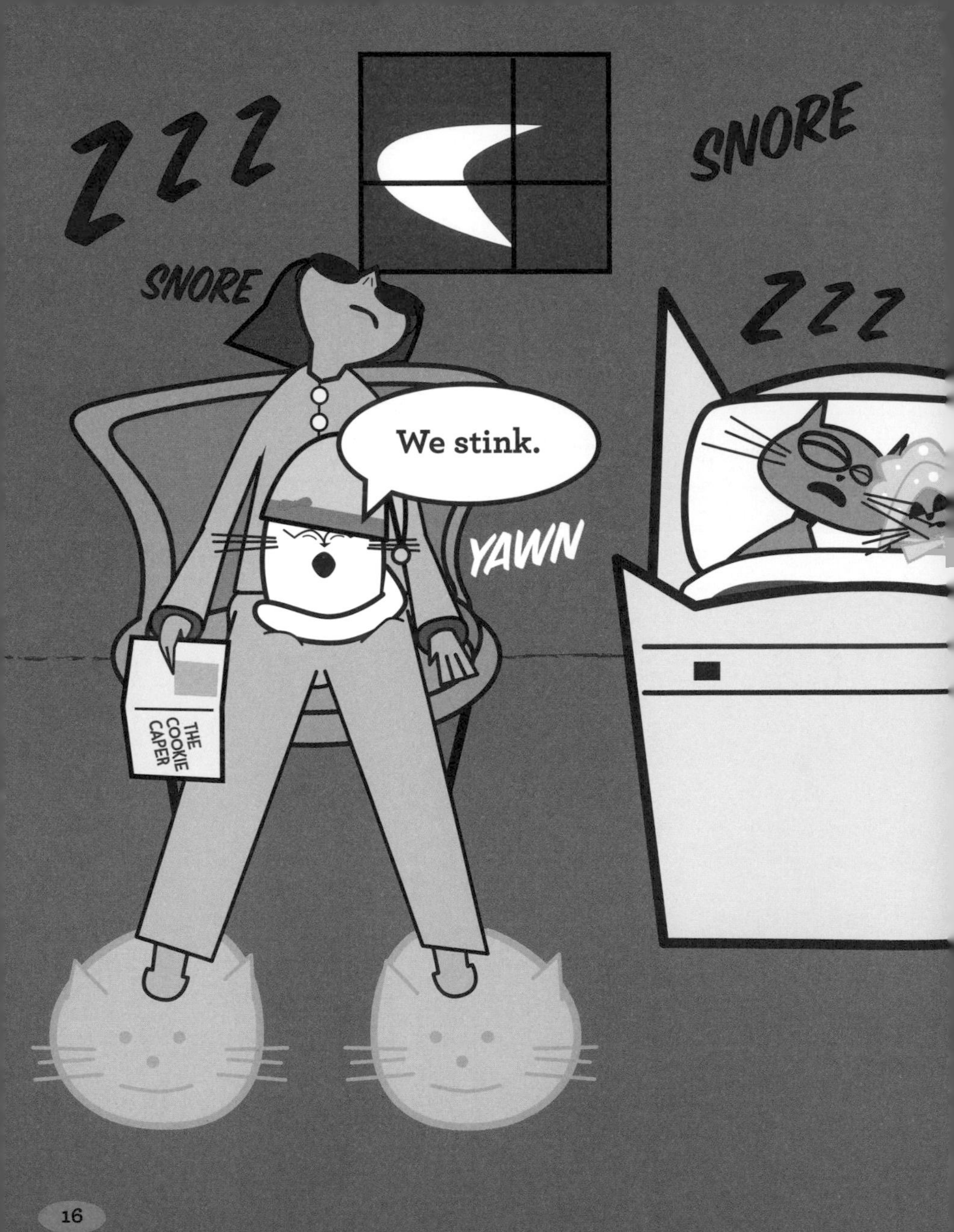
Z Z Z
SNORE
SNORE
Z Z Z
We stink.
YAWN
THE COOKIE CAPER

Chapter One: GHOST SHOP

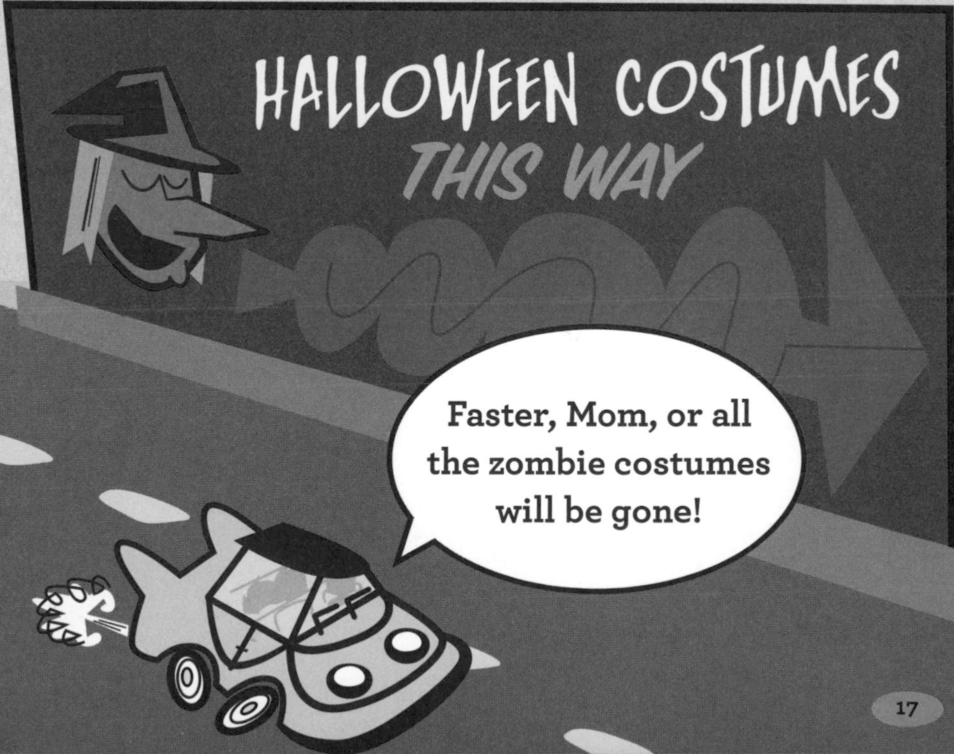
HALLOWEEN COSTUMES
THIS WAY
Faster, Mom, or all the zombie costumes will be gone!

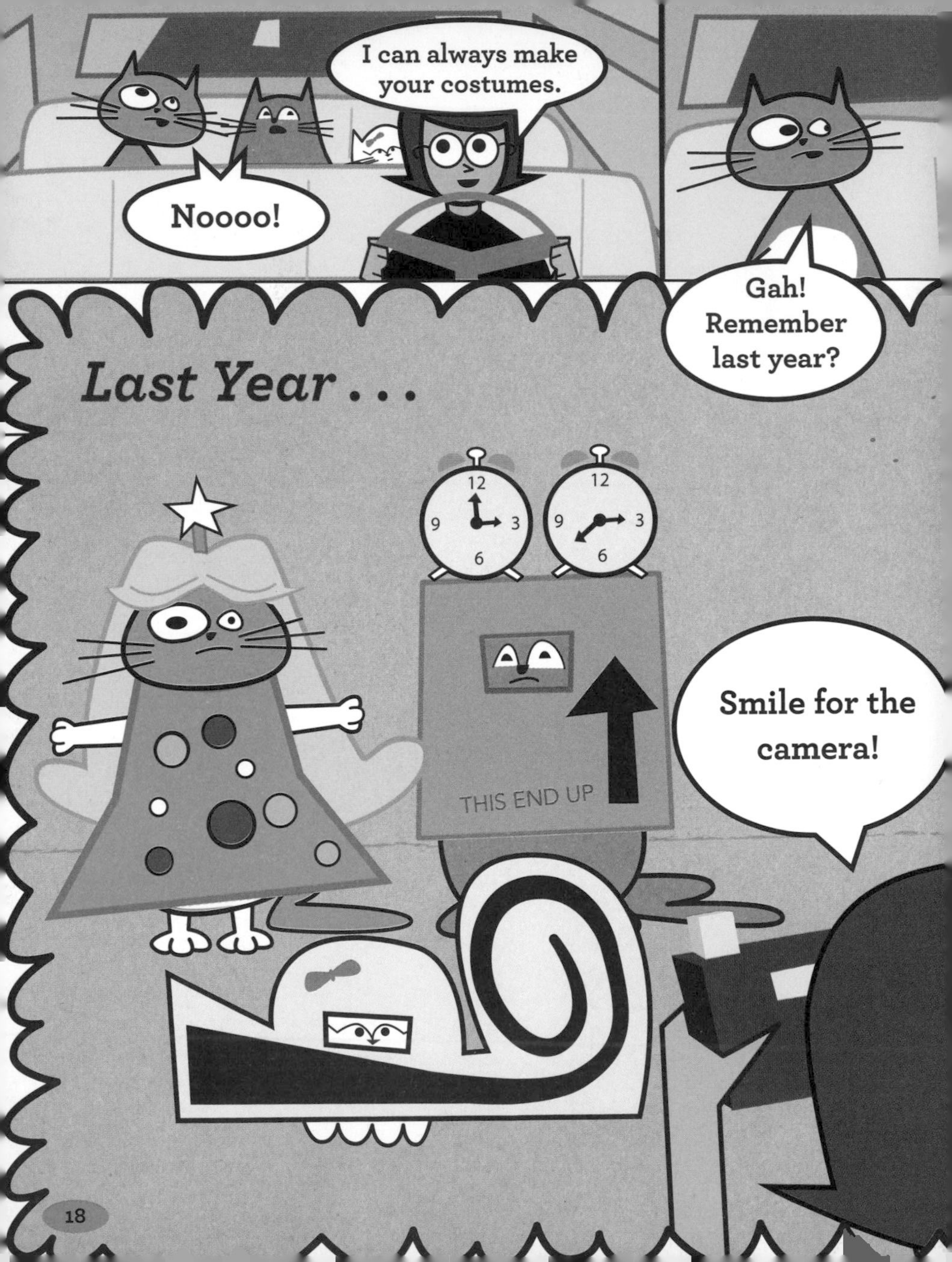

I can always make your costumes.
Noooo!
Gah! Remember last year?
Last Year . . .
12
9
3
6
12
9
3
6
THIS END UP
Smile for the camera!

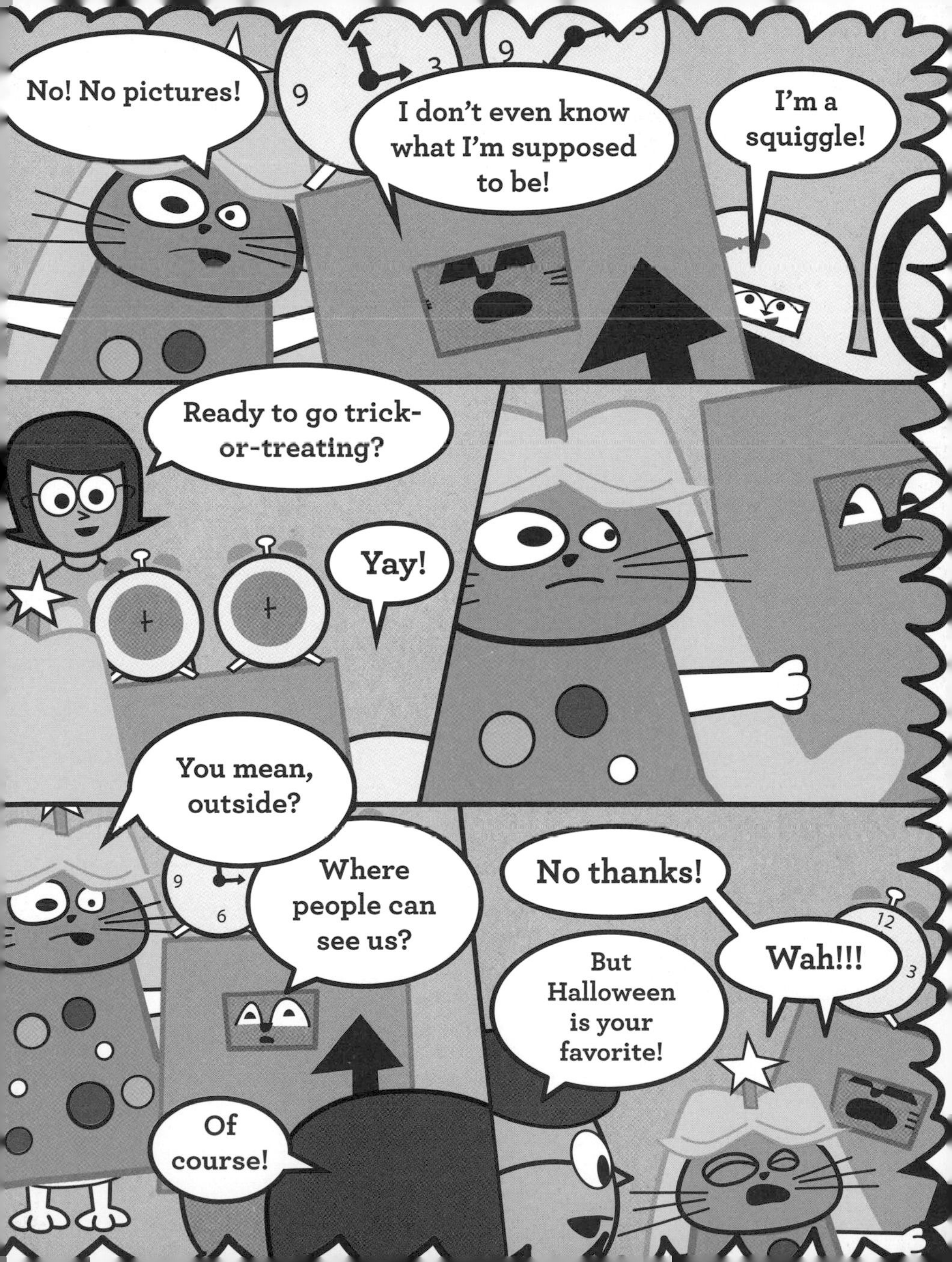
No! No pictures!
I don't even know what I'm supposed to be!
I'm a squiggle!
Ready to go trick-or-treating?
Yay!
You mean, outside?
Where people can see us?
Of course!
No thanks!
Wah!!!
But Halloween is your favorite!

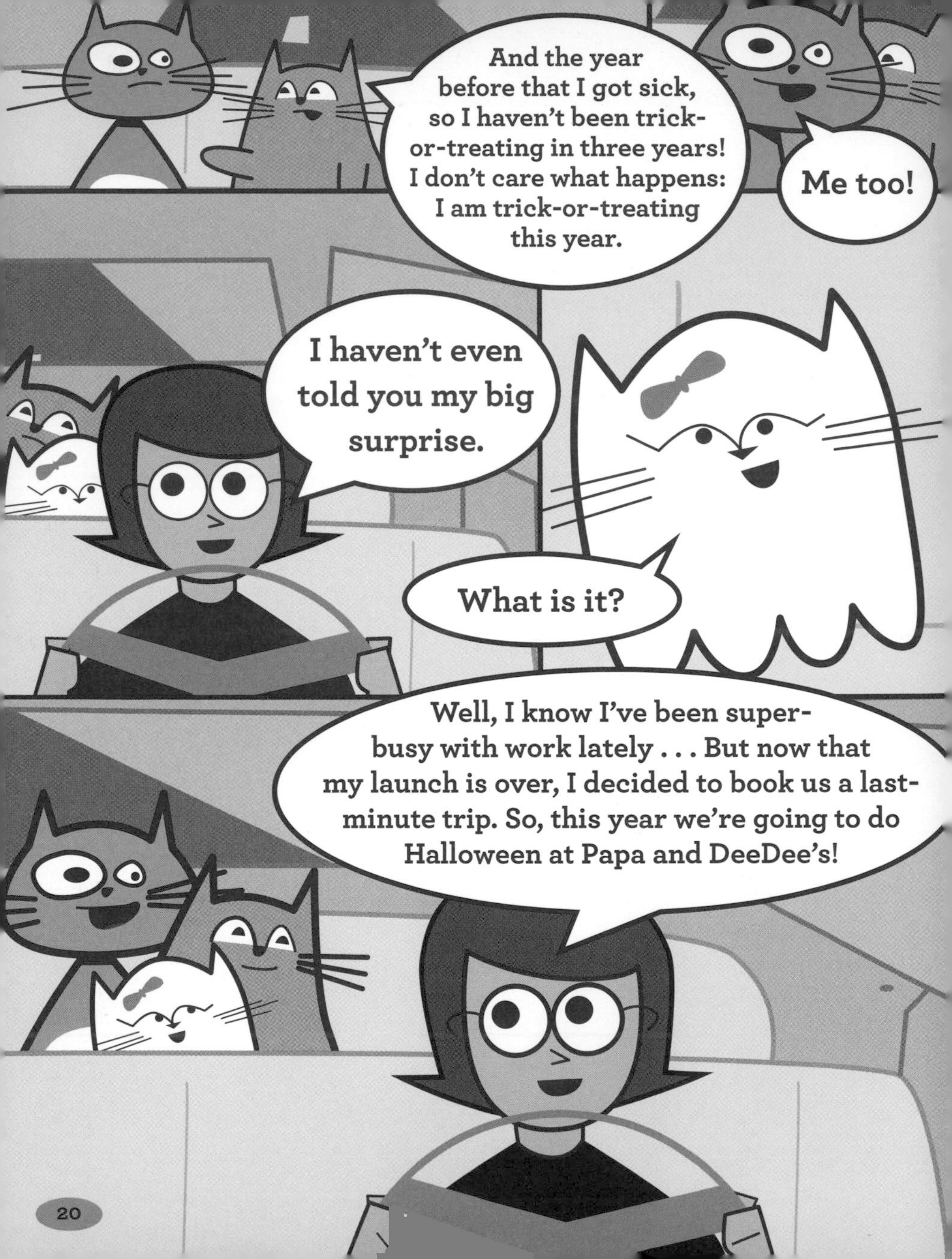
And the year before that I got sick, so I haven't been trick-or-treating in three years! I don't care what happens: I am trick-or-treating this year.
Me too!
I haven't even told you my big surprise.
What is it?
Well, I know I've been super-busy with work lately . . . But now that my launch is over, I decided to book us a last-minute trip. So, this year we're going to do Halloween at Papa and DeeDee's!

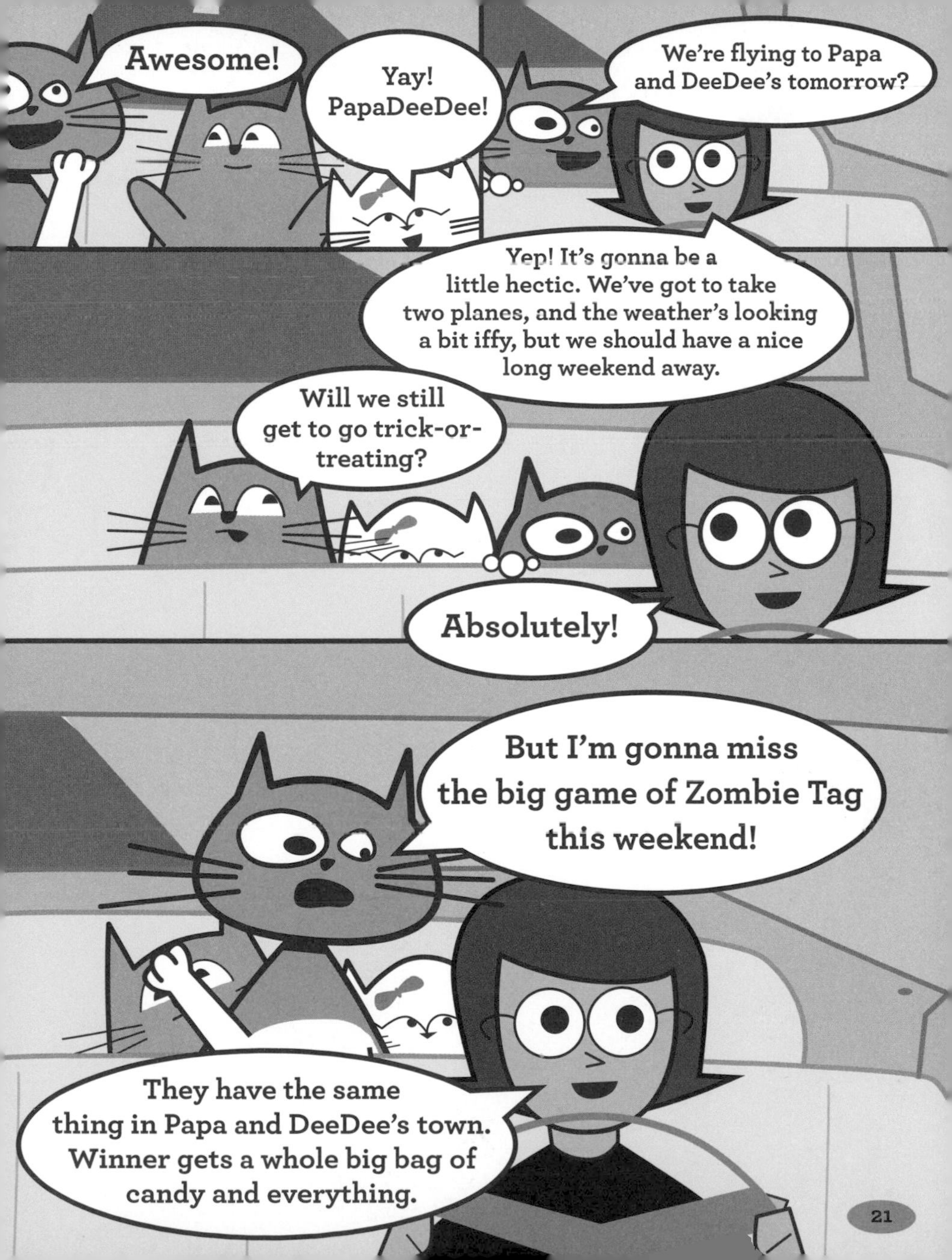
Awesome!
Yay! PapaDeeDee!
We're flying to Papa and DeeDee's tomorrow?
Yep! It's gonna be a little hectic. We've got to take two planes, and the weather's looking a bit iffy, but we should have a nice long weekend away.
Will we still get to go trick-or-treating?
Absolutely!
But I'm gonna miss the big game of Zombie Tag this weekend!
They have the same thing in Papa and DeeDee's town. Winner gets a whole big bag of candy and everything.

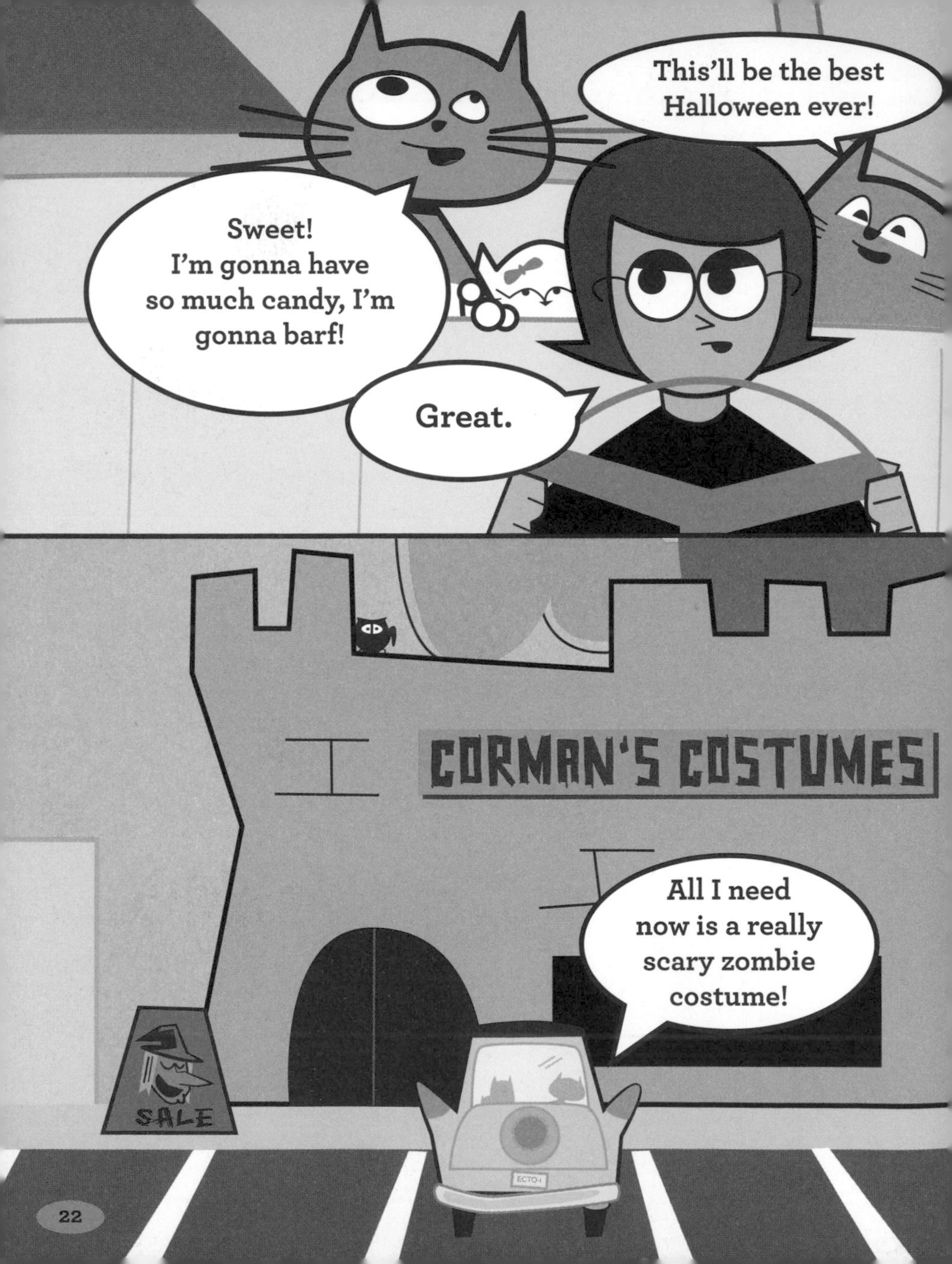
This'll be the best Halloween ever!
Sweet! I'm gonna have so much candy, I'm gonna barf!
Great.
CORMAN'S COSTUMES
All I need now is a really scary zombie costume!
SALE
ECTO-1

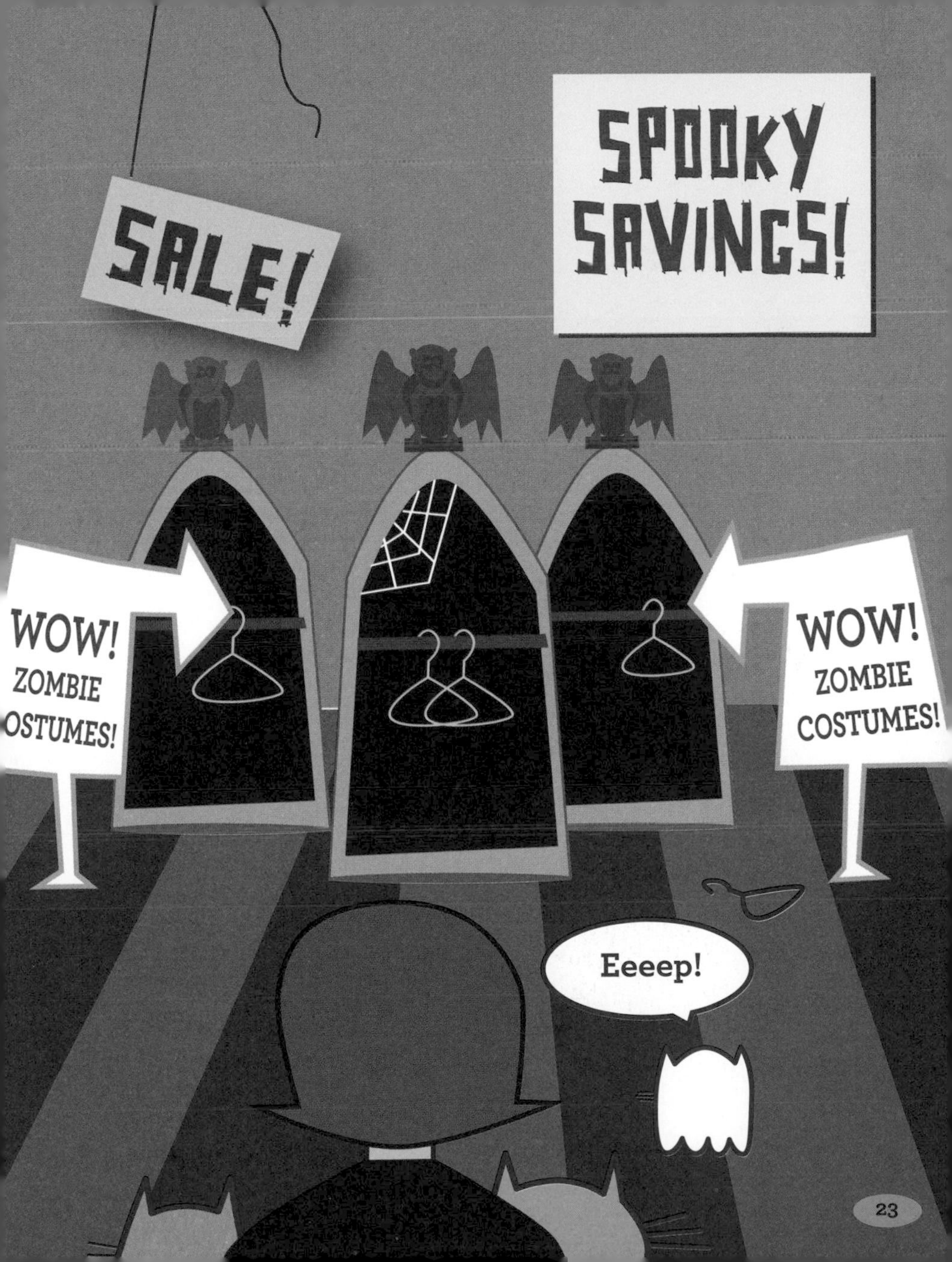
SALE!
SPOOKY SAVINGS!
WOW! ZOMBIE OSTUMES!
WOW! ZOMBIE COSTUMES!
Eeeep!

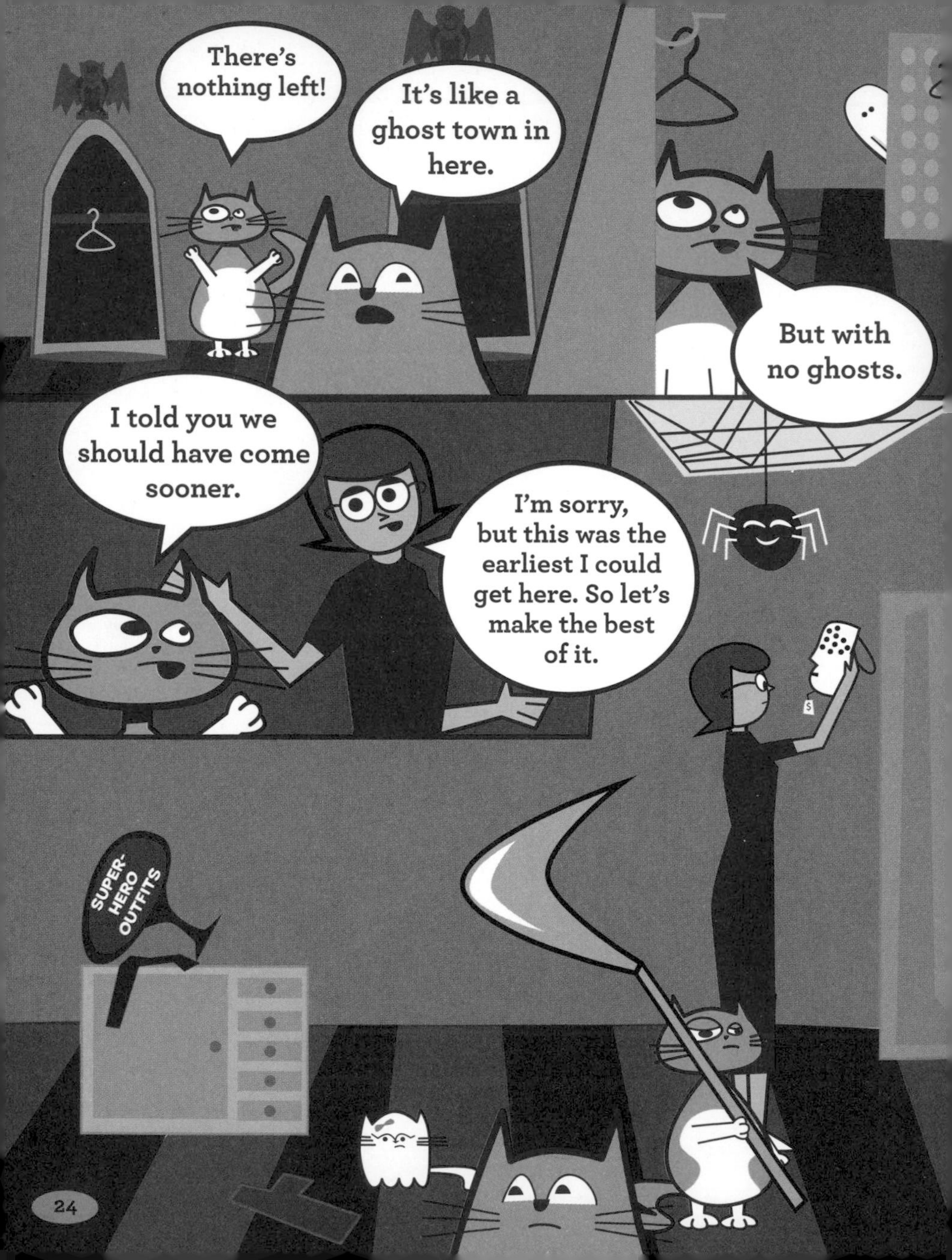
There's nothing left!
It's like a ghost town in here.
But with no ghosts.
I told you we should have come sooner.
I'm sorry, but this was the earliest I could get here. So let's make the best of it.
SUPER-HERO OUTFITS
$

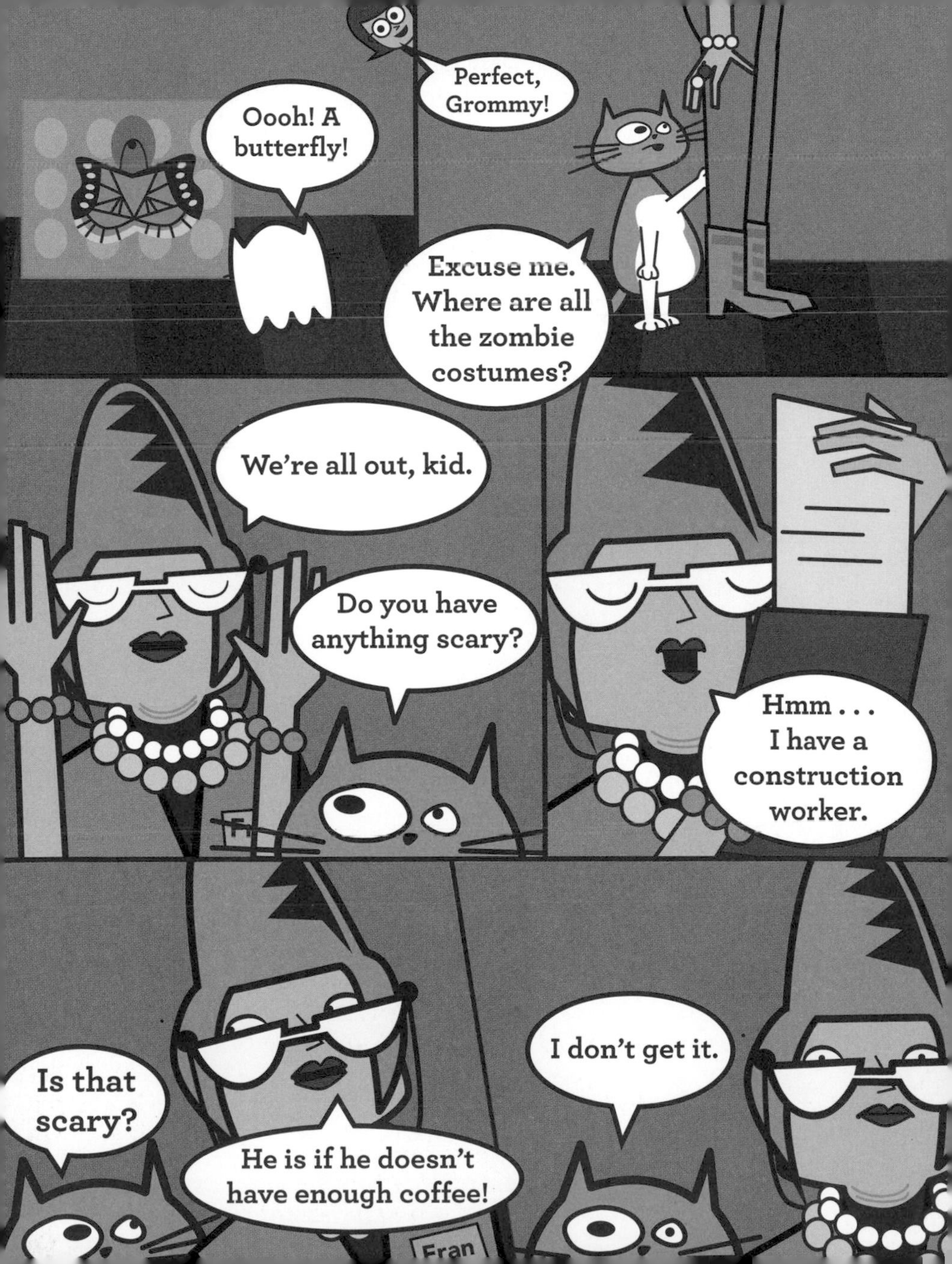
Oooh! A butterfly!
Perfect, Grommy!
Excuse me. Where are all the zombie costumes?
We're all out, kid.
Do you have anything scary?
Hmm . . . I have a construction worker.
Is that scary?
He is if he doesn't have enough coffee!
I don't get it.
Fran

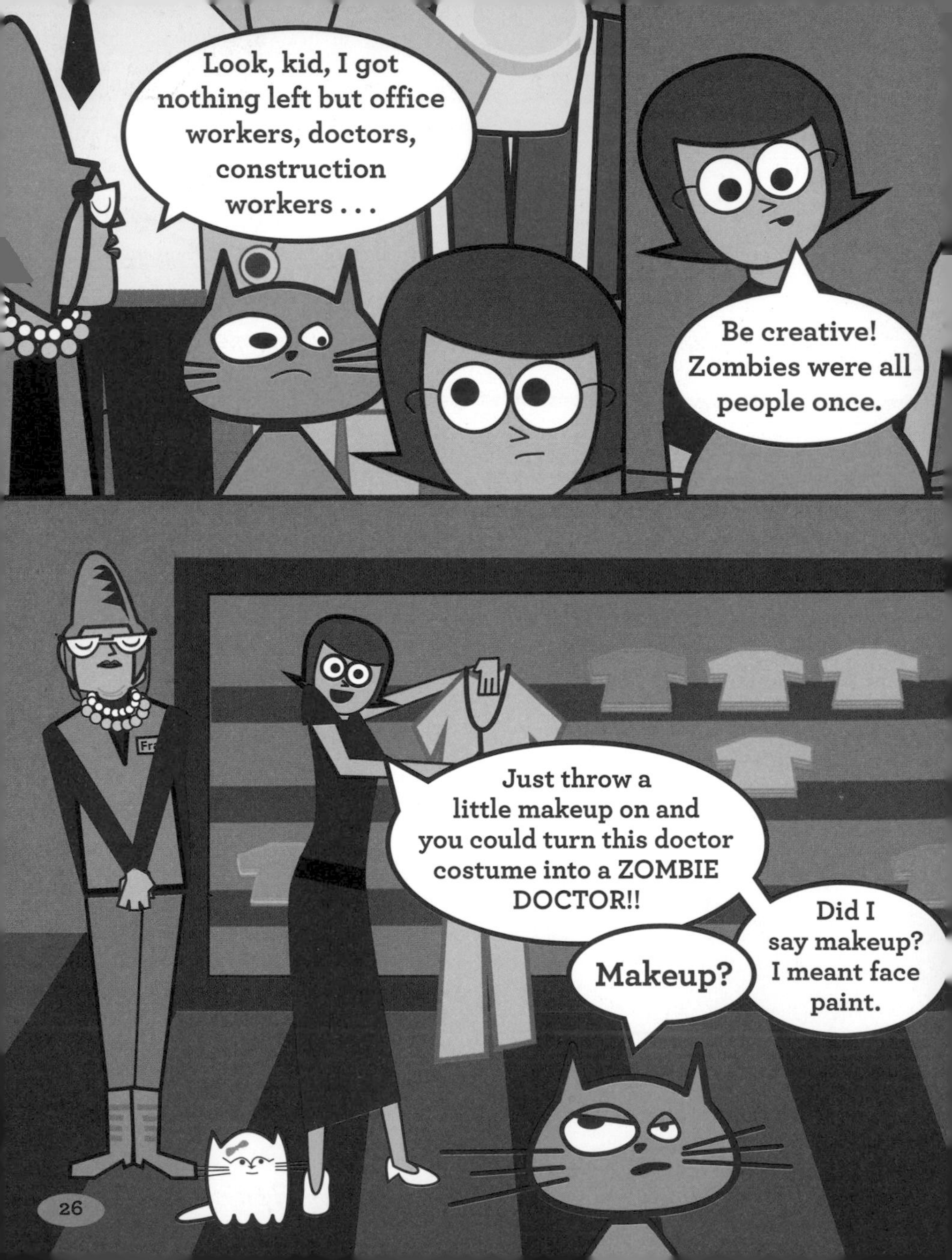

Look, kid, I got nothing left but office workers, doctors, construction workers . . .
Be creative! Zombies were all people once.
Fr
Just throw a little makeup on and you could turn this doctor costume into a ZOMBIE DOCTOR!!
Makeup?
Did I say makeup? I meant face paint.

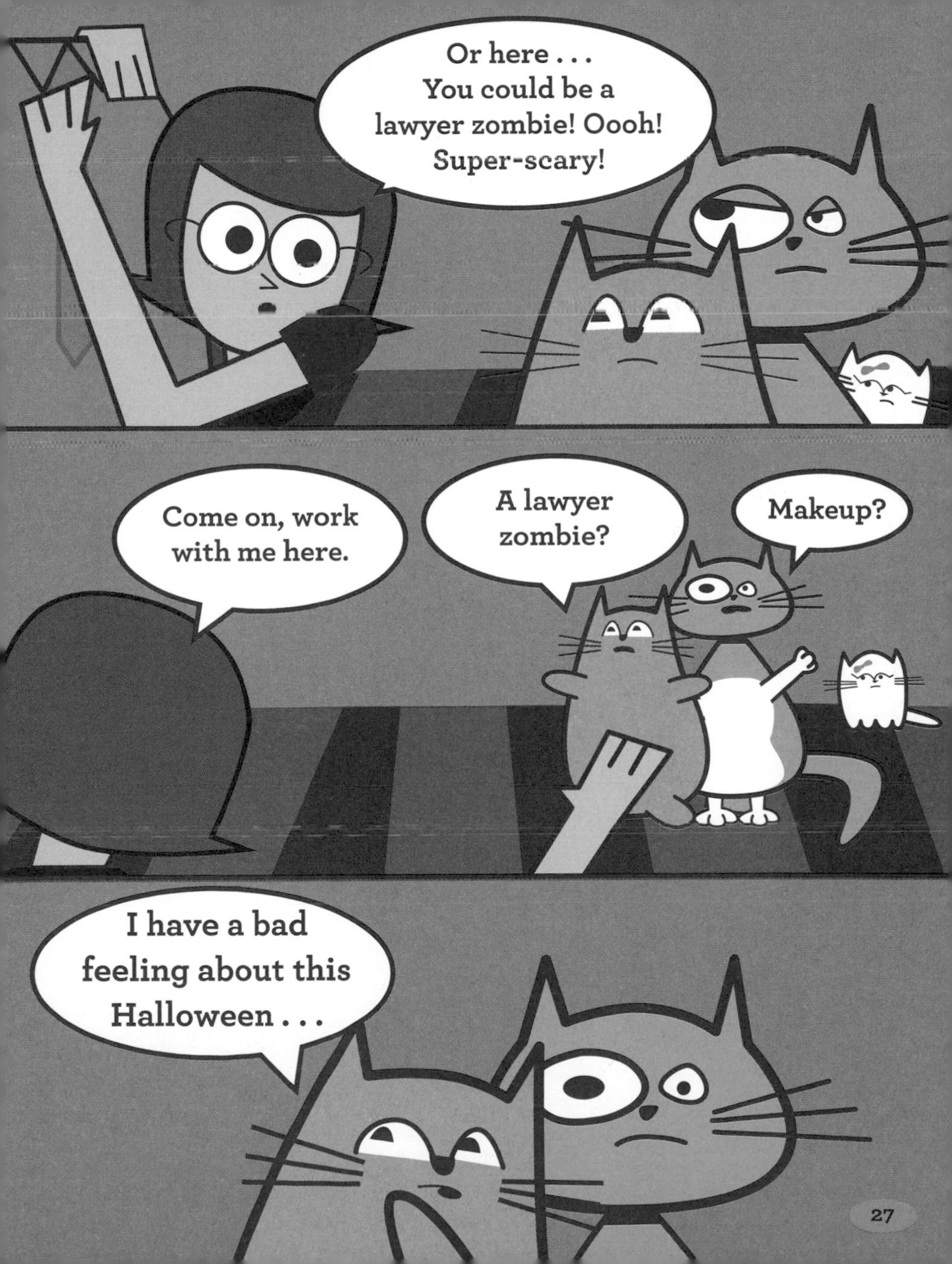

Or here . . . You could be a lawyer zombie! Oooh! Super-scary!
Come on, work with me here.
A lawyer zombie?
Makeup?
I have a bad feeling about this Halloween . . .

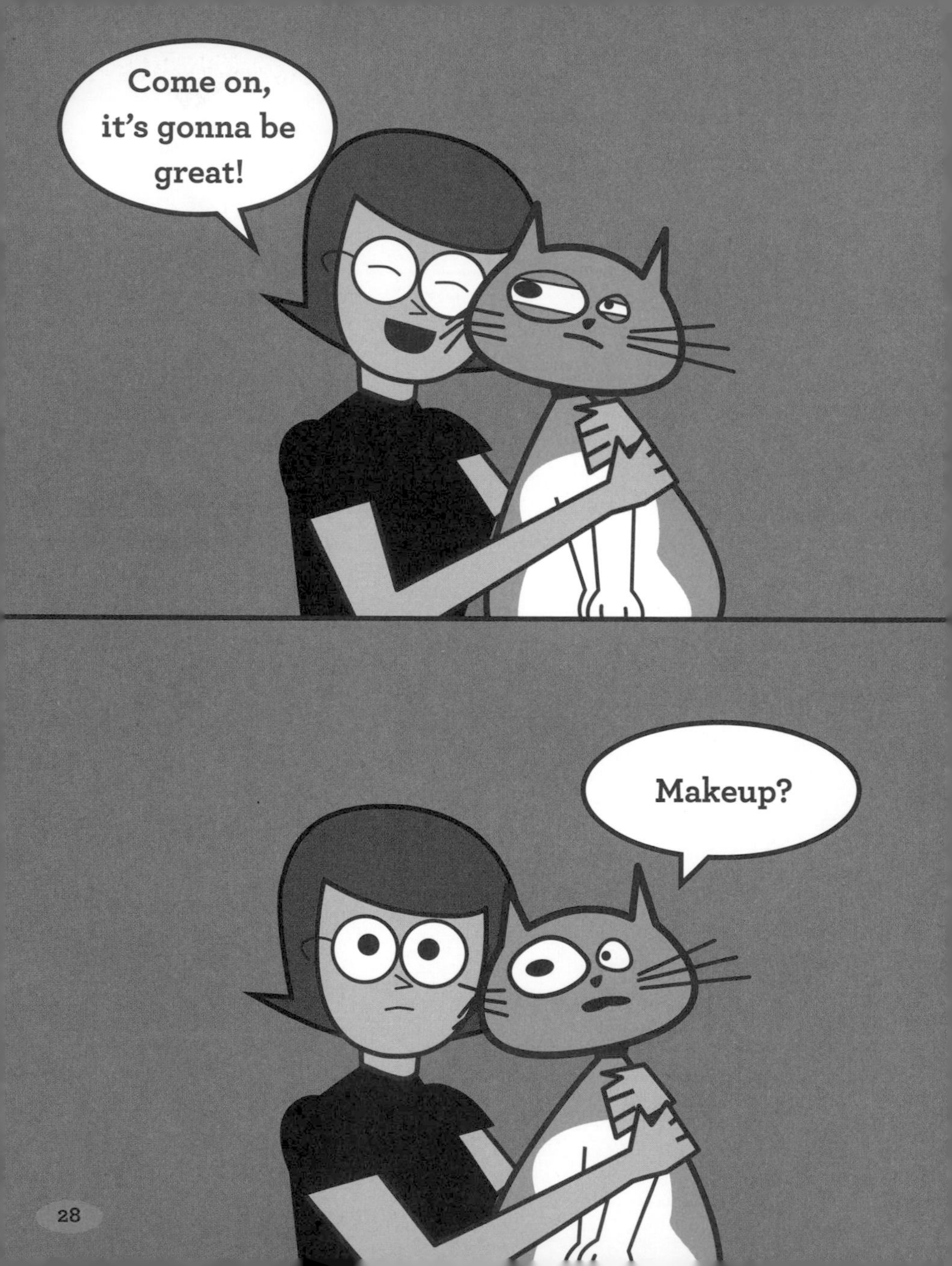
Come on, it's gonna be great!
Makeup?

Chapter Two: MAD DASH FOR MOMMY

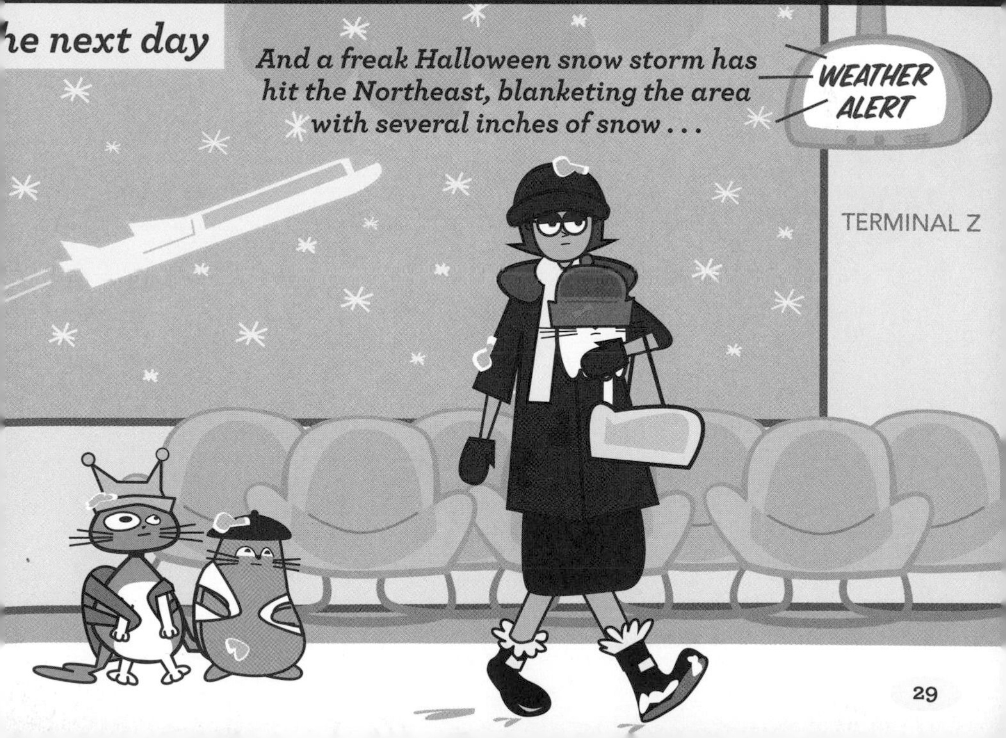
he next day
And a freak Halloween snow storm has hit the Northeast, blanketing the area with several inches of snow . . .
WEATHER ALERT
TERMINAL Z

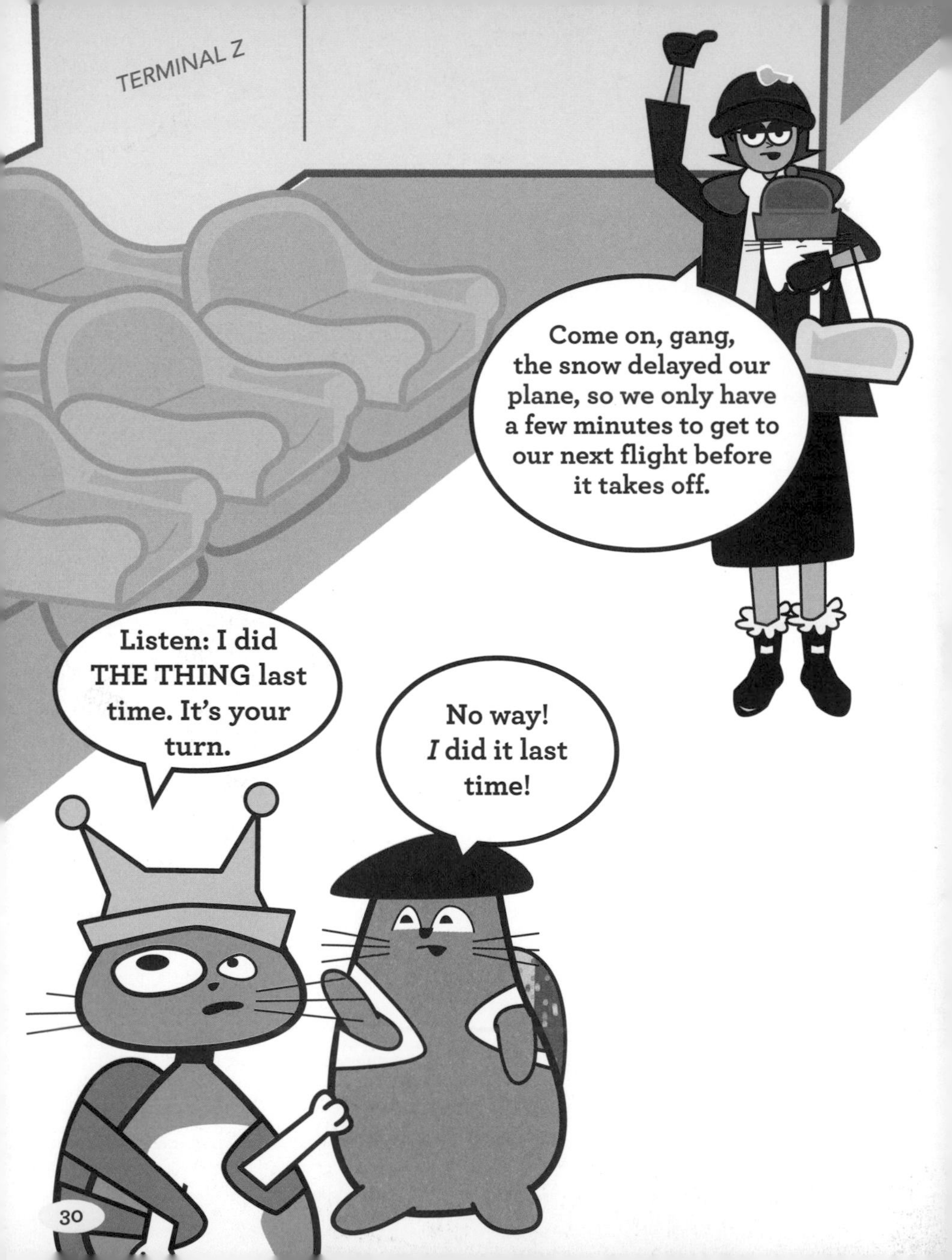
TERMINAL Z
Come on, gang, the snow delayed our plane, so we only have a few minutes to get to our next flight before it takes off.
Listen: I did THE THING last time. It's your turn.
No way! *I* did it last time!

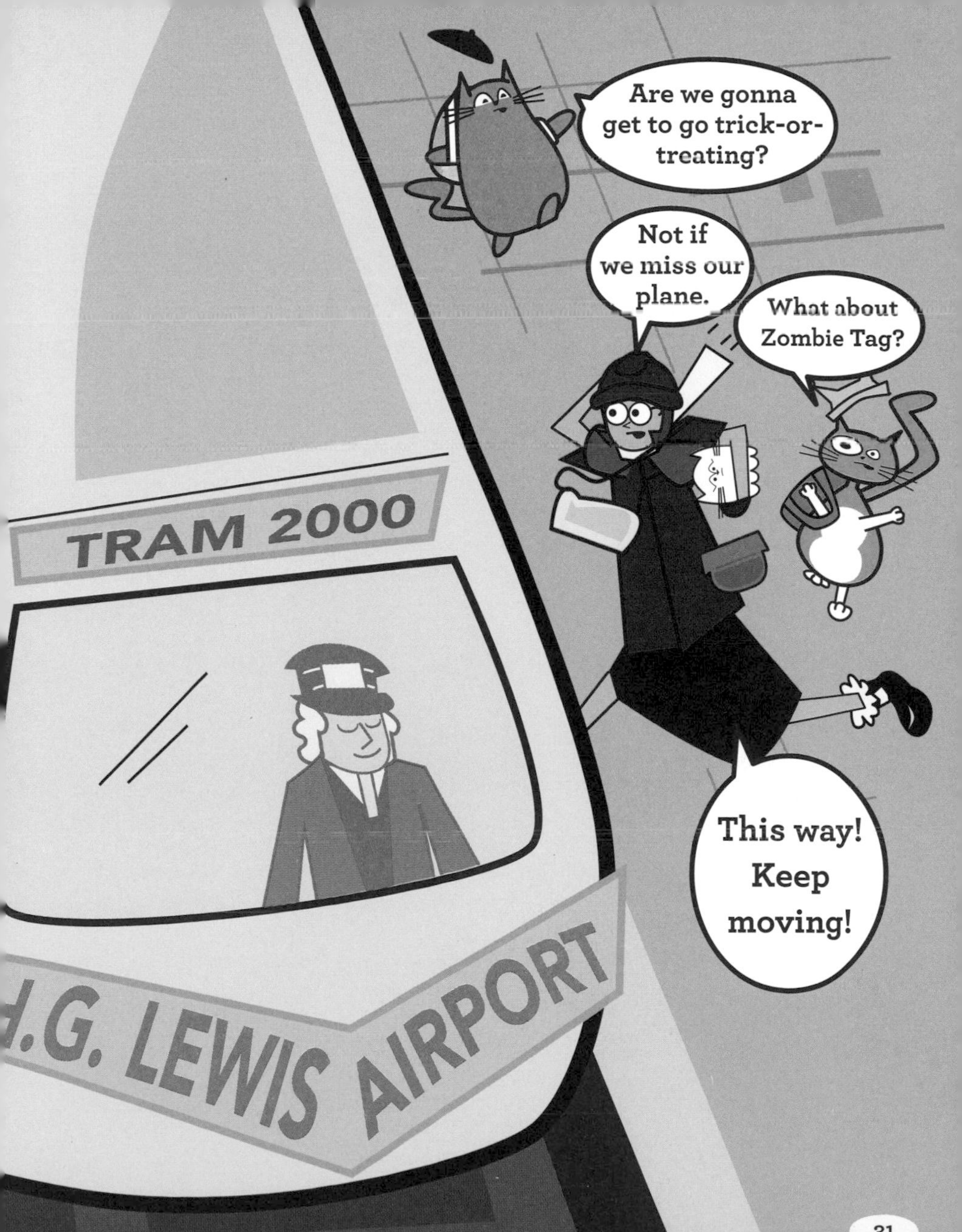
Are we gonna get to go trick-or-treating?
Not if we miss our plane.
What about Zombie Tag?
TRAM 2000
This way! Keep moving!
H.G. LEWIS AIRPORT

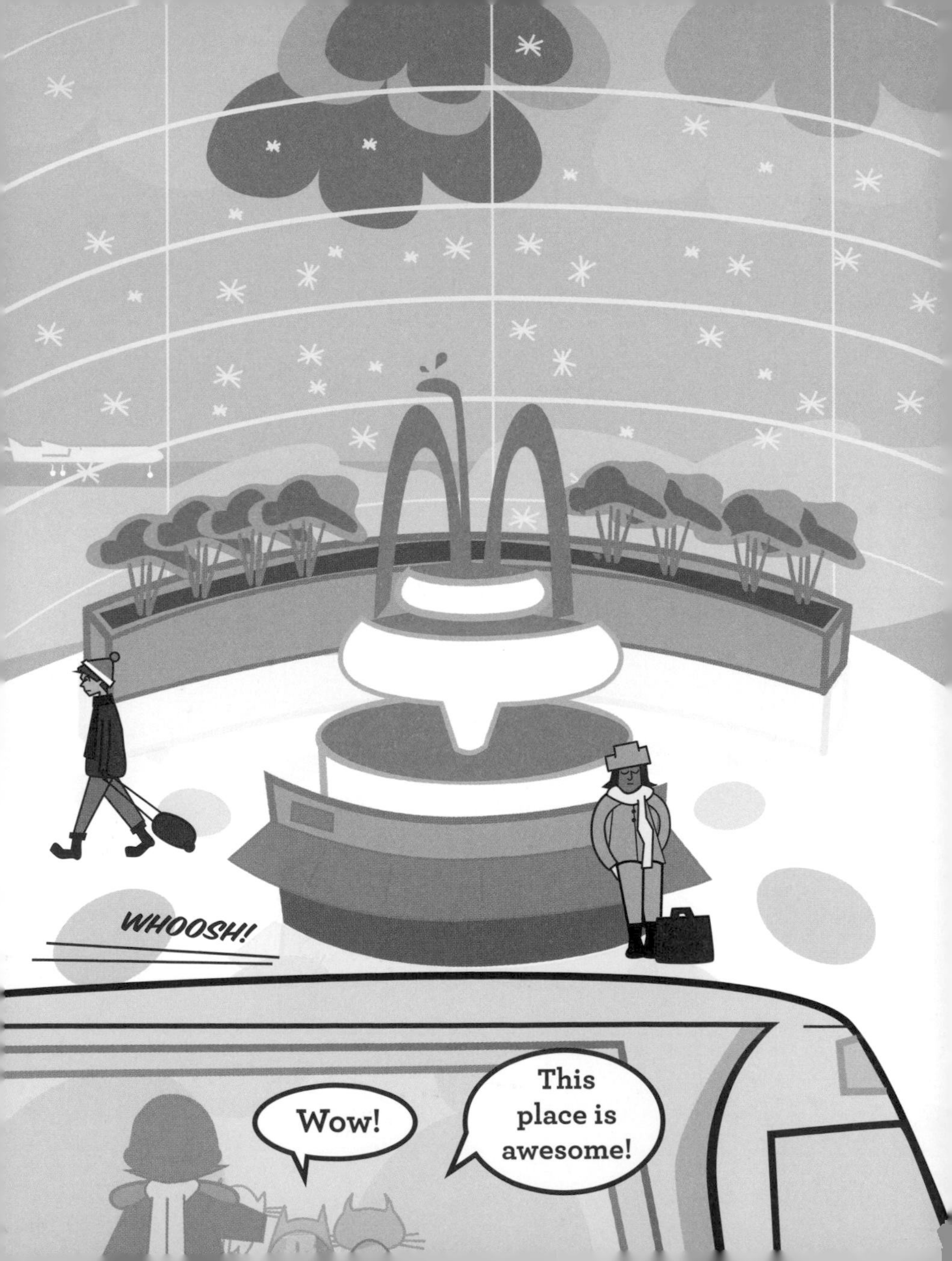
WHOOSH!
Wow!
This place is awesome!

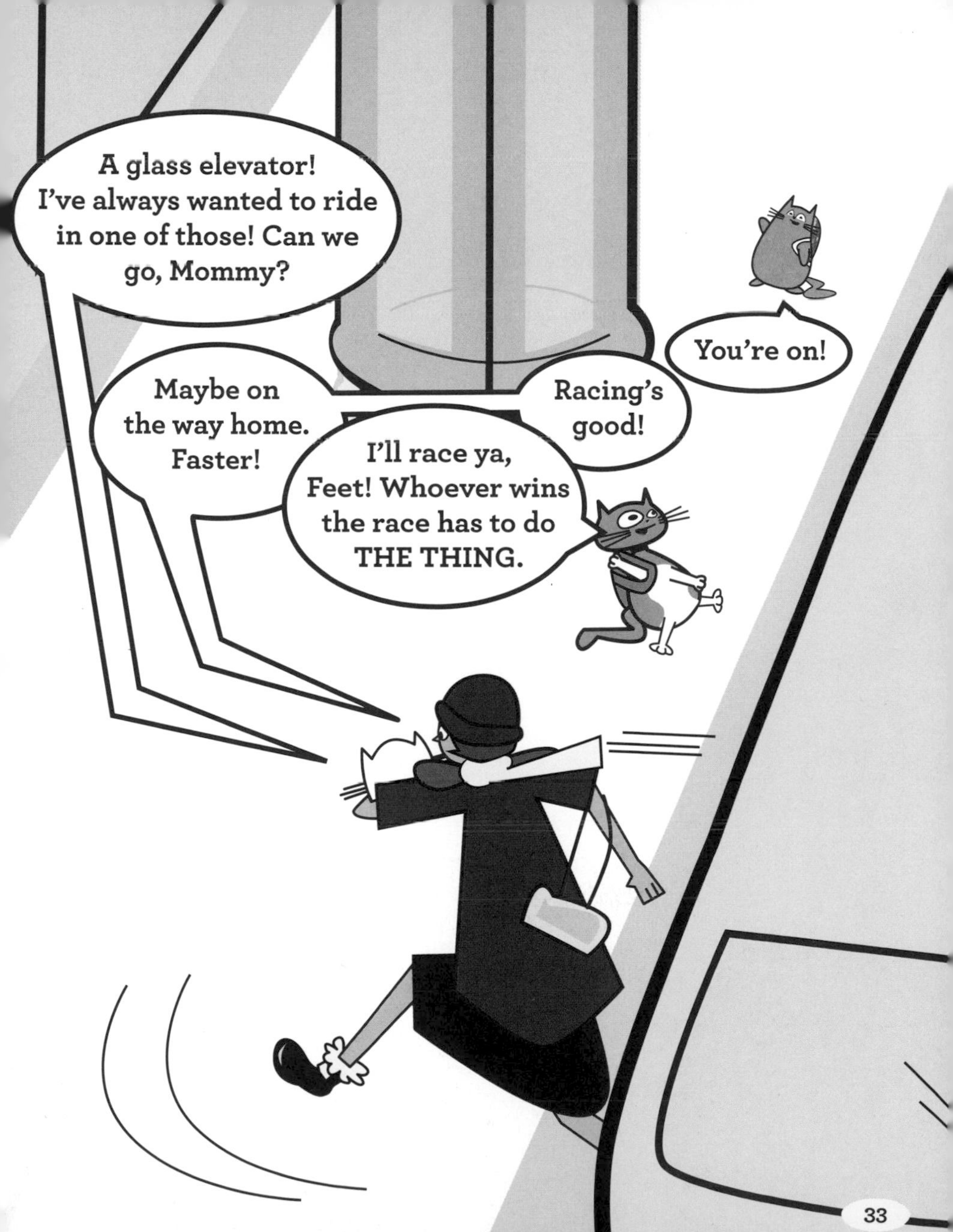
A glass elevator! I've always wanted to ride in one of those! Can we go, Mommy?
Maybe on the way home. Faster!
I'll race ya, Feet! Whoever wins the race has to do THE THING.
Racing's good!
You're on!

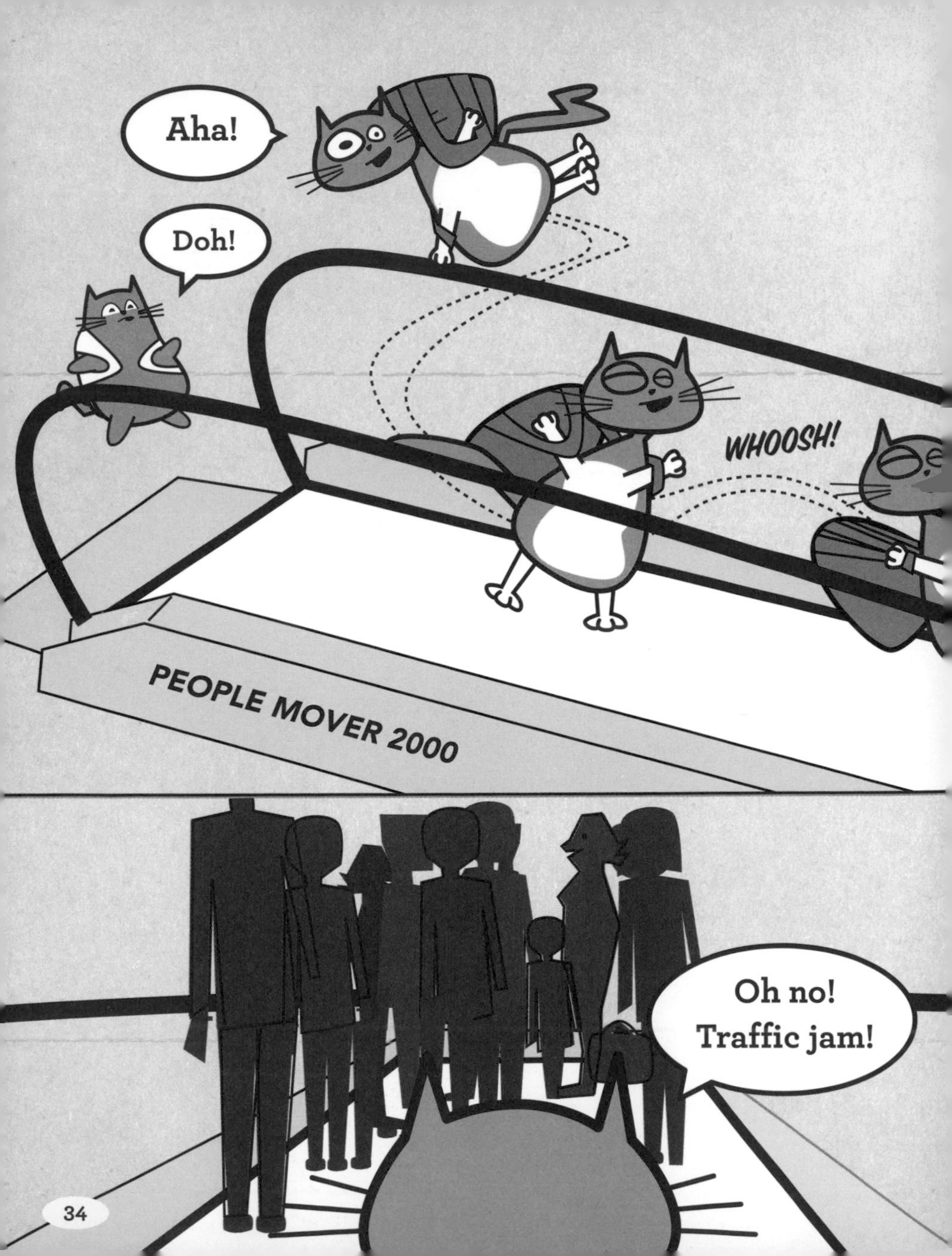
Aha!
Doh!
WHOOSH!
PEOPLE MOVER 2000
Oh no! Traffic jam!

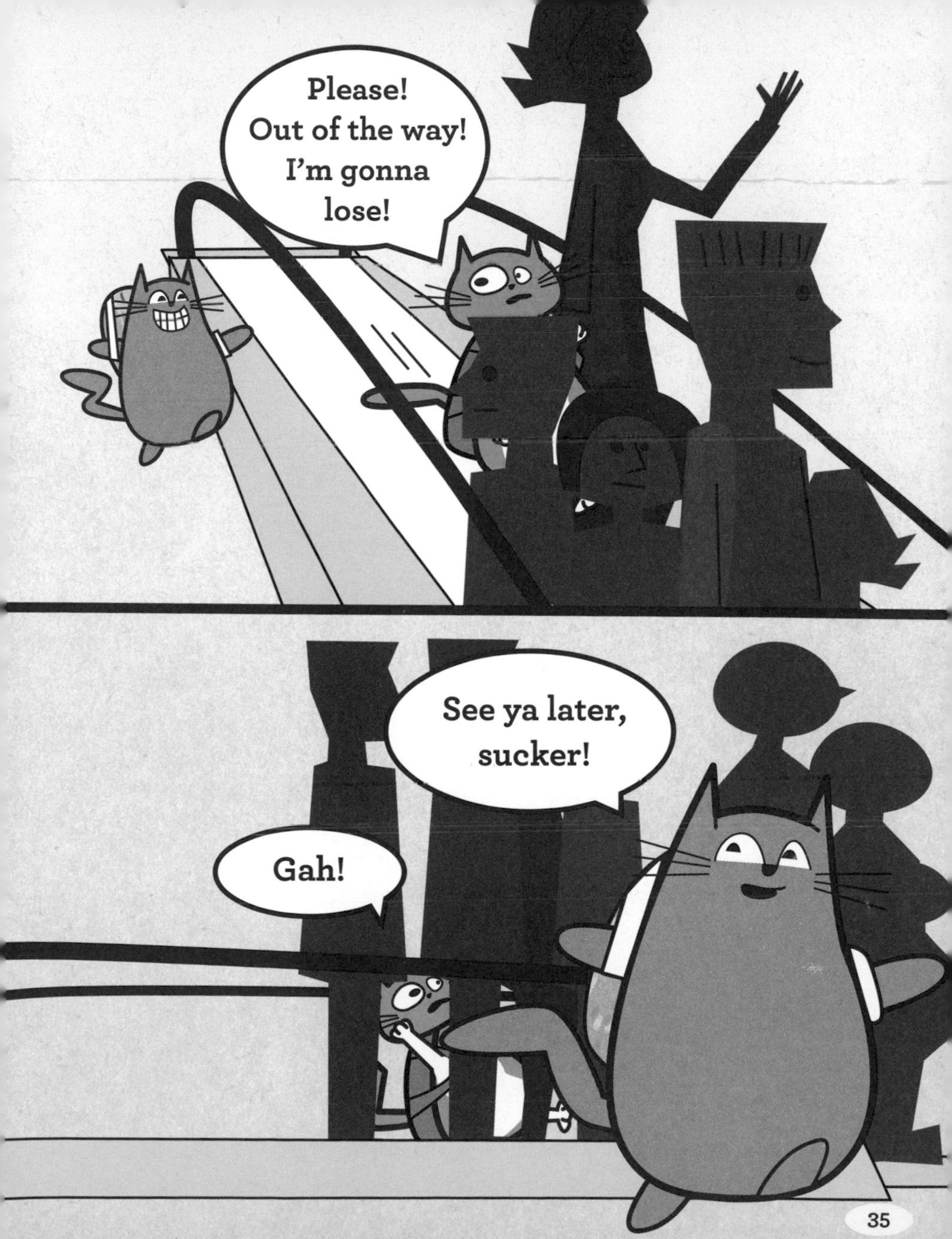
Please!
Out of the way!
I'm gonna
lose!
See ya later,
sucker!
Gah!

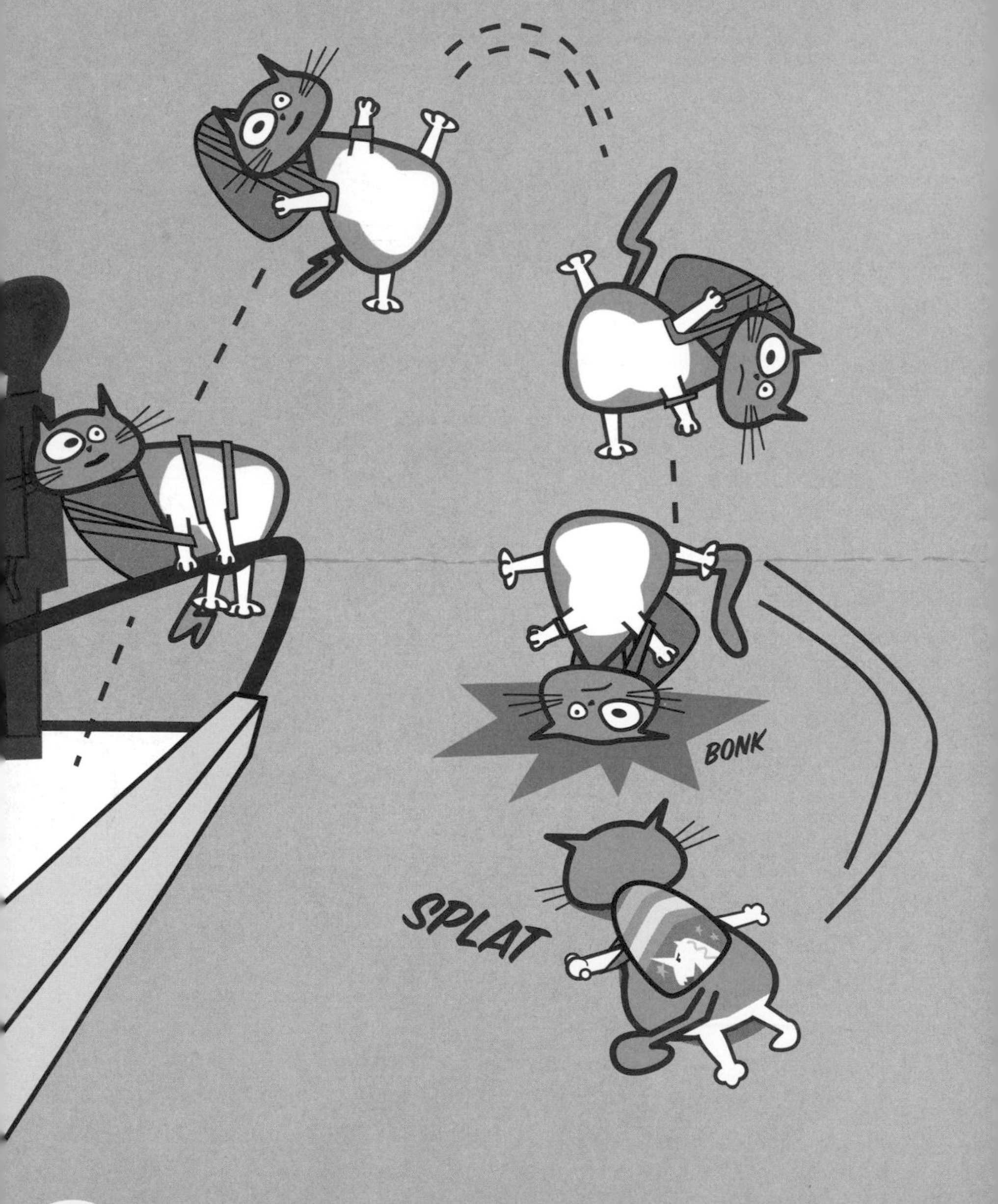
BONK
SPLAT

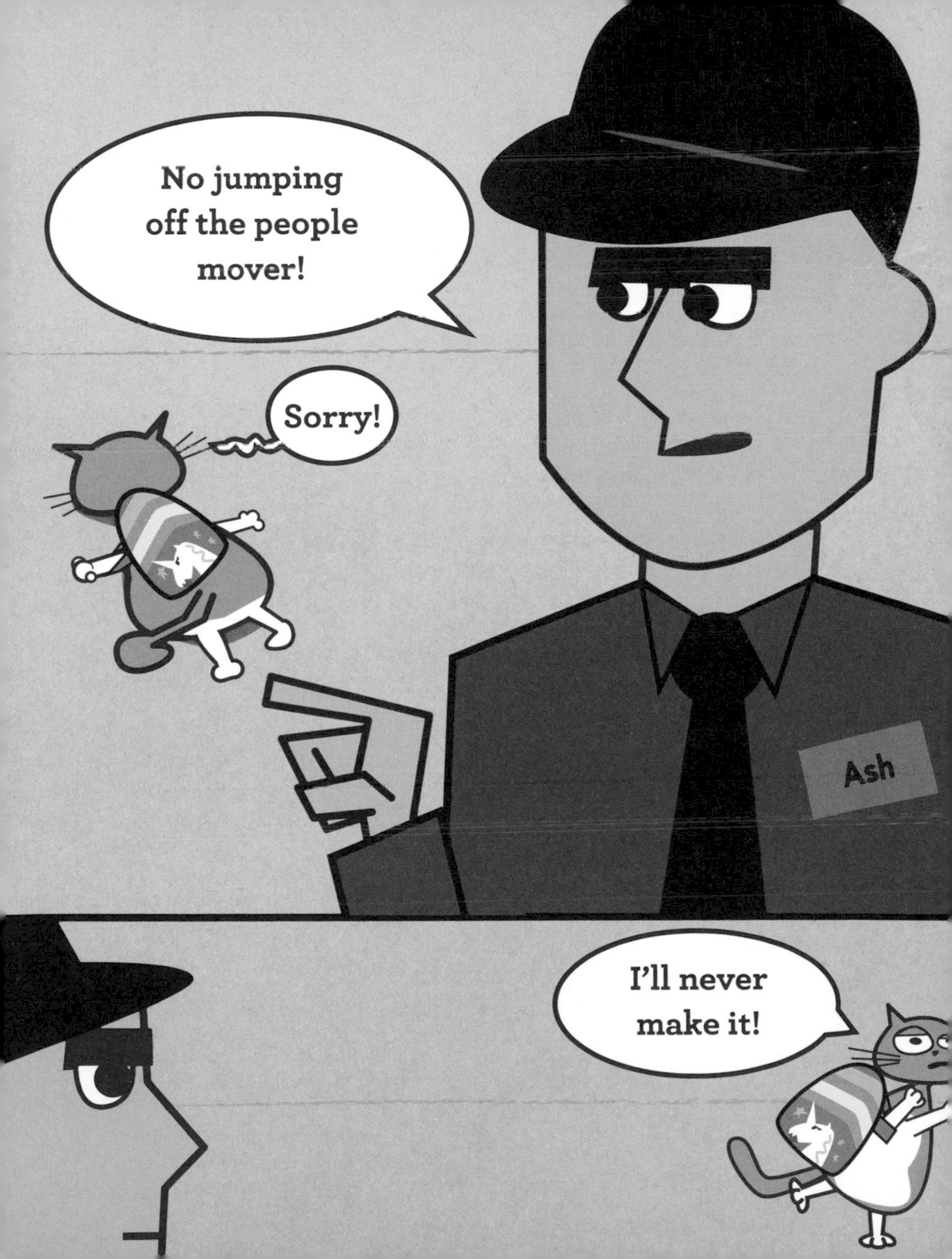
No jumping off the people mover!
Sorry!
Ash
I'll never make it!

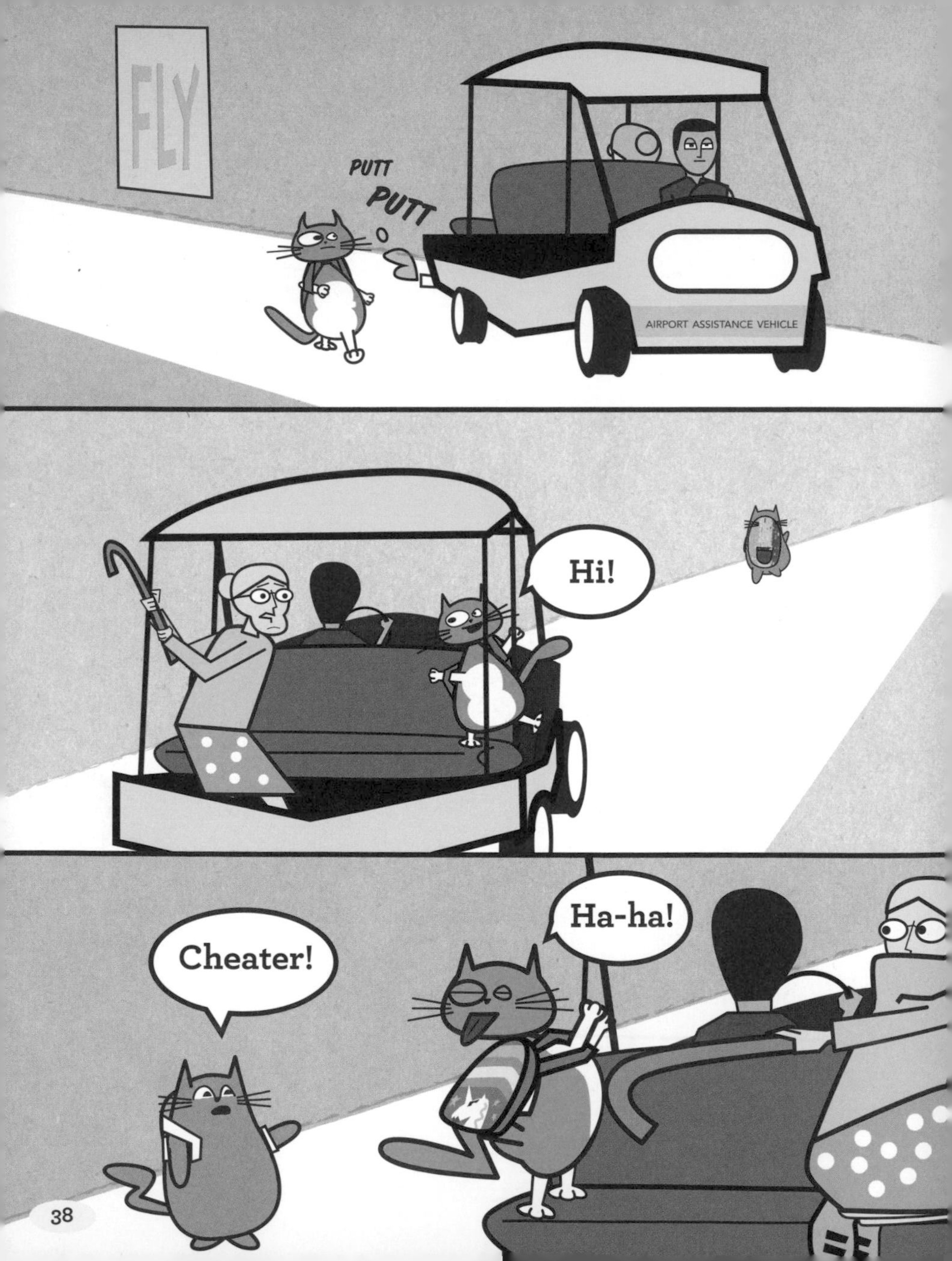
FLY
PUTT
PUTT
AIRPORT ASSISTANCE VEHICLE
Hi!
Cheater!
Ha-ha!

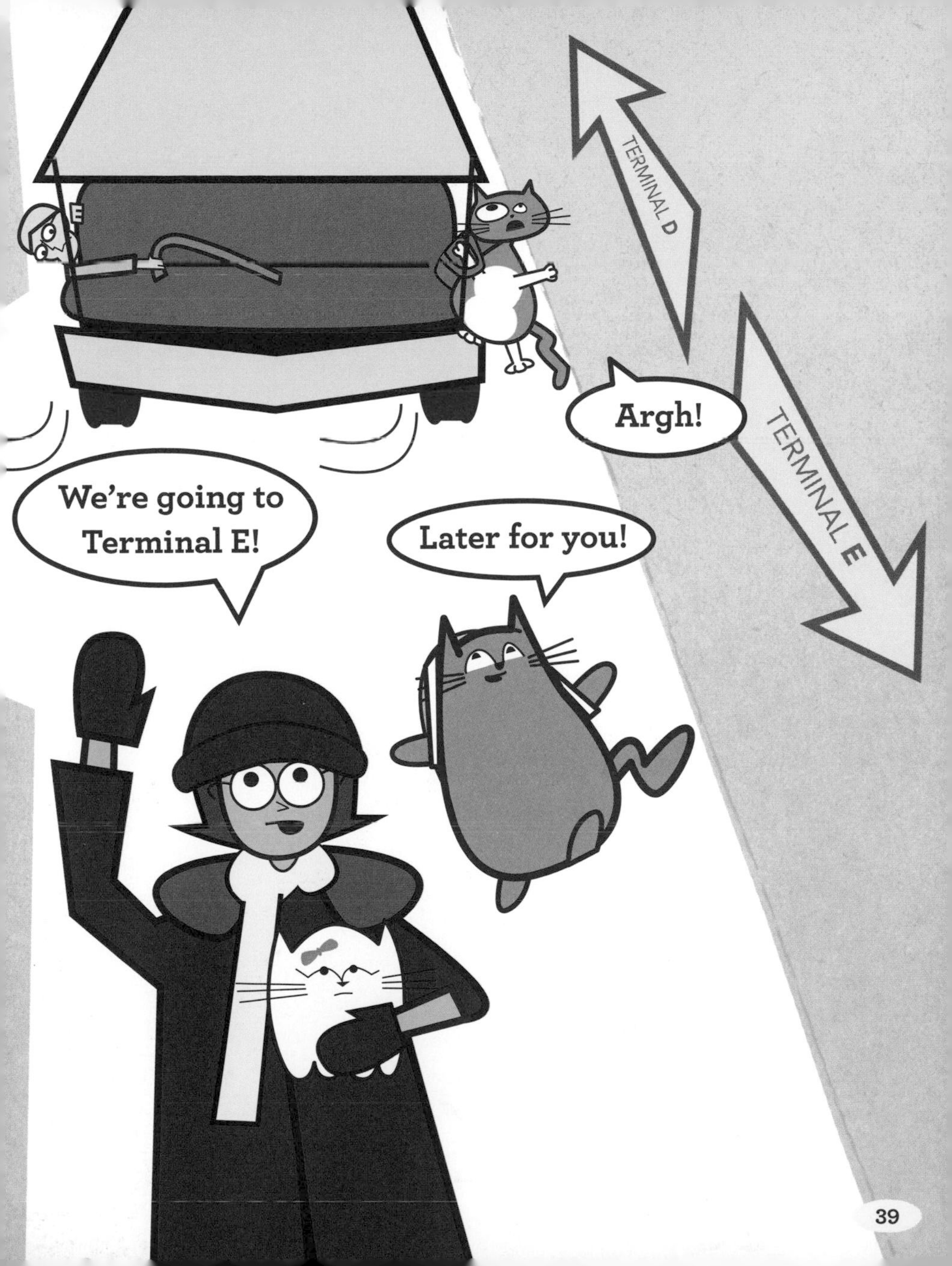
TERMINAL D
Argh!
TERMINAL E
We're going to Terminal E!
Later for you!

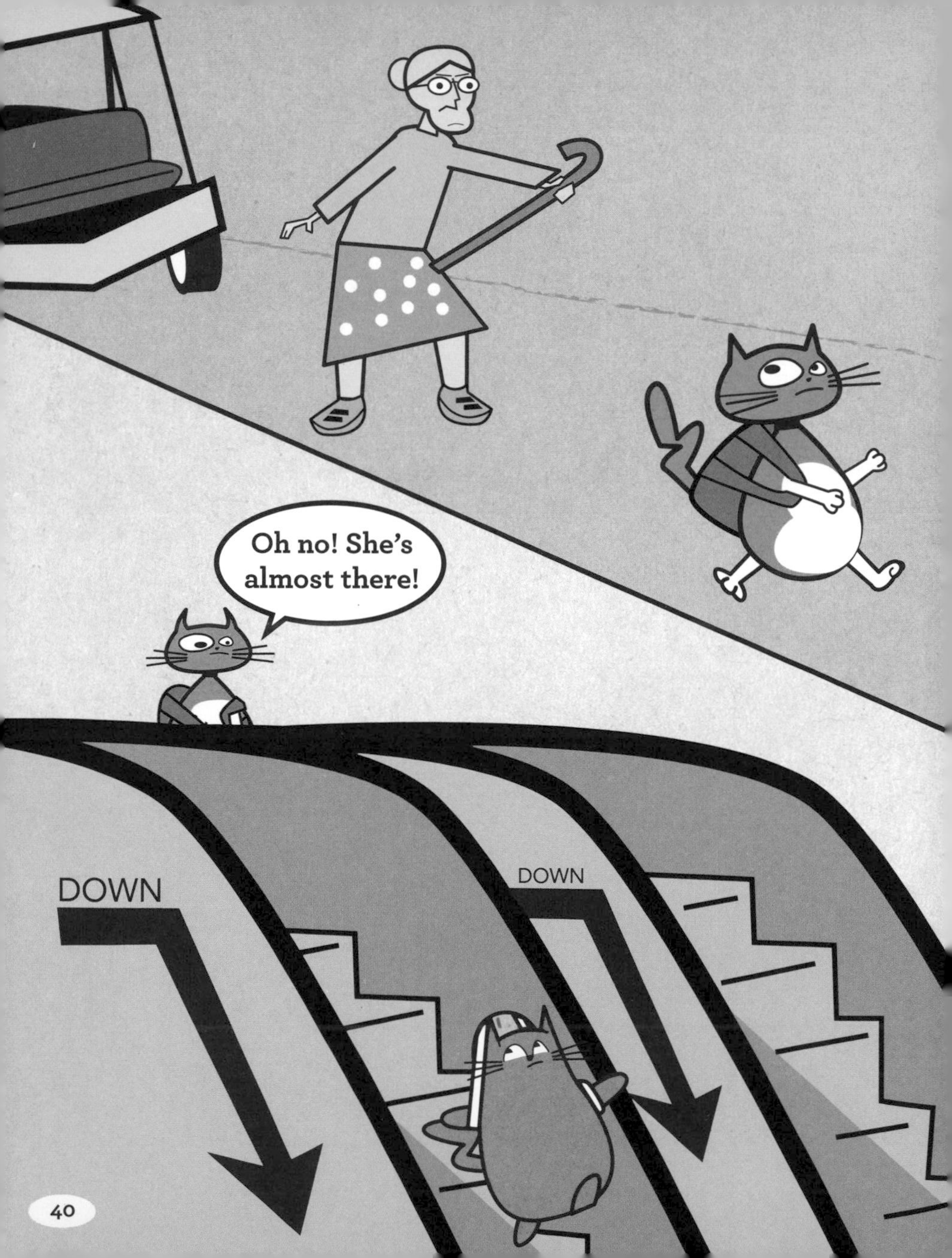

Oh no! She's almost there!
DOWN
DOWN

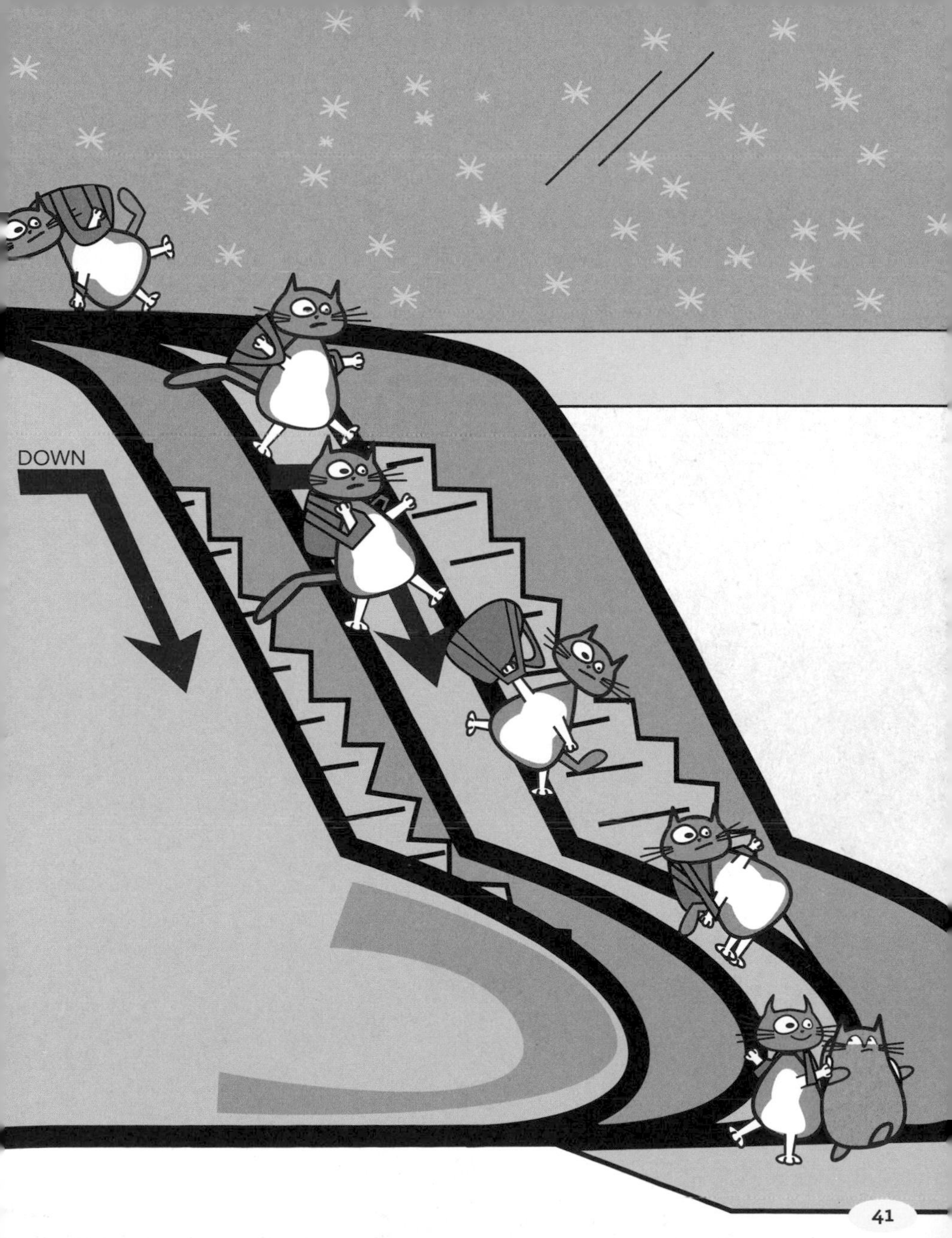
DOWN

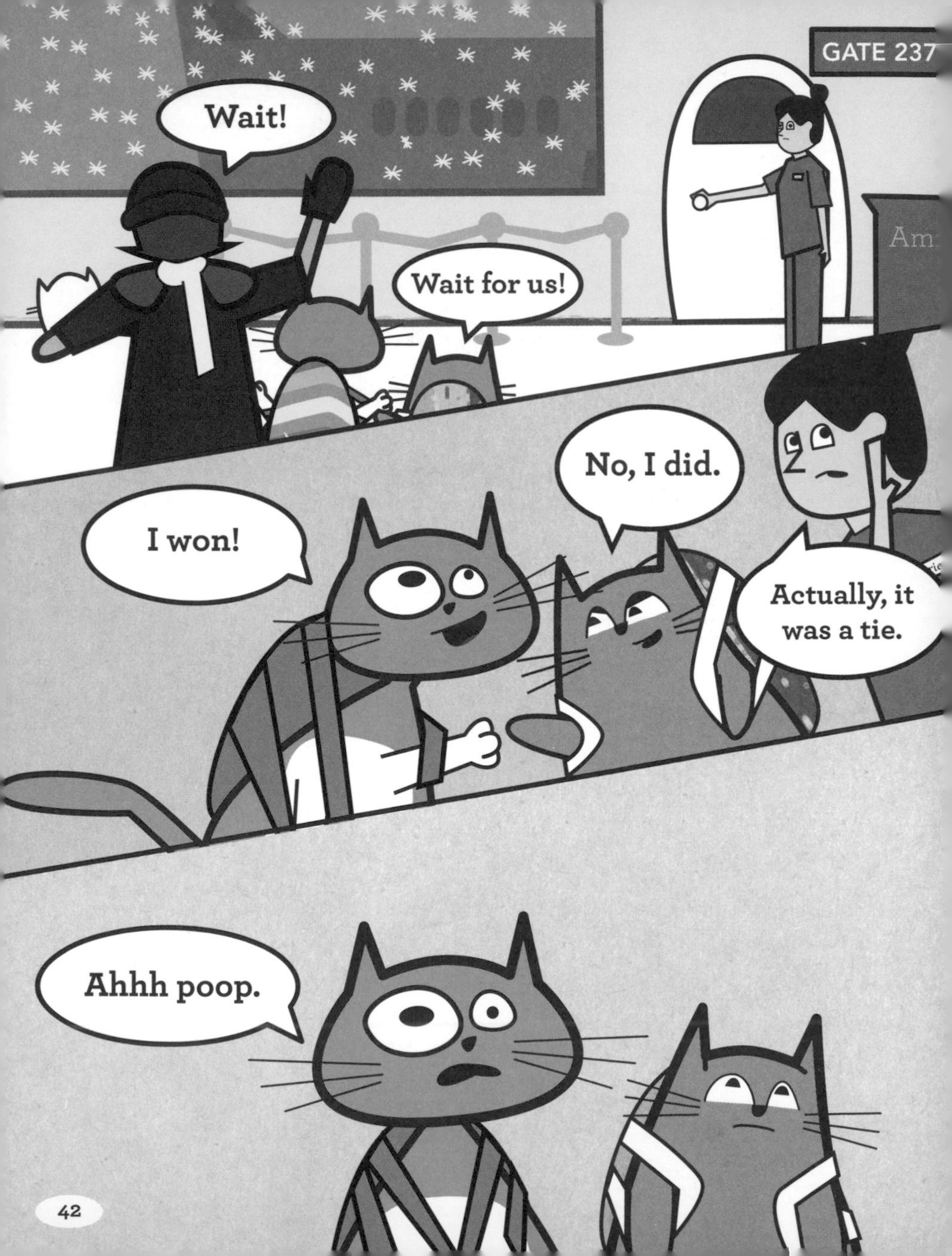
GATE 237
Wait!
Wait for us!
I won!
No, I did.
Actually, it was a tie.
Ahhh poop.

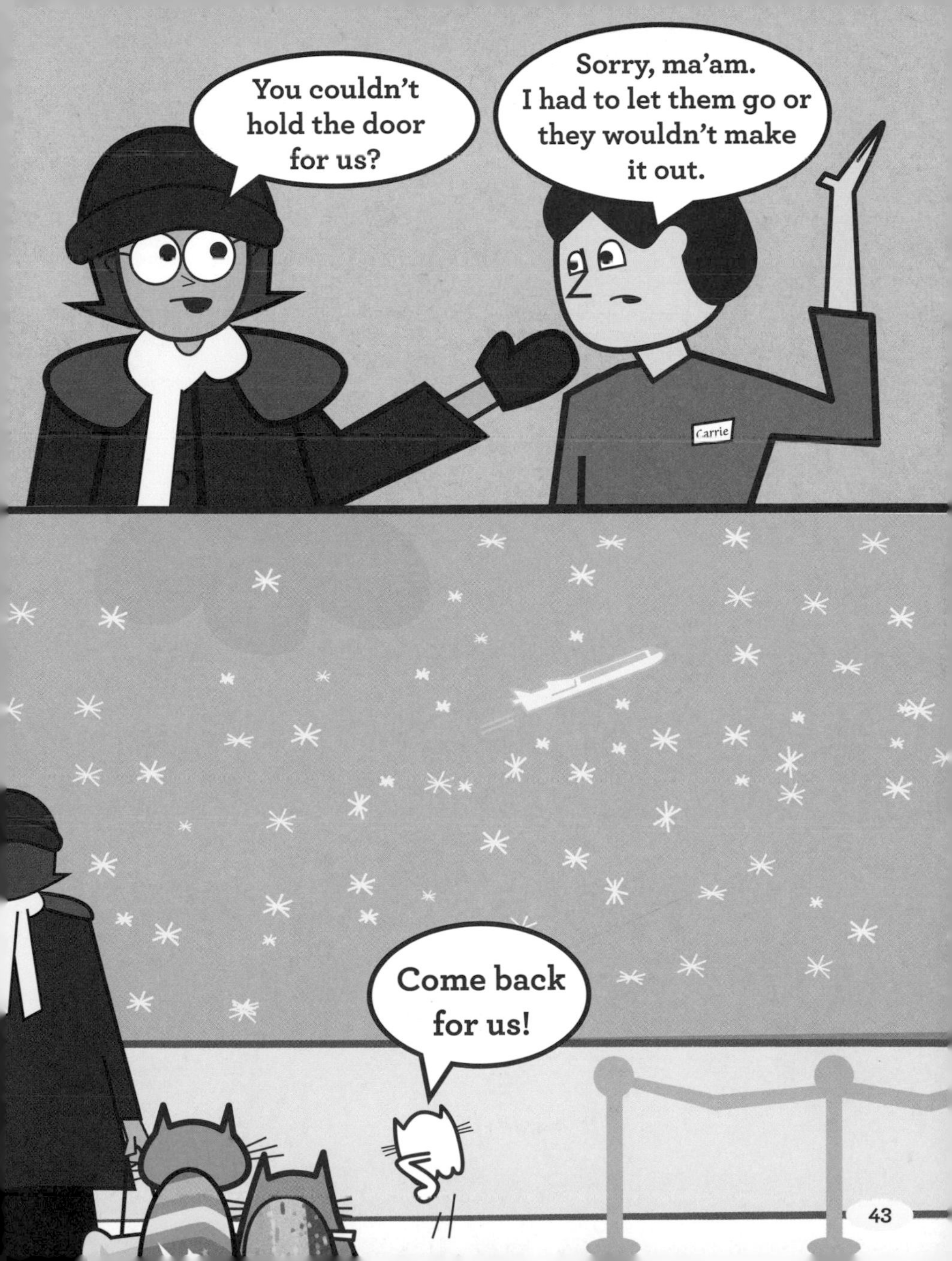
You couldn't hold the door for us?
Sorry, ma'am. I had to let them go or they wouldn't make it out.
Carrie
Come back for us!

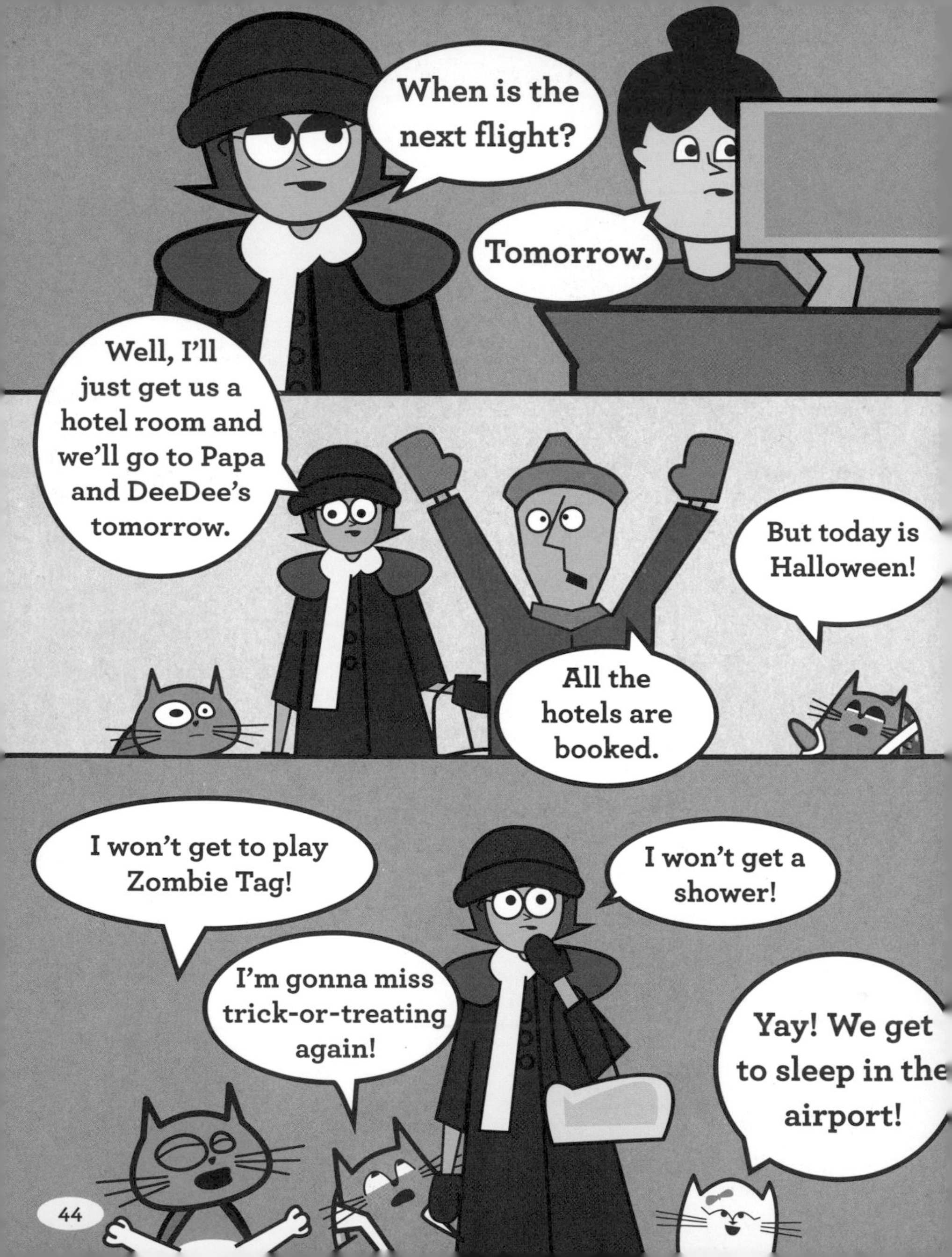
When is the next flight?
Tomorrow.
Well, I'll just get us a hotel room and we'll go to Papa and DeeDee's tomorrow.
But today is Halloween!
All the hotels are booked.
I won't get to play Zombie Tag!
I won't get a shower!
I'm gonna miss trick-or-treating again!
Yay! We get to sleep in the airport!

Chapter Three: AIRPORT OLYMPICS

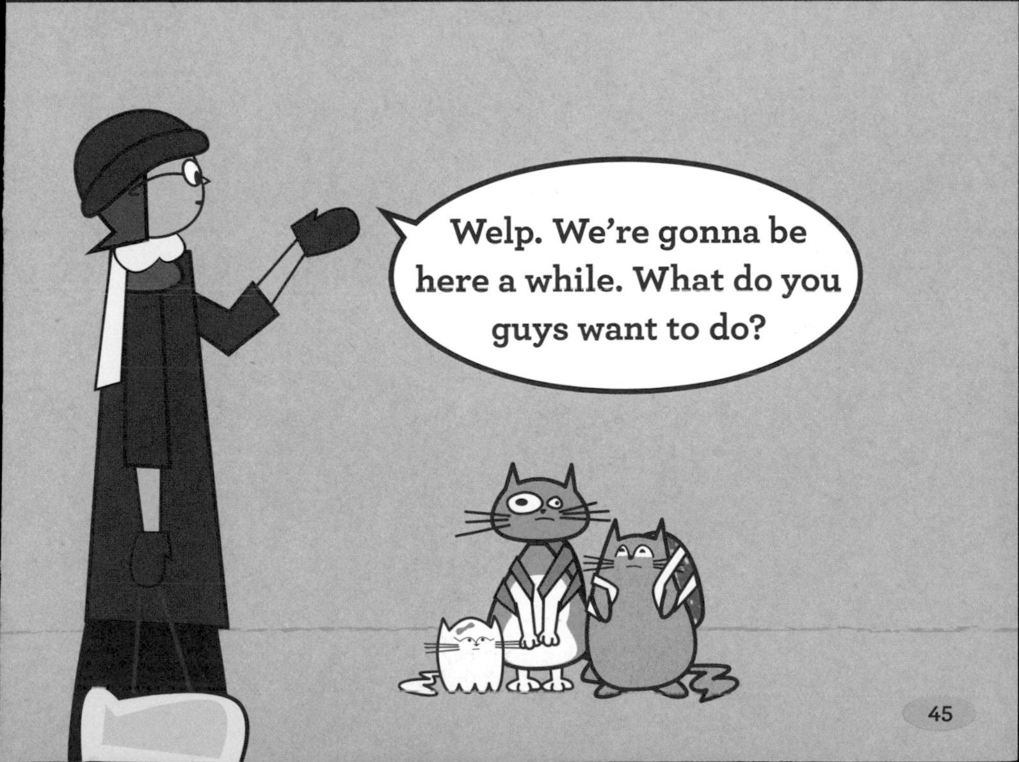
Welp. We're gonna be here a while. What do you guys want to do?

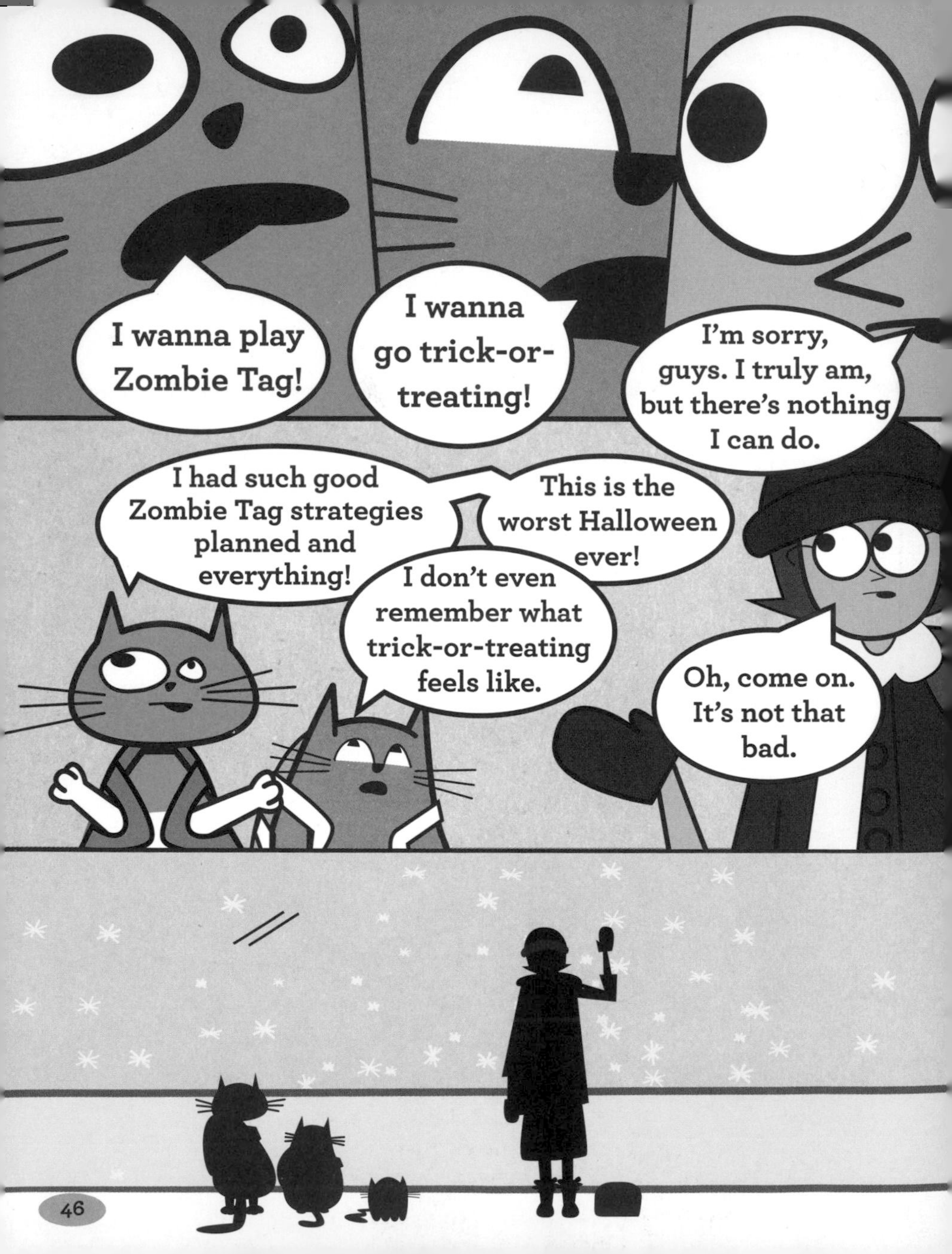
I wanna play Zombie Tag!
I wanna go trick-or-treating!
I'm sorry, guys. I truly am, but there's nothing I can do.
I had such good Zombie Tag strategies planned and everything!
This is the worst Halloween ever!
I don't even remember what trick-or-treating feels like.
Oh, come on. It's not that bad.

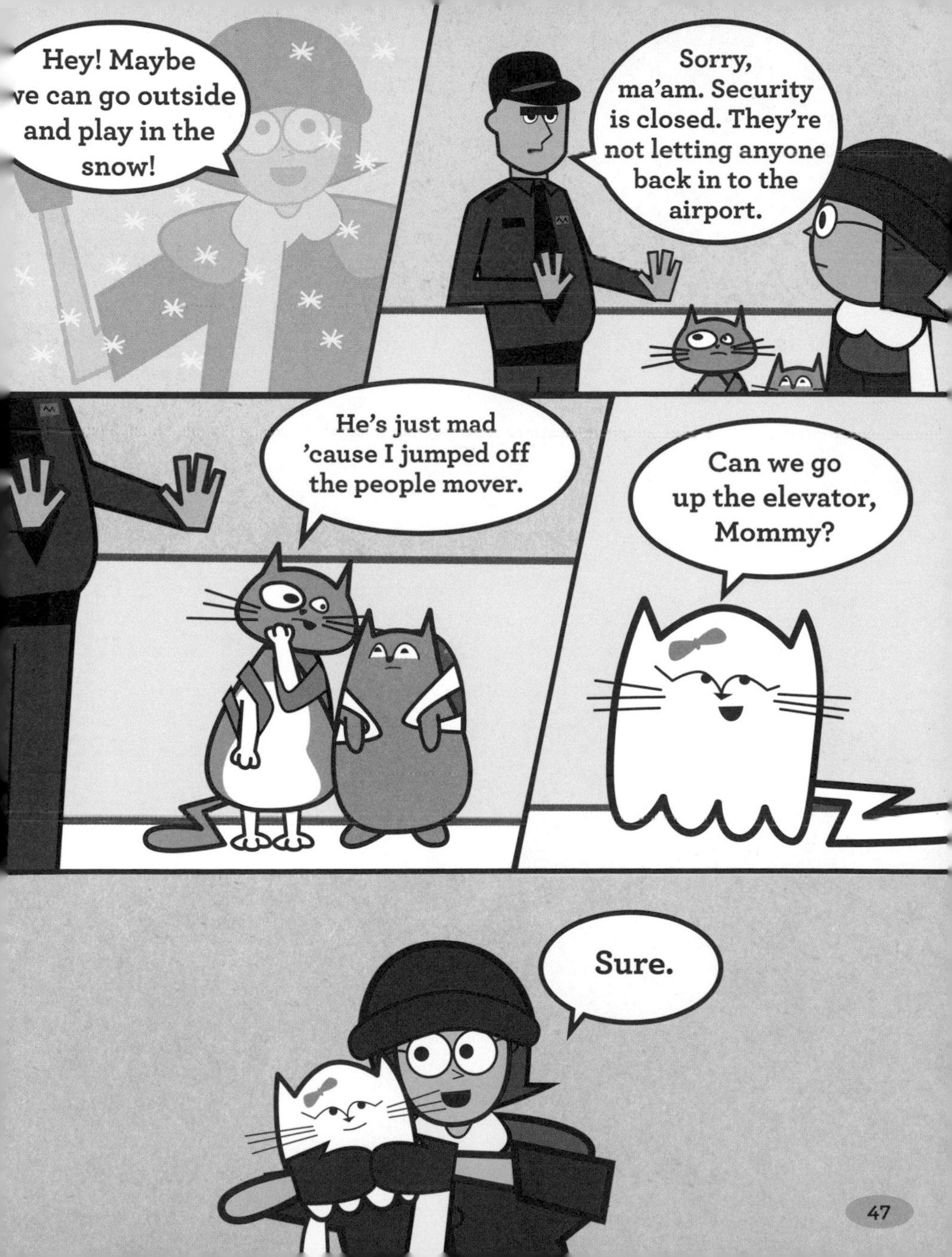
Hey! Maybe we can go outside and play in the snow!
Sorry, ma'am. Security is closed. They're not letting anyone back in to the airport.
He's just mad 'cause I jumped off the people mover.
Can we go up the elevator, Mommy?
Sure.

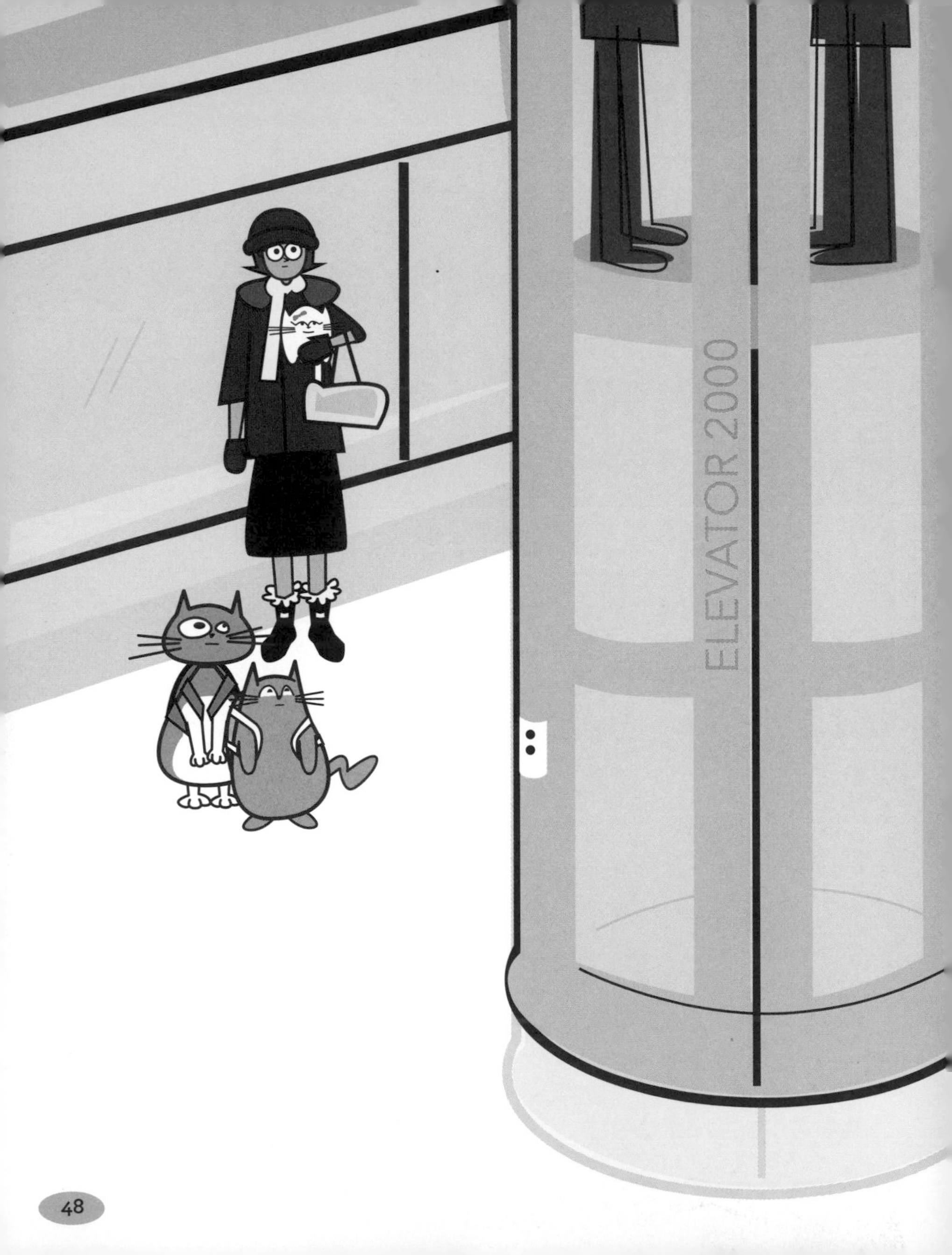
ELEVATOR 2000

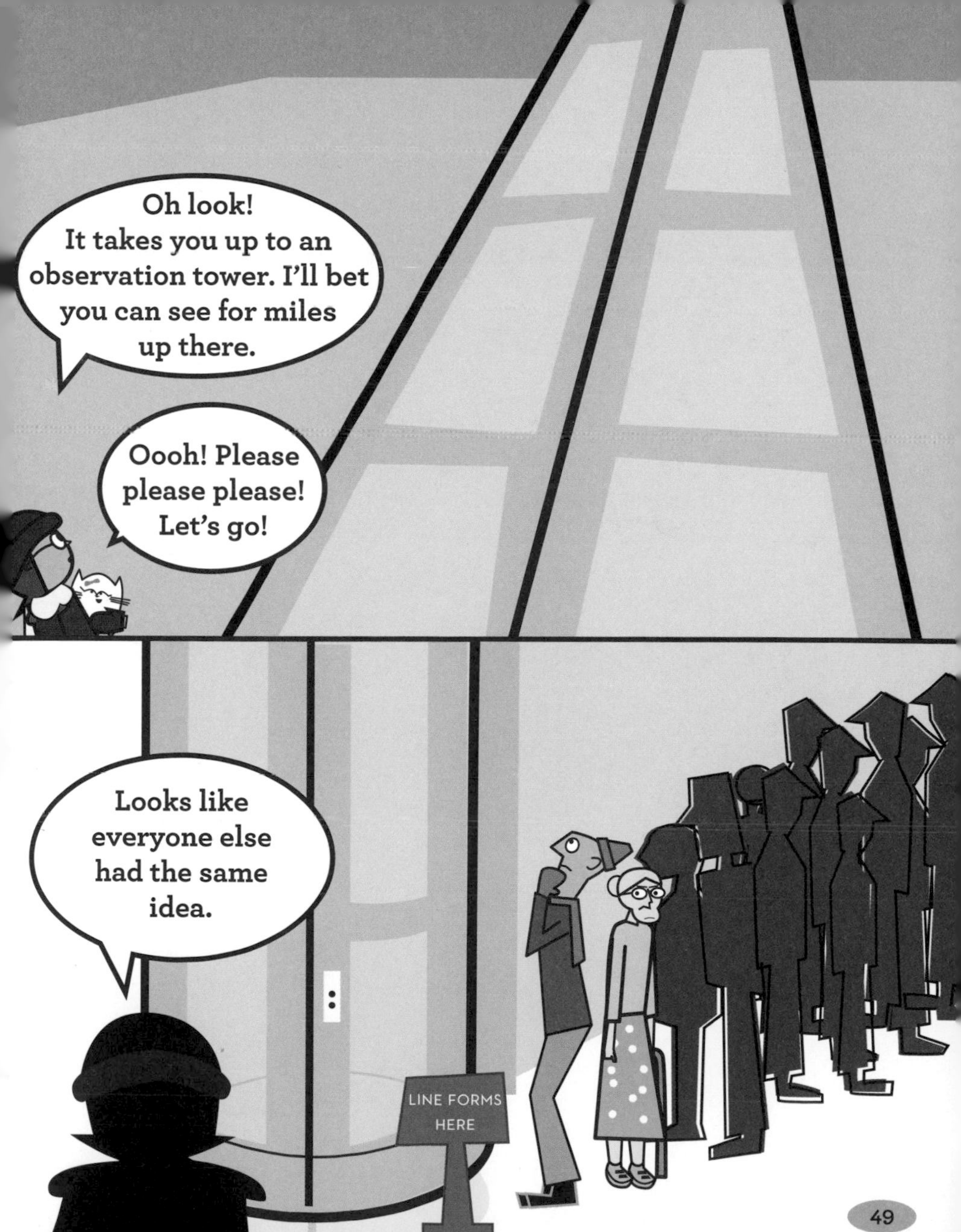
Oh look! It takes you up to an observation tower. I'll bet you can see for miles up there.
Oooh! Please please please! Let's go!
Looks like everyone else had the same idea.
LINE FORMS HERE

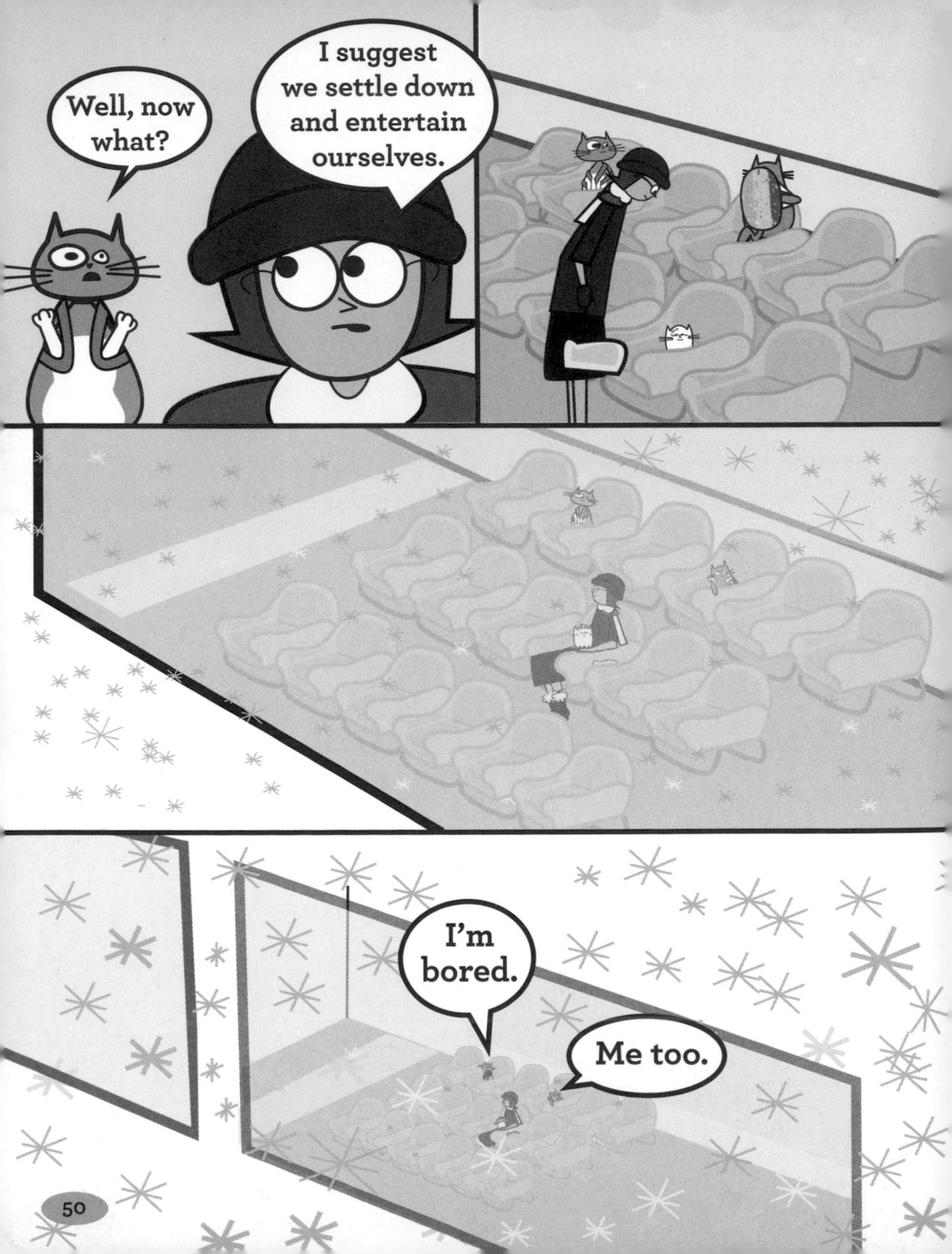
Well, now what?
I suggest we settle down and entertain ourselves.
I'm bored.
Me too.

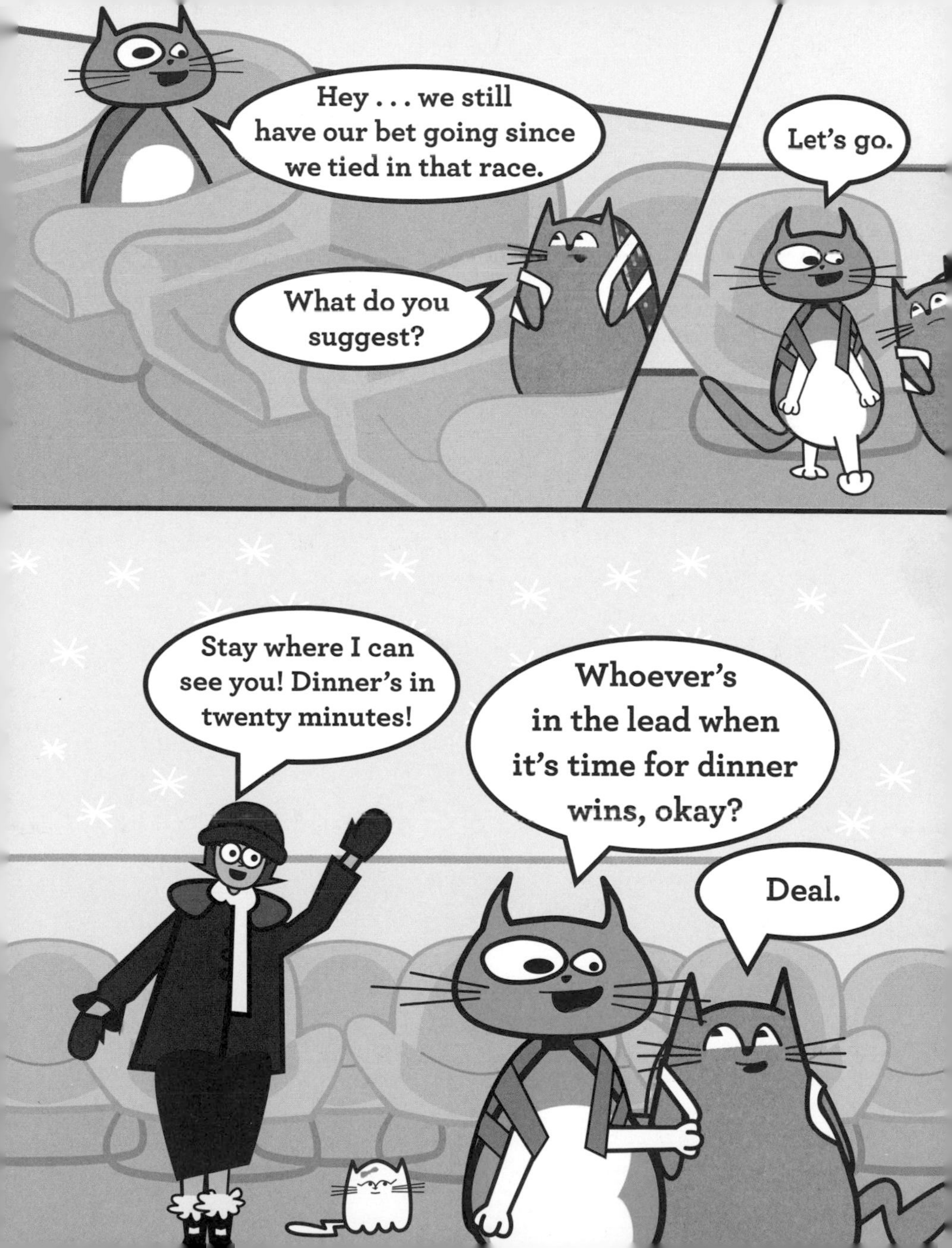
Hey . . . we still have our bet going since we tied in that race.
What do you suggest?
Let's go.
Stay where I can see you! Dinner's in twenty minutes!
Whoever's in the lead when it's time for dinner wins, okay?
Deal.

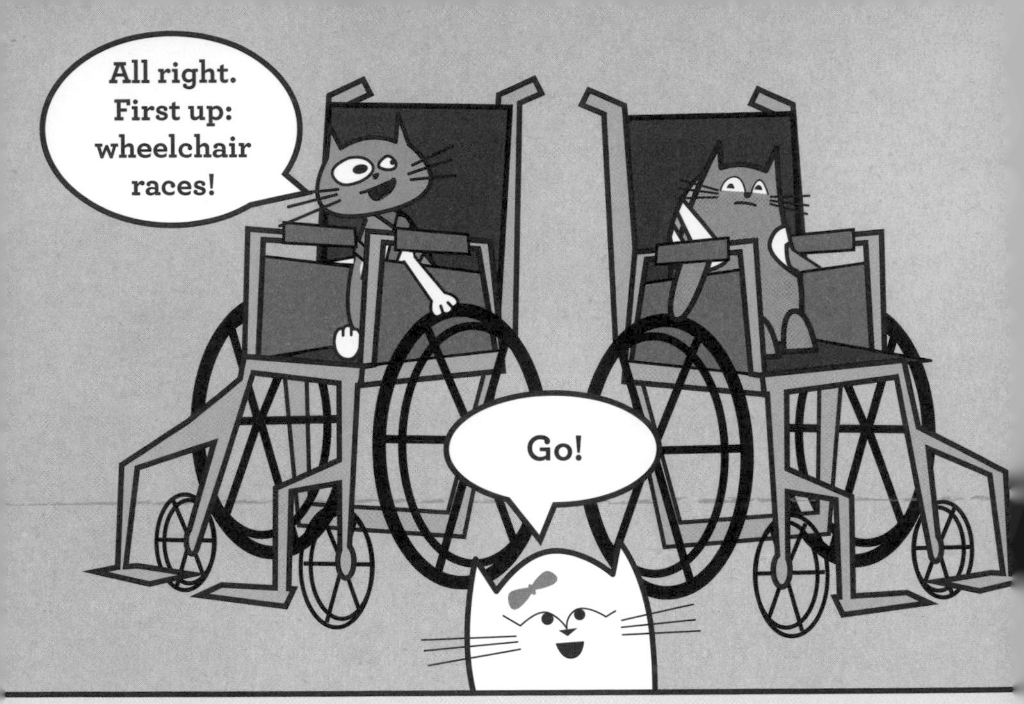
All right.
First up:
wheelchair
races!
Go!

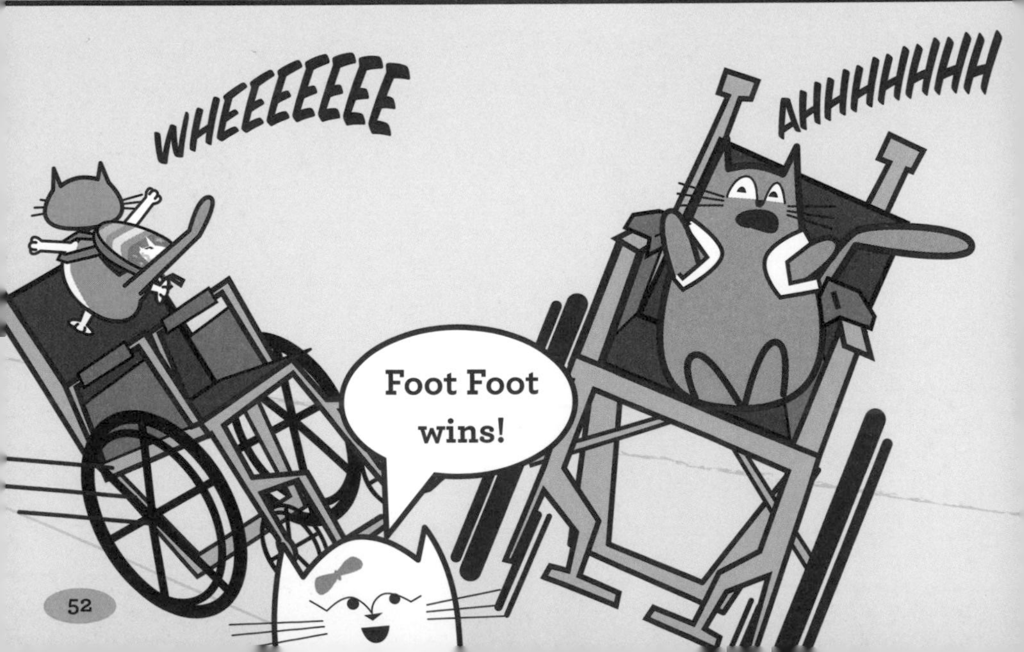
WHEEEEEEEE
AHHHHHHHH
Foot Foot
wins!

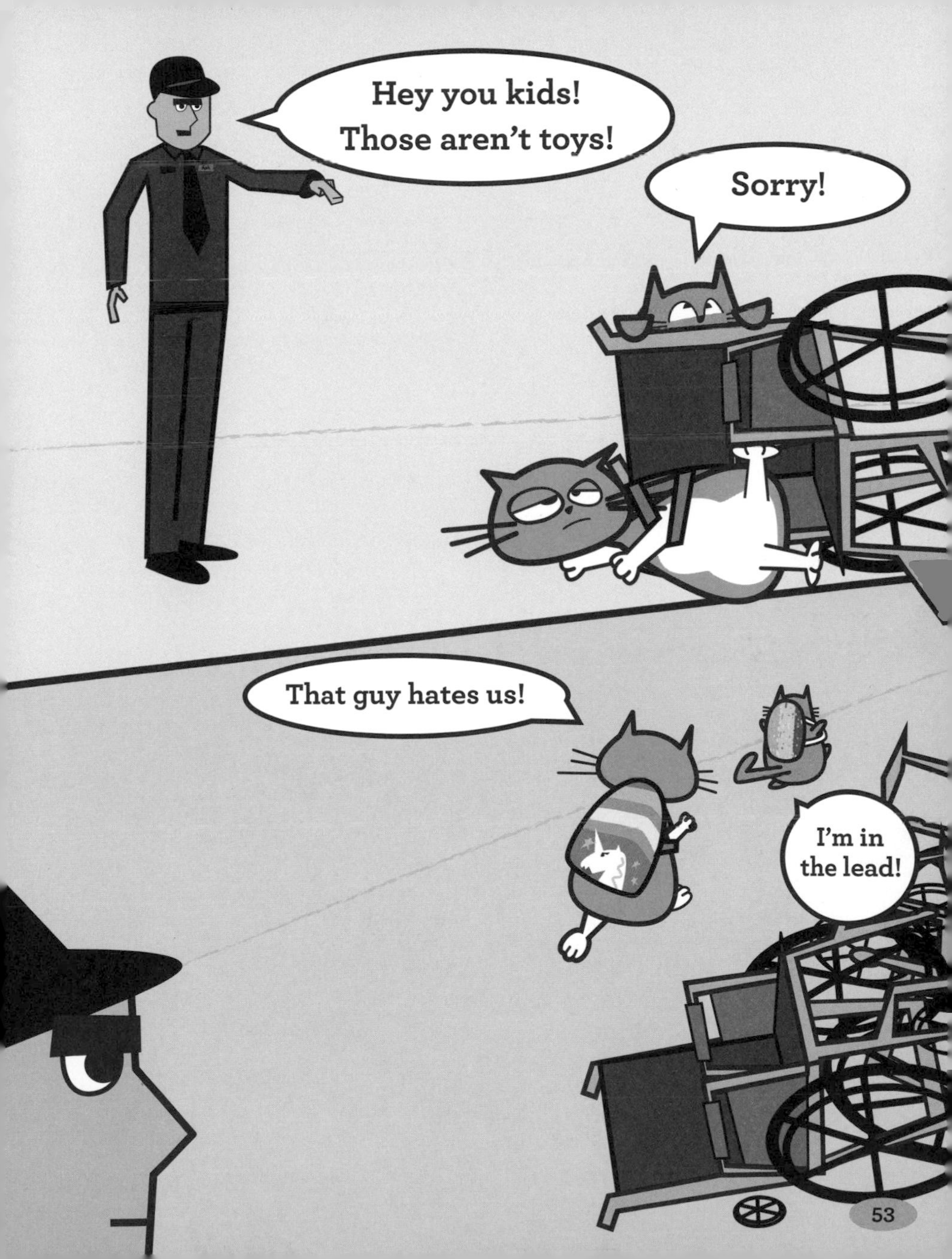
Hey you kids! Those aren't toys!
Sorry!
That guy hates us!
I'm in the lead!

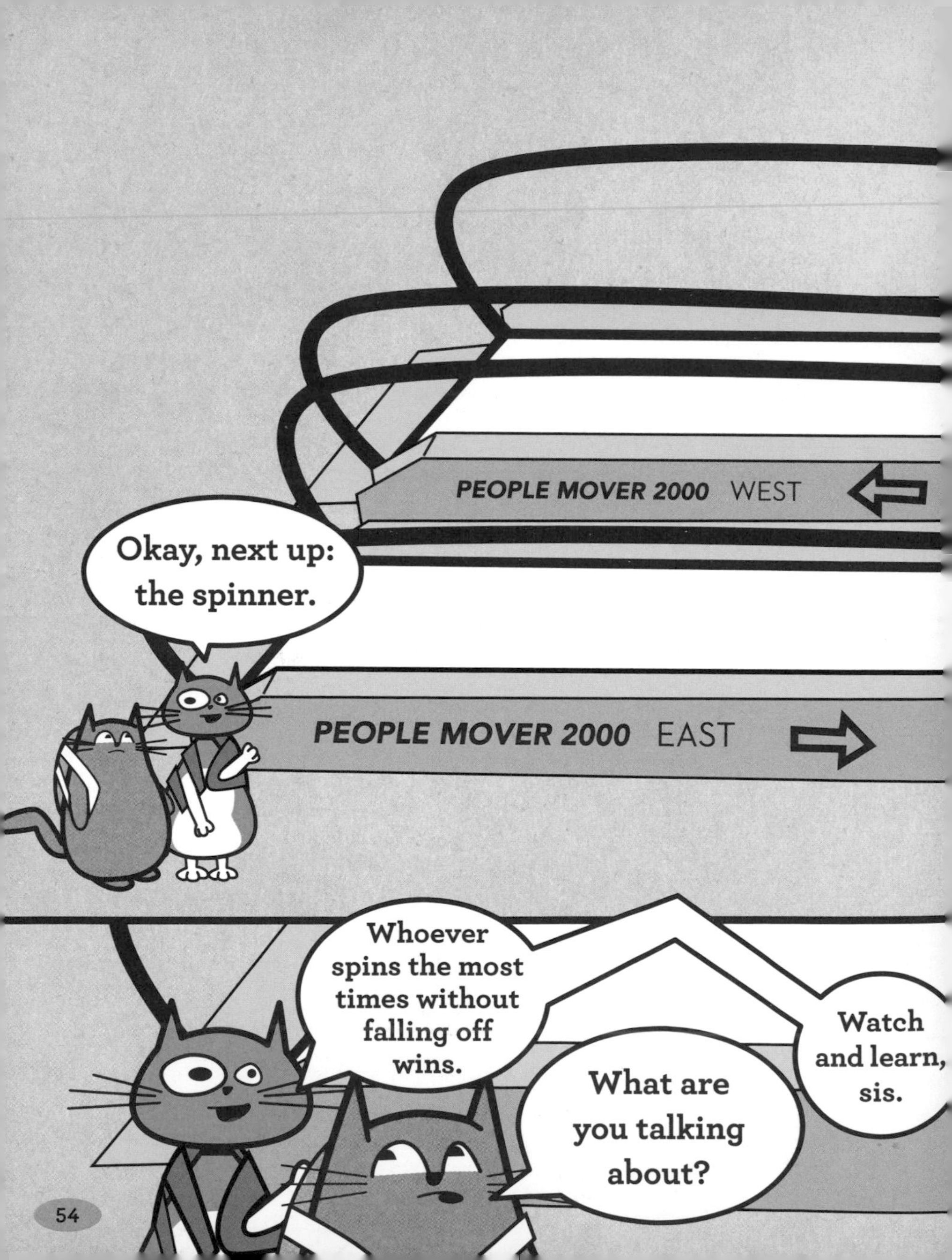
PEOPLE MOVER 2000 WEST
Okay, next up: the spinner.
PEOPLE MOVER 2000 EAST
Whoever spins the most times without falling off wins.
What are you talking about?
Watch and learn, sis.

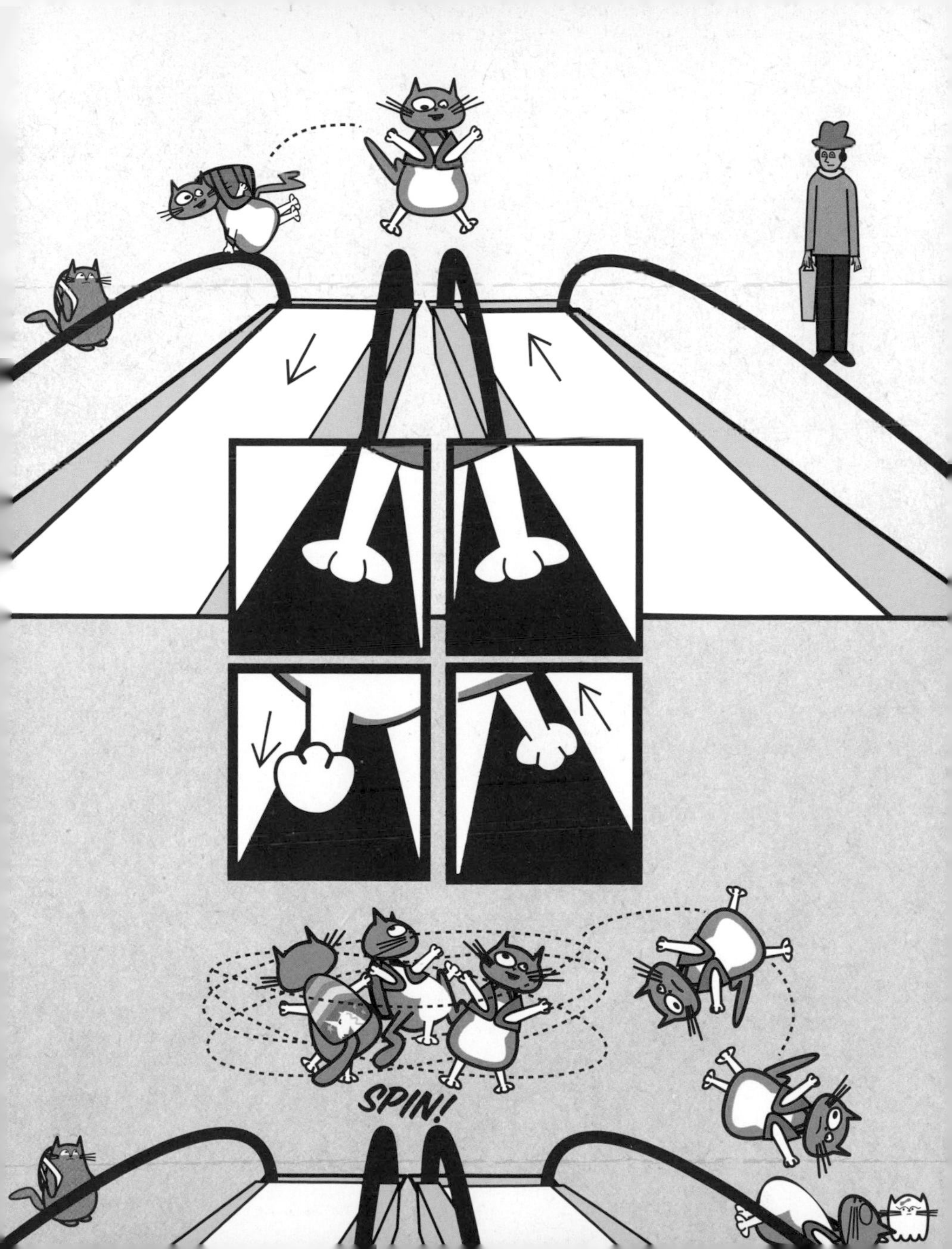
SPIN!

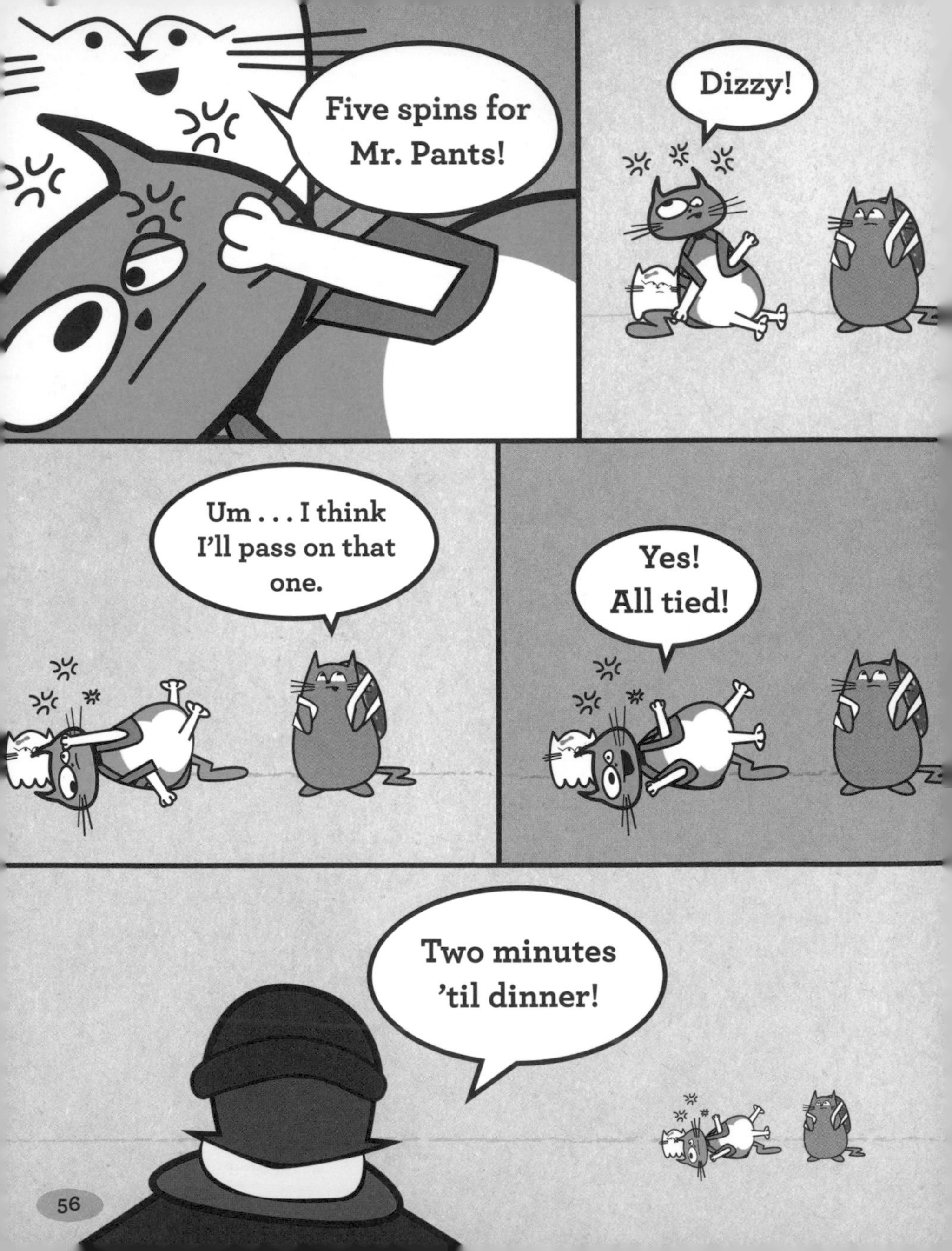
Five spins for Mr. Pants!
Dizzy!
Um . . . I think I'll pass on that one.
Yes! All tied!
Two minutes 'til dinner!

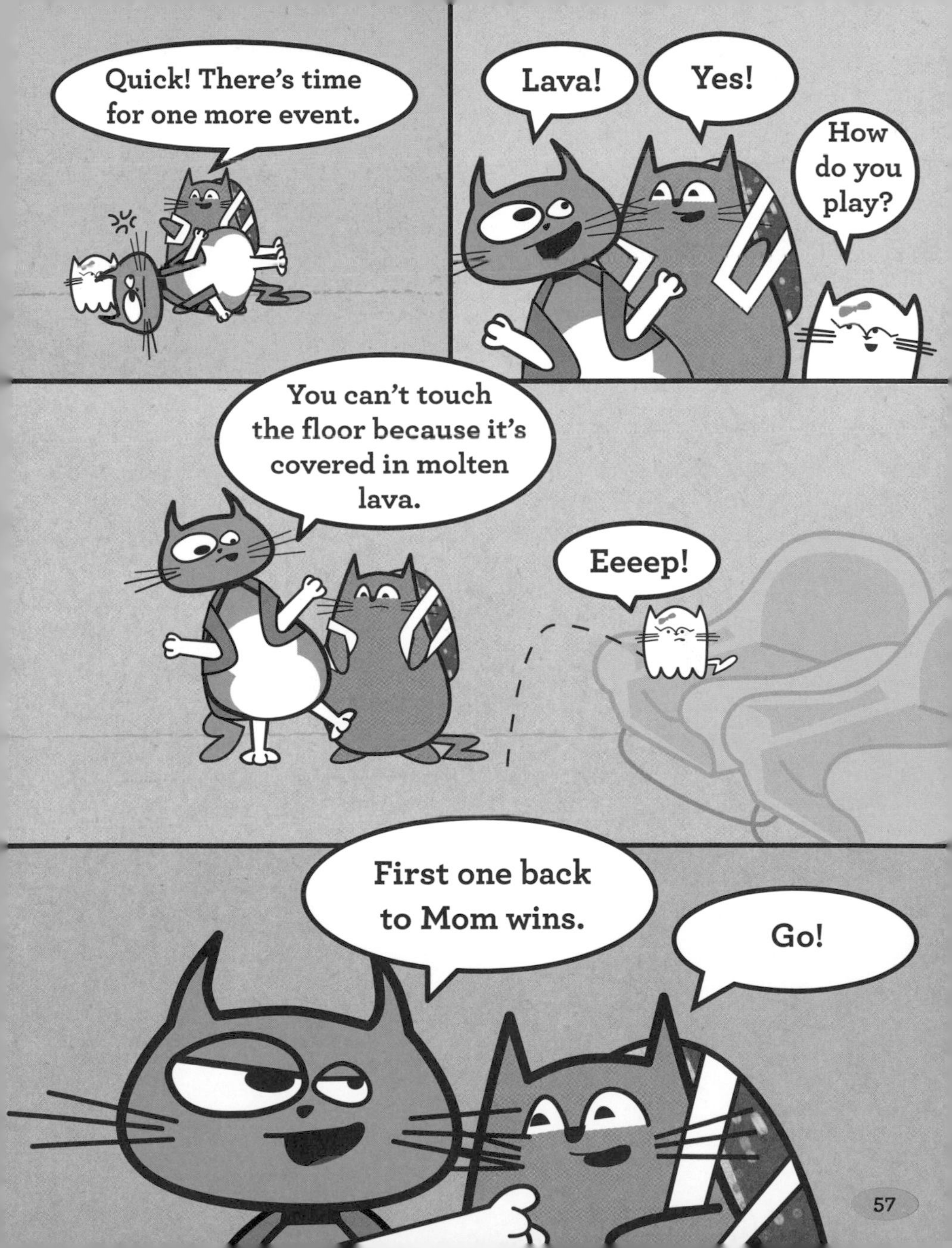
Quick! There's time for one more event.
Lava!
Yes!
How do you play?
You can't touch the floor because it's covered in molten lava.
Eeeep!
First one back to Mom wins.
Go!

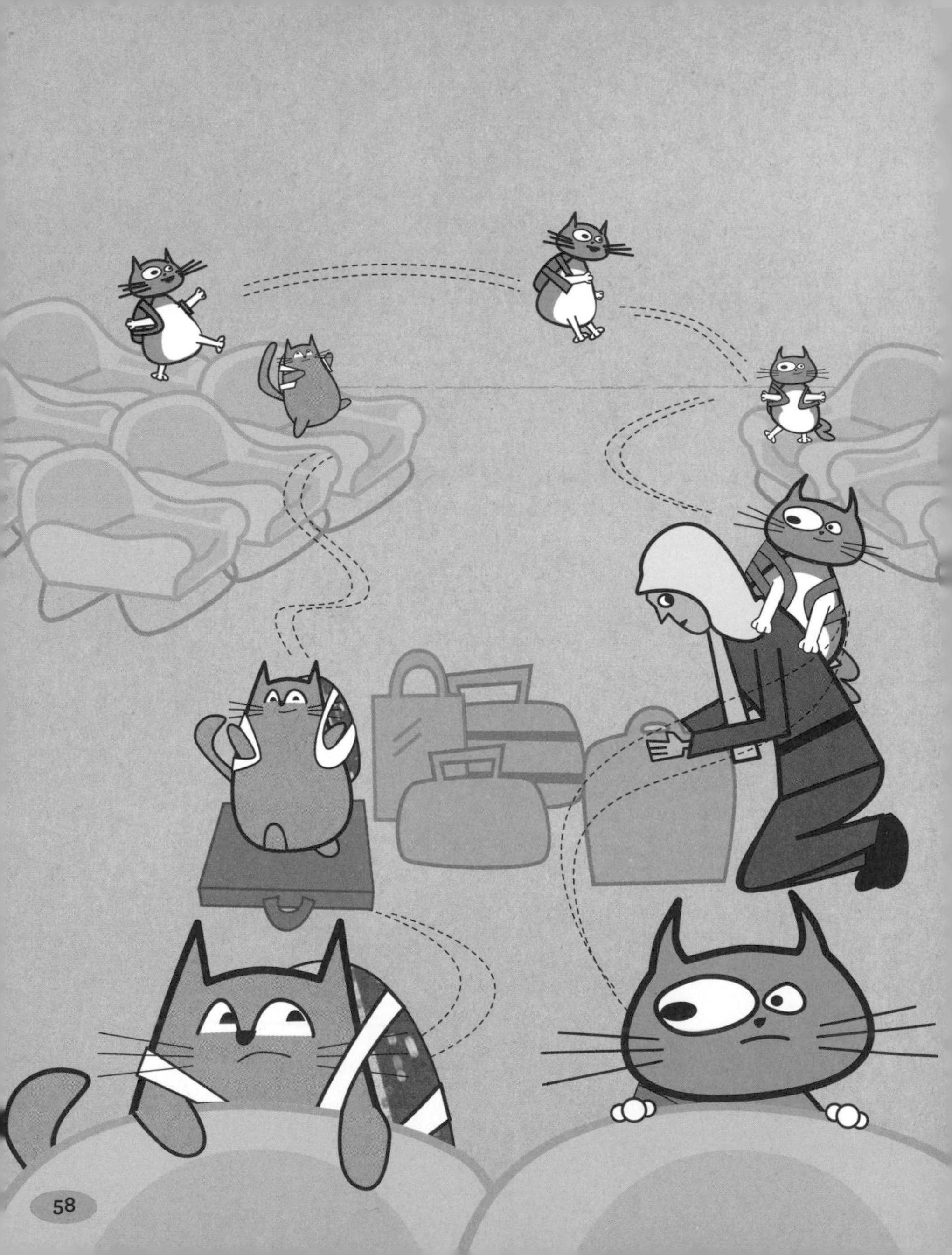

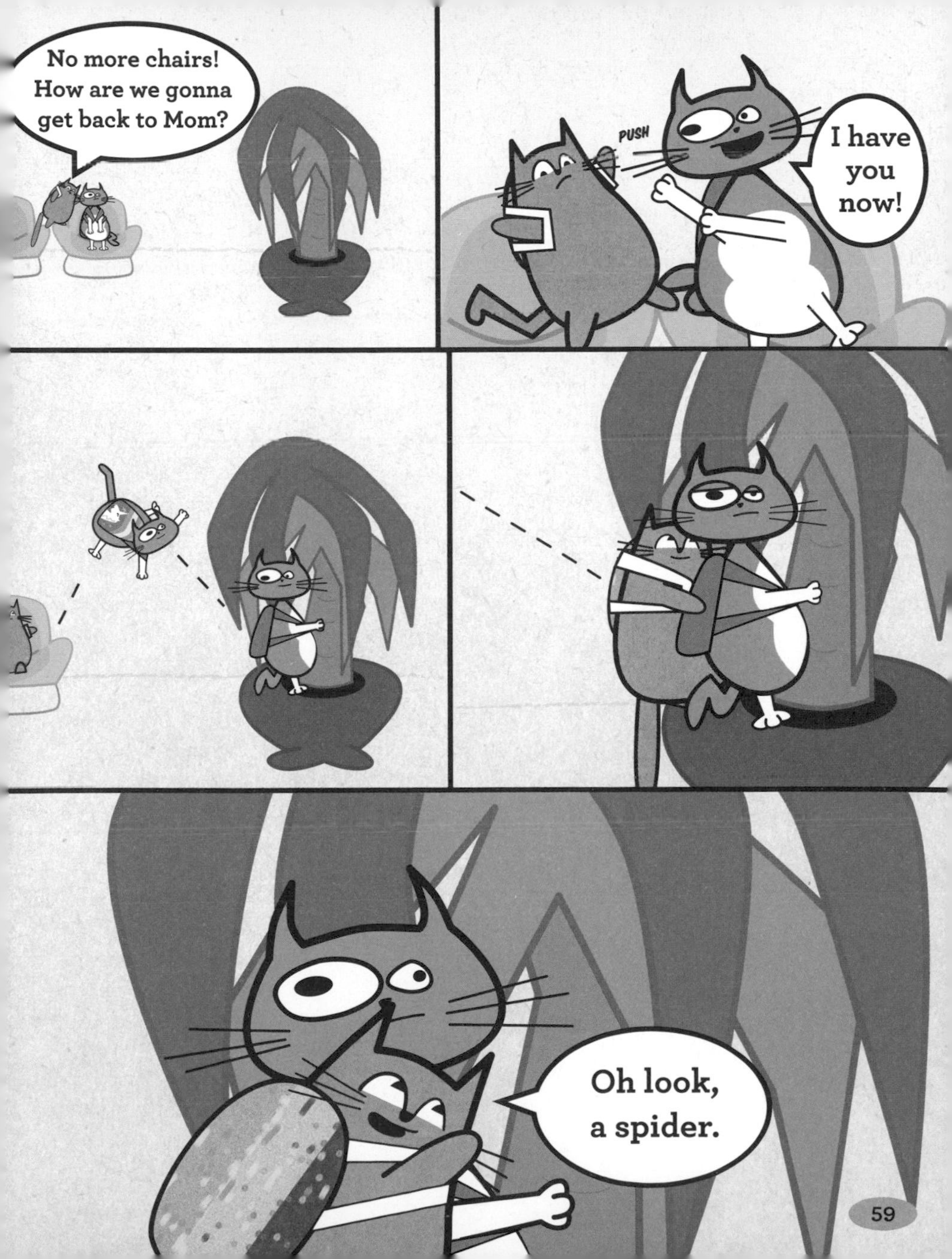
No more chairs! How are we gonna get back to Mom?
PUSH
I have you now!
Oh look, a spider.

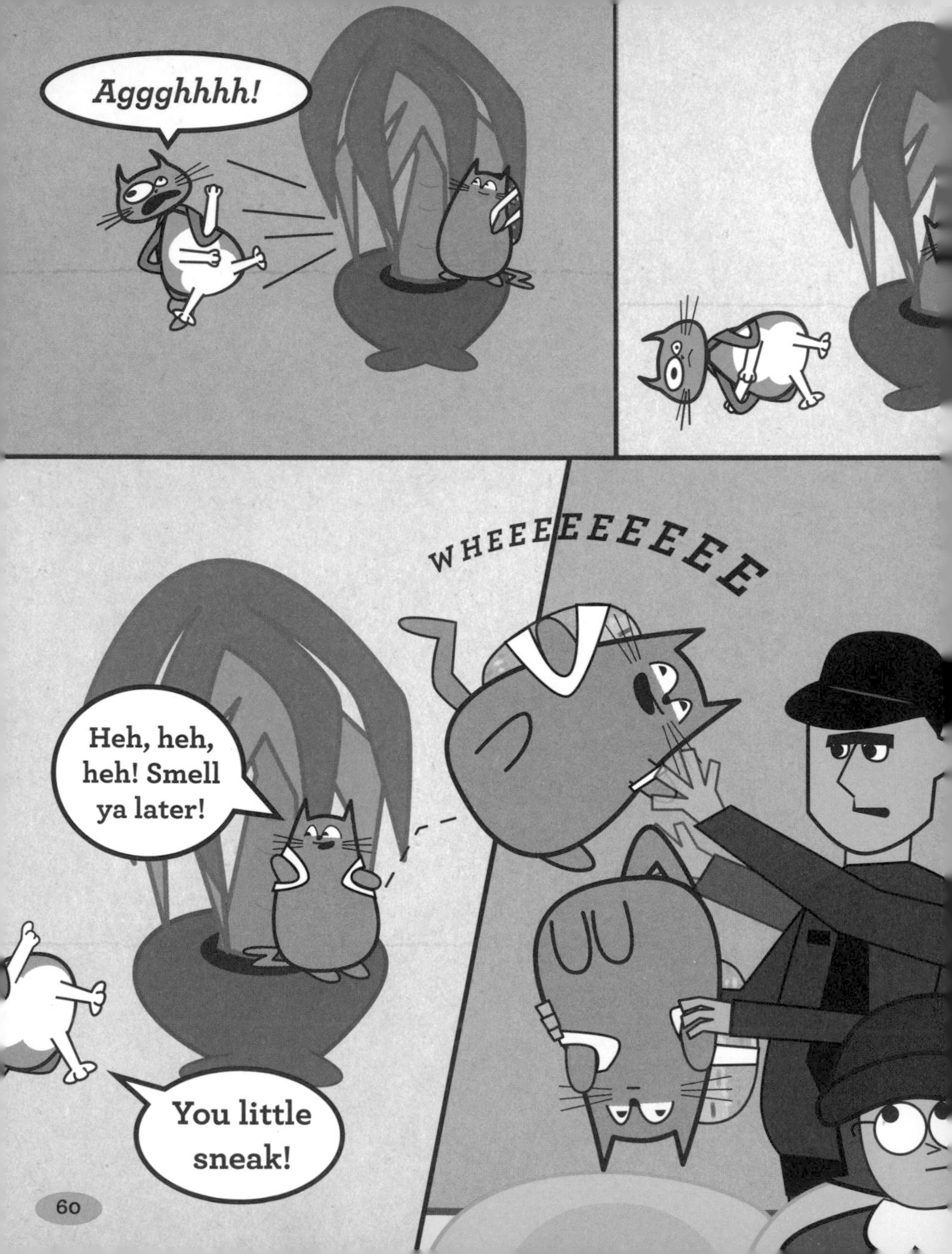
Aggghhhh!
Heh, heh, heh! Smell ya later!
WHEEEEEEEEEE
You little sneak!

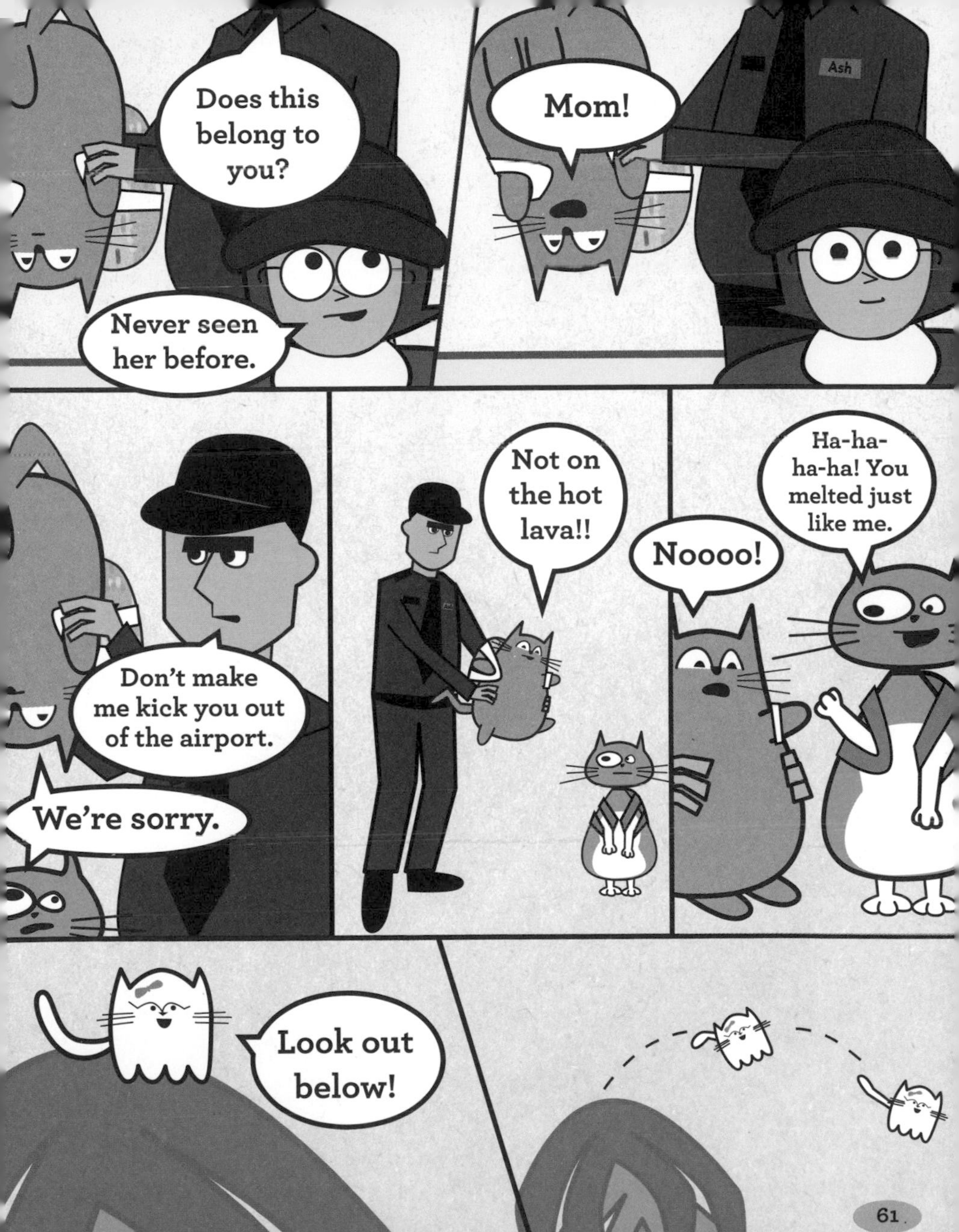
Does this belong to you?
Never seen her before.
Ash
Mom!
Don't make me kick you out of the airport.
We're sorry.
Not on the hot lava!!
Noooo!
Ha-ha-ha-ha! You melted just like me.
Look out below!

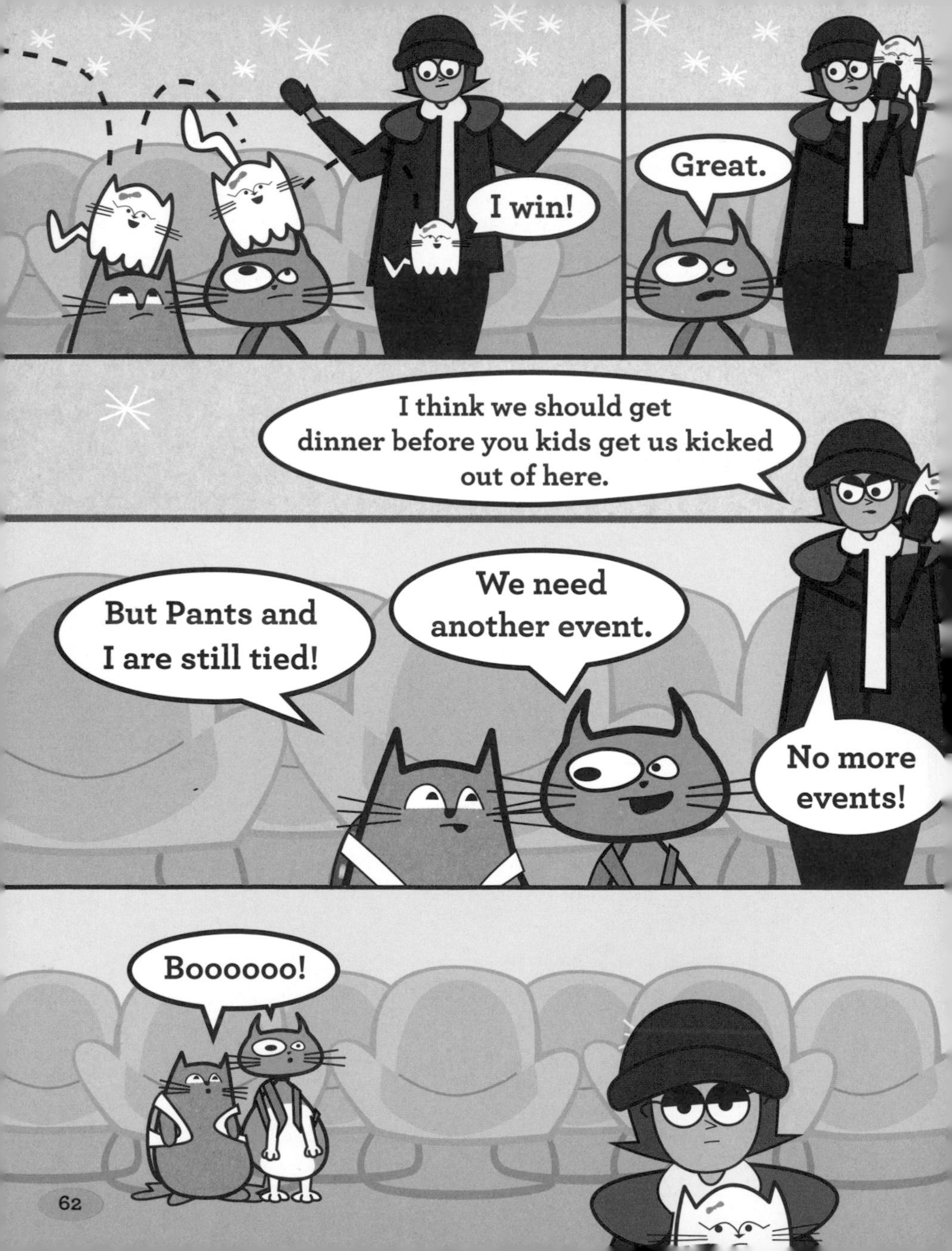
I win!
Great.
I think we should get dinner before you kids get us kicked out of here.
But Pants and I are still tied!
We need another event.
No more events!
Boooooo!

Chapter Four: TRICK OR FEET

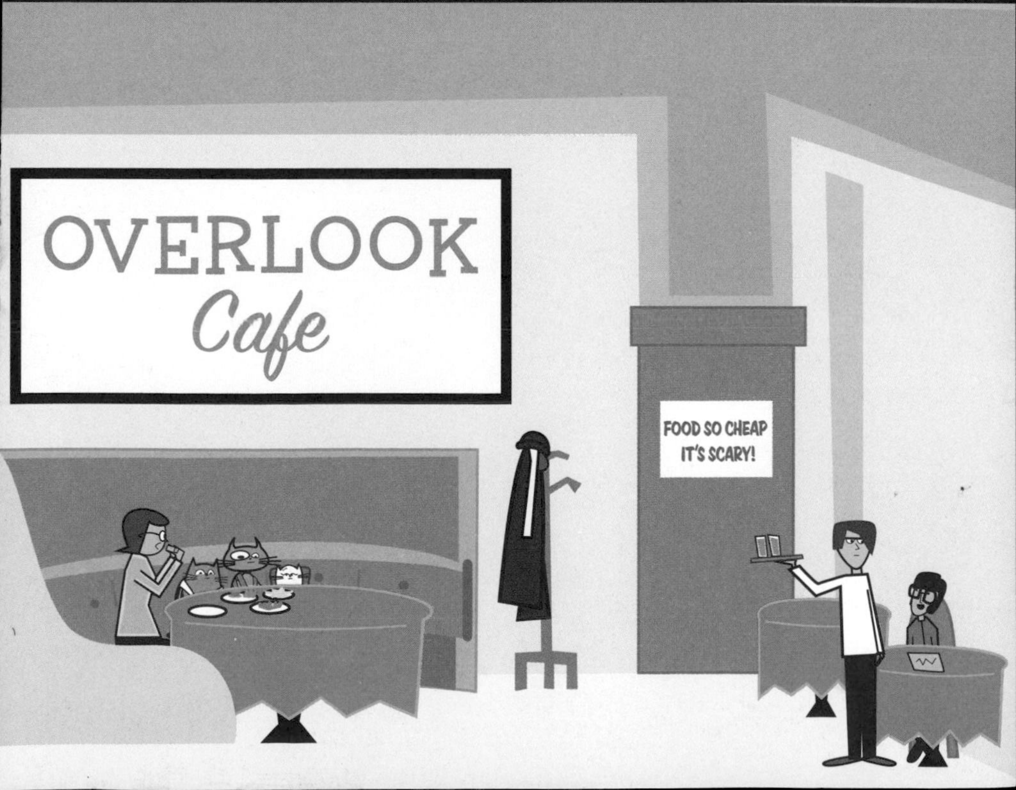
OVERLOOK
Cafe
FOOD SO CHEAP
IT'S SCARY!

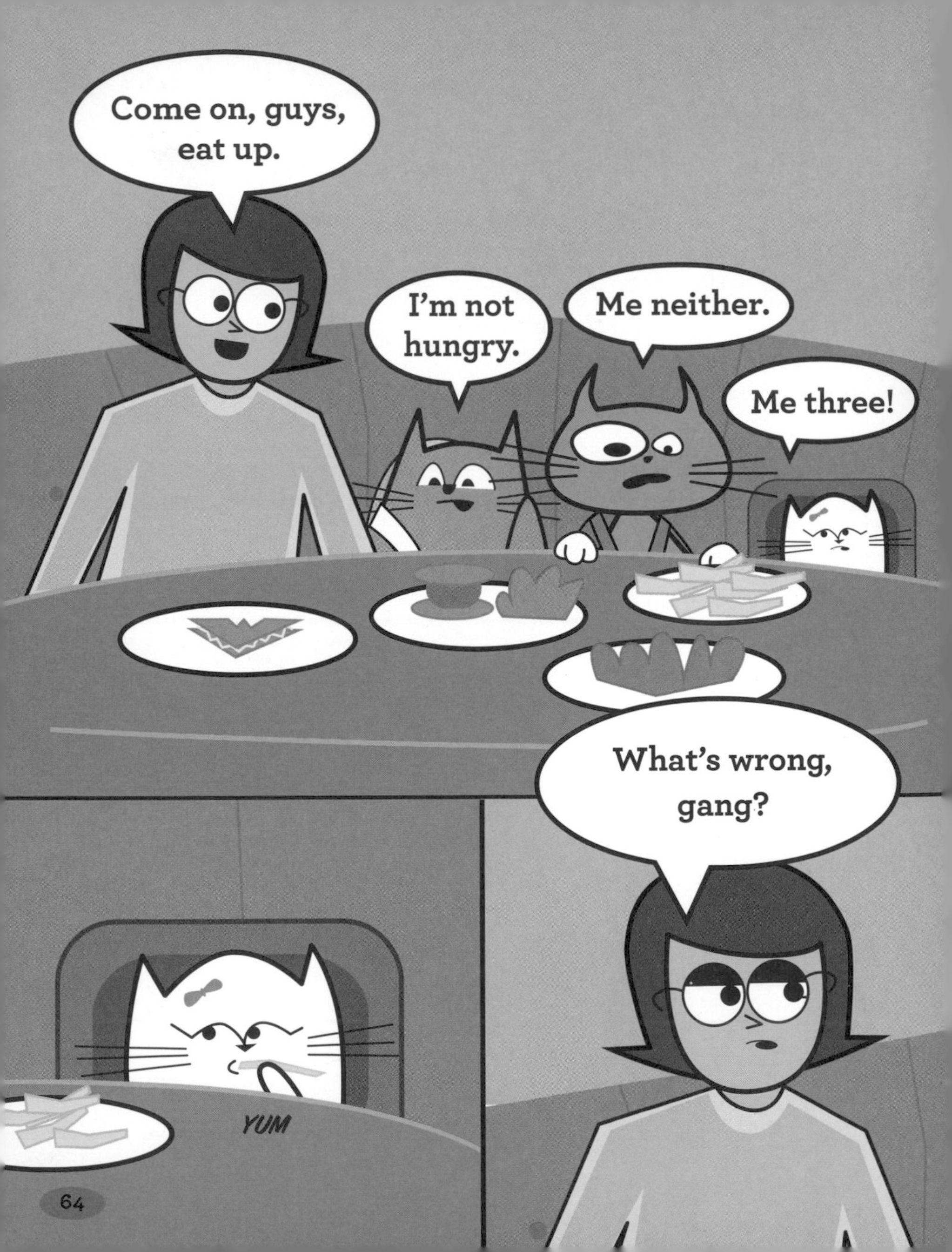
Come on, guys, eat up.
I'm not hungry.
Me neither.
Me three!
What's wrong, gang?
YUM

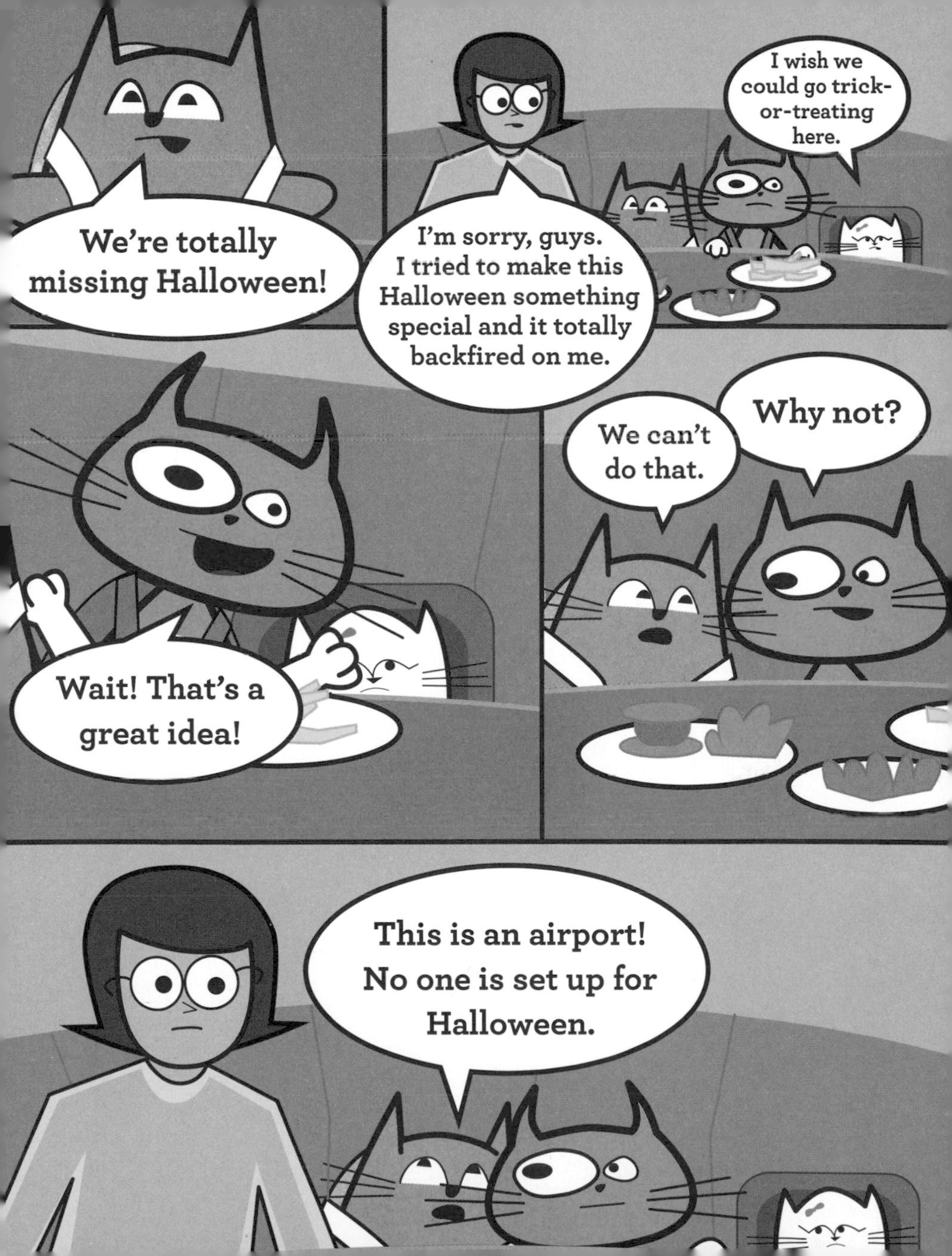
We're totally missing Halloween!
I'm sorry, guys. I tried to make this Halloween something special and it totally backfired on me.
I wish we could go trick-or-treating here.
Wait! That's a great idea!
We can't do that.
Why not?
This is an airport! No one is set up for Halloween.

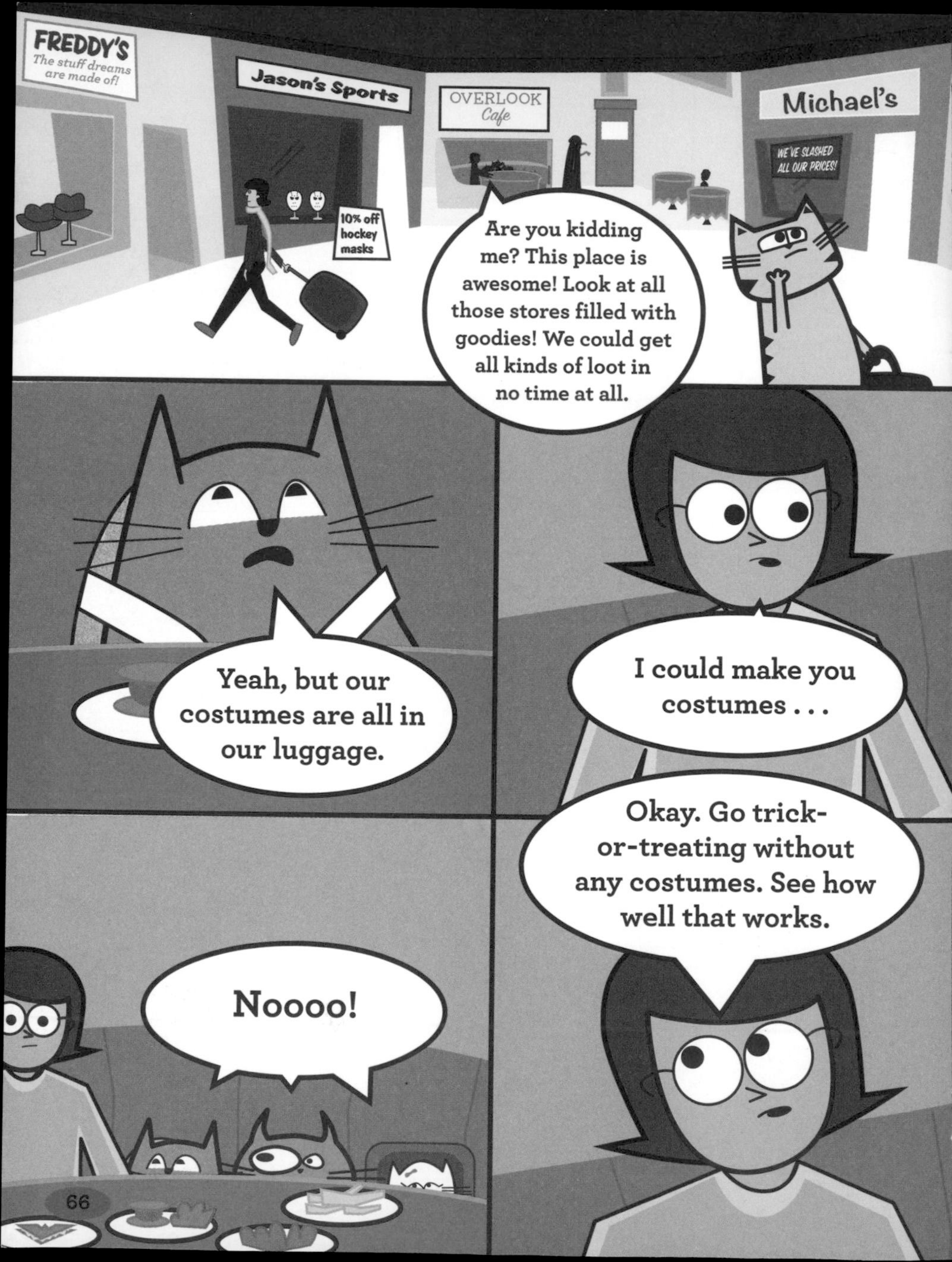
FREDDY'S
The stuff dreams are made of!
Jason's Sports
OVERLOOK Cafe
Michael's
WE'VE SLASHED ALL OUR PRICES!
10% off hockey masks
Are you kidding me? This place is awesome! Look at all those stores filled with goodies! We could get all kinds of loot in no time at all.
Yeah, but our costumes are all in our luggage.
I could make you costumes . . .
Okay. Go trick-or-treating without any costumes. See how well that works.
Noooo!

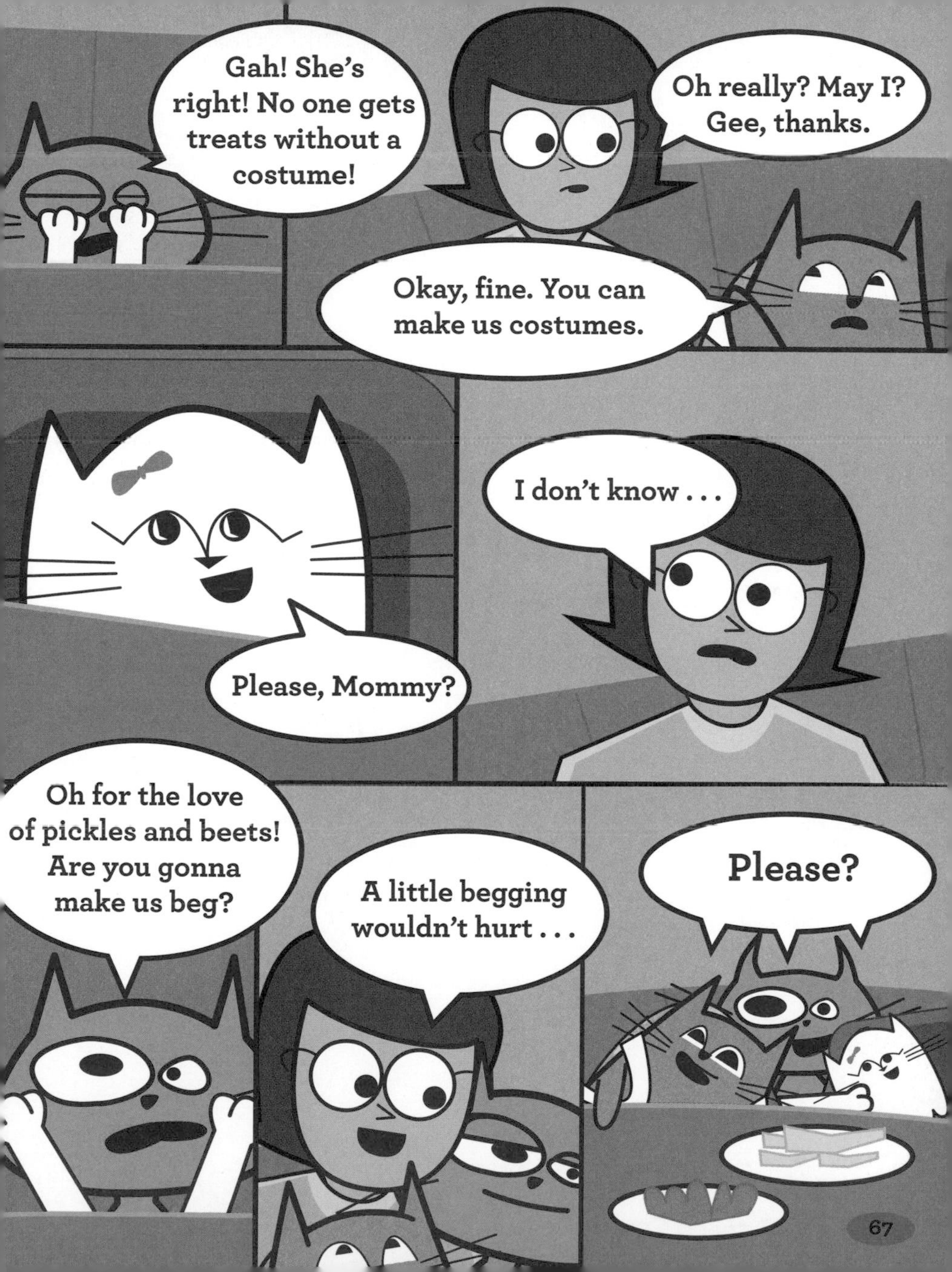
Gah! She's right! No one gets treats without a costume!
Oh really? May I? Gee, thanks.
Okay, fine. You can make us costumes.
I don't know . . .
Please, Mommy?
Oh for the love of pickles and beets! Are you gonna make us beg?
A little begging wouldn't hurt . . .
Please?

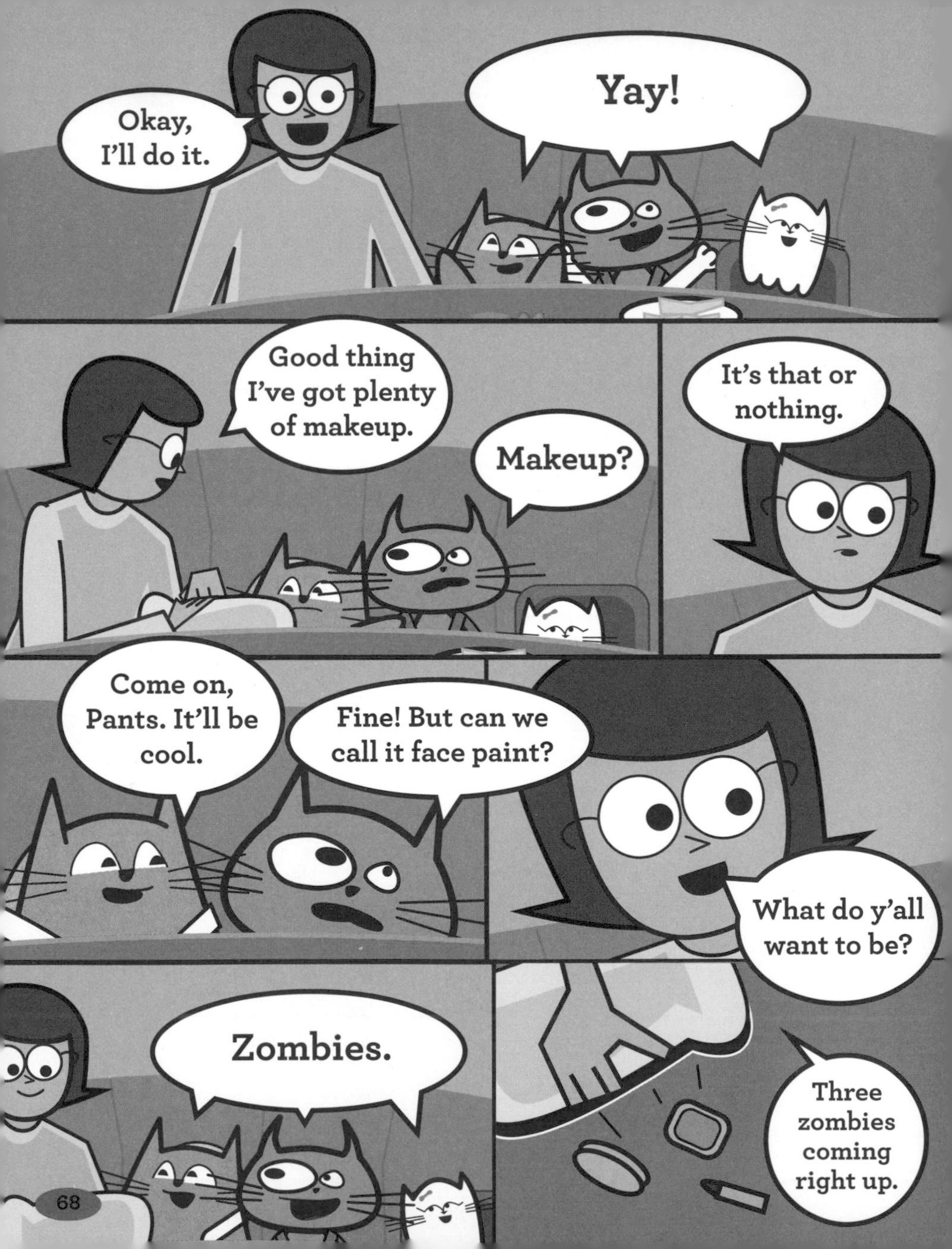
Okay, I'll do it.
Yay!
Good thing I've got plenty of makeup.
Makeup?
It's that or nothing.
Come on, Pants. It'll be cool.
Fine! But can we call it face paint?
What do y'all want to be?
Zombies.
Three zombies coming right up.

Ten minutes later . . .

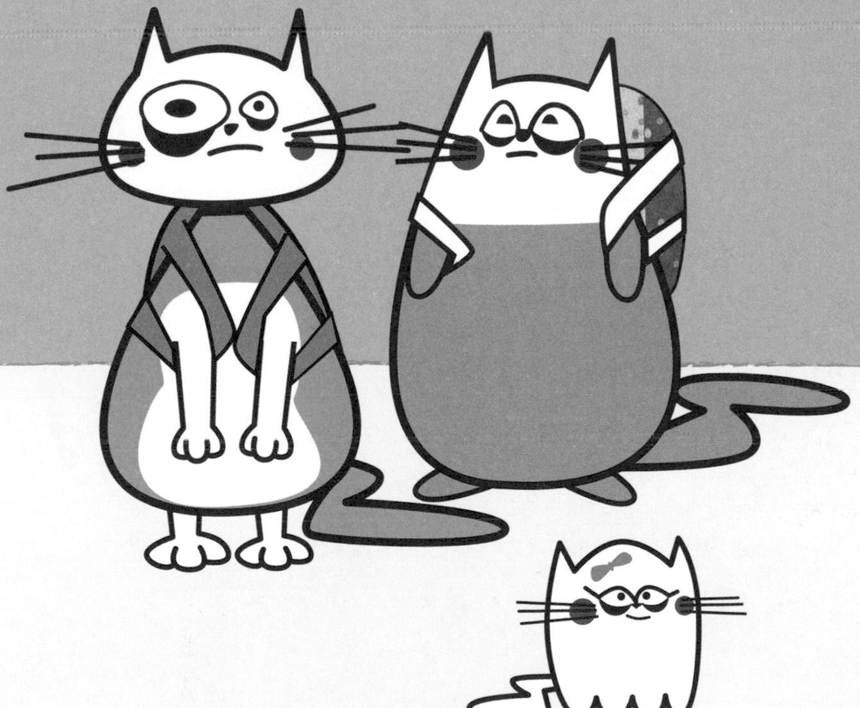

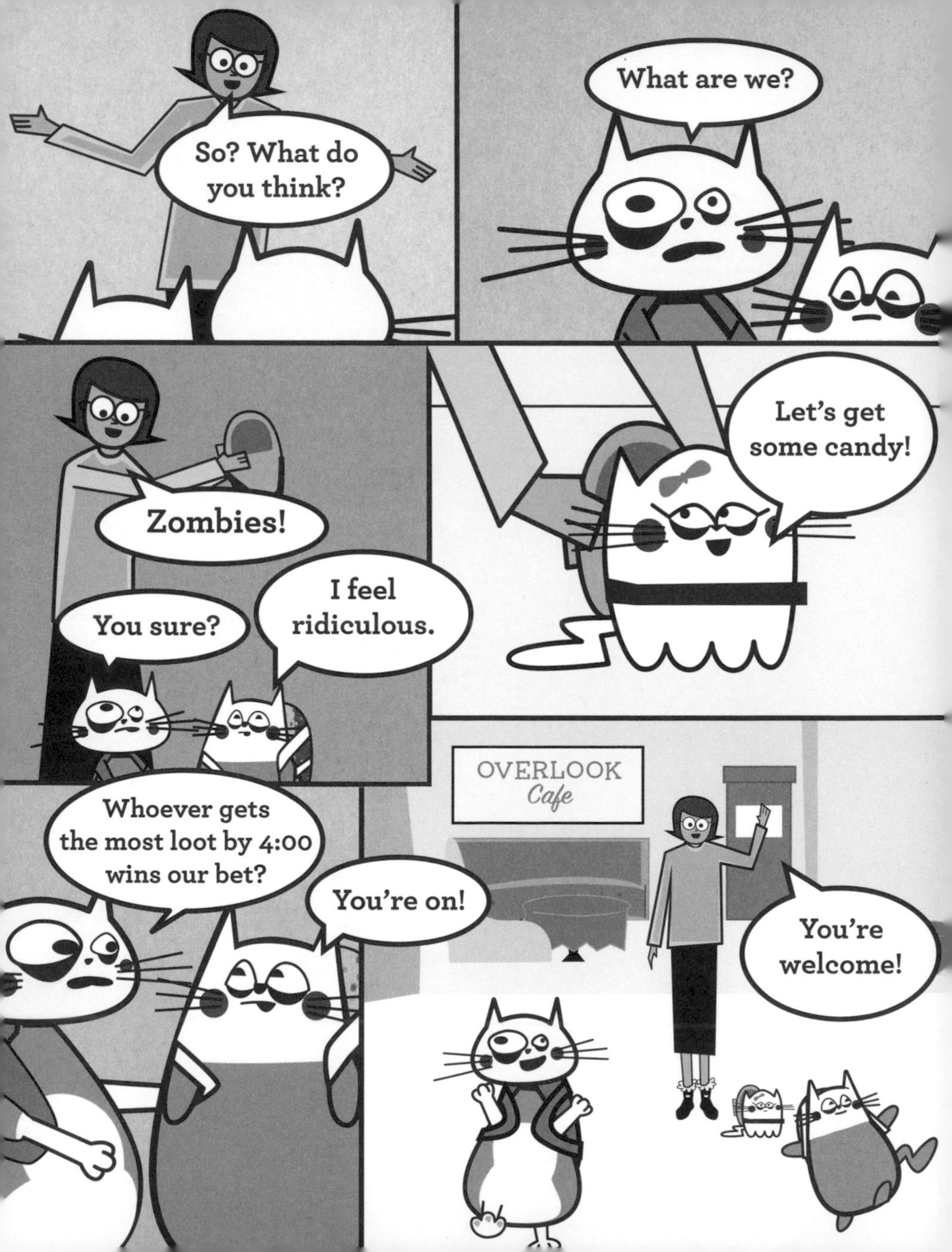
So? What do you think?
What are we?
Zombies!
You sure?
I feel ridiculous.
Let's get some candy!
Whoever gets the most loot by 4:00 wins our bet?
You're on!
OVERLOOK Cafe
You're welcome!

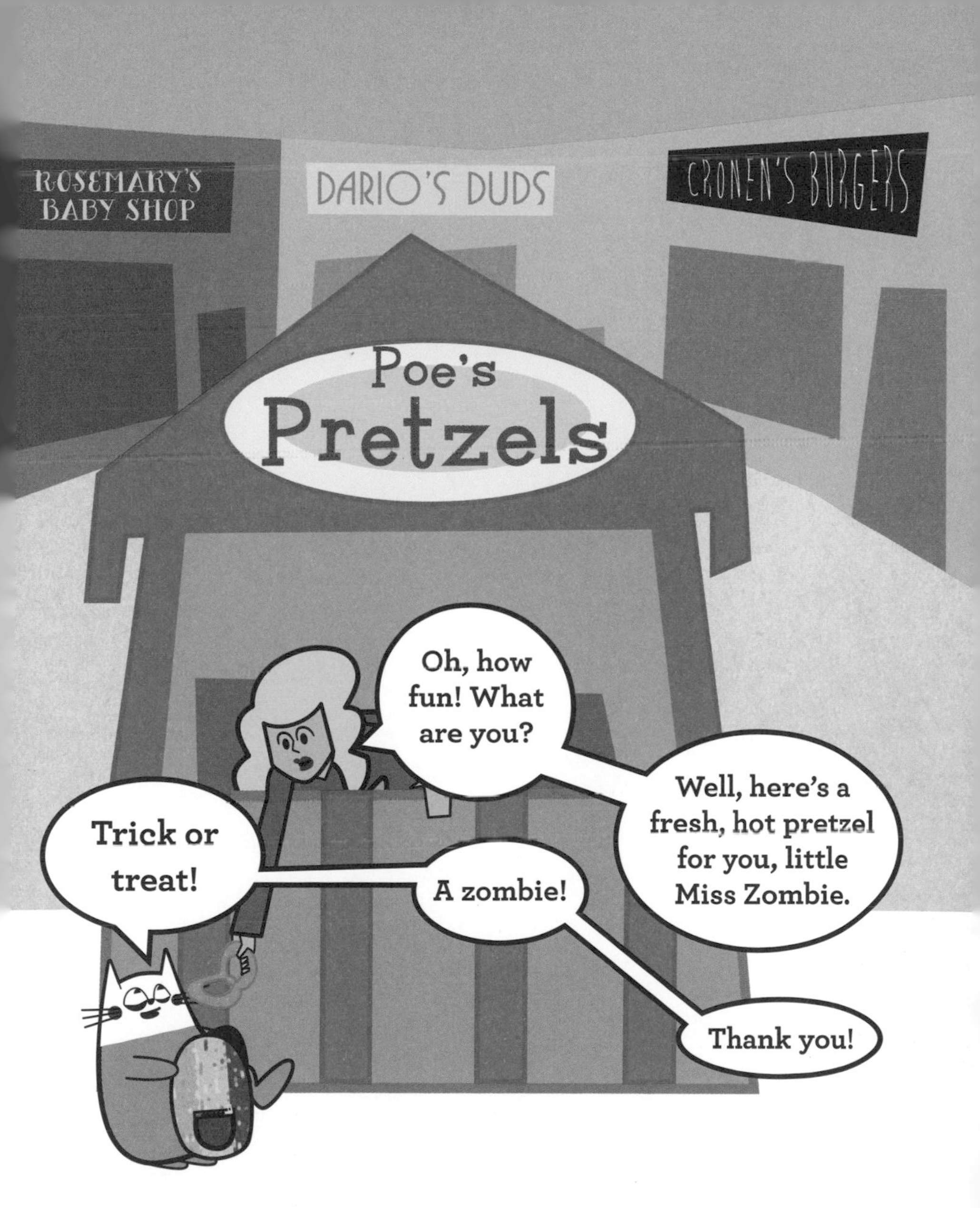
ROSEMARY'S BABY SHOP
DARIO'S DUDS
CRONEN'S BURGERS
Poe's Pretzels
Trick or treat!
Oh, how fun! What are you?
A zombie!
Well, here's a fresh, hot pretzel for you, little Miss Zombie.
Thank you!

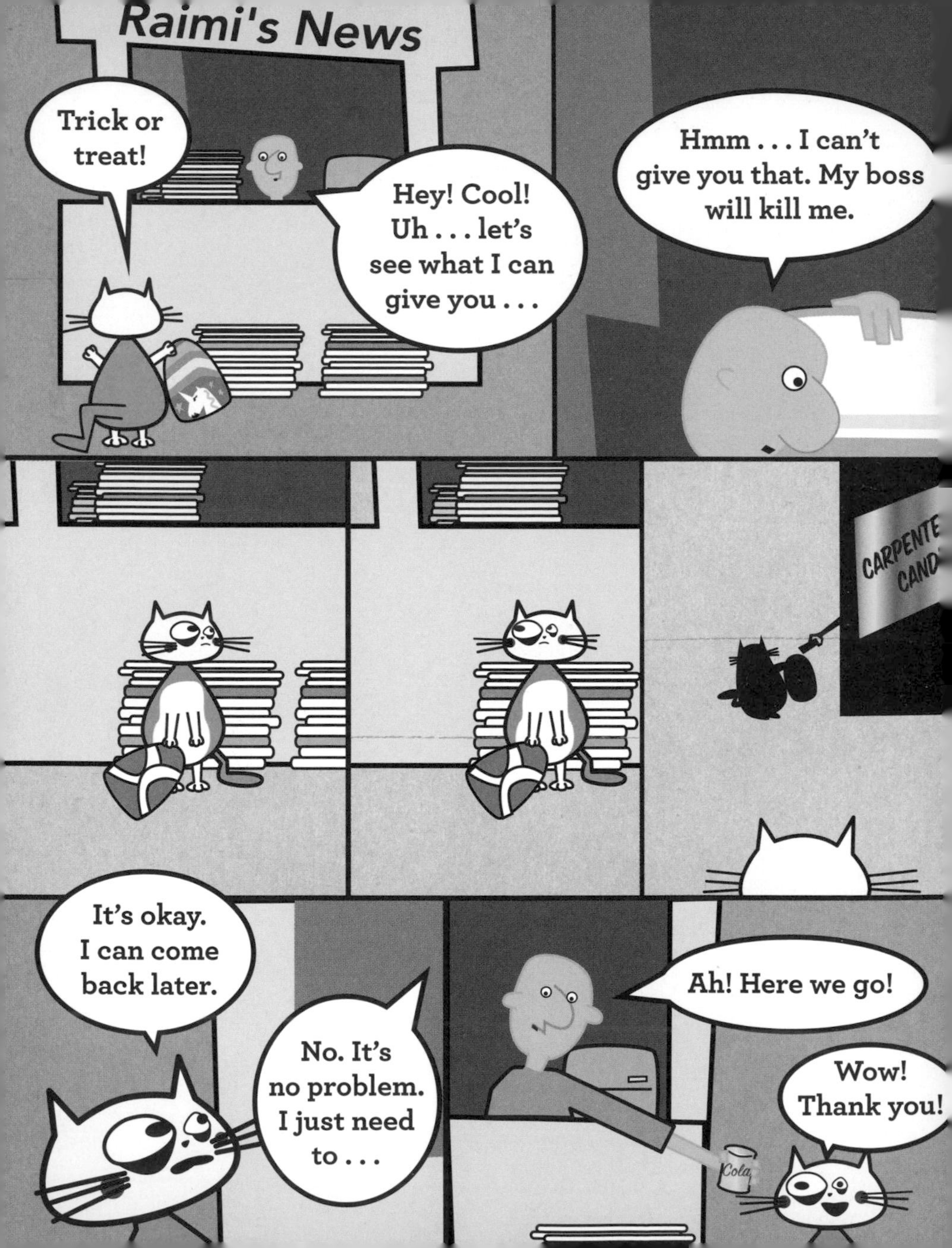
Raimi's News
Trick or treat!
Hey! Cool! Uh . . . let's see what I can give you . . .
Hmm . . . I can't give you that. My boss will kill me.
CARPENTE CAND
It's okay. I can come back later.
No. It's no problem. I just need to . . .
Ah! Here we go!
Cola
Wow! Thank you!

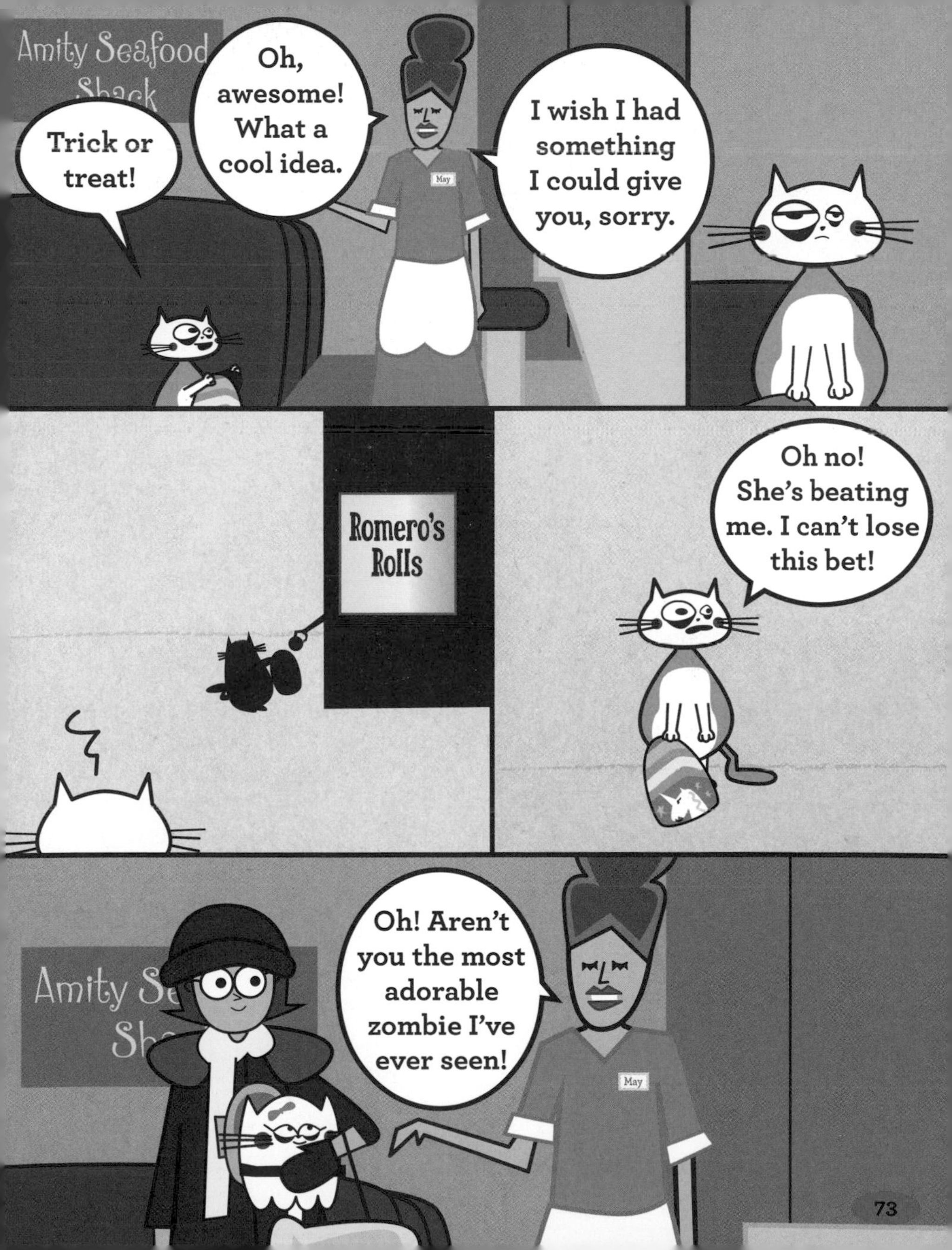
Amity Seafood Shack
Trick or treat!
Oh, awesome! What a cool idea.
May
I wish I had something I could give you, sorry.
Romero's Rolls
Oh no! She's beating me. I can't lose this bet!
Amity Se
Sh
Oh! Aren't you the most adorable zombie I've ever seen!
May

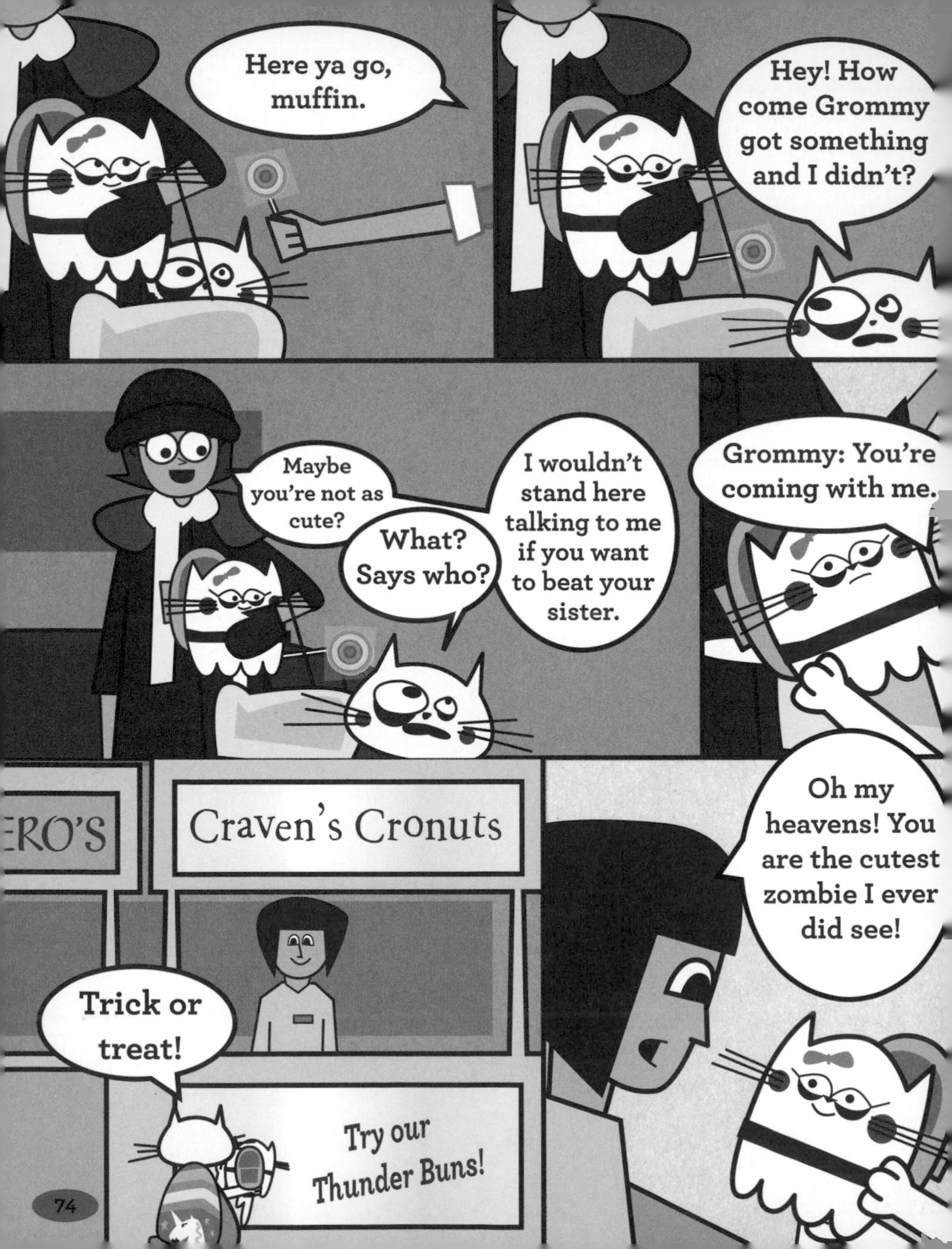

Here ya go, muffin.
Hey! How come Grommy got something and I didn't?
Maybe you're not as cute?
What? Says who?
I wouldn't stand here talking to me if you want to beat your sister.
Grommy: You're coming with me.
ERO'S
Craven's Cronuts
Trick or treat!
Try our Thunder Buns!
Oh my heavens! You are the cutest zombie I ever did see!

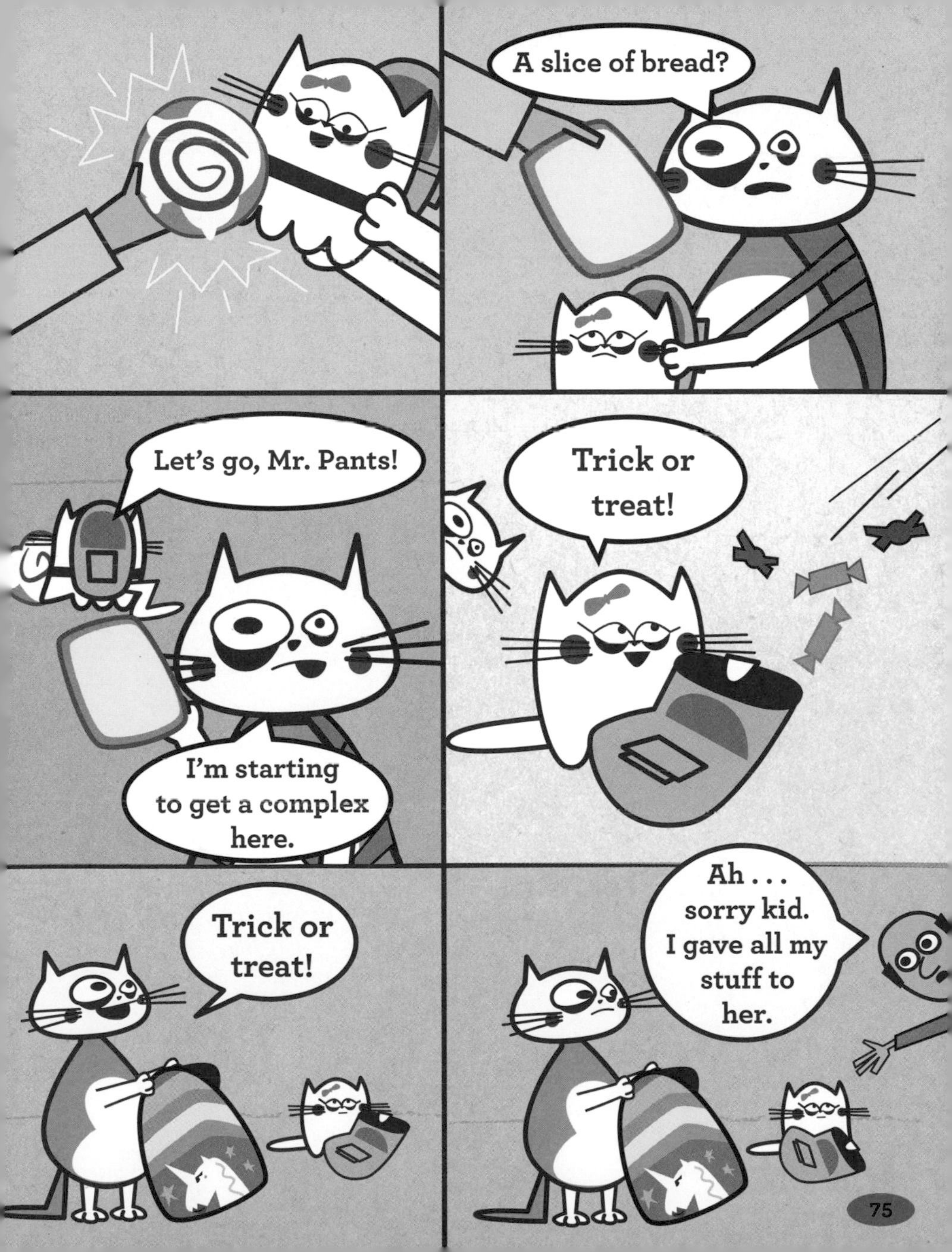
A slice of bread?
Let's go, Mr. Pants!
I'm starting to get a complex here.
Trick or treat!
Trick or treat!
Ah . . . sorry kid. I gave all my stuff to her.

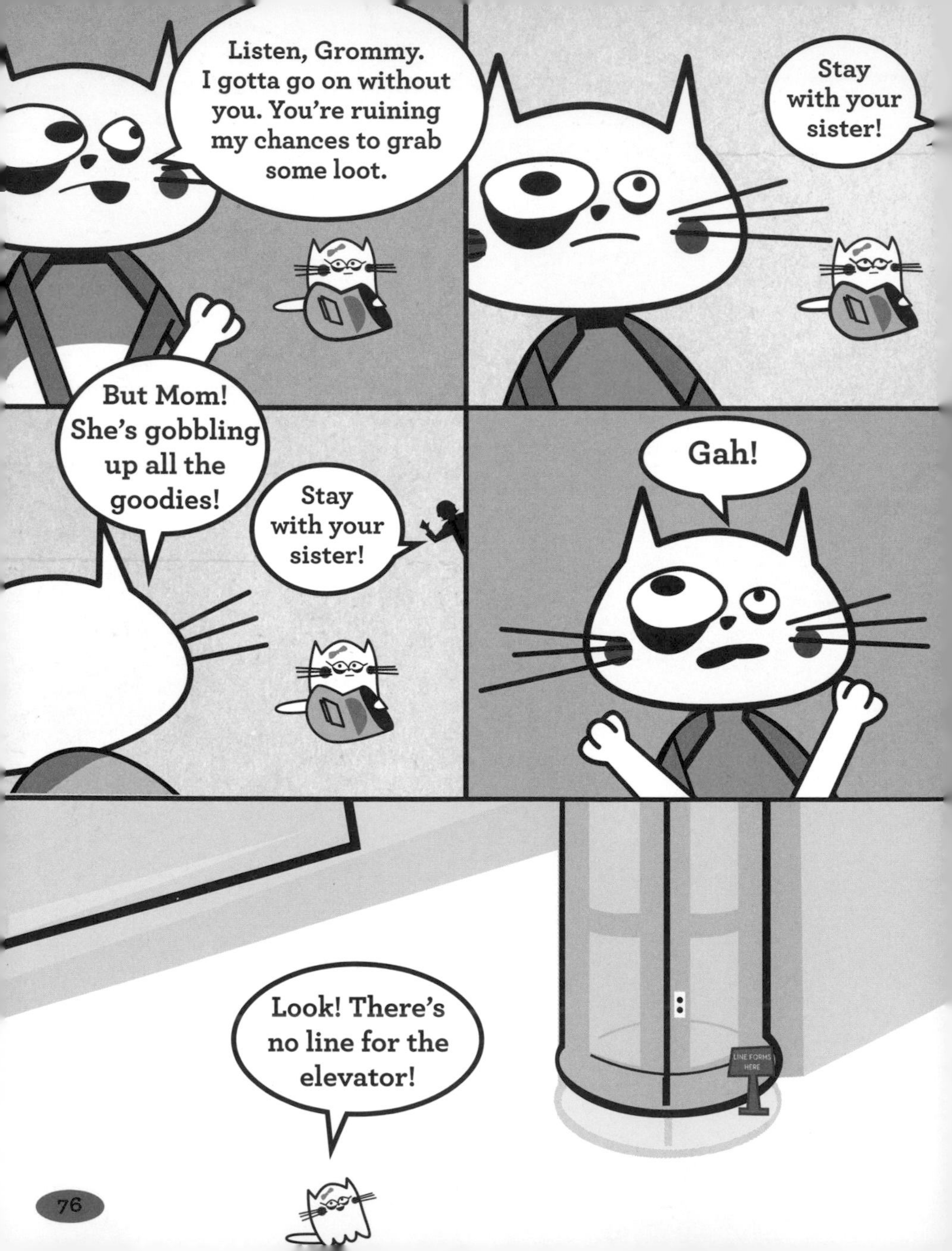
Listen, Grommy. I gotta go on without you. You're ruining my chances to grab some loot.
Stay with your sister!
But Mom! She's gobbling up all the goodies!
Stay with your sister!
Gah!
Look! There's no line for the elevator!
LINE FORMS HERE

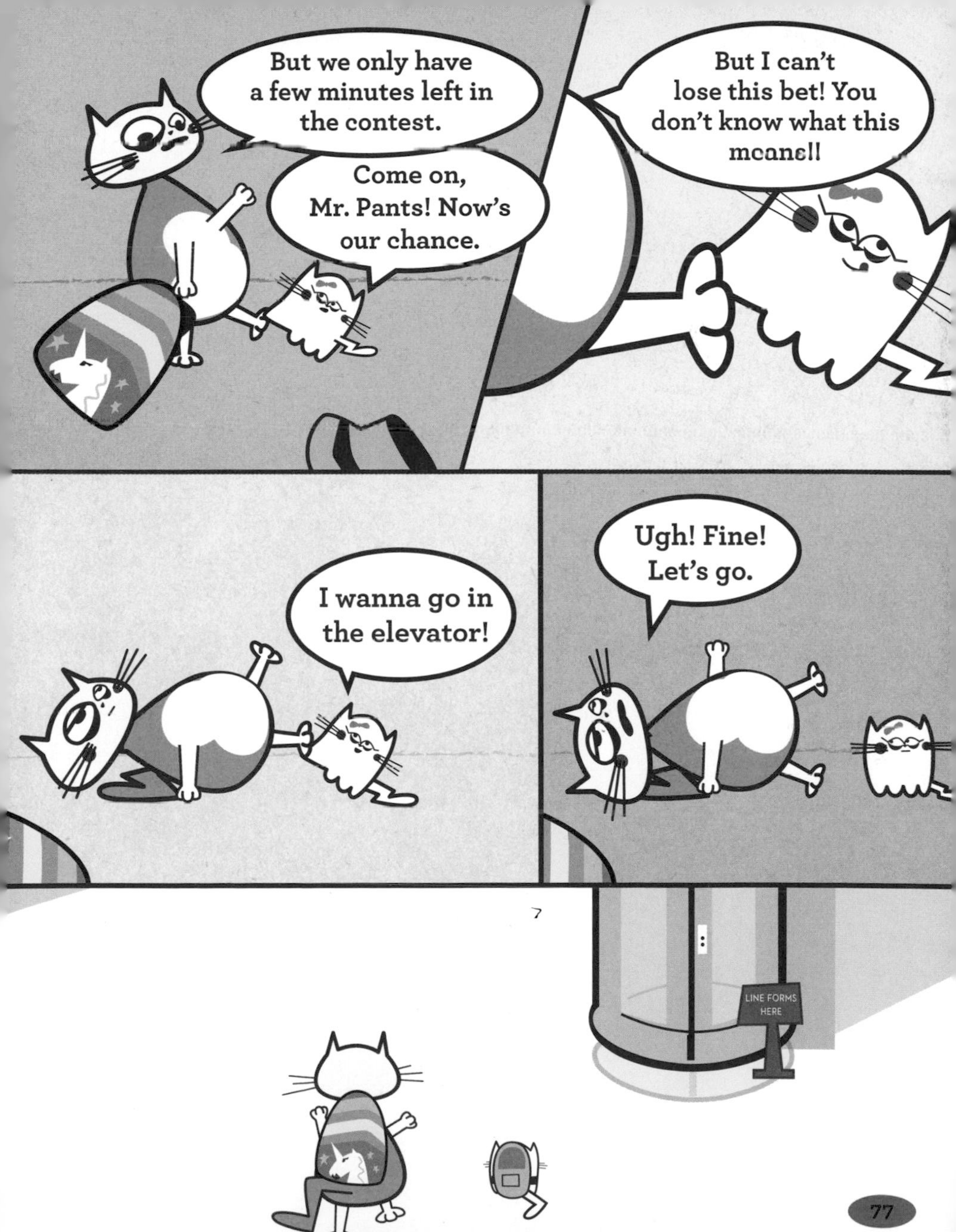
But we only have a few minutes left in the contest.
Come on, Mr. Pants! Now's our chance.
But I can't lose this bet! You don't know what this means!!
I wanna go in the elevator!
Ugh! Fine! Let's go.
LINE FORMS HERE

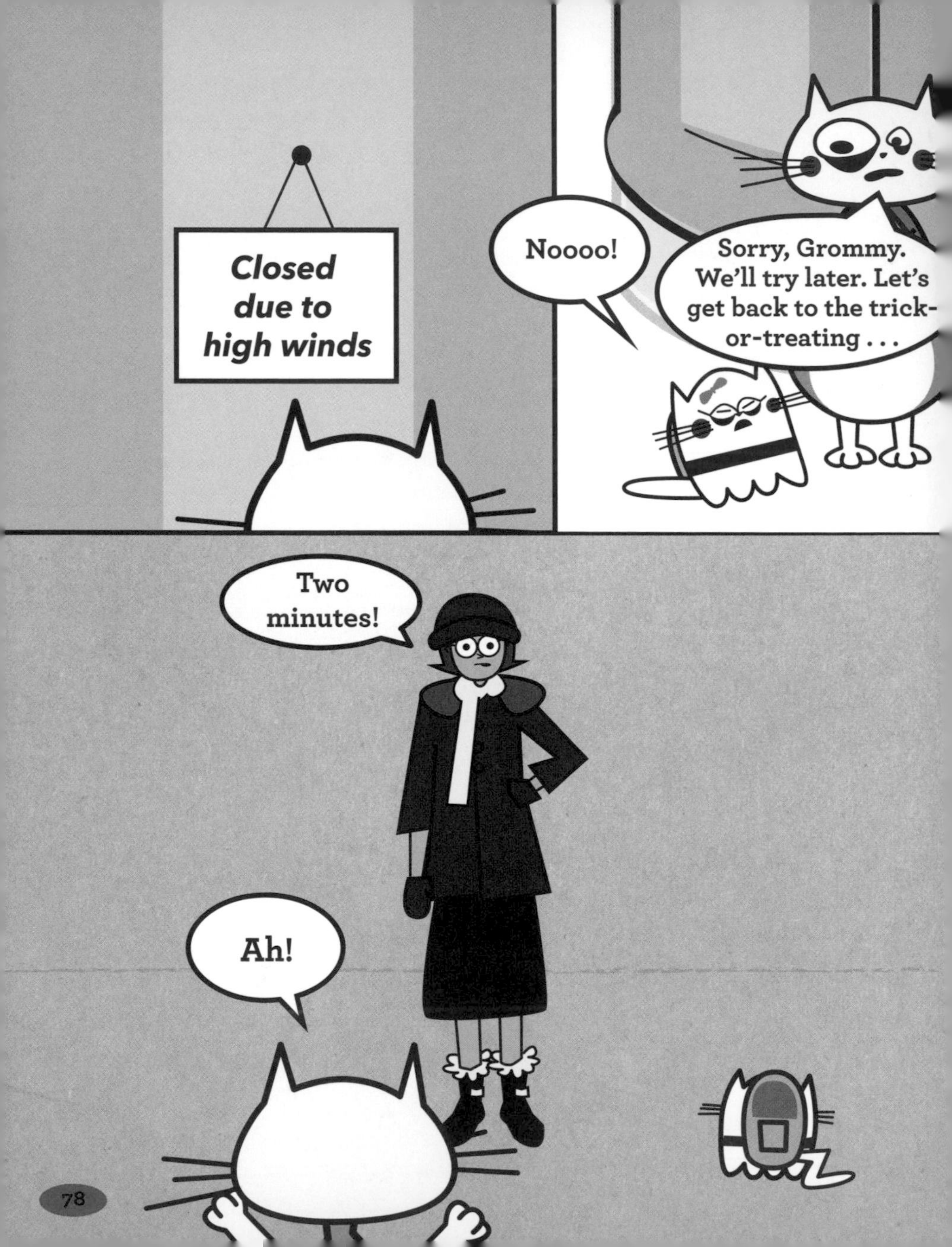
Closed due to high winds
Noooo!
Sorry, Grommy. We'll try later. Let's get back to the trick-or-treating . . .
Two minutes!
Ah!

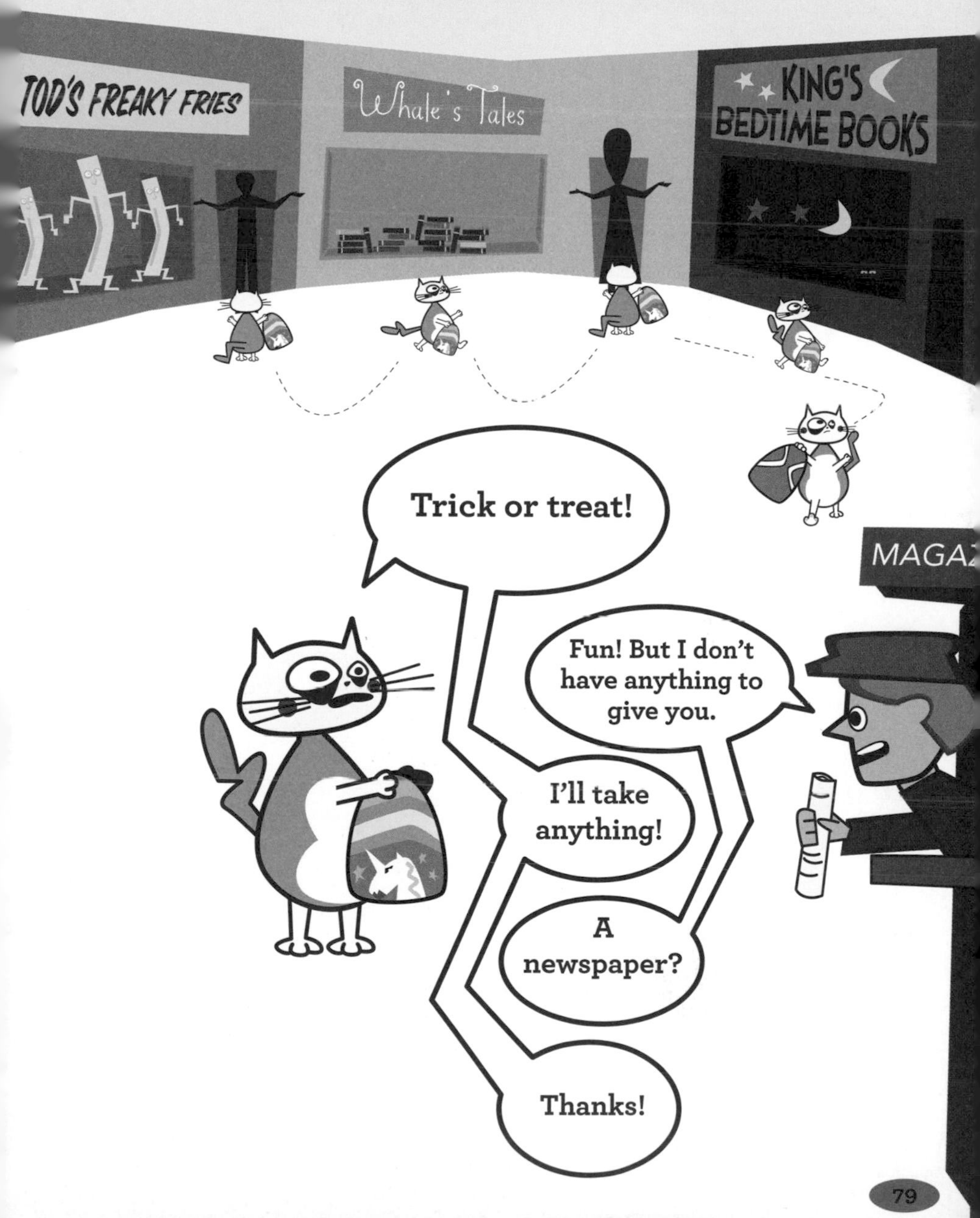
TOD'S FREAKY FRIES
Whale's Tales
KING'S BEDTIME BOOKS
MAGA
Trick or treat!
Fun! But I don't have anything to give you.
I'll take anything!
A newspaper?
Thanks!

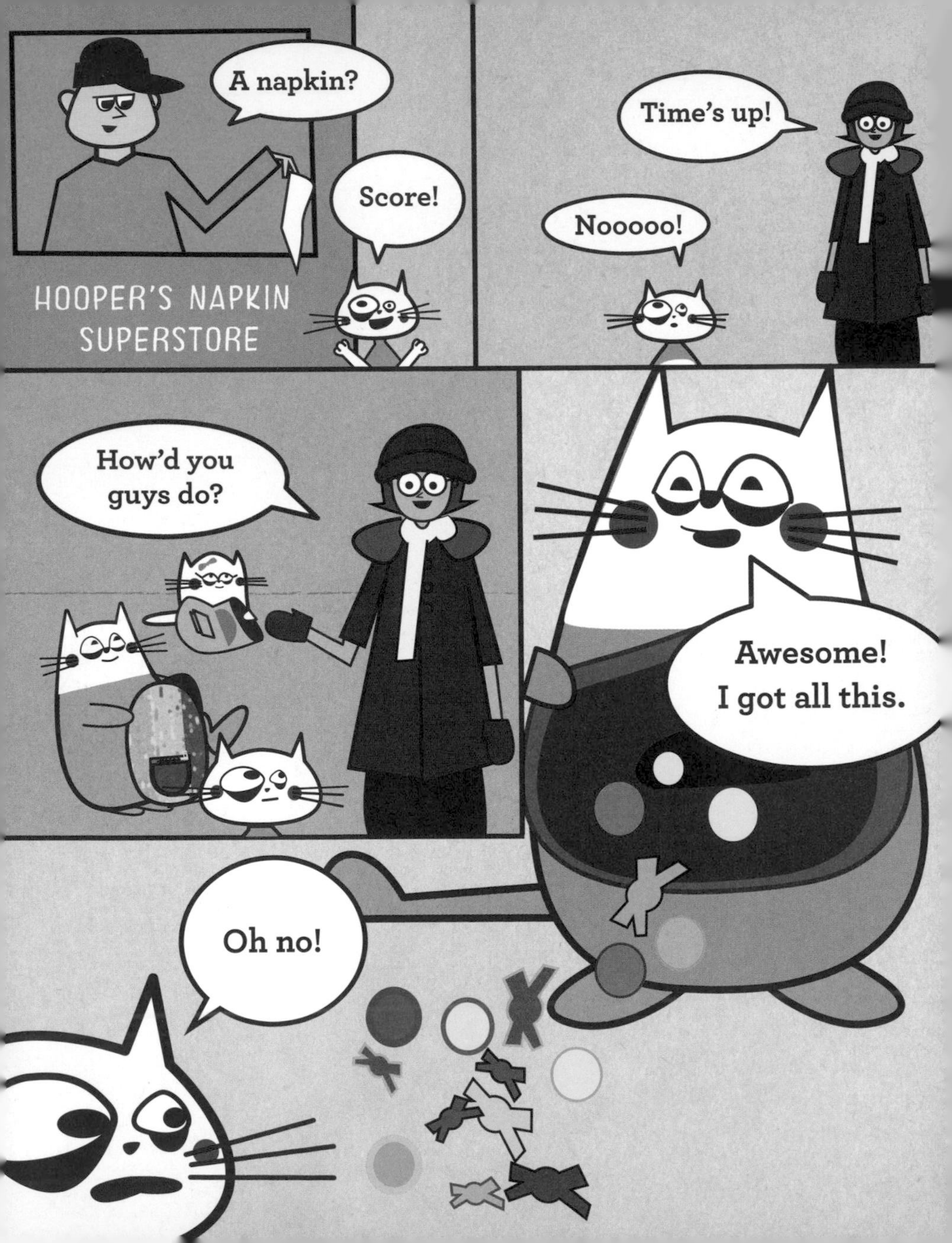
A napkin?
HOOPER'S NAPKIN SUPERSTORE
Score!
Time's up!
Nooooo!
How'd you guys do?
Awesome! I got all this.
Oh no!

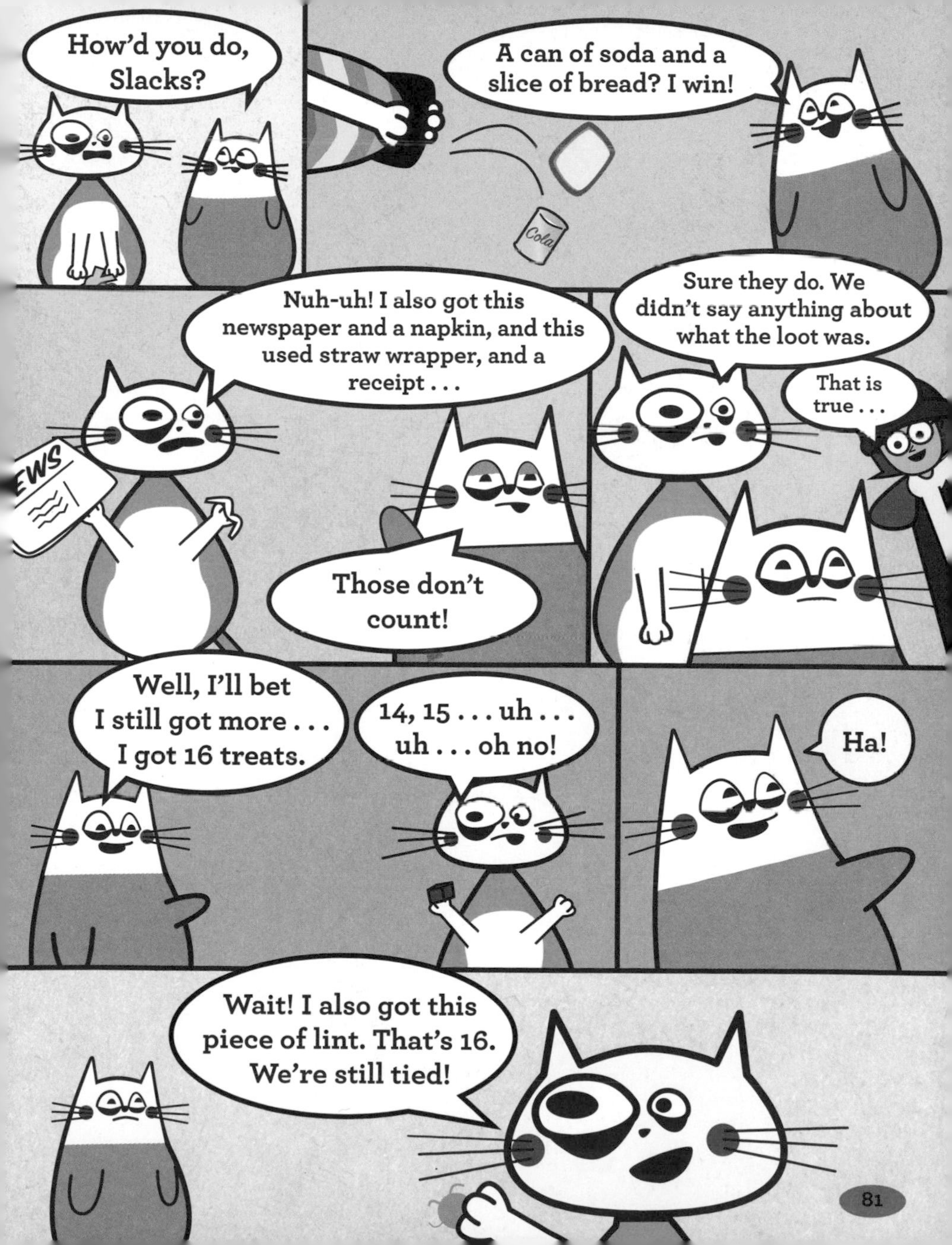
How'd you do, Slacks?
A can of soda and a slice of bread? I win!
Cola
Nuh-uh! I also got this newspaper and a napkin, and this used straw wrapper, and a receipt . . .
EWS
Those don't count!
Sure they do. We didn't say anything about what the loot was.
That is true . . .
Well, I'll bet I still got more . . . I got 16 treats.
14, 15 . . . uh . . . uh . . . oh no!
Ha!
Wait! I also got this piece of lint. That's 16. We're still tied!

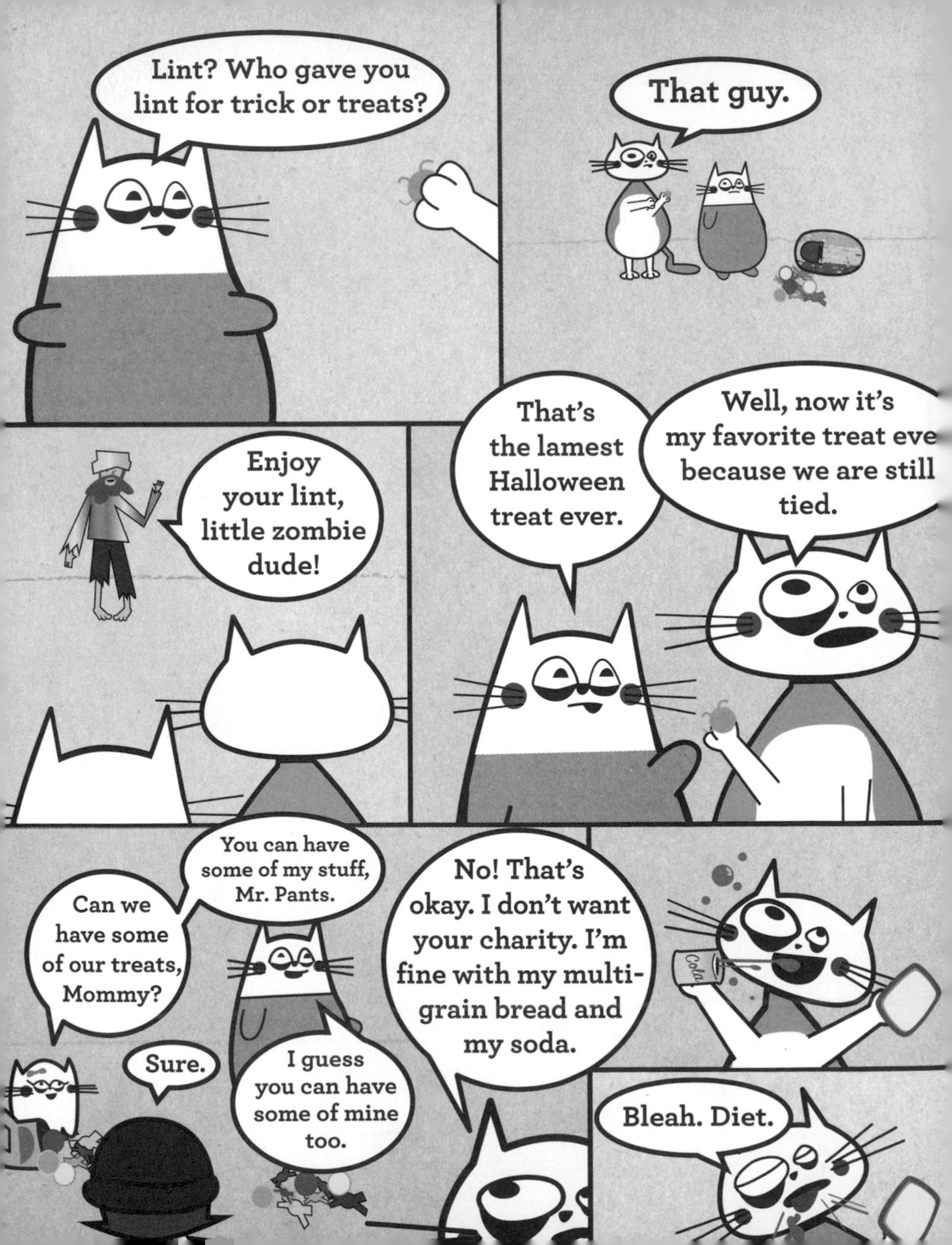
Lint? Who gave you lint for trick or treats?
That guy.
Enjoy your lint, little zombie dude!
That's the lamest Halloween treat ever.
Well, now it's my favorite treat eve because we are still tied.
Can we have some of our treats, Mommy?
Sure.
You can have some of my stuff, Mr. Pants.
I guess you can have some of mine too.
No! That's okay. I don't want your charity. I'm fine with my multi-grain bread and my soda.
Cola
Bleah. Diet.

Chapter Five:
PANTS vs. ZOMBIES

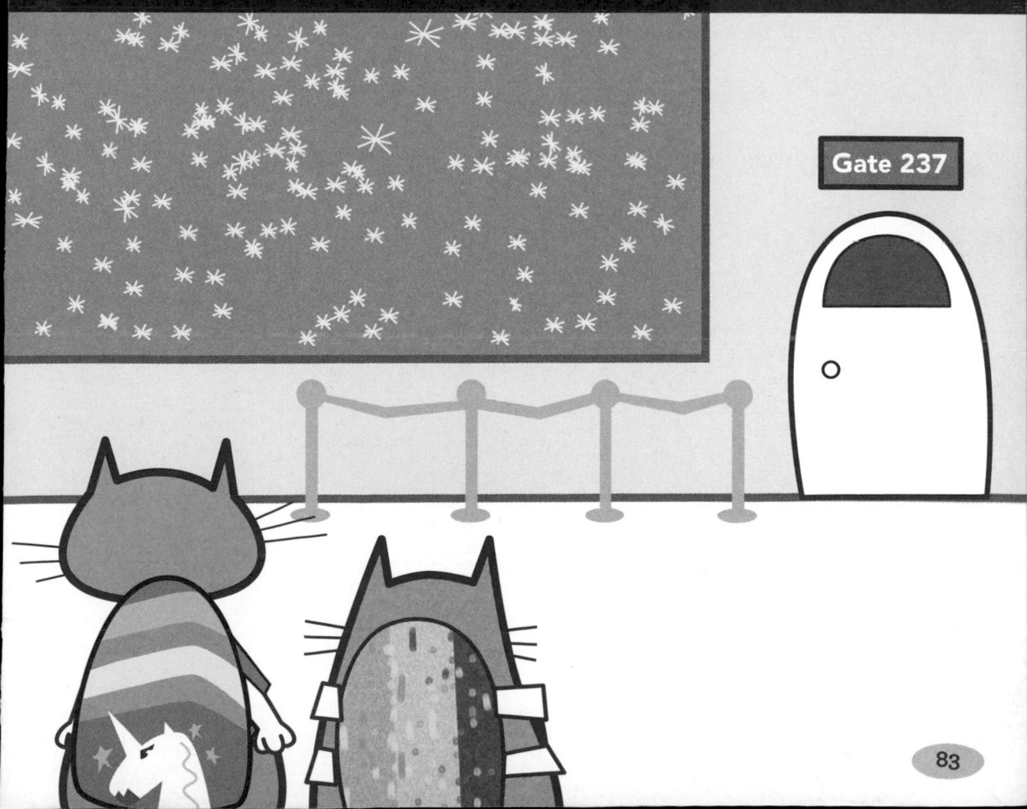

Gate 237

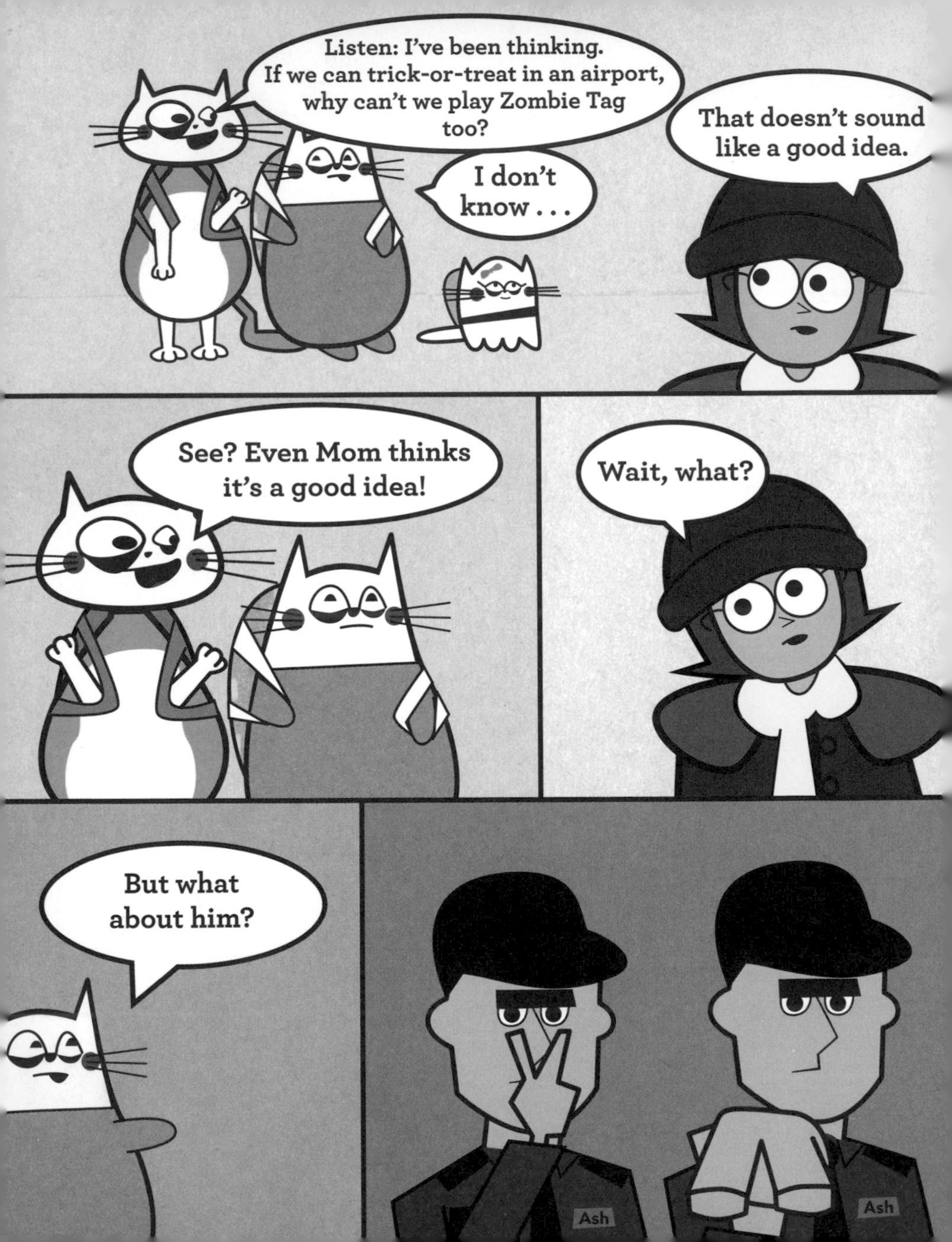
Listen: I've been thinking. If we can trick-or-treat in an airport, why can't we play Zombie Tag too?
I don't know . . .
That doesn't sound like a good idea.
See? Even Mom thinks it's a good idea!
Wait, what?
But what about him?
Ash
Ash

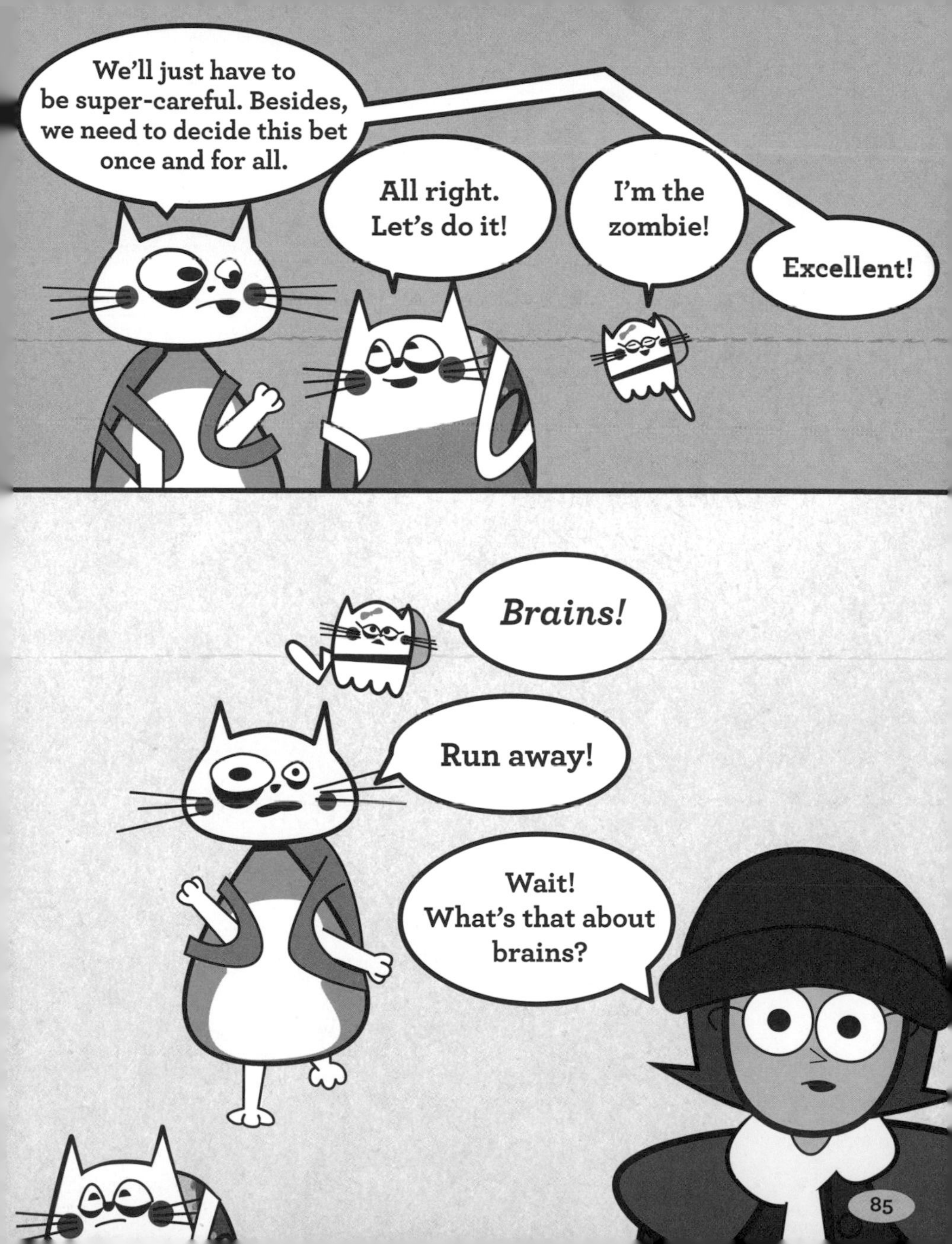
We'll just have to be super-careful. Besides, we need to decide this bet once and for all.
All right. Let's do it!
I'm the zombie!
Excellent!
Brains!
Run away!
Wait! What's that about brains?

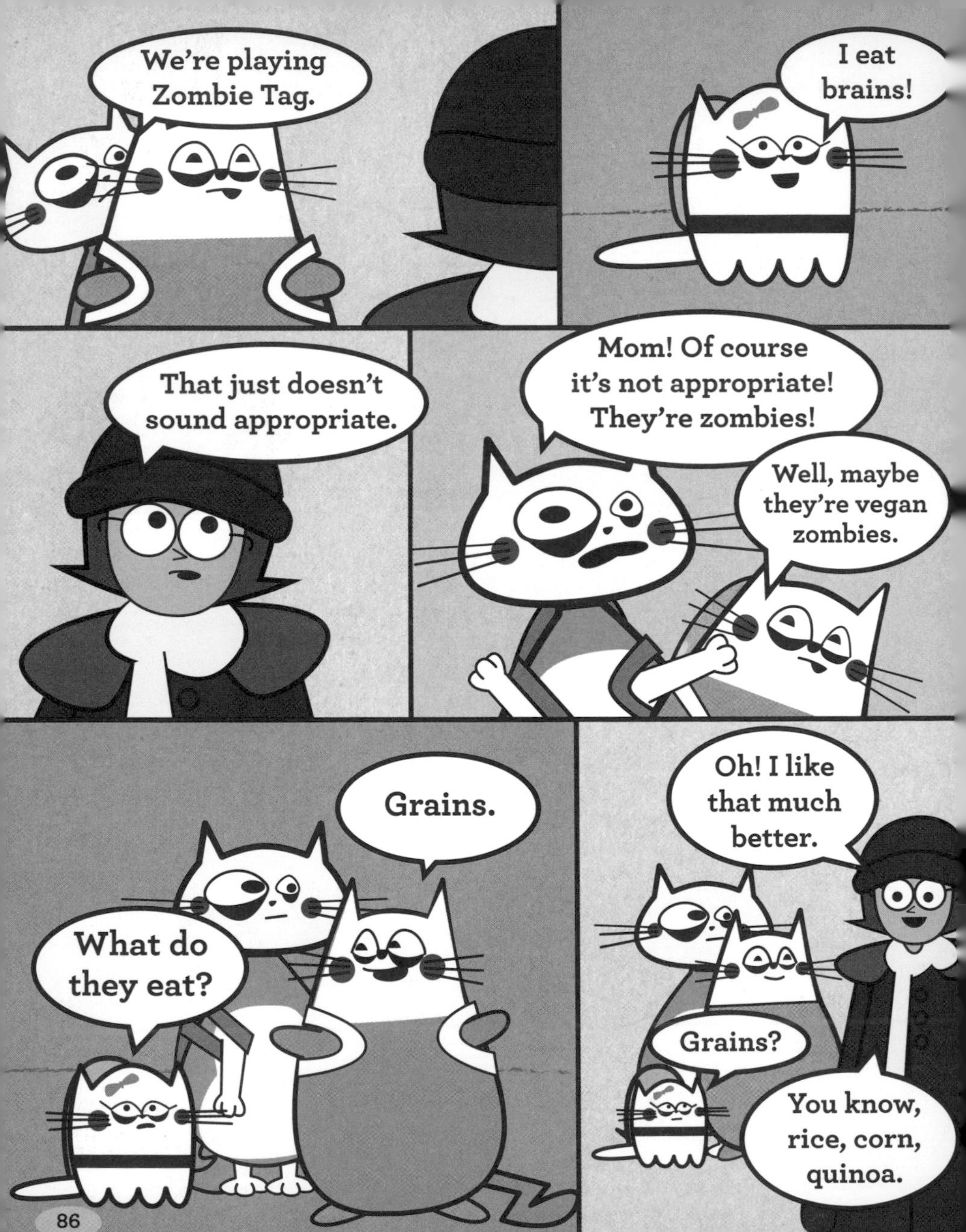
We're playing Zombie Tag.
I eat brains!
That just doesn't sound appropriate.
Mom! Of course it's not appropriate! They're zombies!
Well, maybe they're vegan zombies.
What do they eat?
Grains.
Oh! I like that much better.
Grains?
You know, rice, corn, quinoa.

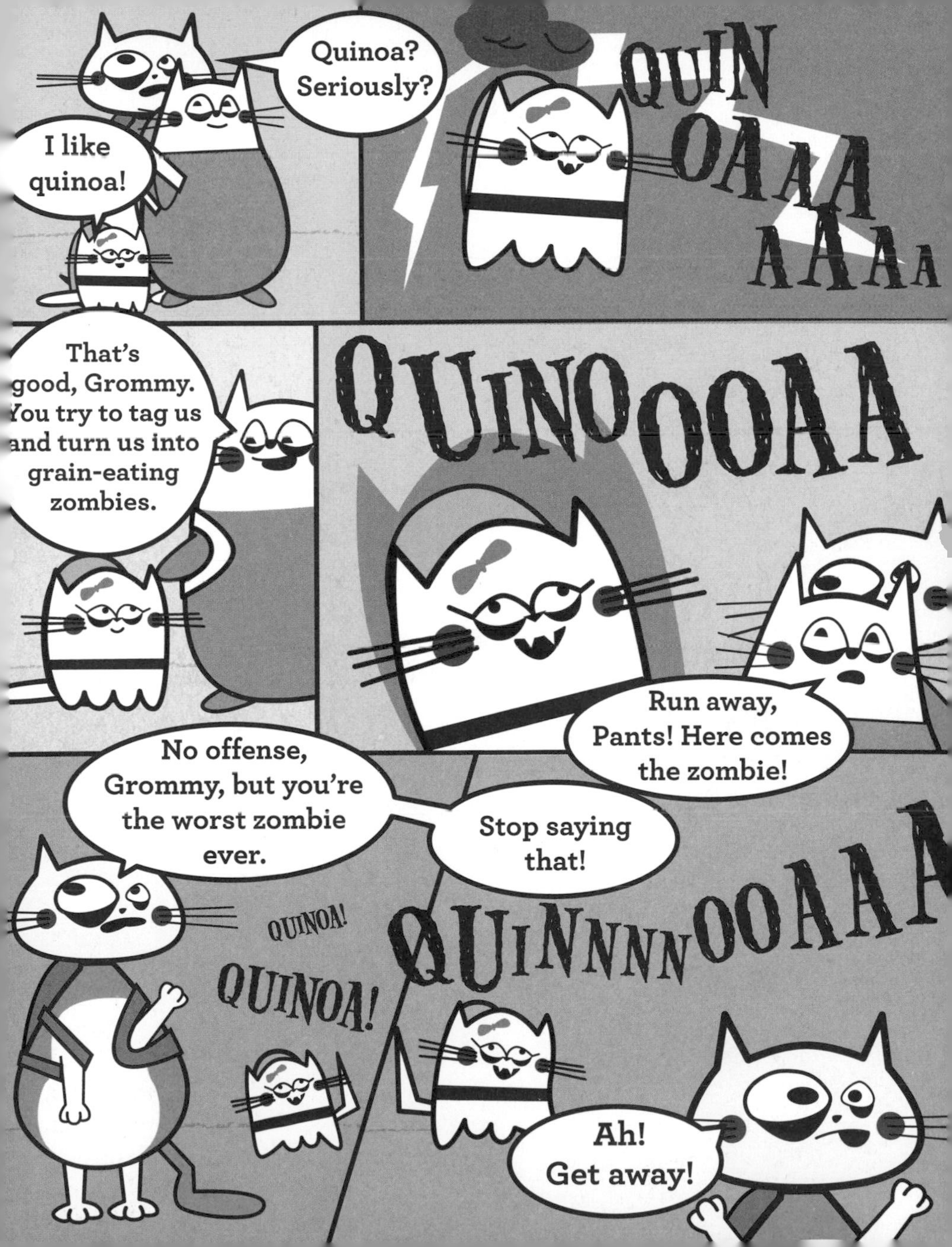
Quinoa? Seriously?
I like quinoa!
QUIN OAAA AAAA
That's good, Grommy. You try to tag us and turn us into grain-eating zombies.
QUINOOOAA
Run away, Pants! Here comes the zombie!
No offense, Grommy, but you're the worst zombie ever.
Stop saying that!
QUINOA!
QUINOA!
QUINNNNOOAAA
Ah! Get away!

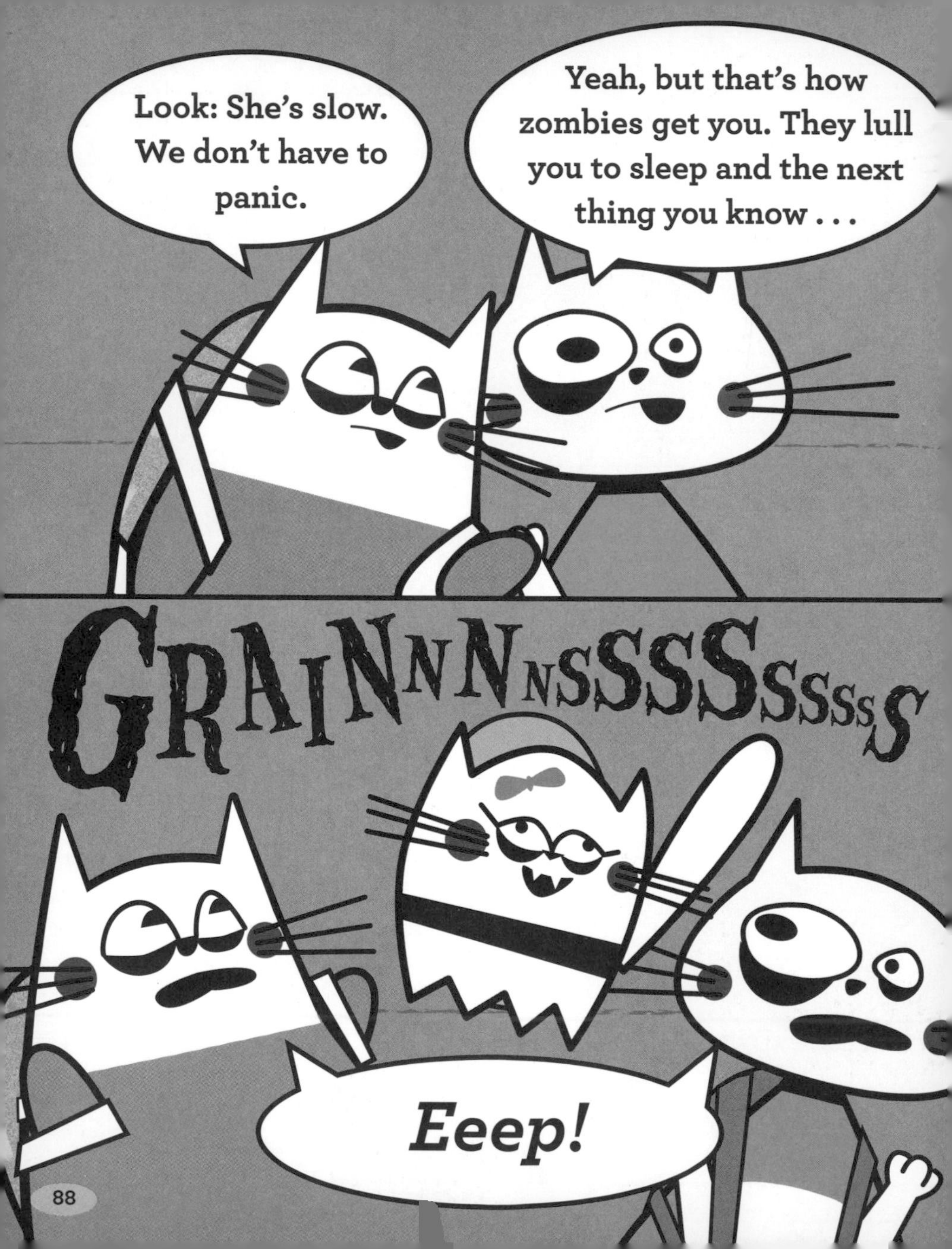
Look: She's slow. We don't have to panic.
Yeah, but that's how zombies get you. They lull you to sleep and the next thing you know . . .
GRAINNNNNSSSSSSSSSS
Eeep!

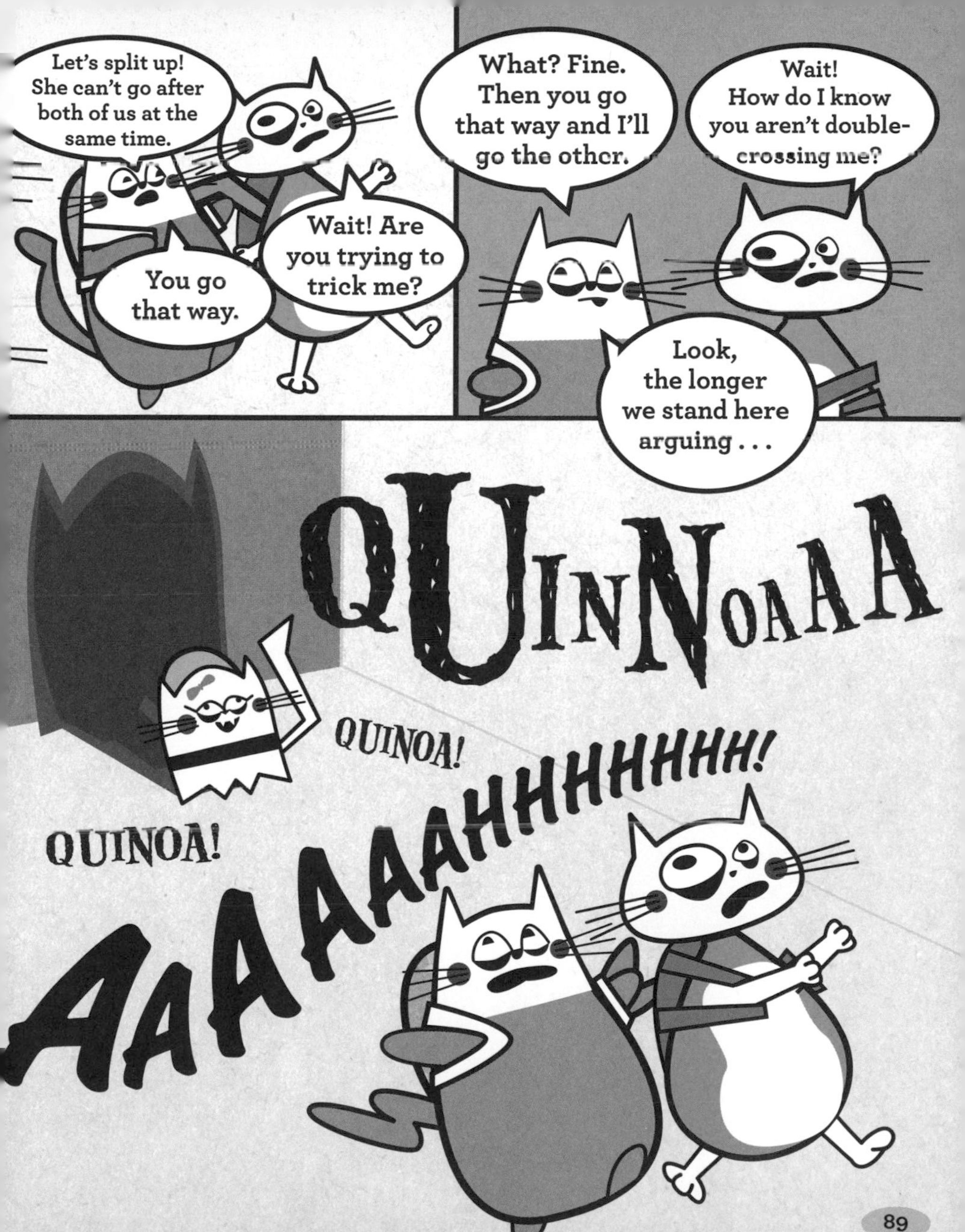
Let's split up! She can't go after both of us at the same time.
You go that way.
Wait! Are you trying to trick me?
What? Fine. Then you go that way and I'll go the other.
Wait! How do I know you aren't double-crossing me?
Look, the longer we stand here arguing . . .
QUINNoaAA
QUINOA!
QUINOA!
AAAAAAHHHHHHHH!

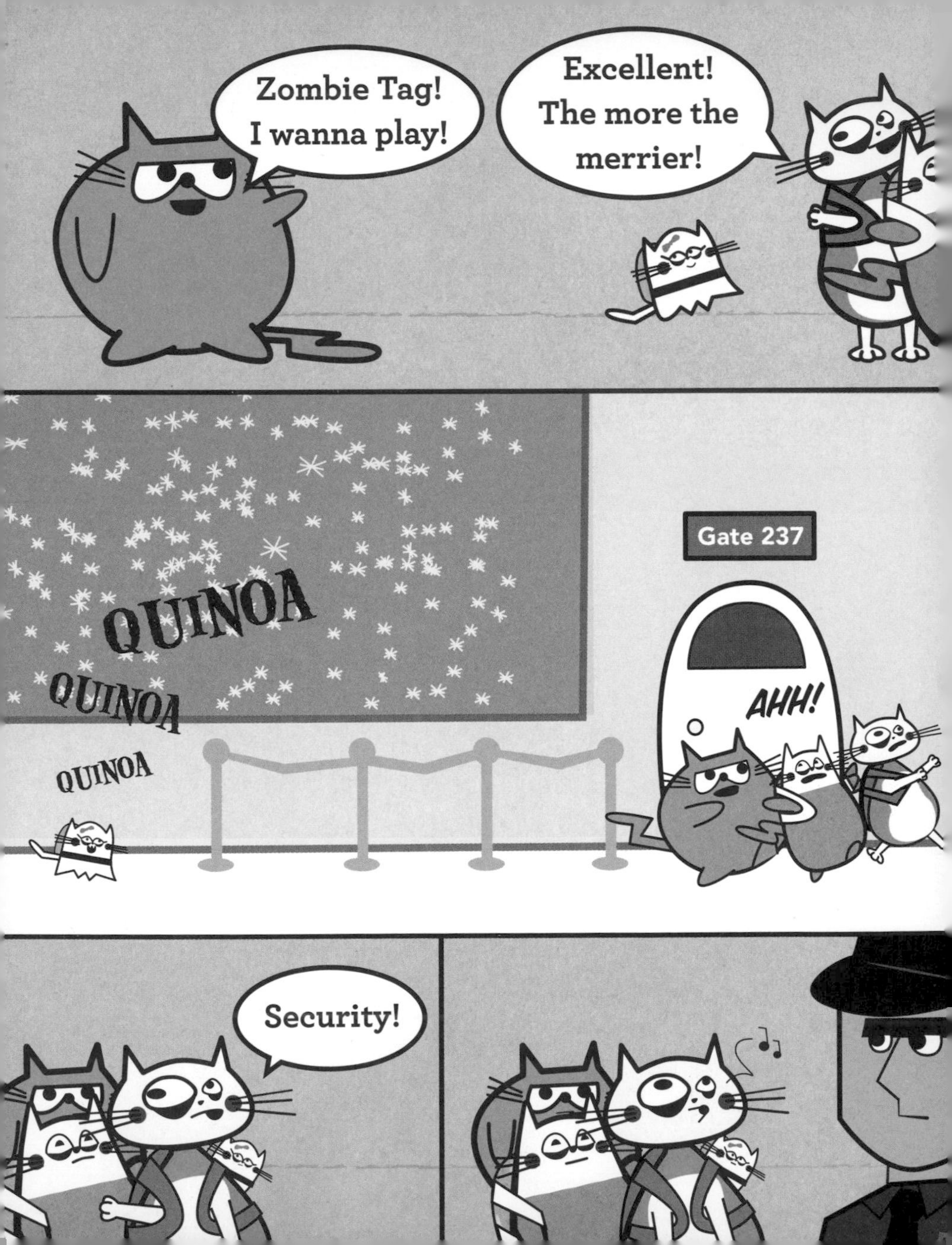
Zombie Tag! I wanna play!
Excellent! The more the merrier!
QUINOA
QUINOA
QUINOA
Gate 237
AHH!
Security!

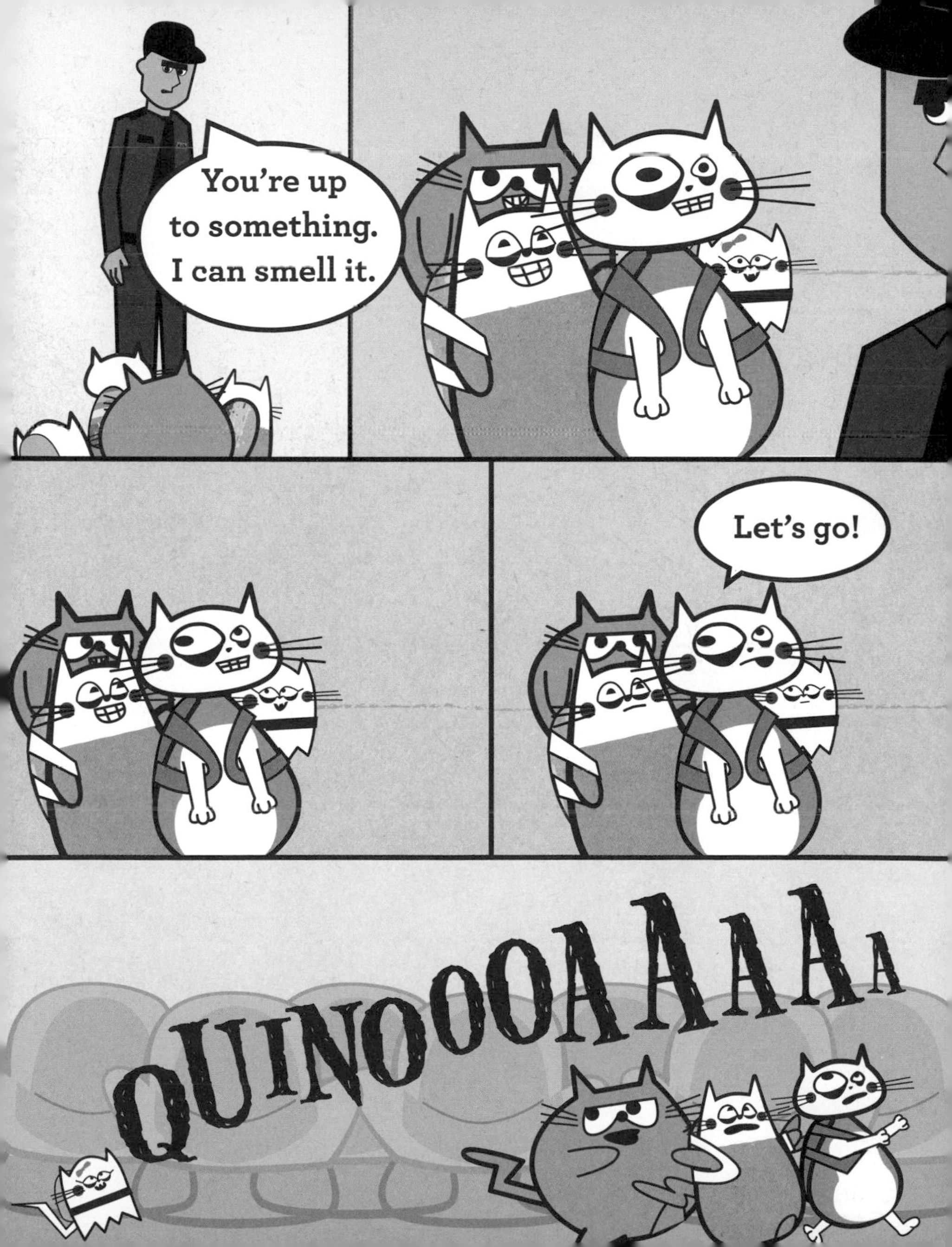
You're up to something. I can smell it.
Let's go!
QUINOOOOAAAAA

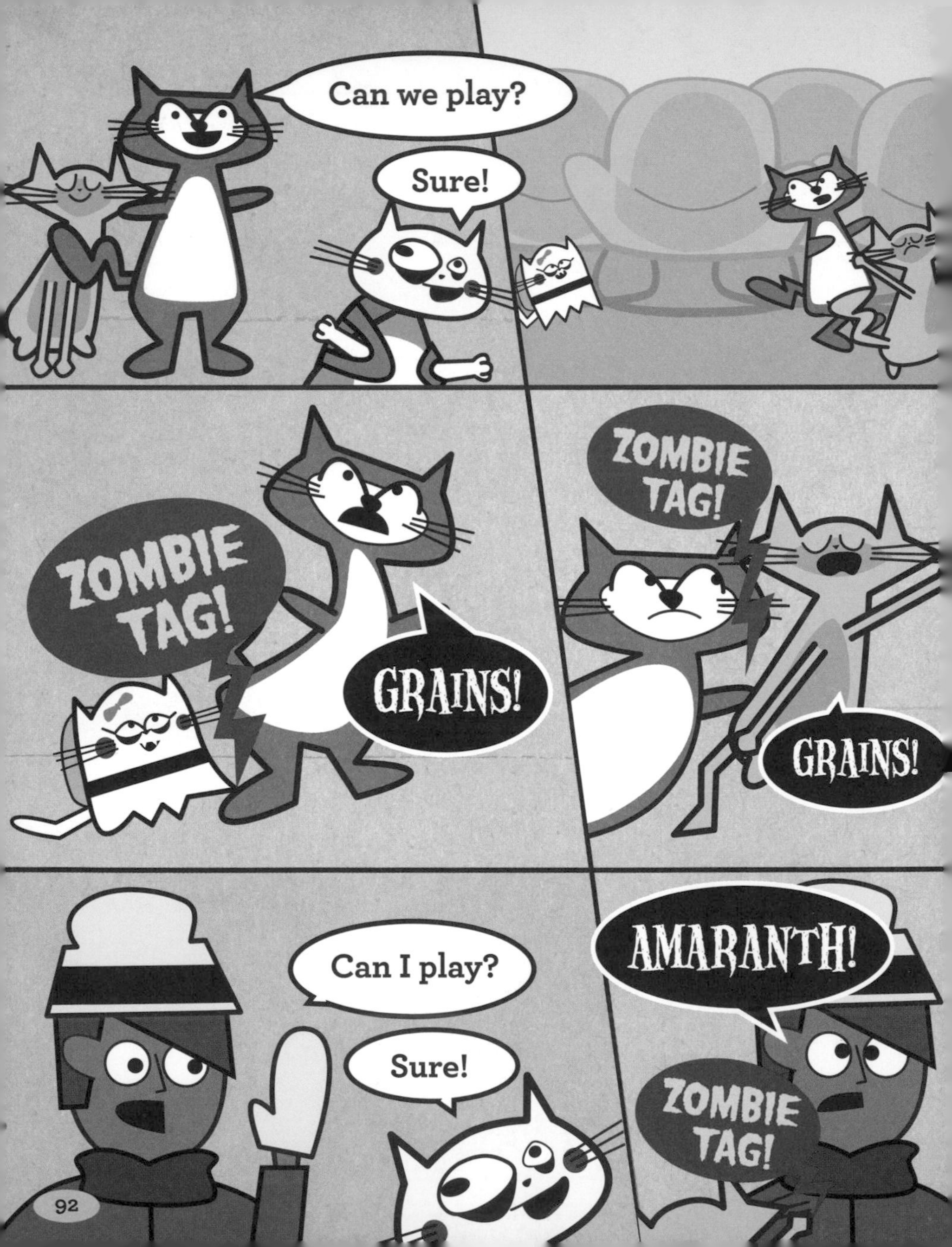
Can we play?
Sure!
ZOMBIE TAG!
GRAINS!
ZOMBIE TAG!
GRAINS!
Can I play?
Sure!
AMARANTH!
ZOMBIE TAG!

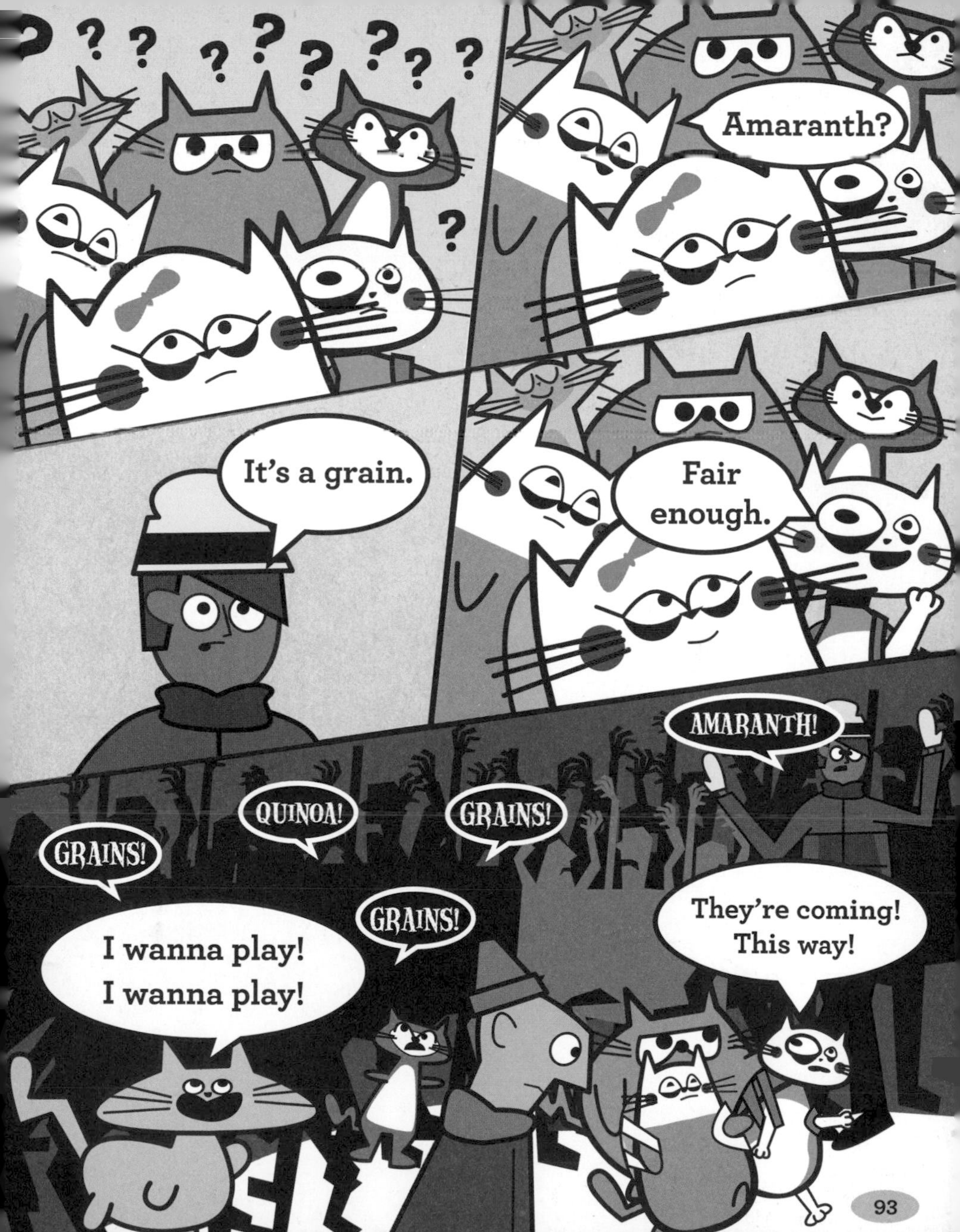

Amaranth?
It's a grain.
Fair enough.
AMARANTH!
QUINOA!
GRAINS!
GRAINS!
GRAINS!
I wanna play! I wanna play!
They're coming! This way!

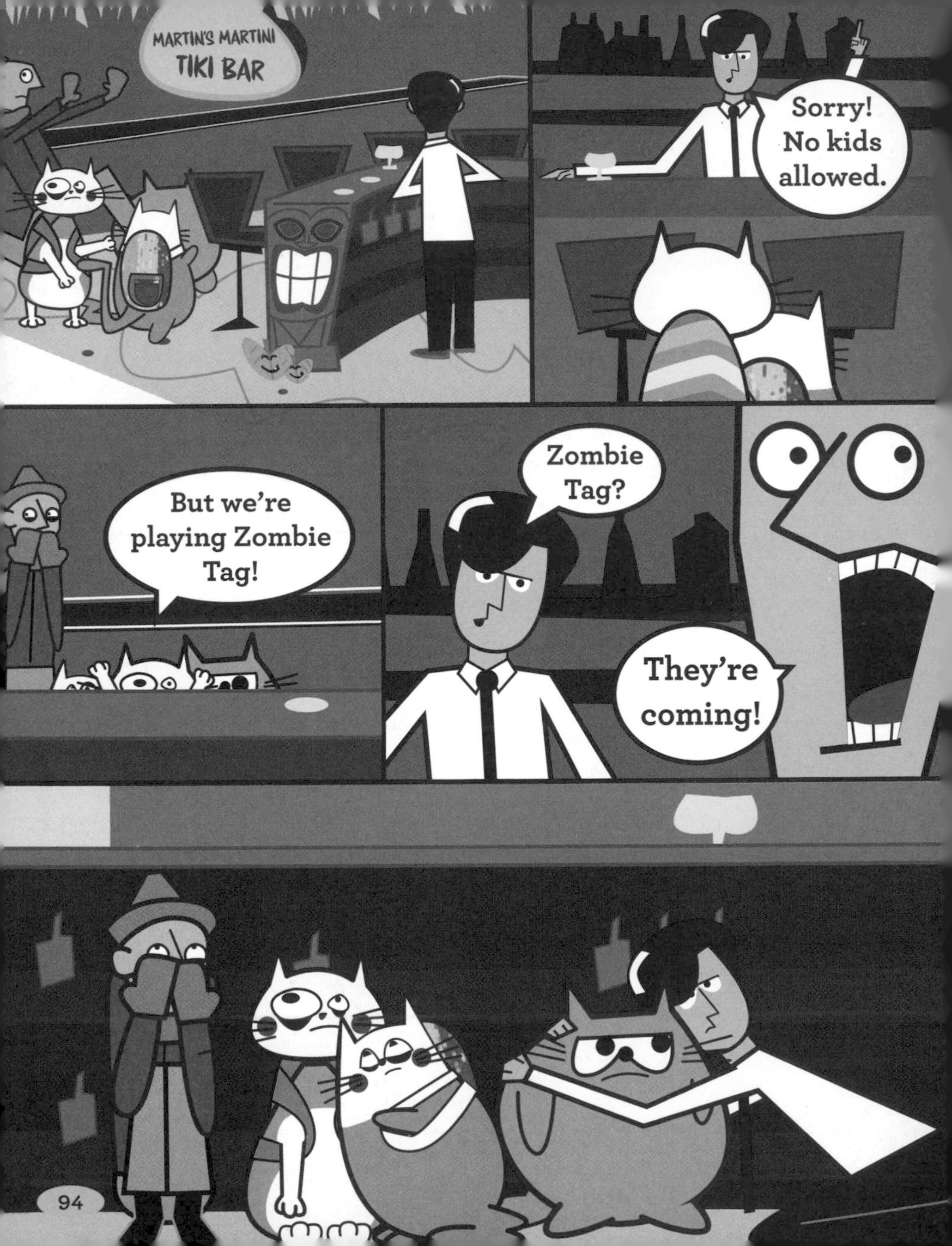
MARTIN'S MARTINI
TIKI BAR
Sorry! No kids allowed.
But we're playing Zombie Tag!
Zombie Tag?
They're coming!

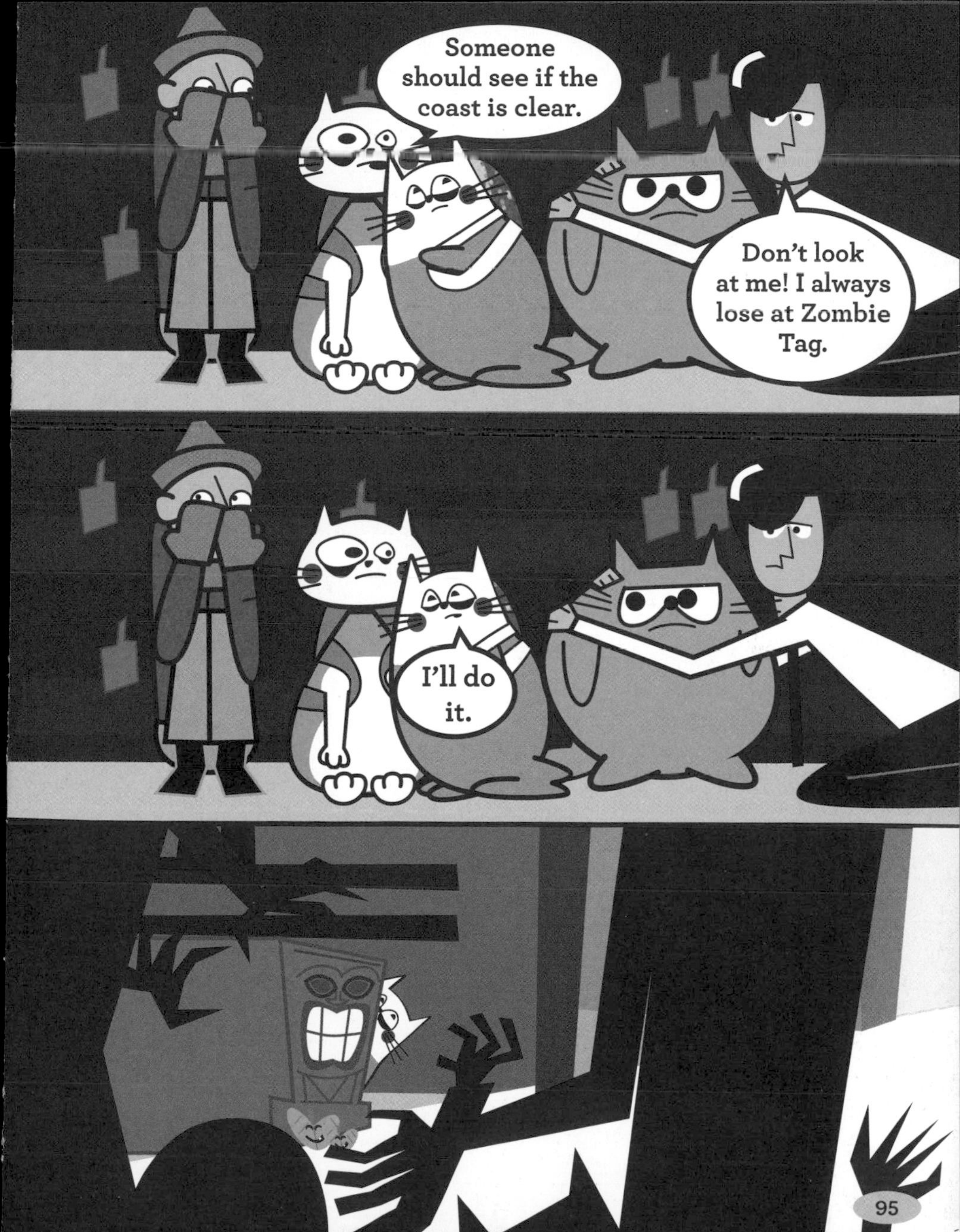
Someone should see if the coast is clear.
Don't look at me! I always lose at Zombie Tag.
I'll do it.

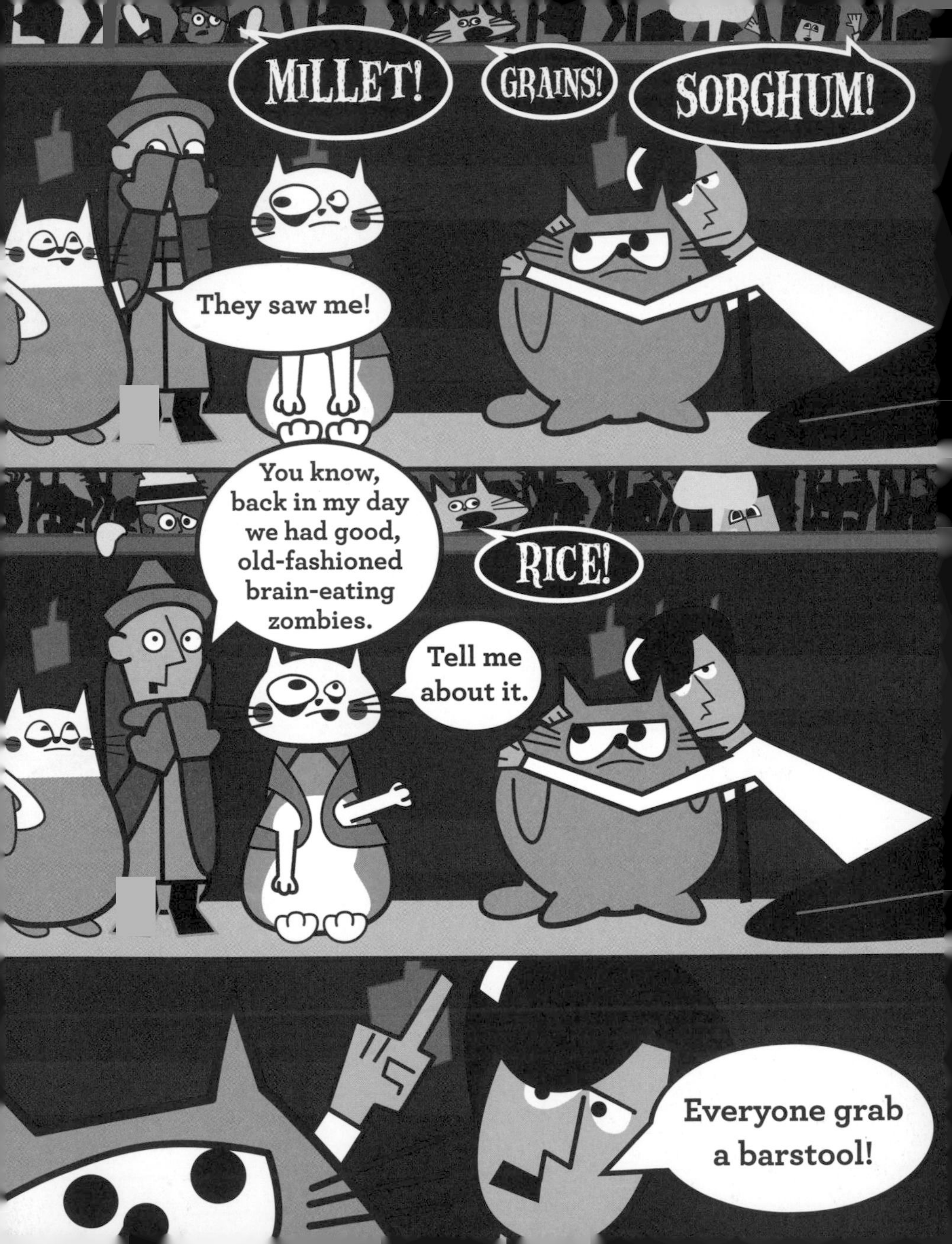
MILLET!
GRAINS!
SORGHUM!
They saw me!
You know, back in my day we had good, old-fashioned brain-eating zombies.
RICE!
Tell me about it.
Everyone grab a barstool!

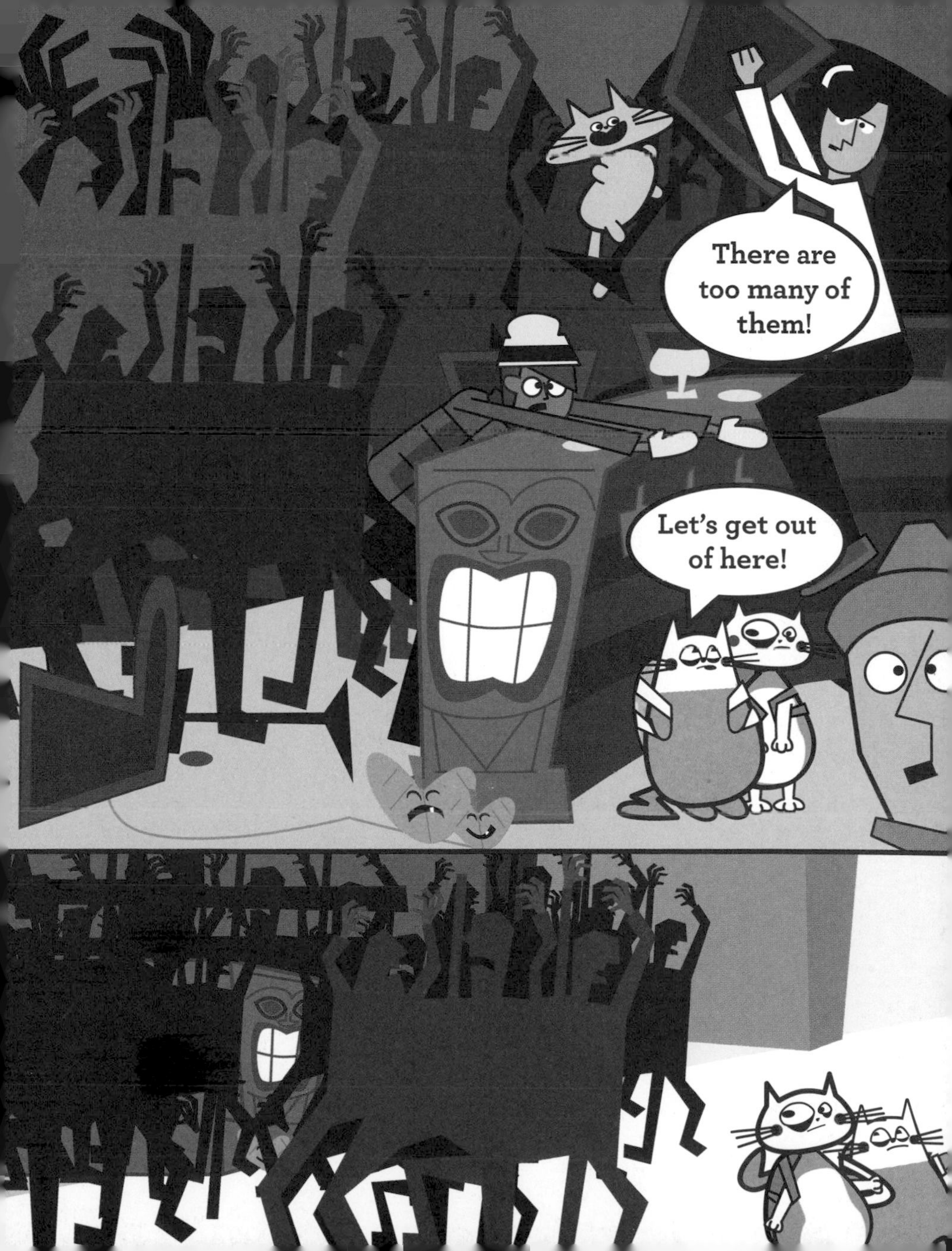
There are too many of them!
Let's get out of here!

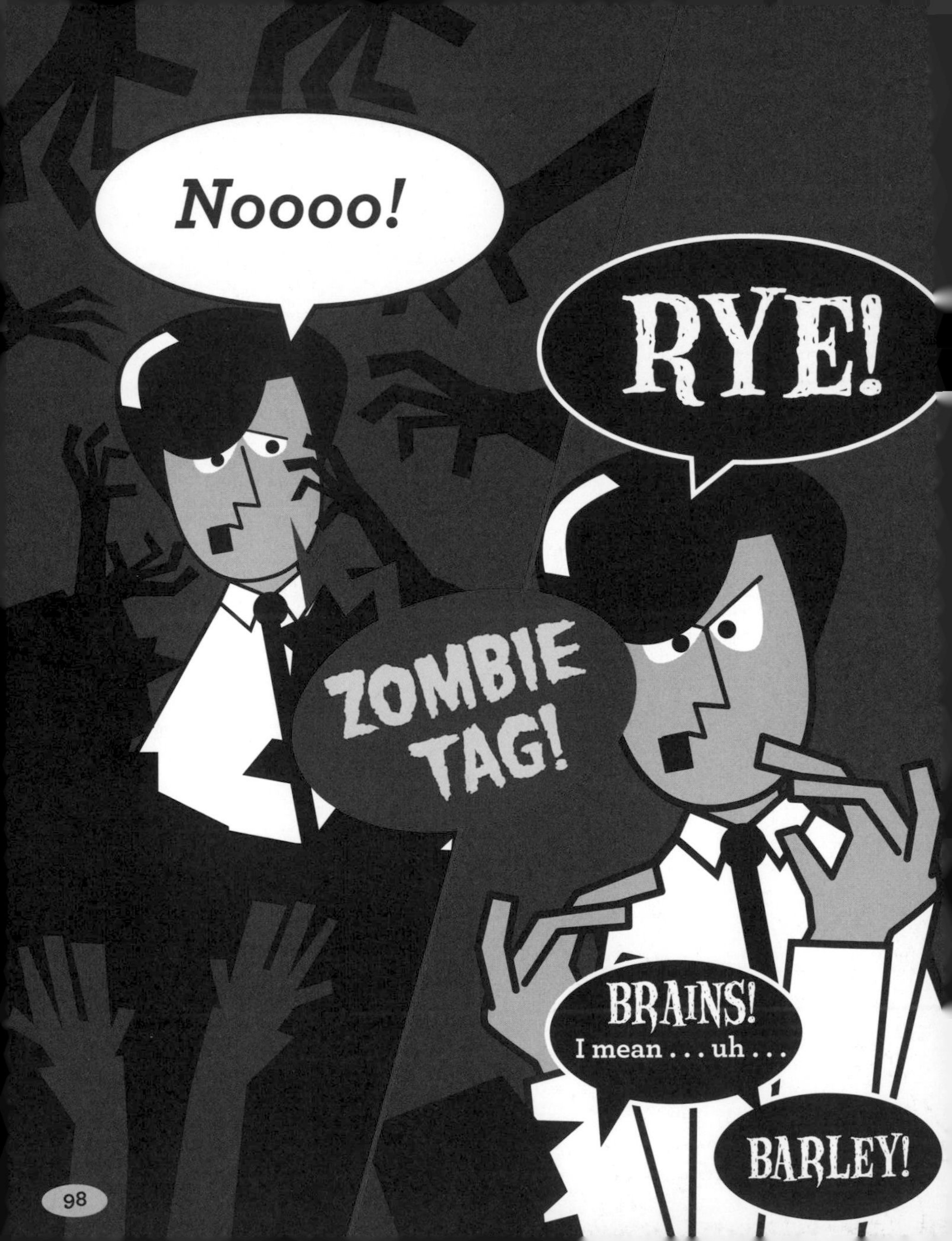
Noooo!
RYE!
ZOMBIE TAG!
BRAINS!
I mean . . . uh . . .
BARLEY!

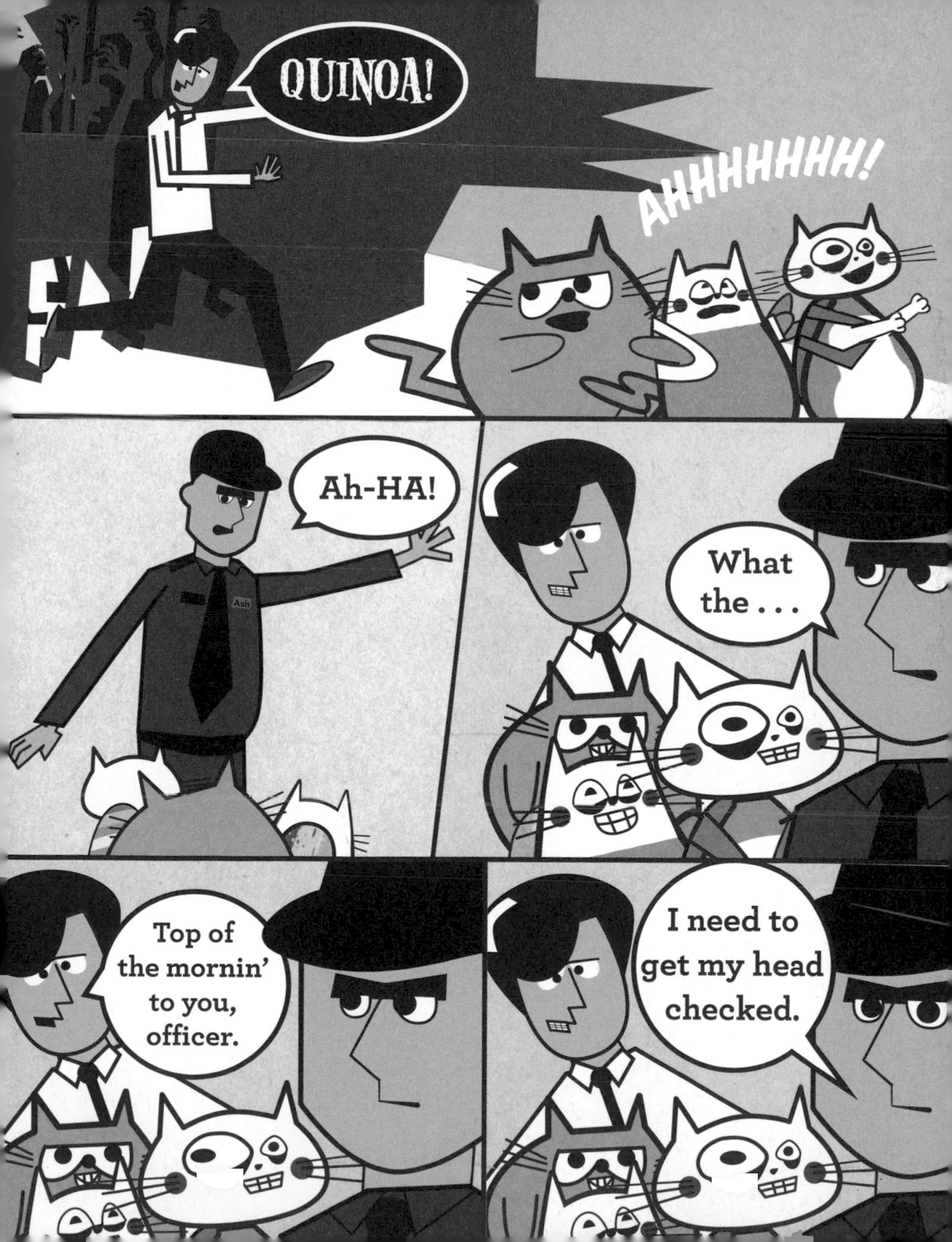
QUINOA!
AHHHHHHHH!
Ah-HA!
Ash
What the . . .
Top of the mornin' to you, officer.
I need to get my head checked.

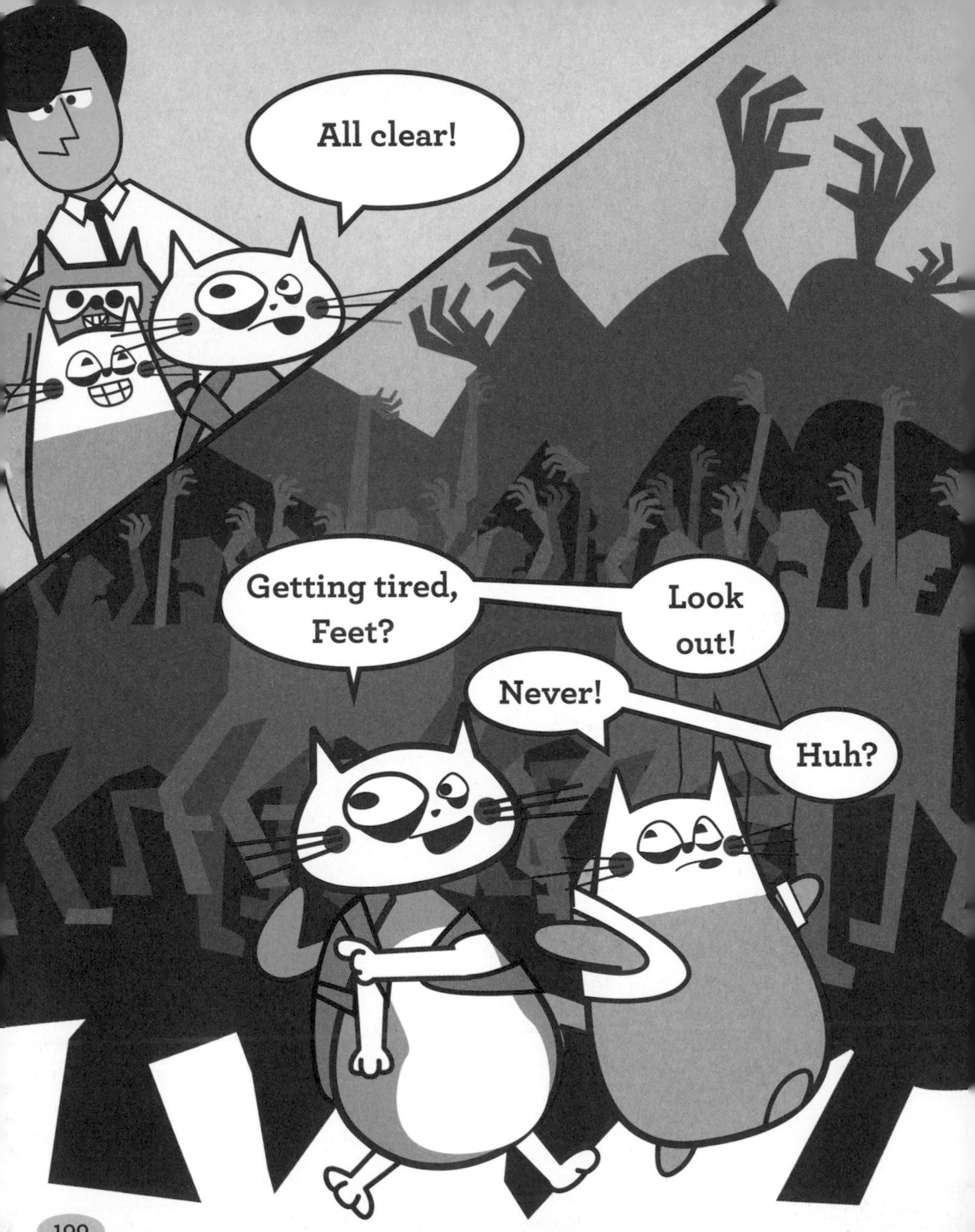
All clear!
Getting tired, Feet?
Look out!
Never!
Huh?

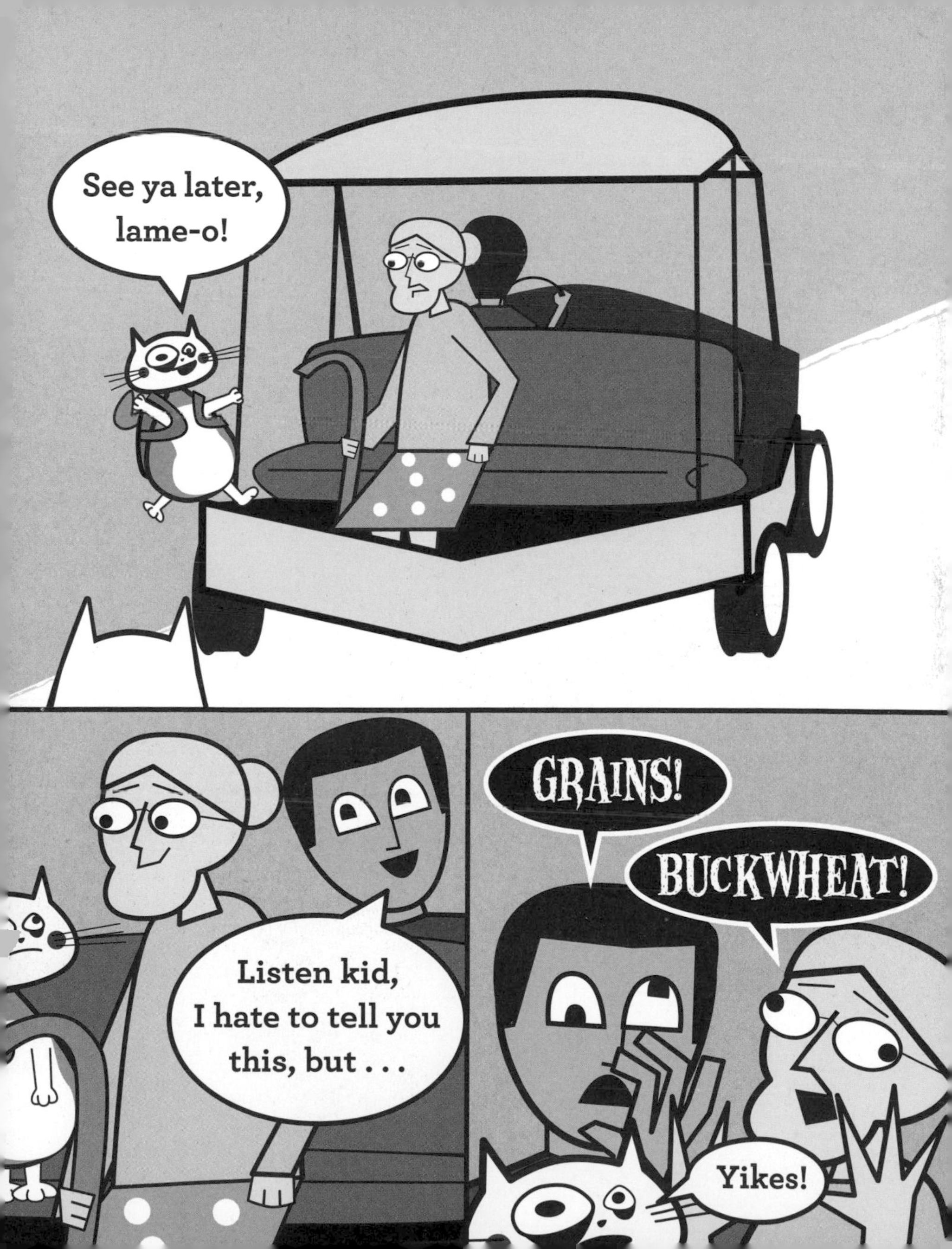
See ya later, lame-o!
Listen kid, I hate to tell you this, but . . .
GRAINS!
BUCKWHEAT!
Yikes!

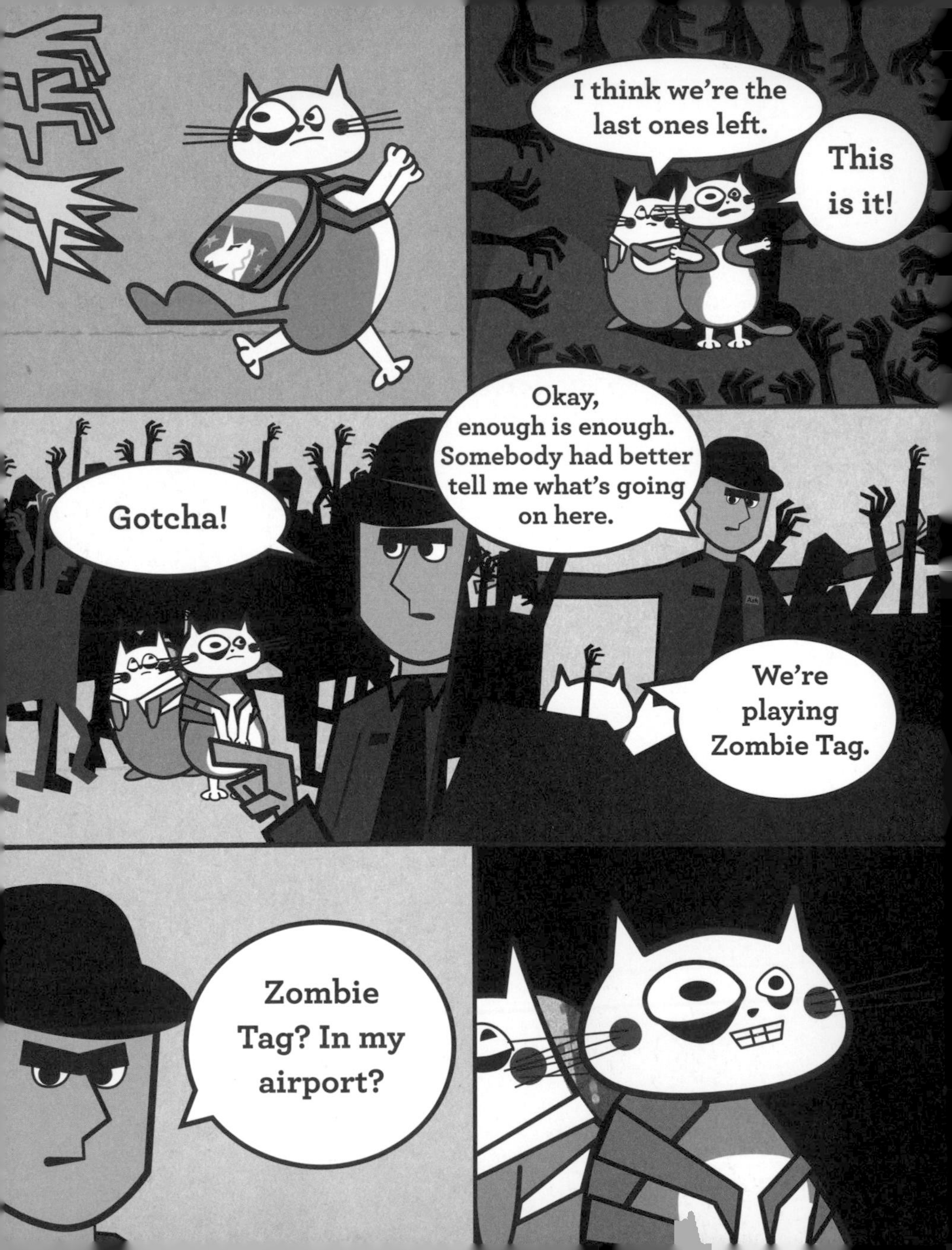
I think we're the last ones left.
This is it!
Gotcha!
Okay, enough is enough. Somebody had better tell me what's going on here.
We're playing Zombie Tag.
Zombie Tag? In my airport?

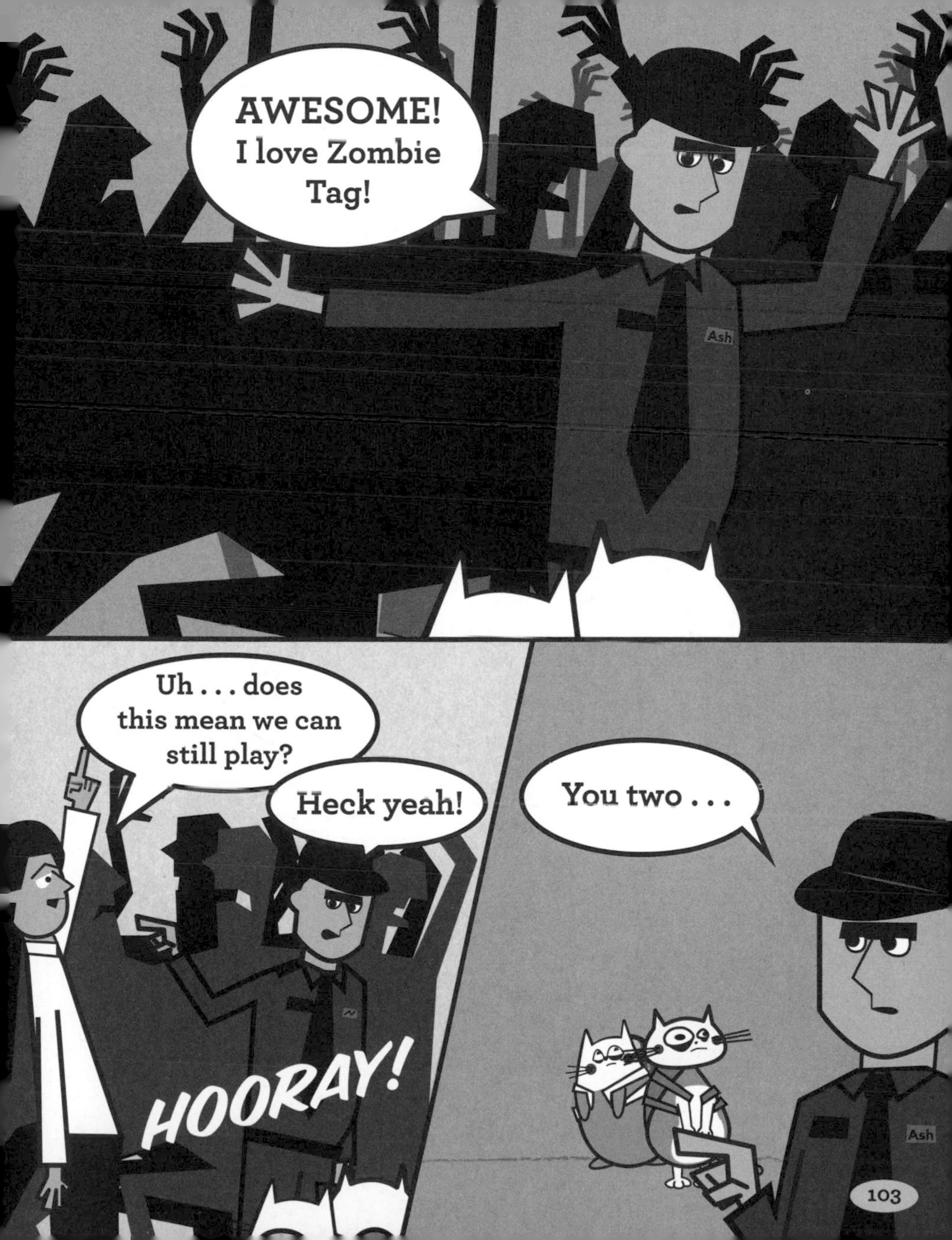
AWESOME! I love Zombie Tag!
Ash
Uh . . . does this mean we can still play?
Heck yeah!
HOORAY!
You two . . .
Ash

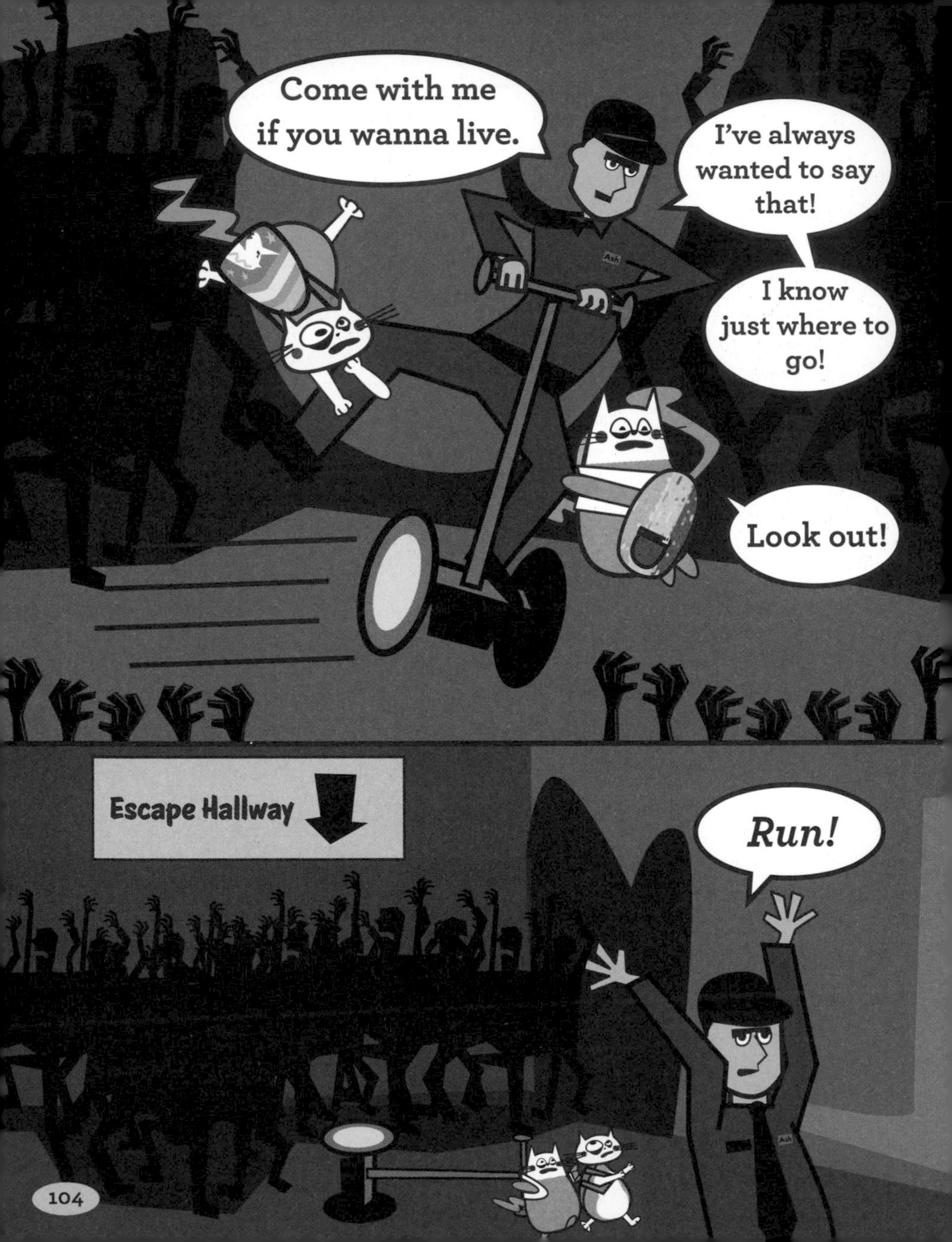
Come with me
if you wanna live.
I've always
wanted to say
that!
I know
just where to
go!
Look out!
Escape Hallway
Run!

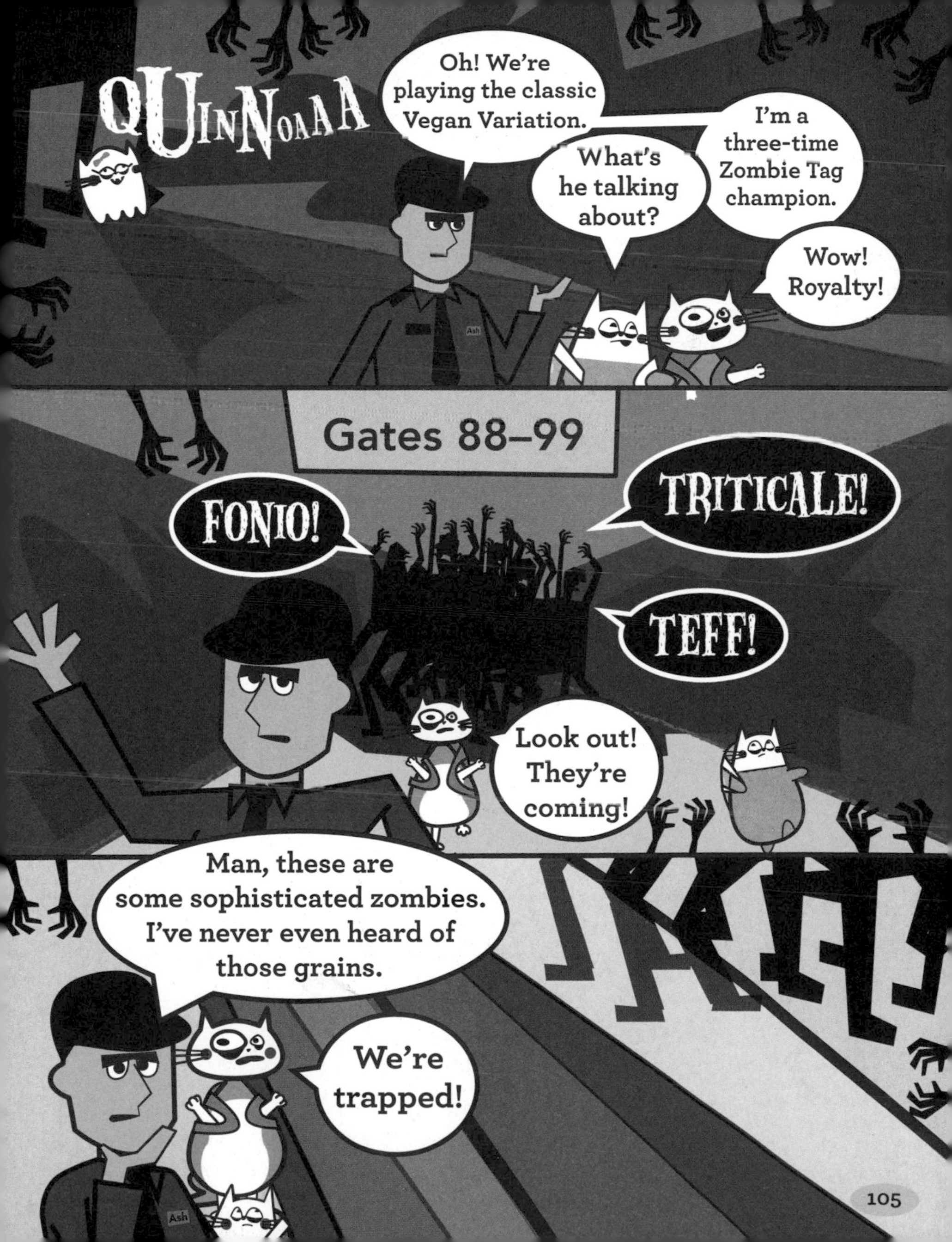

QUINNOAAA
Oh! We're playing the classic Vegan Variation.
What's he talking about?
I'm a three-time Zombie Tag champion.
Wow! Royalty!
Ash
Gates 88–99
FONIO!
TRITICALE!
TEFF!
Look out! They're coming!
Man, these are some sophisticated zombies. I've never even heard of those grains.
We're trapped!
Ash

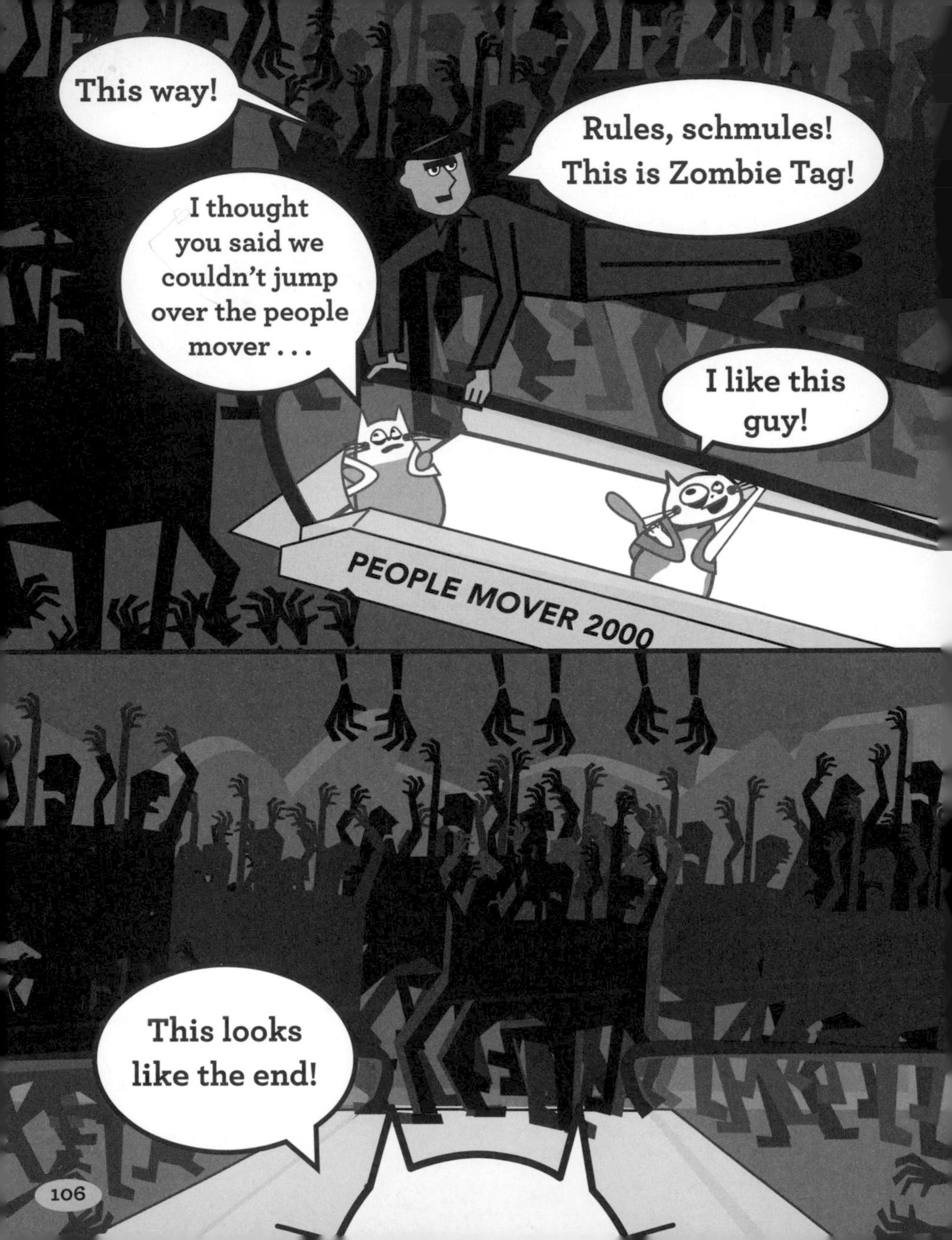
This way!
Rules, schmules! This is Zombie Tag!
I thought you said we couldn't jump over the people mover . . .
I like this guy!
PEOPLE MOVER 2000
This looks like the end!

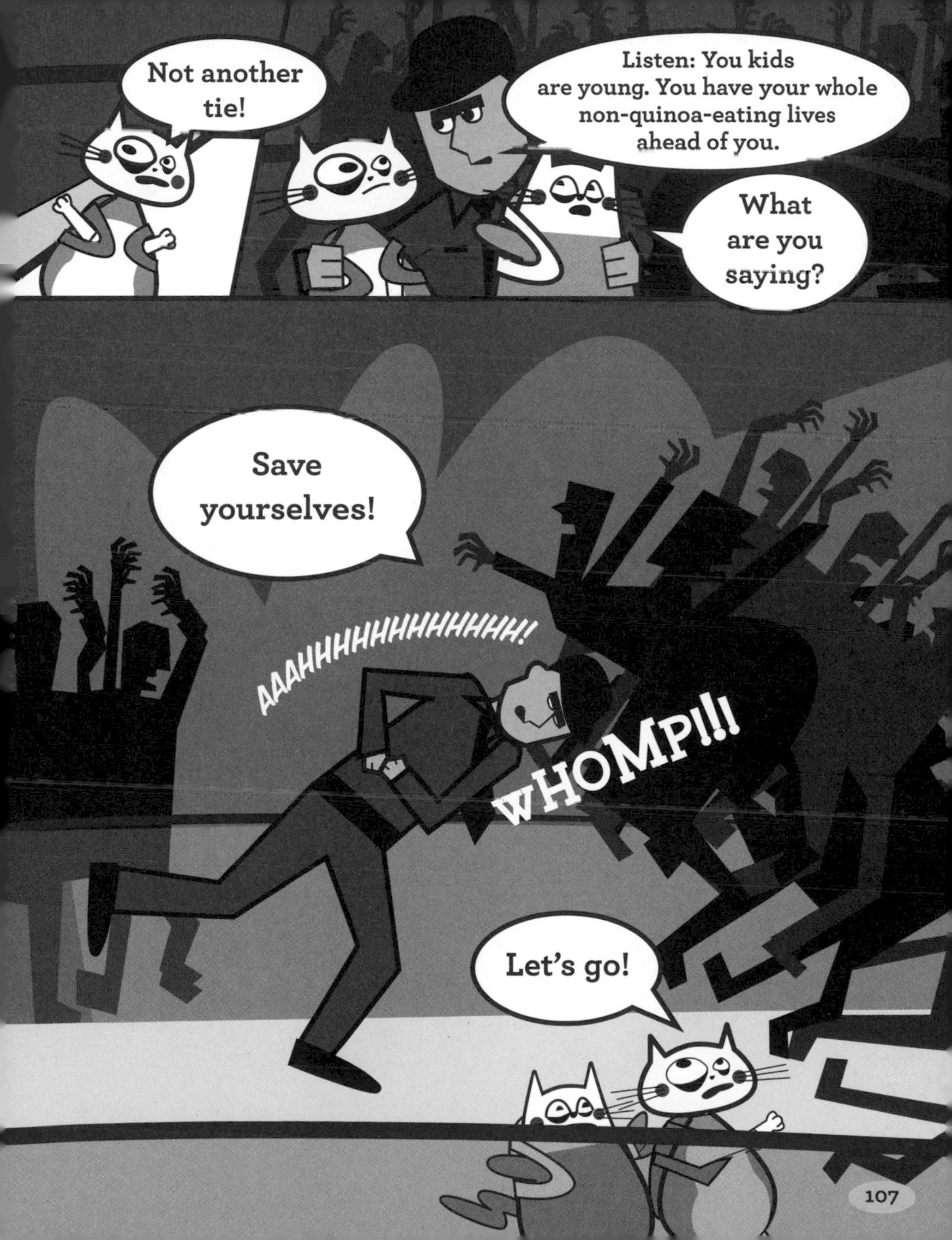
Not another tie!
Listen: You kids are young. You have your whole non-quinoa-eating lives ahead of you.
What are you saying?
Save yourselves!
AAAHHHHHHHHHHHHH!
WHOMP!!!
Let's go!

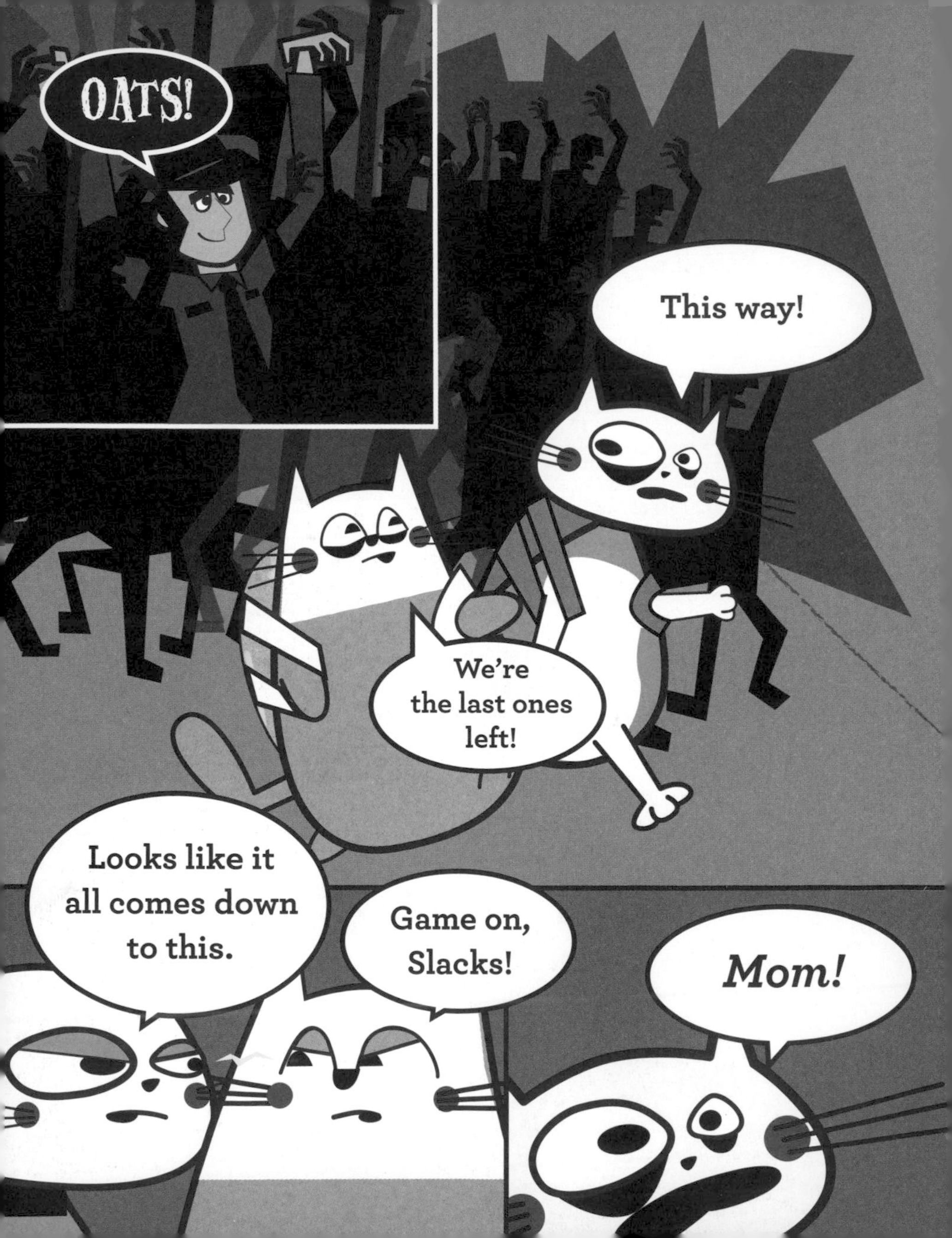
OATS!
This way!
We're the last ones left!
Looks like it all comes down to this.
Game on, Slacks!
Mom!

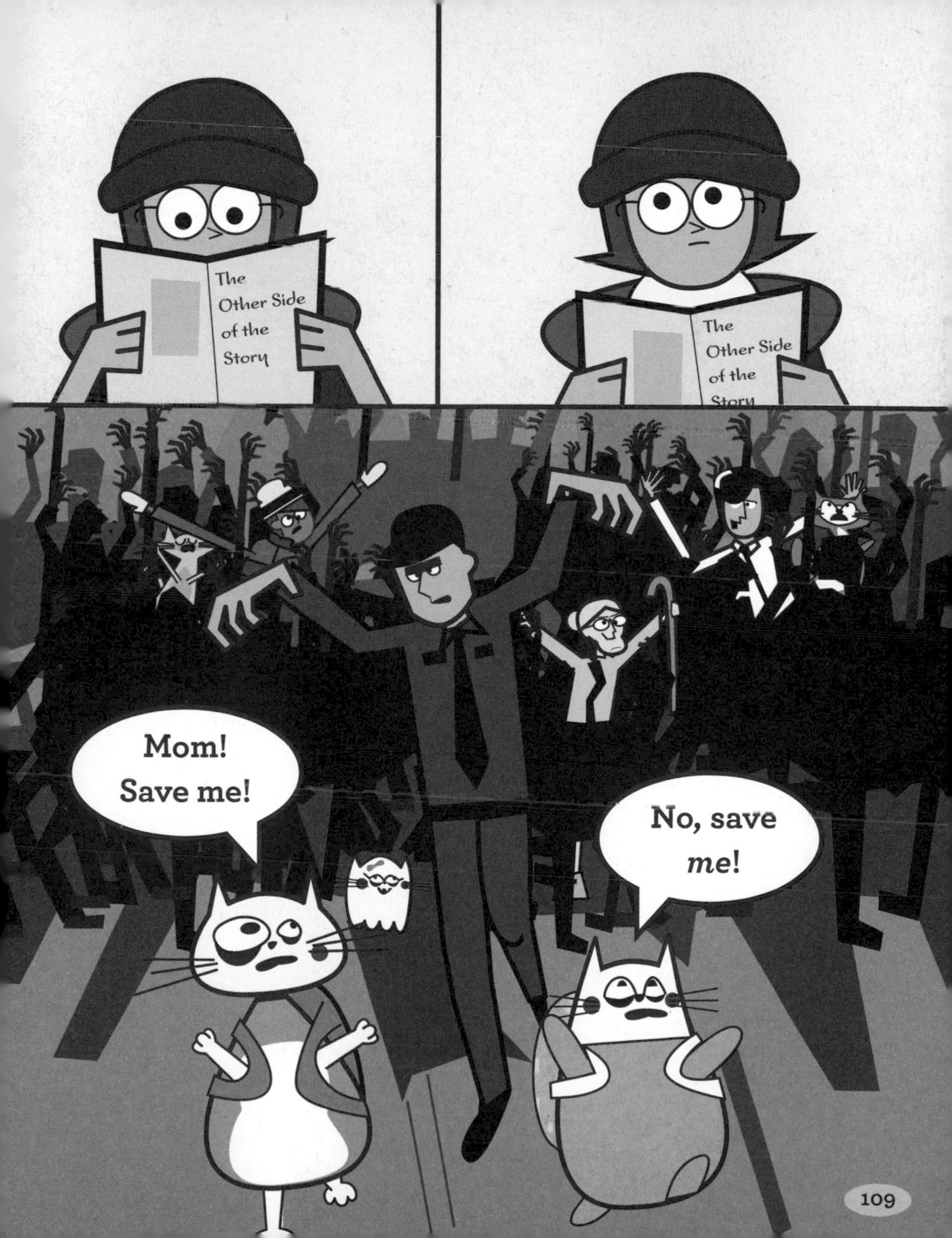
The Other Side of the Story
The Other Side of the Story
Mom! Save me!
No, save *me*!

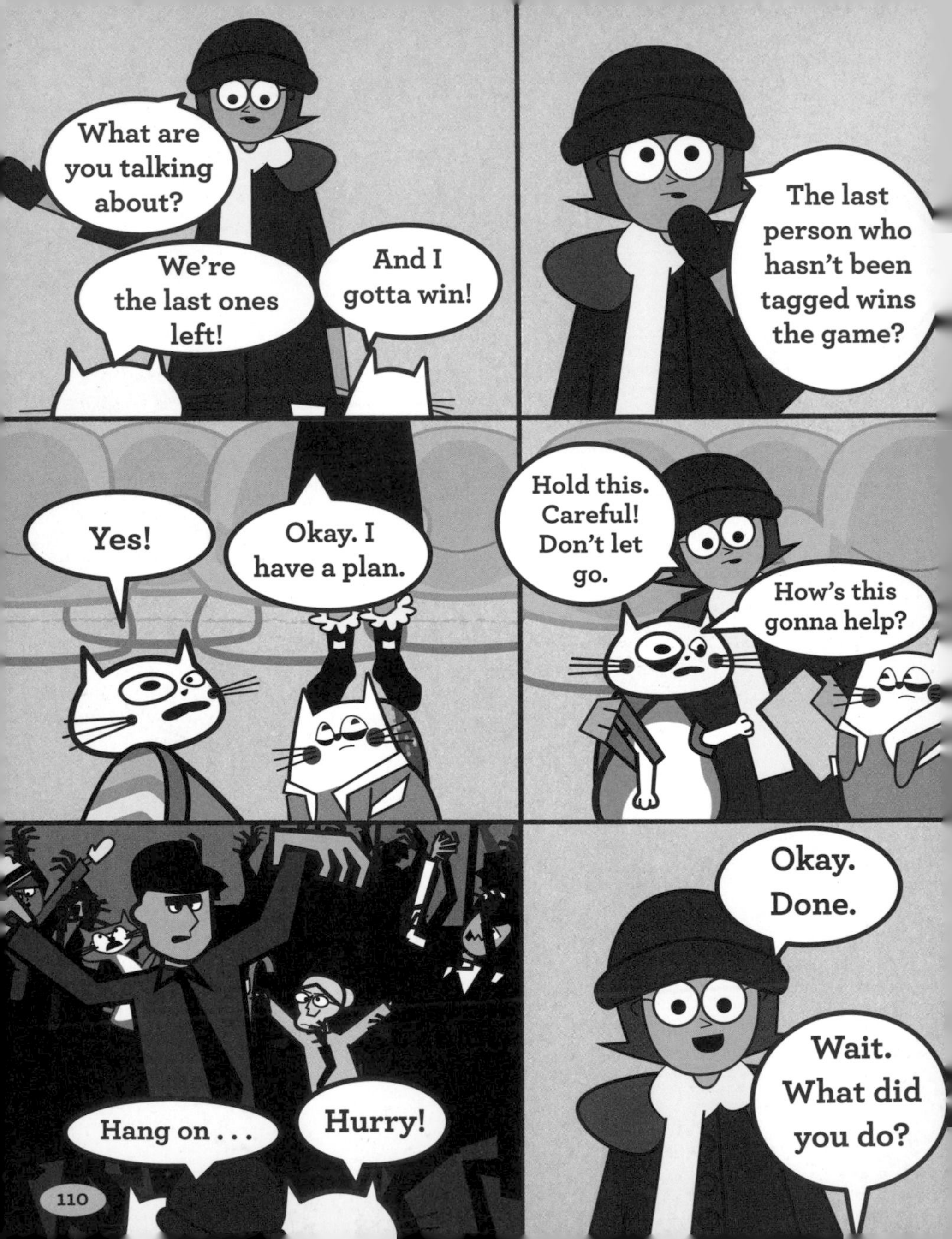
What are you talking about?
We're the last ones left!
And I gotta win!
The last person who hasn't been tagged wins the game?
Yes!
Okay. I have a plan.
Hold this. Careful! Don't let go.
How's this gonna help?
Hang on . . .
Hurry!
Okay. Done.
Wait. What did you do?

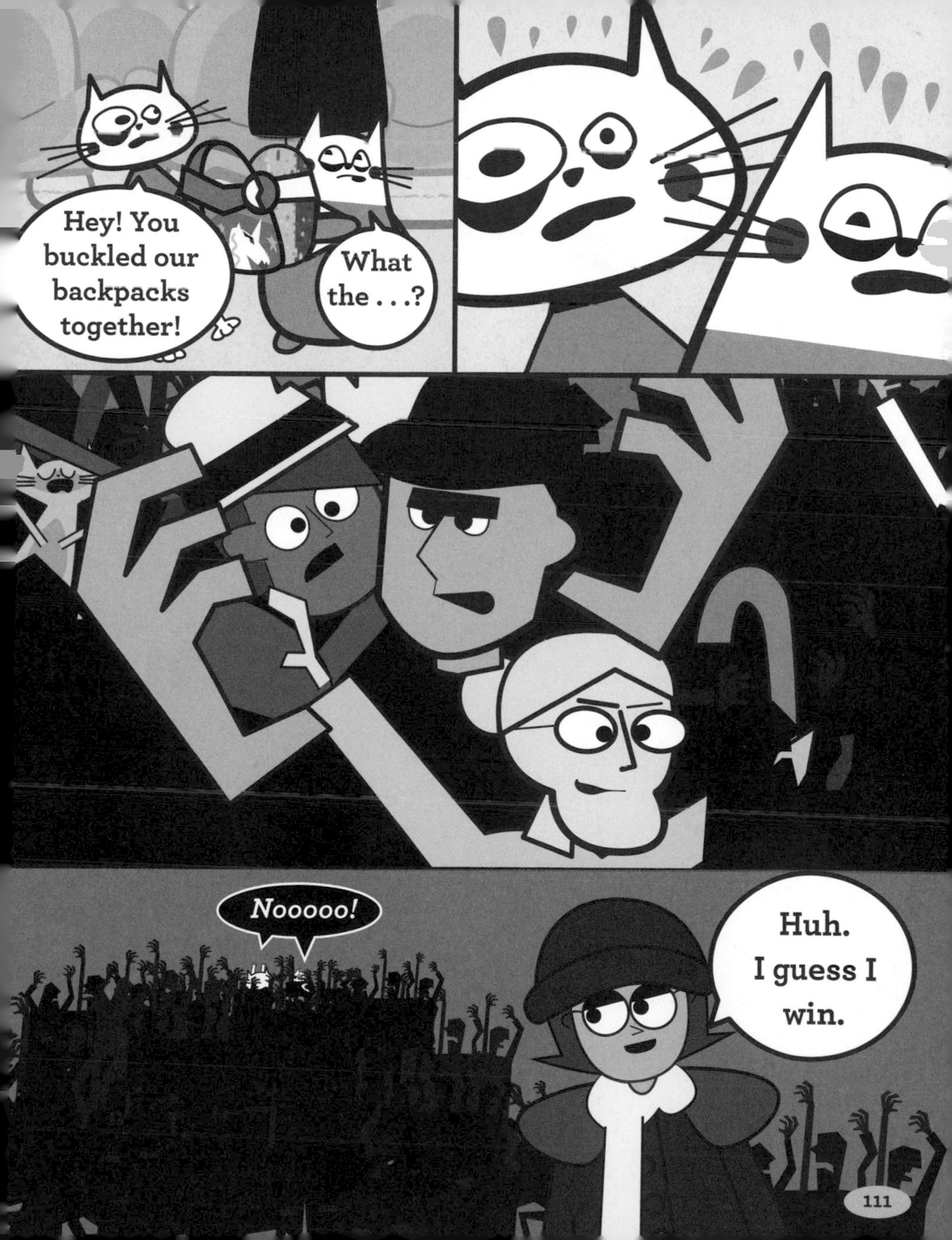
Hey! You buckled our backpacks together!
What the . . .?
Nooooo!
Huh. I guess I win.

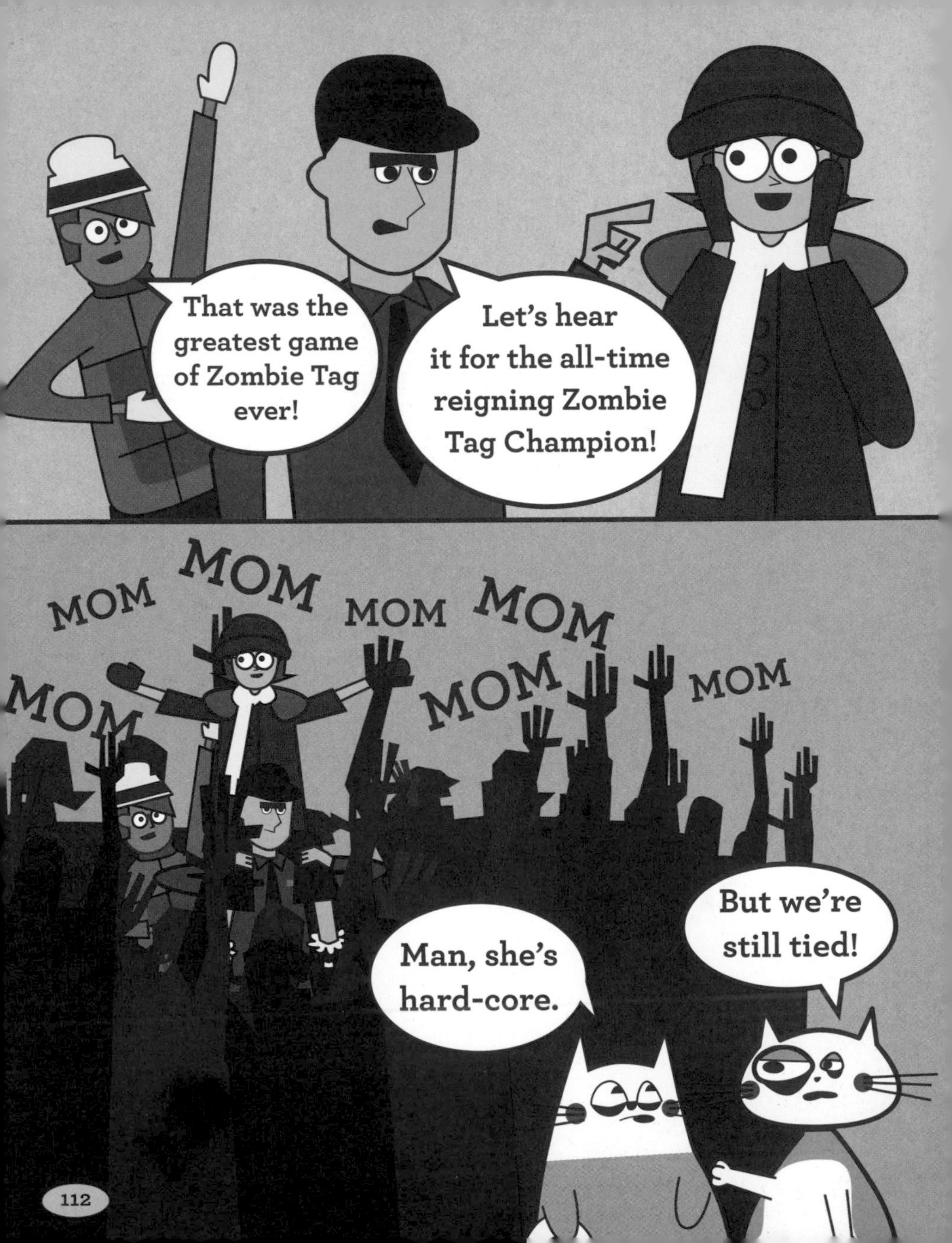
That was the greatest game of Zombie Tag ever!
Let's hear it for the all-time reigning Zombie Tag Champion!
MOM
MOM
MOM
MOM
MOM
MOM
MOM
Man, she's hard-core.
But we're still tied!

Chapter Six:

THE BEDTIME ADVENTURE

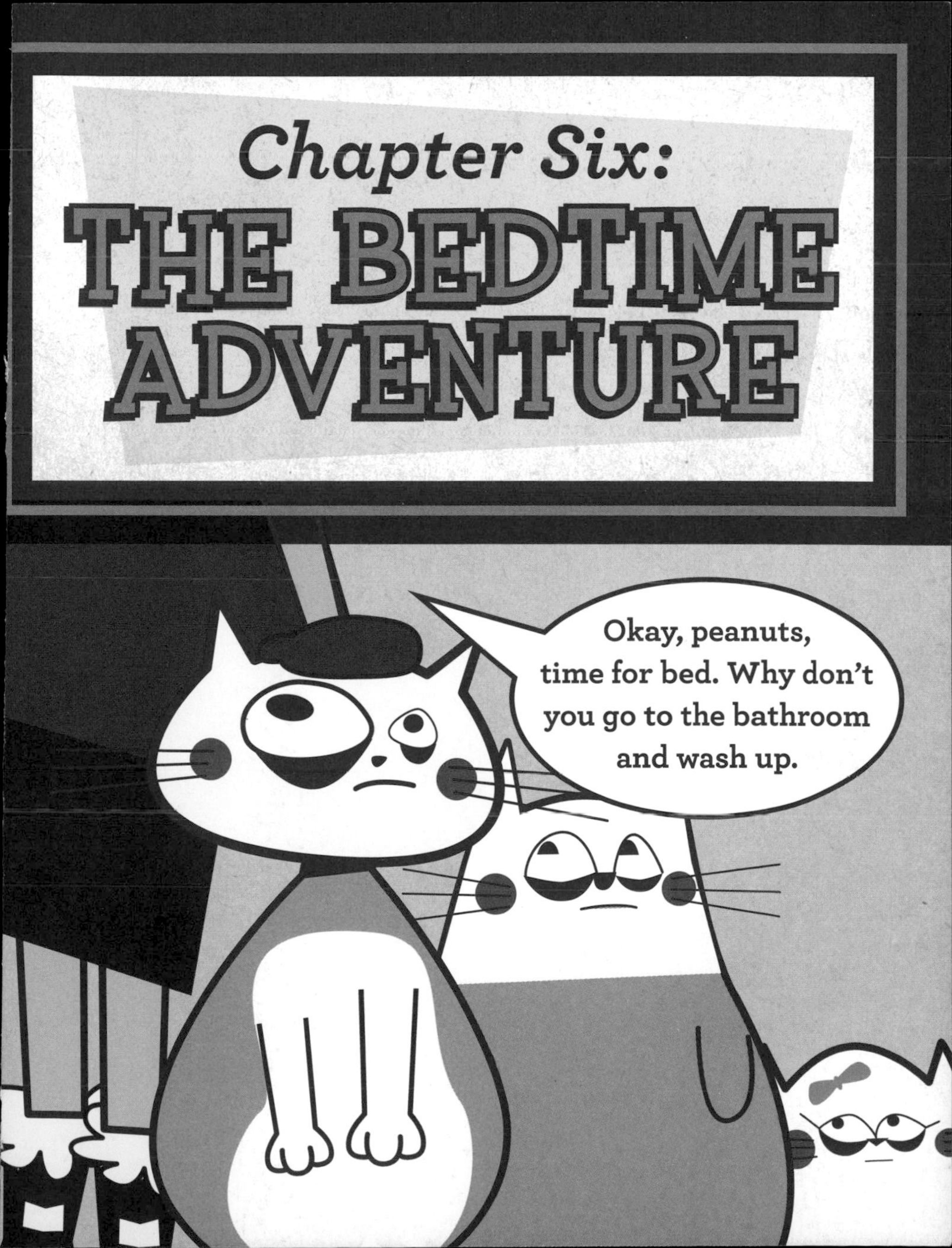
Okay, peanuts, time for bed. Why don't you go to the bathroom and wash up.

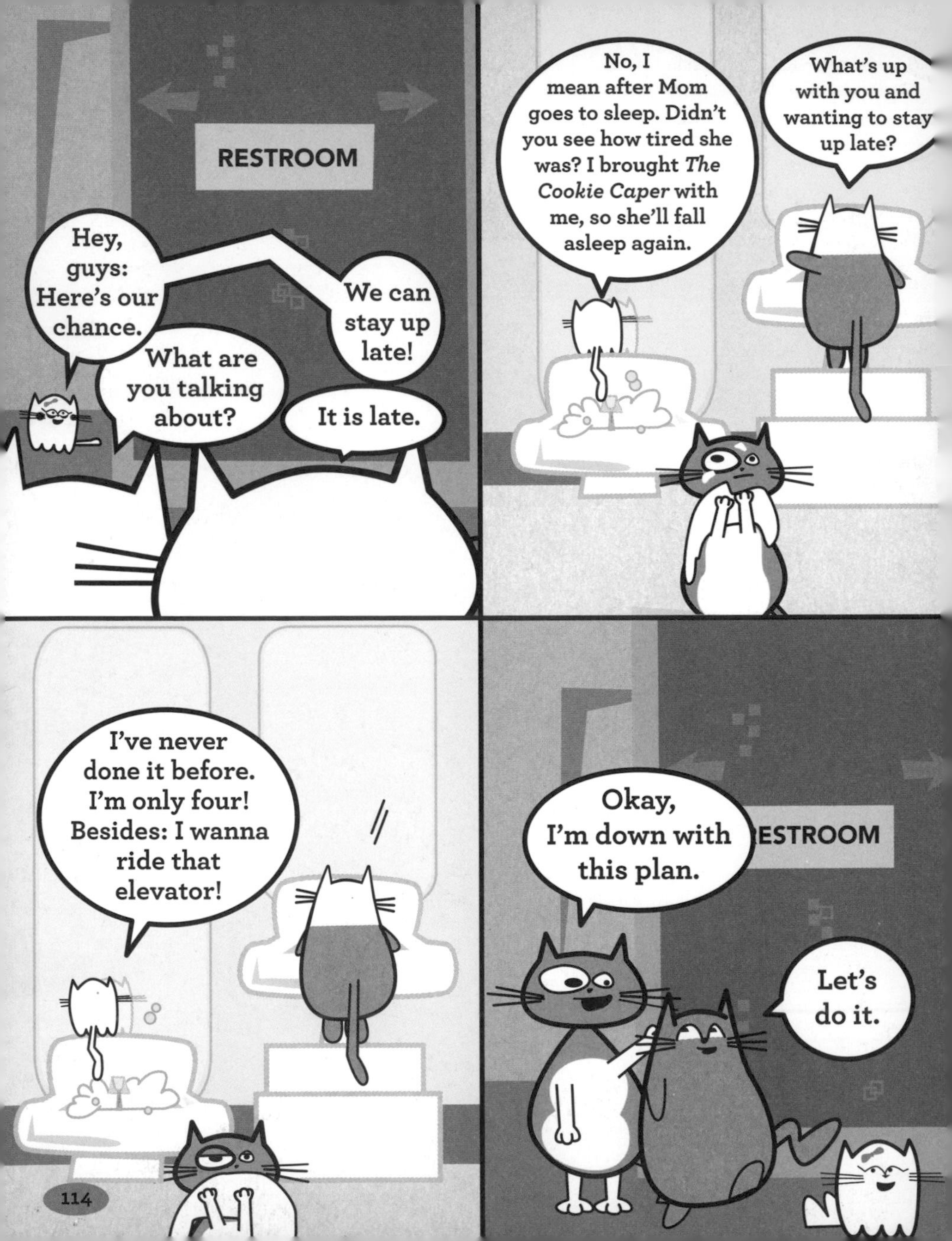

RESTROOM
Hey, guys: Here's our chance.
We can stay up late!
What are you talking about?
It is late.
No, I mean after Mom goes to sleep. Didn't you see how tired she was? I brought *The Cookie Caper* with me, so she'll fall asleep again.
What's up with you and wanting to stay up late?
I've never done it before. I'm only four! Besides: I wanna ride that elevator!
Okay, I'm down with this plan.
ESTROOM
Let's do it.

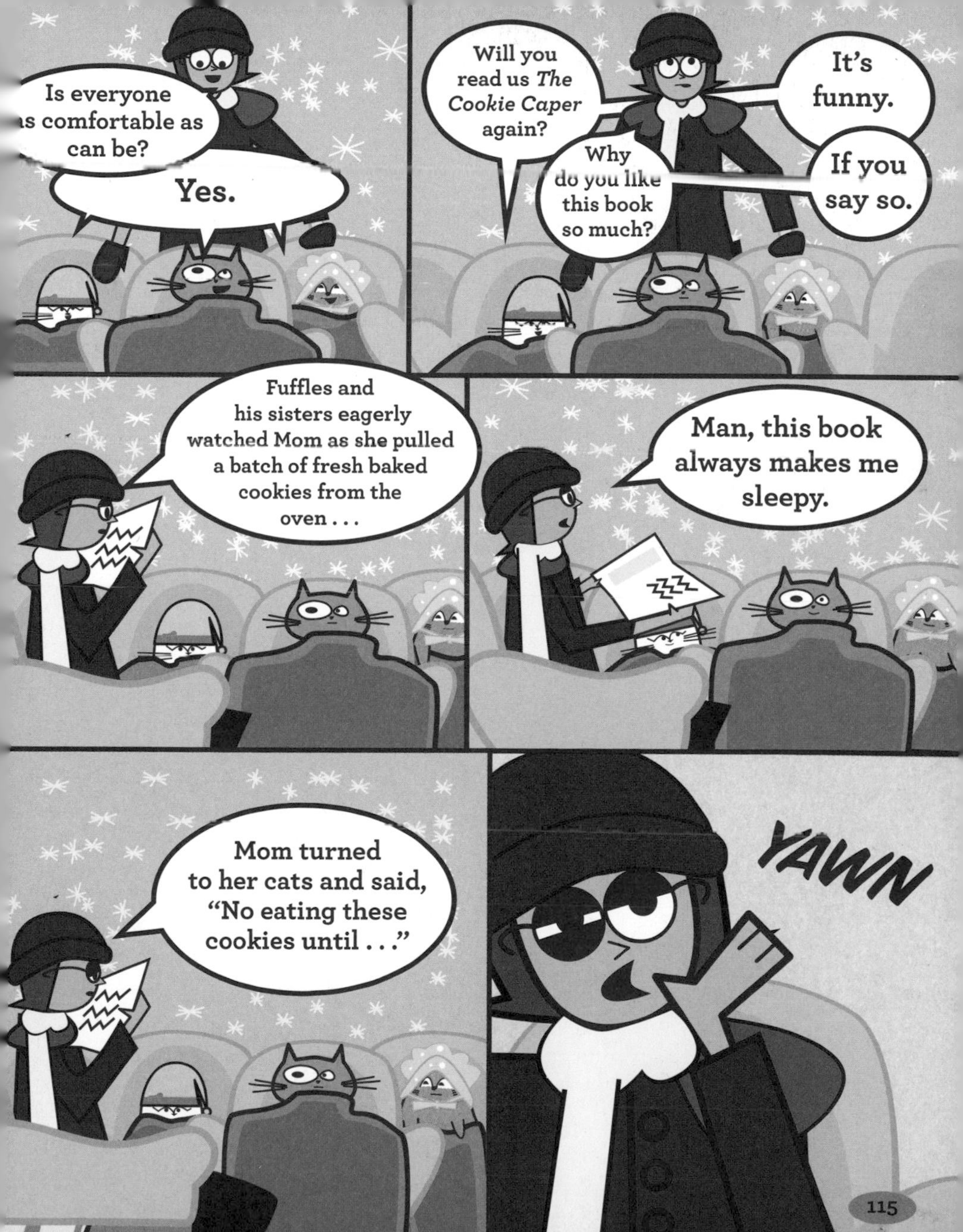
Is everyone as comfortable as can be?
Yes.
Will you read us *The Cookie Caper* again?
Why do you like this book so much?
It's funny.
If you say so.
Fuffles and his sisters eagerly watched Mom as she pulled a batch of fresh baked cookies from the oven . . .
Man, this book always makes me sleepy.
Mom turned to her cats and said, "No eating these cookies until . . ."
YAWN

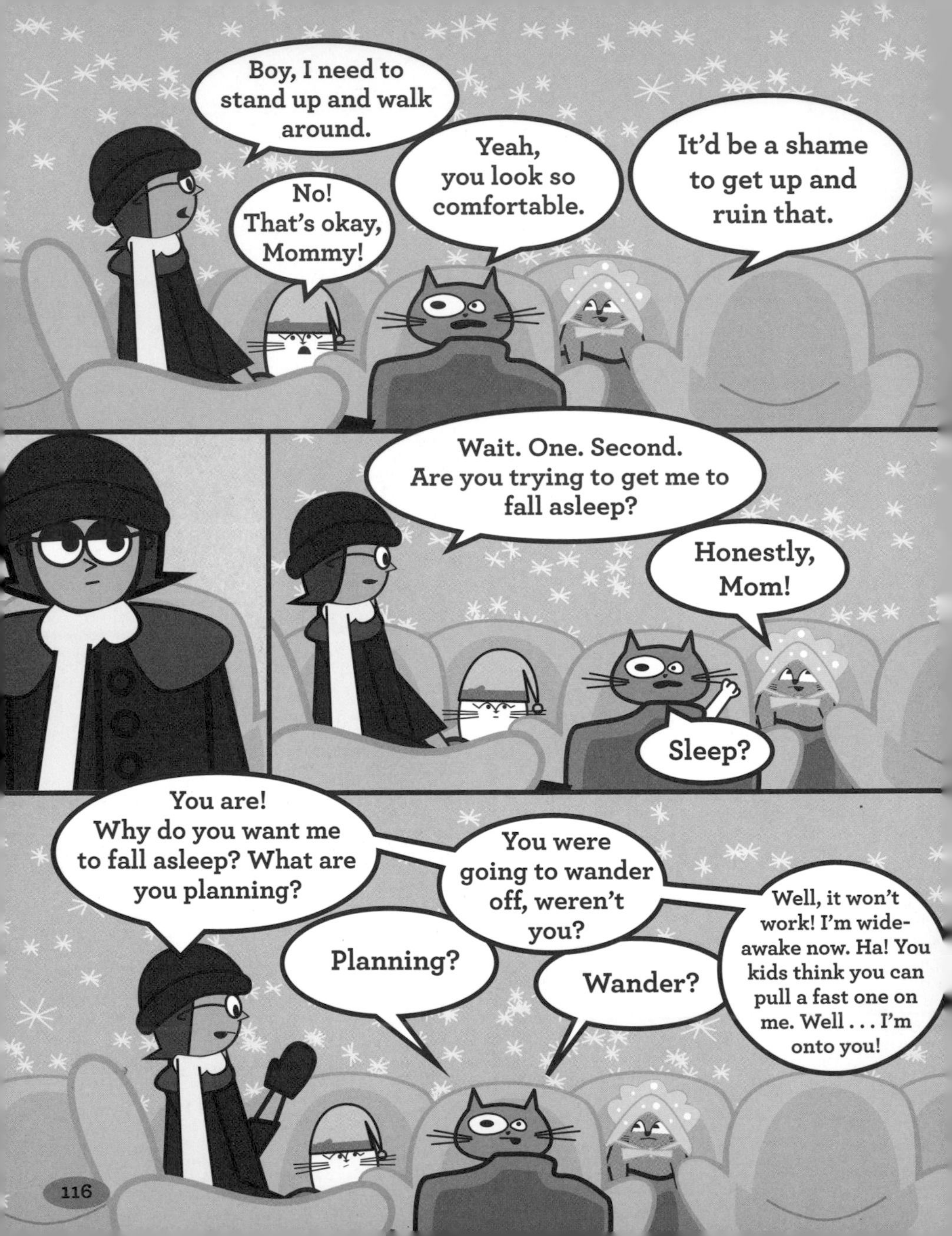
Boy, I need to stand up and walk around.
No! That's okay, Mommy!
Yeah, you look so comfortable.
It'd be a shame to get up and ruin that.
Wait. One. Second. Are you trying to get me to fall asleep?
Honestly, Mom!
Sleep?
You are! Why do you want me to fall asleep? What are you planning?
Planning?
You were going to wander off, weren't you?
Wander?
Well, it won't work! I'm wide-awake now. Ha! You kids think you can pull a fast one on me. Well . . . I'm onto you!

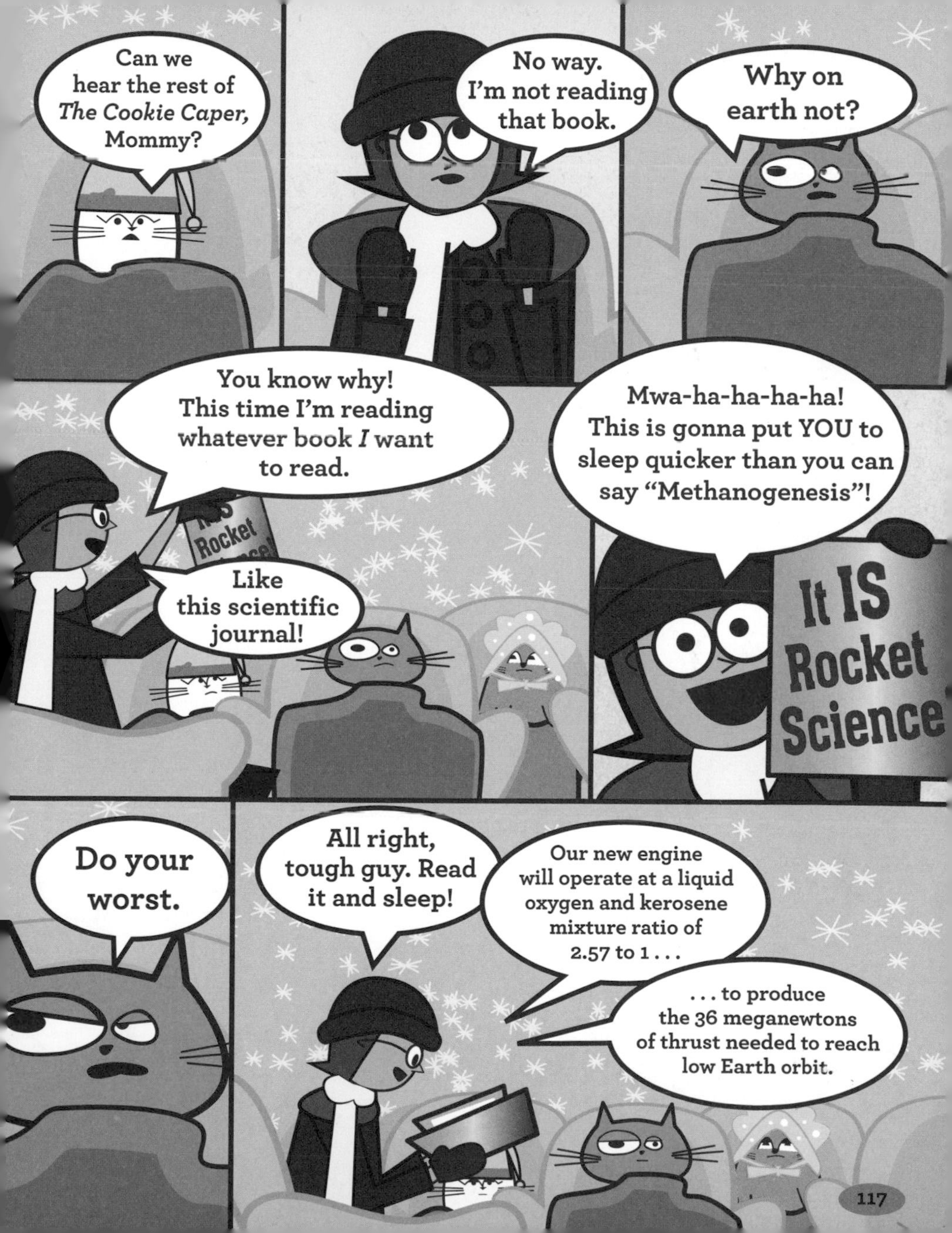
Can we hear the rest of *The Cookie Caper,* Mommy?
No way. I'm not reading that book.
Why on earth not?
You know why! This time I'm reading whatever book *I* want to read.
Rocket
Like this scientific journal!
Mwa-ha-ha-ha-ha! This is gonna put YOU to sleep quicker than you can say "Methanogenesis"!
It IS Rocket Science
Do your worst.
All right, tough guy. Read it and sleep!
Our new engine will operate at a liquid oxygen and kerosene mixture ratio of 2.57 to 1 . . .
. . . to produce the 36 meganewtons of thrust needed to reach low Earth orbit.

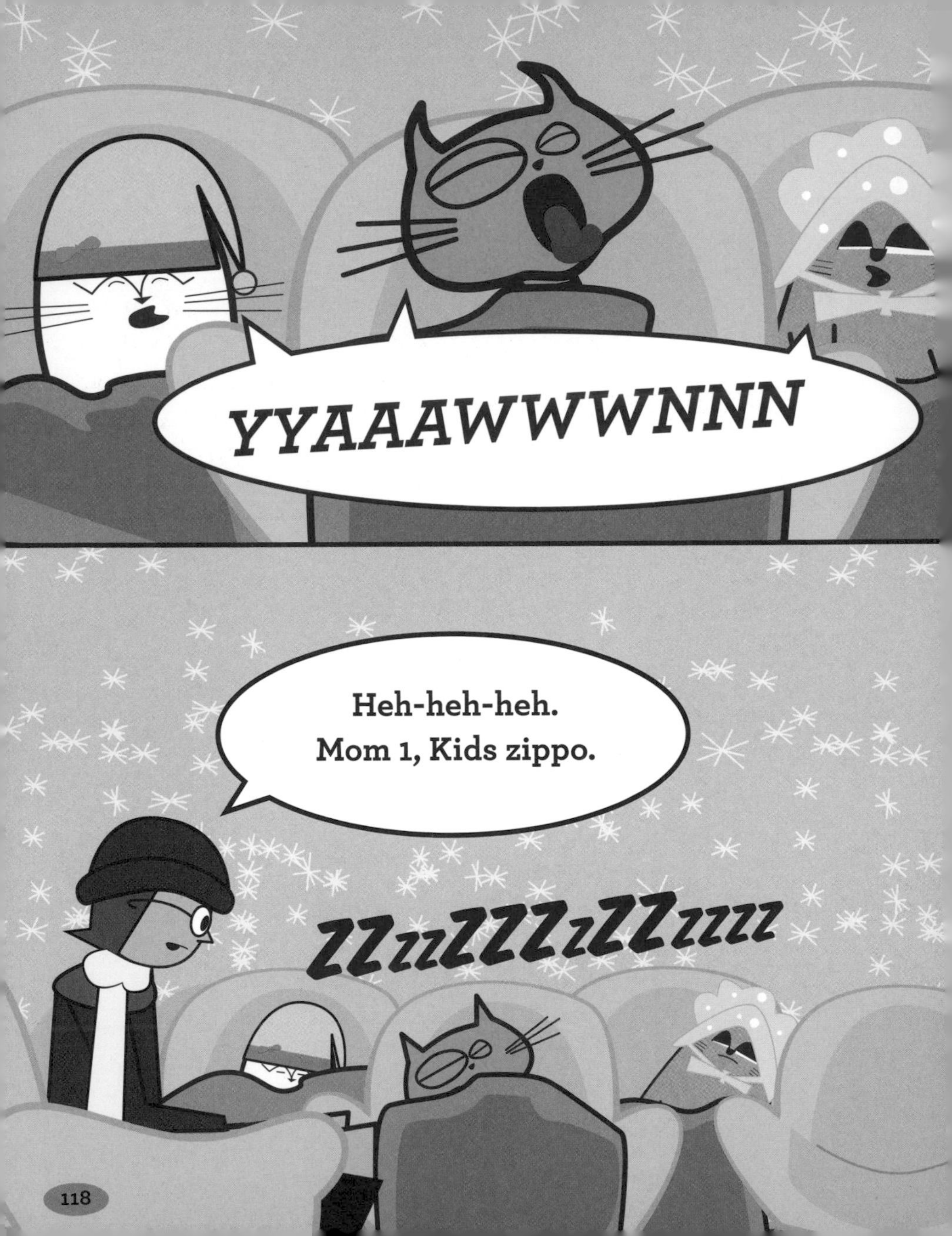
YYAAAWWWNNN
Heh-heh-heh.
Mom 1, Kids zippo.
ZZzzZZZzZZzzzz

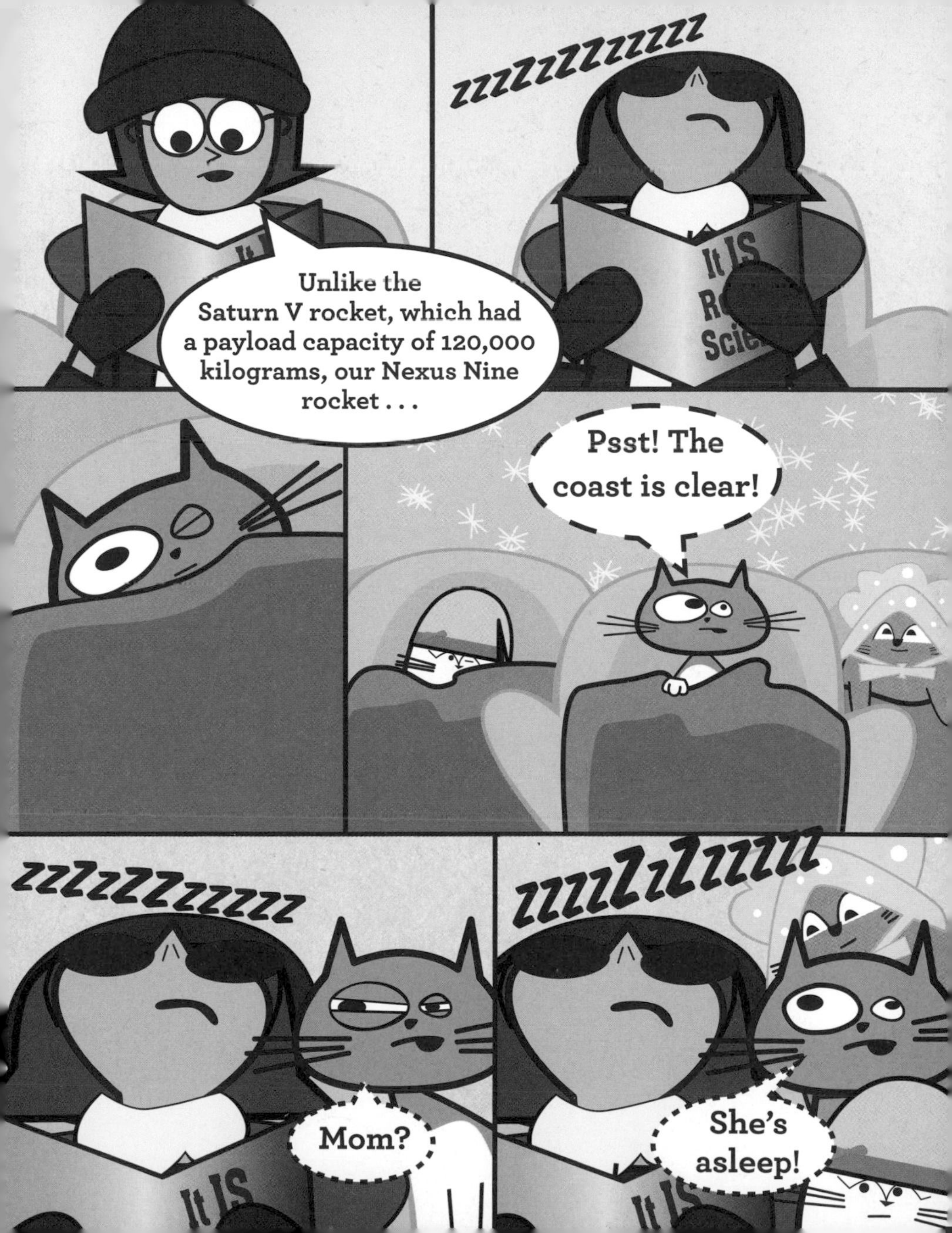
Unlike the Saturn V rocket, which had a payload capacity of 120,000 kilograms, our Nexus Nine rocket . . .
zzzZzzZZZzzzzz
Psst! The coast is clear!
zzZzzZZzzzzzz
Mom?
zzzzZzZzzzzz
She's asleep!

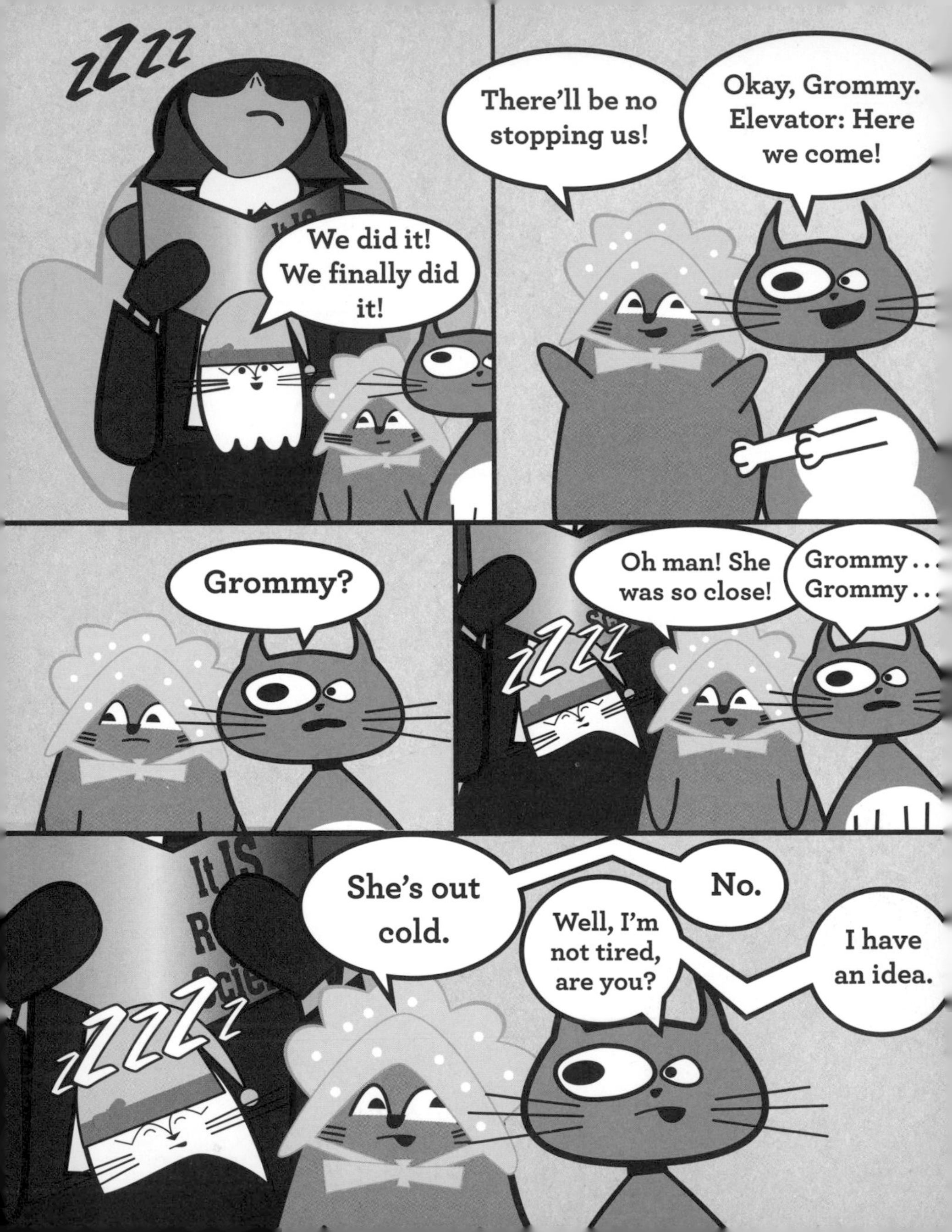
zZZZ
We did it! We finally did it!
There'll be no stopping us!
Okay, Grommy. Elevator: Here we come!
Grommy?
zZZZ
Oh man! She was so close!
Grommy . . . Grommy . . .
zZZZz
She's out cold.
Well, I'm not tired, are you?
No.
I have an idea.

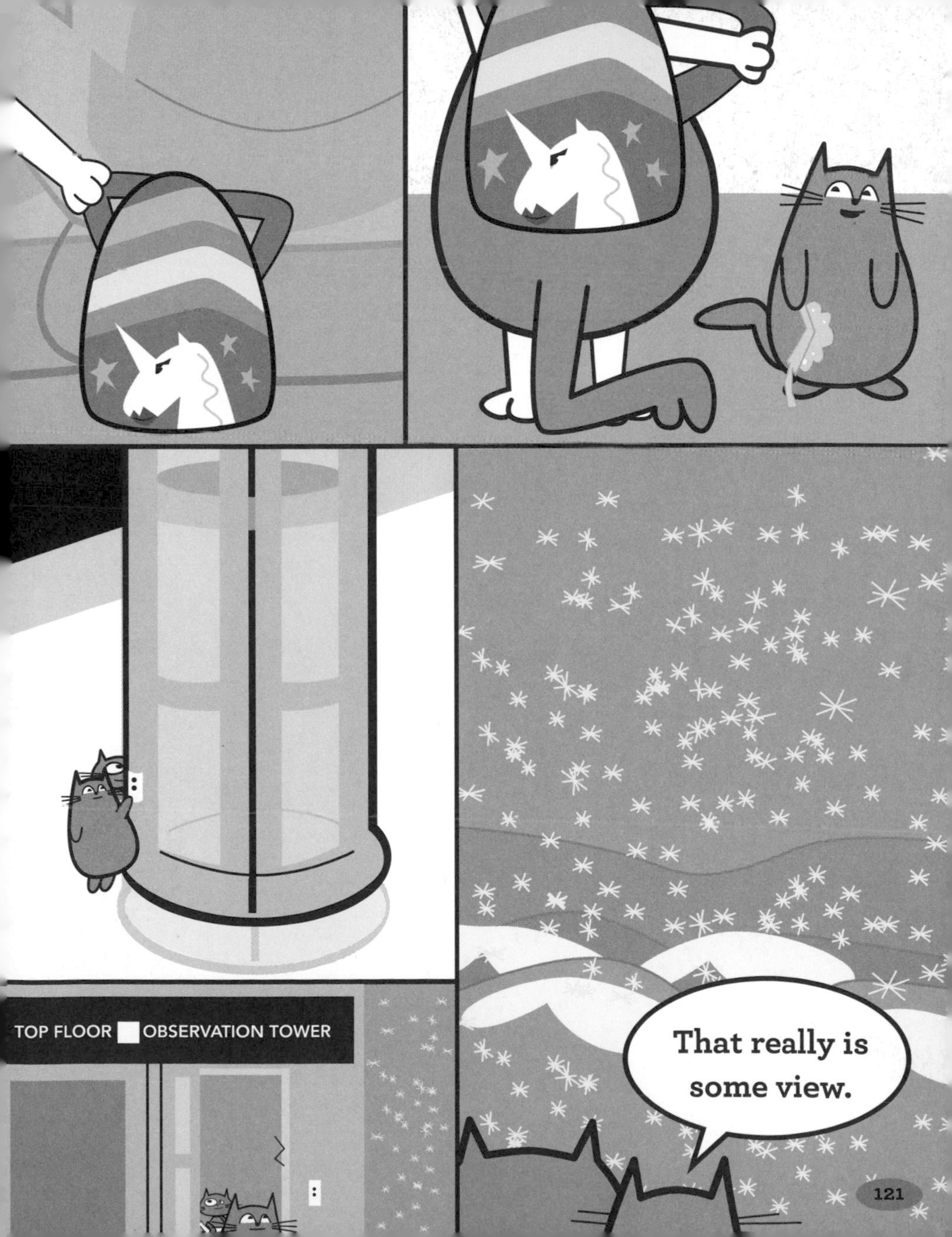
TOP FLOOR OBSERVATION TOWER
That really is some view.

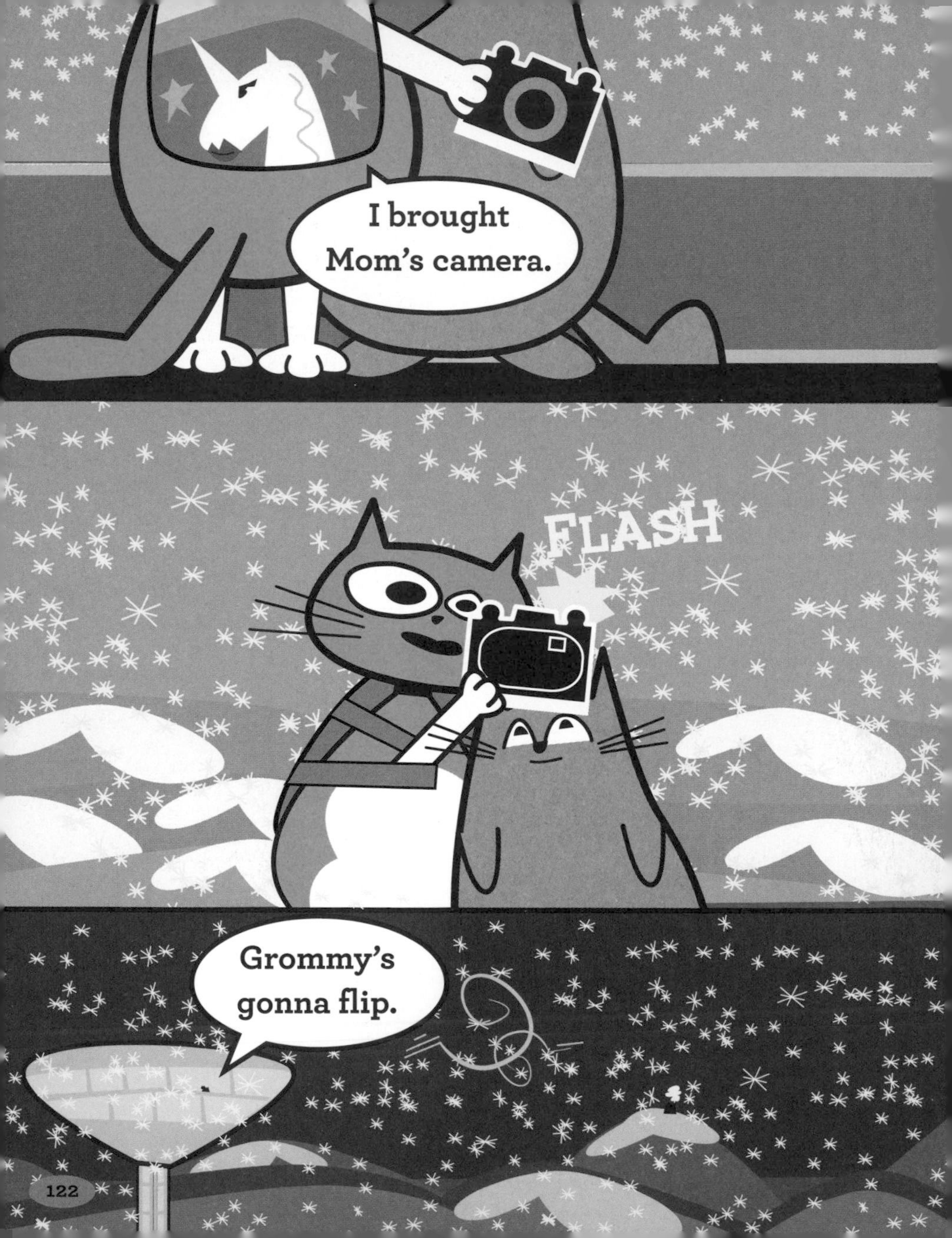
I brought Mom's camera.
FLASH
Grommy's gonna flip.

Chapter Seven:
GROMMY MAKES IT

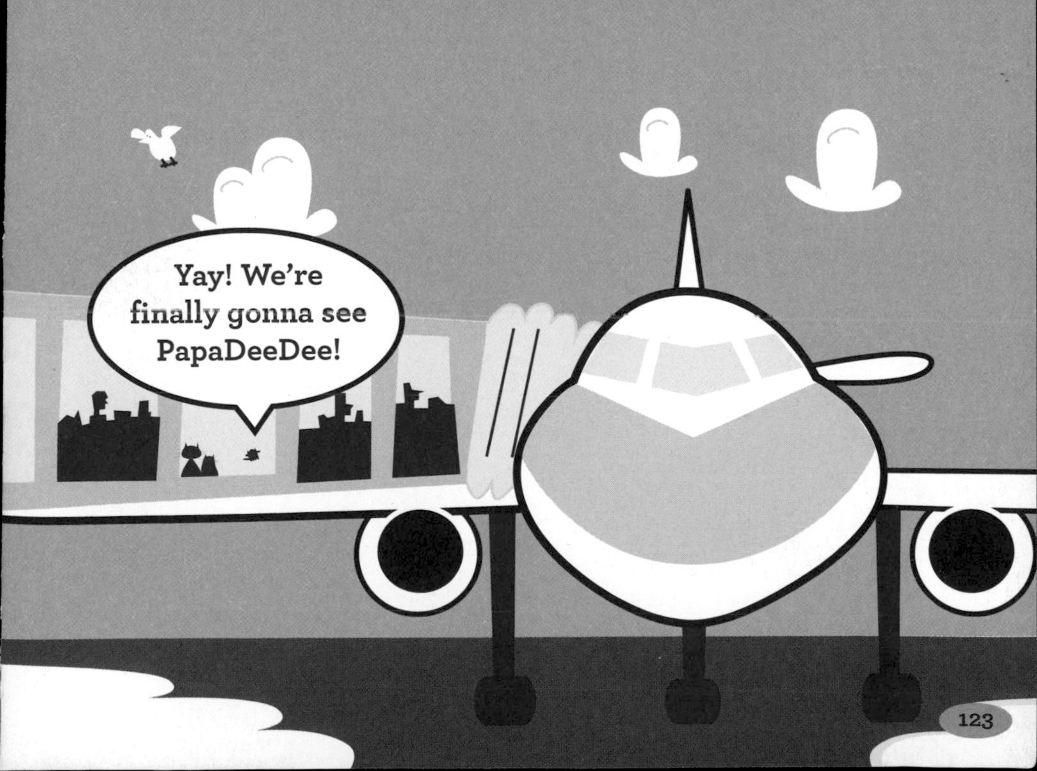

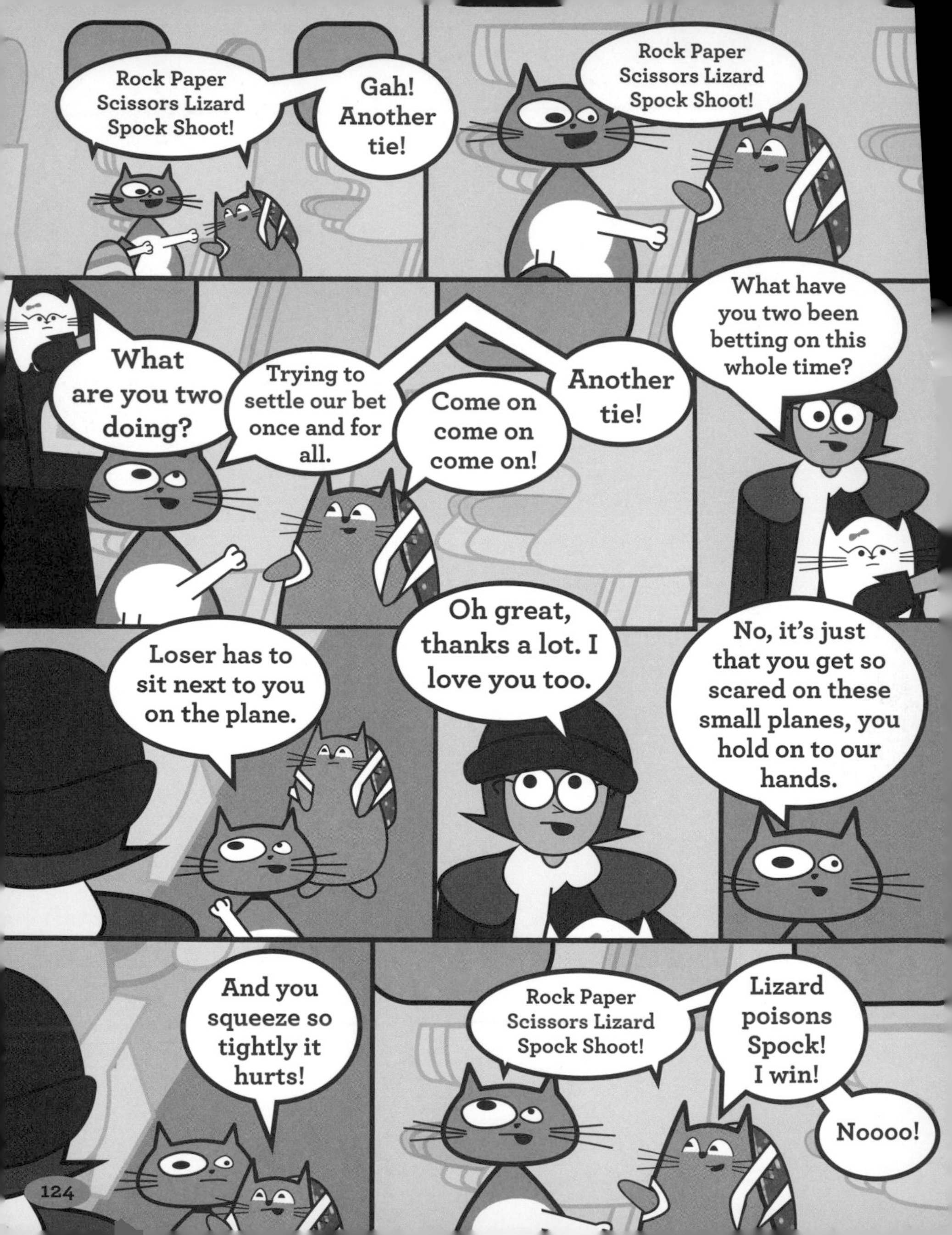
Rock Paper Scissors Lizard Spock Shoot!
Gah! Another tie!
Rock Paper Scissors Lizard Spock Shoot!
What are you two doing?
Trying to settle our bet once and for all.
Come on come on come on!
Another tie!
What have you two been betting on this whole time?
Loser has to sit next to you on the plane.
Oh great, thanks a lot. I love you too.
No, it's just that you get so scared on these small planes, you hold on to our hands.
And you squeeze so tightly it hurts!
Rock Paper Scissors Lizard Spock Shoot!
Lizard poisons Spock! I win!
Noooo!

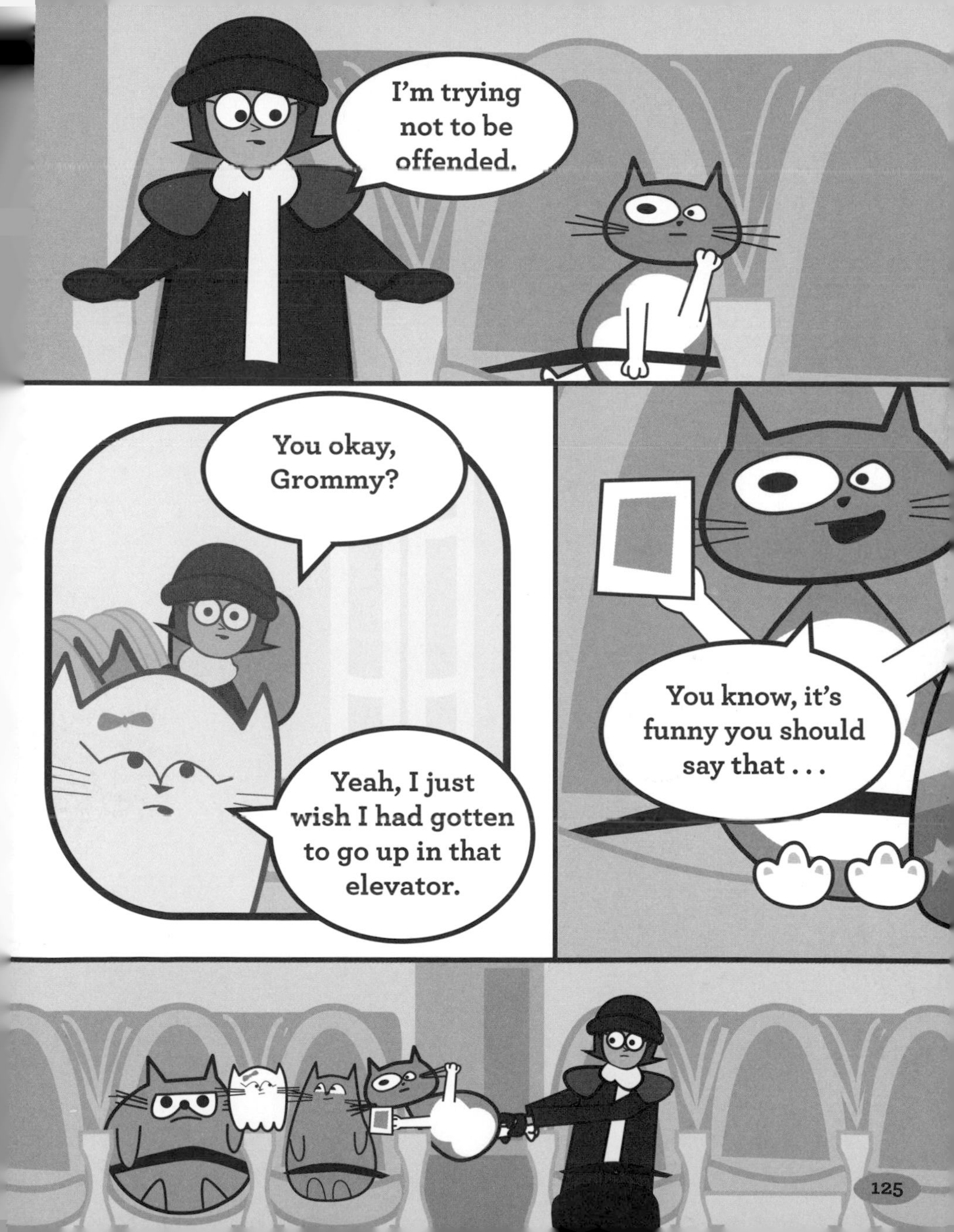
I'm trying not to be offended.
You okay, Grommy?
Yeah, I just wish I had gotten to go up in that elevator.
You know, it's funny you should say that . . .

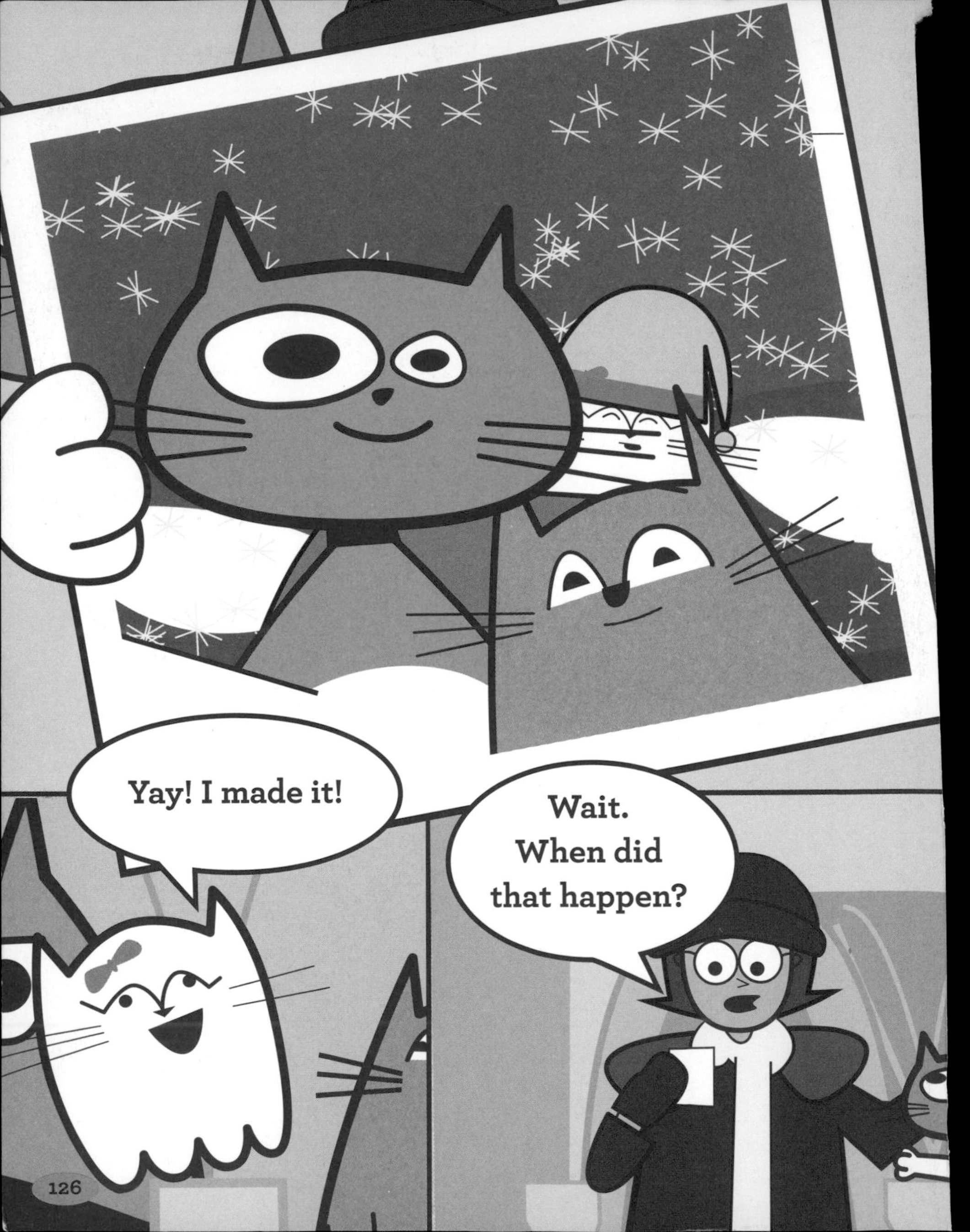
Yay! I made it!
Wait. When did that happen?

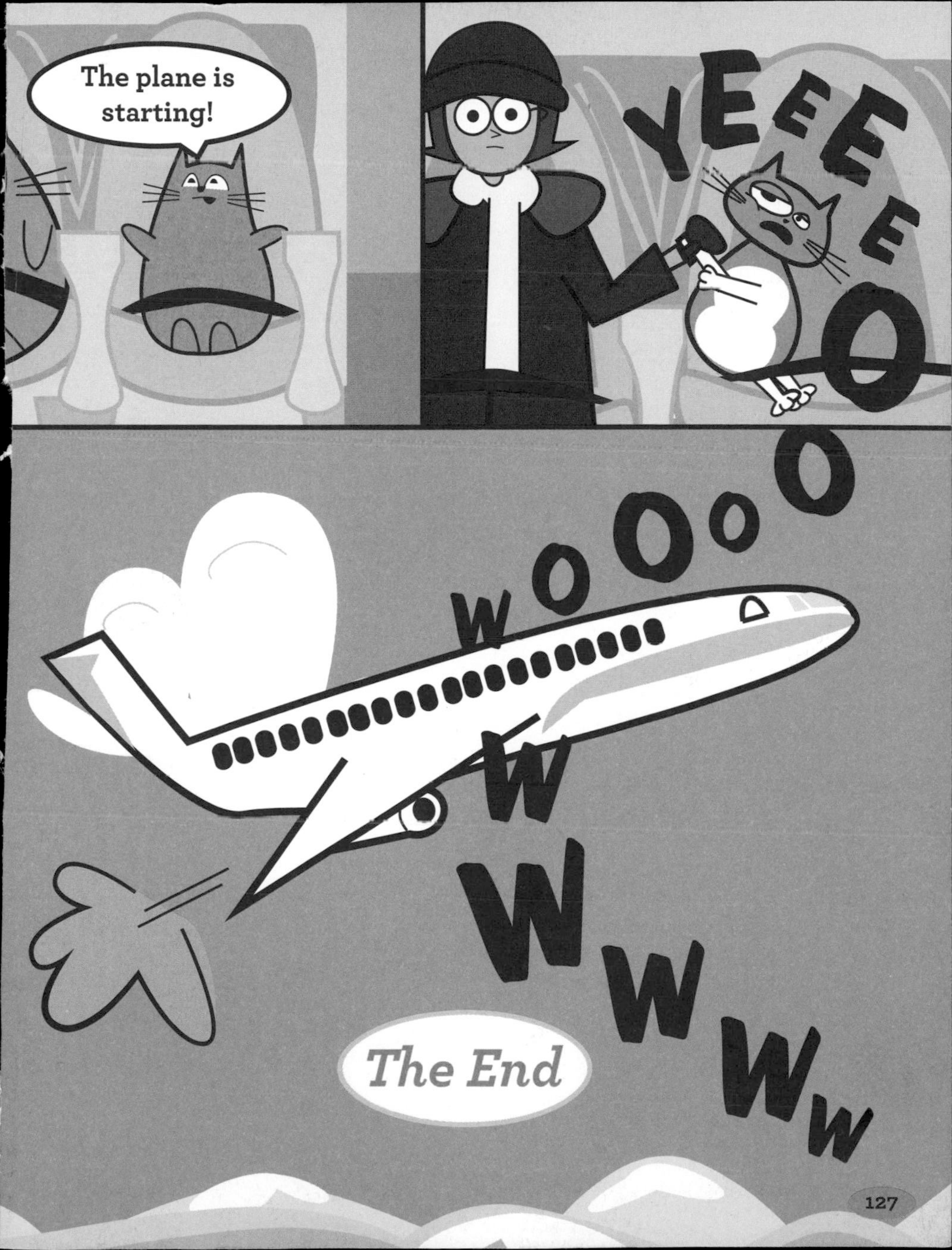
The plane is starting!
YEEEEOOOoOOW
WWWWw
The End

About the Authors:

Don't try playing vegan zombie tag with SCOTT MCCORMICK in an airport. He's already scouted out all the cool hiding places. But if you do—and if you're lucky enough to tag him—he's got dibs on saying "triticale." Scott lives in North Carolina.

R. H. LAZZELL enjoys the changing leaves in the autumn and watching spooky movies. He is currently running from zombies in New Jersey.

Find out more at PANTSANDFOOTFOOT.COM

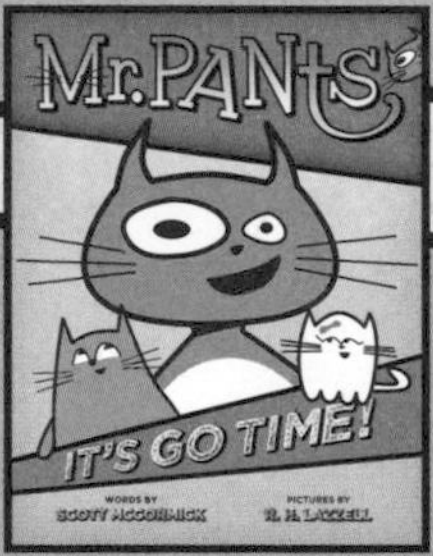
Mr.PANTS
IT'S GO TIME!

Read more Mr. Pants books!

"Laugh-out-loud hilarious."—*Booklist*

"Fans will wait excitedly for the next book in this fun, rollicking series."—*School Library Journal*

"Readers . . . will find plenty to recognize in this family's harried day of activities and errands, while enjoying Mr. Pants's lighthearted comeuppances."—*Publishers Weekly*

"Young readers will enjoy the cartoony, colorful silliness."
—*Booklist*

"A great choice for readers who are graduating from Mo Willems's early readers and just discovering Doreen Cronin's easy-reader chapter books."
—*School Library Journal*

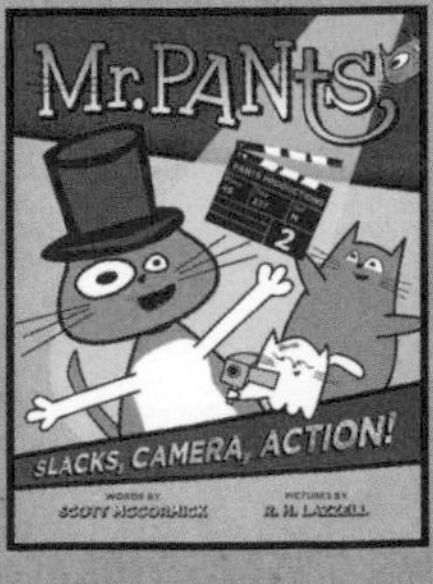
Mr.PANTS
SLACKS, CAMERA, ACTION!